CHILDREN OF PARANOIA

CHILDREN OF PARANOIA

Trevor Shane

 NEW AMERICAN LIBRARY

New American Library
Published by New American Library, a division of
Penguin Group (USA) Inc., 375 Hudson Street,
New York, New York 10014, USA
Penguin Group (Canada), 90 Eglinton Avenue East, Suite 700, Toronto,
Ontario M4P 2Y3, Canada (a division of Pearson Penguin Canada Inc.)
Penguin Books Ltd., 80 Strand, London WC2R 0RL, England
Penguin Ireland, 25 St. Stephen's Green, Dublin 2,
Ireland (a division of Penguin Books Ltd.)
Penguin Group (Australia), 250 Camberwell Road, Camberwell, Victoria 3124,
Australia (a division of Pearson Australia Group Pty. Ltd.)
Penguin Books India Pvt. Ltd., 11 Community Centre, Panchsheel Park,
New Delhi - 110 017, India
Penguin Group (NZ), 67 Apollo Drive, Rosedale, Auckland 0632,
New Zealand (a division of Pearson New Zealand Ltd.)
Penguin Books (South Africa) (Pty.) Ltd., 24 Sturdee Avenue,
Rosebank, Johannesburg 2196, South Africa

Penguin Books Ltd., Registered Offices:
80 Strand, London WC2R 0RL, England

Published by New American Library, a division of Penguin Group (USA) Inc. Previously published in a
Dutton edition.

First New American Library Printing, August 2012
10 9 8 7 6 5 4 3 2 1

 REGISTERED TRADEMARK—MARCA REGISTRADA

NAL Trade Paperback ISBN: 978-0-451-23691-3

THE LIBRARY OF CONGRESS HAS CATALOGED THE HARDCOVER EDITION OF THIS TITLE AS FOLLOWS:

Shane, Trevor.
Children of paranoia/Trevor Shane.
p. cm.
ISBN 978-0-525-95237-4
I. Title.
PS3619.H35465C47 2011
813'.6—dc22   2011010262

Set in Janson Text LT Std
Designed by Leonard Telesca

Printed in the United States of America

PUBLISHER'S NOTE
This is a work of fiction. Names, characters, places, and incidents either are the product of the author's
imagination or are used fictitiously, and any resemblance to actual persons, living or dead, business
establishments, events, or locales is entirely coincidental.
    The publisher does not have any control over and does not assume any responsibility for author or
third-party Web sites or their content.

For my son, Leo, who inspired me before I even knew he existed.

CHILDREN OF PARANOIA BOOK I

Christopher,
You need to know who you are.
You need to know where you come from.
It's the only way you'll be able to fight them if
they come after you.

Love always,
Your mother

PART I

Prologue

Dear Maria,

I doubt that you expected this journal to amount to much when you gave it to me, but here it is. I wrote it for you. When you gave it to me, you said that you wanted to understand me. I'm still not sure you'll understand what I've done but I have hope.

You're a big part of this story now, bigger than I expected when I started. I just kept on writing. So here it is. Here I am on a few hundred ratty pages.

I don't know if I've sinned or if sin even exists. If it does, then I guess I've committed more than my share. Maybe I should care, but I don't. All that I care about now is that you and Christopher are safe. Everything else will take care of itself.

I love you.

Love,
Joe

One

It's hard to decide where to start. I know you're supposed to start at the beginning, but how do I know where the beginning is? It's hard for me. I've always had a much better sense for endings. But I guess it starts in Brooklyn, standing in the dark on a street corner, waiting for a woman to finish closing up her shop.

When she first stepped out of the building, I backed into the shadows. She took a few quick glances in each direction but I knew that all she could see was the empty street. Seeing nothing, she turned her attention back to locking up. She had spent the last hour cleaning up, wiping down the counter, and putting the bottles of wine that the customers had rearranged back in order. Now she stood there on the street outside, her long day over. She was ready to go home to her family. She pulled down the metal grate meant to protect her store, attached a padlock to the grate, placed the key in her purse, and then stepped back again. She took another quick glance in both directions. Still nothing. She reached into her purse and pulled out a loose cigarette. She lit the cigarette, took one deep draw, turned to her left, and began walking down the dark street toward home.

So far everything was exactly as I had been told. She had no escorts. She exhibited no suspicions. Her husband was away on business. This one was supposed to be easy. For once, it looked like it might actually work out that way.

I waited until she was a full block away before stepping out of the darkness where I had been waiting. I turned to my right and began to walk down the opposite side of the street from her. She walked quickly, each stride deliberate but relaxed. Every few steps, she would take another draw from her cigarette. She was wearing a long black skirt, black sneakers, and a purple blouse. She was attractive, but I did my best to block this from my mind. I concentrated on pacing myself so that I would move just fast enough to catch up to her by the time she turned toward her apartment, but not so fast as to arouse suspicion. This wasn't the first time I'd done this. I busted my cherry years ago. It wouldn't be the last time either. I was certain of that even then. The thought didn't bother me. I had a job to do.

I was less than a quarter of a block behind her when she turned left down the street toward her apartment. I watched as she flipped the butt of her cigarette onto the sidewalk and put it out with a twist of her foot. Then she started down the even quieter, tree-lined street that she lived on. When I was sure that she couldn't see me, I jogged across the street. As I did, I pulled a pair of thin black leather gloves out of my bag and slipped them onto my hands. It was darker on the side street. There were fewer streetlights.

She was moving quickly now. Faster than I suspect she normally would. I don't think she saw me but she must have sensed something. This was normal. It was some sort of sixth sense, a sinking feeling of impending tragedy. She didn't dare look back, not yet. With a few long strides, I closed the distance between us to little more than ten feet.

It was clear now that she knew I was following her. She still hadn't seen me. She simply felt me behind her. She could have screamed now but I knew that she wouldn't. She wouldn't risk the embarrassment. After all, I might have been one of her neighbors returning home just like she was. She'd been out of the game for a while. She'd lost the ability to trust her instincts.

I watched as she put her hand back into her purse. She could have been reaching for anything. I watched her hand. If she pulled out a gun, Mace, even a cell phone, I would have had to move faster than I wanted to. I would have had to grab her wrist, twist it, and force her to let whatever she was holding go. I didn't have to, though. I heard a slight jingling sound. She was just reaching for her keys.

There were shadows on the sidewalk from the trees and she stepped quickly between the darkness and the light. Three more houses and she would make a left turn toward her brownstone. I did my best to control my pulse. Adrenaline—adrenaline that I hoped I wouldn't need—began to flow through my system. Physically her reaction likely mirrored mine. She began to walk faster but she still refused to run. I kept my strides long and even and was able to close the gap between us until I was almost touching her.

By now she knew. She must have. I was a mere pace and a half behind her. She must have been all but resigned to her fate. Certain thoughts would be flying through her head, regrets, thoughts about what she could have done differently to save herself. I'm sure she was thinking that it was stupid for her to walk home alone at night even though she'd done it hundreds of times before. It had been years. Years of pleasant walks home through the quiet Brooklyn streets after an honest day's work. This was her home. Twelve years. Two children. Who knows how many fond memories? Could she still scream? What if her screams woke up her kids? She wouldn't want to frighten them. I knew. So what could she have done differently? She could have hugged her kids this morning. She could have told them how much she loved them. She could have not yelled at the poor four-year-old Eric after he spilled his Cheerios on the kitchen floor.

I thought back to that moment, earlier in the day, as I watched her through her kitchen window from the stoop across the street. I would have liked to have said something to her. I would have liked to let her know how much she would regret yelling at her kid like that. Let him spill, I thought when it happened, let him spill. Of course, I didn't say a word.

Now, one building from her home, I ran through my plan again in my head. As I did so, she turned left and pushed open the small gate that led to her apartment. I was close enough behind her that I was able to catch the gate before it clicked closed. I could hear her breathing now. I could hear the sounds of the television from her apartment. The babysitter must have been watching TV.

I couldn't see her face but could imagine her expression. At that moment, her face would be full of one of two things, panic or determination. I had seen both before. I could only hope for determination. Panic could make things messy. She was about to place her foot on the first of the steps that led up to her apartment door. Before she could, I reached forward and grabbed her wrist tightly. I went for the hand with the keys so that she would not be able to use them as a weapon. She'd been taught that at some point, I'm sure. "Go for the eyes," she was taught. All women are. After grabbing her wrist, I spun her toward me and, after giving her a chance to release only a small gasp of air, I placed my free hand over her mouth.

There we were then, face-to-face. For one brief moment she would get a clear look at my face in the light. This would confirm only one thing in her mind. She did not know me. I pushed her back into the shadows next to the stairs. As we moved, I slipped the keys from her hand and dropped them into the soft soil next to the entrance to the garden apartment. Her place was a typical Brooklyn brownstone, where the garden apartment door was slightly inset below the stairs to the main entrance. I continued to push her backward until her back was pressed hard against the door. We were quickly swallowed by shadows. No one could see us. No one would see her die. Each step of my plan had gone off without a hitch.

In one quick, coordinated motion, I took both my hand holding her wrist and my hand covering her mouth and wrapped them around her neck. Wasting no time I squeezed. I worked quickly enough that, even if she developed the courage to scream, no sound would come. I watched her face as I cut the air off between her lungs and her brain. She stared into my eyes as I clenched my gloved hands around her throat. Her face began to slowly turn color as her mouth opened and closed, trying in vain to capture one last breath of air. She didn't fight much. No kicking, no punching, just gasping. A few tears began to roll down her cheeks as her face turned from a reddish color to the initial shades of blue. Even through my gloves, I could now feel her pulse in my hands, as her heart began its furious work to try to get oxygen to her brain. I could feel her pulse in my thumbs and my pinkies. I felt no pulse beyond that. My index fingers could only feel the tightening muscles in her neck. Now her thoughts, if she could still piece together a coherent thought, were surely of her sons, wondering if they were okay, wondering if she could hear them one last time, hear their little voices, hear their laughter. No luck. The only sound from the apartment was the television.

A small stream of blood began to flow from her left nostril as her eyes began to glaze over. First, the blood balled up inside her nose, and then, when the force of gravity became too much, it trickled quickly down to her lips. The last thing she would taste would be her own blood. Not once did she take her eyes off mine. Her eyes were not questioning. She didn't know me, but she knew why I had to kill her. Seconds later, she was gone.

I eased her body down to the ground and stood back up. She was slumped against the door in the shadows, her knees bent under her, the blood already beginning to dry on her face. Her eyes were open but were lifeless. I felt almost nothing. I was numb. I felt no pleasure in doing what I'd done. I had gone through stages in the past. We all go through stages—different feelings. Power. Pride. Guilt. But

I didn't feel any of that. All I felt was satisfaction in a job well done. This one was supposed to be easy. I guess it was.

I backed away from the body, stepped back into the light, turned, and began walking casually away. They would find the body in a few hours. The babysitter would soon wonder why the kids' mother was so late coming home from work. She would call her parents, who would call the wine shop. Eventually the parents would come over and call the police, who would find the body. As I walked away my pulse returned to normal. I took my gloves off and placed them back in my bag. I would leave town tomorrow and this crime would remain unsolved. The neighborhood would go into a minor panic for a few weeks. Then things would settle down again. To all but her family, the events of this night would merely become a tale children tell to each other, like a ghost story around a campfire, real death co-opted into urban legend. Her family, like her, wouldn't question why she was killed. The same way I didn't question why I killed her. It's simple, really. I killed her because I am good and she was evil. At least that's what they told me, Maria.

I'd be lying if I didn't admit that sometimes I still believe it.

Two

I woke up the next morning and went through my normal routine. Exercise. Two hundred push-ups, four hundred sit-ups. Breakfast and then an eight-mile run. I was up early enough that the streets were barren. I had gotten back to my host's apartment in Jersey City at about one-thirty in the morning. I got four hours of sleep, woke up, and started my day. It was a travel day. I wanted to get started as early as my body could handle. I had a flight to catch out of Philadelphia in the early afternoon and was anxious to leave. I was always anxious to leave after a job. Maybe there was something in me that regretted doing what I did. I don't know. The plan was for me to take a bus from Jersey City to the parking lot of a shopping mall in the New Jersey suburbs. Once there, my friends would pick me up and drive me to the airport.

The early morning air was crisp. I found myself running through a light fog that had settled in around the four-story brownstones that lined the Jersey City streets. I ran hard, trying to drive all thoughts from my mind. As I ran, I kept an eye out for anything suspicious, gazing to my left and my right as I took each step, looking for anything odd or out of place, trying to make eye contact with the vendors opening up their stores to see if there was even the slightest hint of recognition. It wouldn't be long before they realized what had happened. "They" could be anywhere. The night before had been a concerted effort. Three hits in the same night all around the same city. All told, we were leaving five corpses in our wake. I had the easy kill. At this point, I could only assume that my friends had been able to complete their jobs too. If not, I could be waiting for my ride for a long time.

I turned a corner and began running up a steep hill. Ahead of me was a man in front of a dry cleaner unloading a truckful of cleanly pressed shirts and suits. Our eyes met and his face turned sour. I quickly turned down another side street and kept running. I doubted that he recognized me but you can never be too safe. After another block, I turned and looked back, but there was nothing. Paranoia. It was a helpful tool in my profession. I was taught early on that only the paranoid survive. Let your guard down for even a moment and that moment could be your last.

If Jared and Michael's marks went down without much fanfare, they might not realize what had happened until later today. Knowing Jared and Michael, however, their marks probably didn't go down quietly. If their jobs weren't clean, then there was likely already a team of people out looking for us. Three jobs and five bodies in one night was sure to stir up trouble. I guess stirring up trouble was the point.

The police didn't worry me. Sure, the cops were going to be investigating, and New York cops were some of the best, but the cops had a protocol to follow. They had a system. Seemingly mindless, senseless killings by perpetrators who come into town for a night or two and leave without a trace were not their forte. Motive? What motive? Anyone who could piece the motive together for these killings already knew why each person was killed. Those people were already on a side. Did we have any guys on the inside in New York? I don't know. Probably. Did they? It's just as likely. We are everywhere—so are they.

I turned another corner and started to run back to my host's apartment. I pumped my arms and lifted my knees, kicking it into a higher gear and pushing the last two miles hard.

My host was a nice guy. Roughly thirty years old, he was single and lived in a two-bedroom apartment in Jersey City. He was a computer programmer at some insurance company in downtown Manhattan. He took me out for drinks my first night in town and peppered me with questions. I answered a few and left a lot more unanswered. He knew the drill. He also knew that the more information he could pry from me, the more dangerous it became for him.

I finished my run at a slower pace than normal. I blamed the lack of sleep.

It was nearly noon by the time Jared and Michael pulled up in their rental car. We would have to move pretty quickly for me to make my flight. Jared was driving, so speed wasn't going to be a problem. Jared swung the car around as Michael hung himself out of the passenger-side window. "Joe," he called out to me as the car slowed to a stop, "your chariot has arrived." He spread his arms out wide, welcoming me. "Come here and give me a hug, you ugly bastard."

I picked up my bag and headed toward the car. I had spent the last hour or so people-watching on the sidewalk in front of Macy's. I watched the people as they strolled into the mall, destined to spend their day trying to decide which pair of jeans made their ass look smallest or which television set would best fit in their living rooms. There were moments when I was jealous, but my life, our life, is never going to be normal like that. "You guys are late," I said as I stepped toward Michael's outstretched arms.

"Better late than never," Michael whispered to me as he grabbed me into a big bear hug. "Get in the car. We've got to get moving."

I threw my bag across the backseat and climbed in.

"Jared," I acknowledged my old friend with a quick nod, making eye contact with him in the rearview mirror.

"How're things, Joey? I assume everything went well." He showed me a wide grin.

"Easiest job yet. No hitches. How about you guys?"

"You don't have to assume," Michael said. He threw an edition of the *New York Post* in my lap. "Your lazy ass didn't even make the paper." I looked down at the front page. There, in bold print over a picture of two bloody bodies covered by formerly white blankets, was the headline "Bloodbath in the Bronx." Beneath the picture, in smaller print, were the words "Mets Take Two from the Phillies to Pull within One."

"Holy shit," I said as I flipped to page three to read the story. "You guys are going to get yourselves killed." I looked at the picture and the headline again. "And you're going to get me killed with you."

"They told me and Michael that they wanted us to stir things up. Well, Michael might have gone a little overboard." Jared eyed me in the rearview mirror again. His smile didn't fade. He was proud, proud of Michael, proud of the job we'd just done, proud of all of us. I began to read.

> Last night at 12:35, two men were stabbed to death in front of Yankee Tavern, a crowded bar near Yankee Stadium. Joseph Delenato and Andrew Braxton were walking out of the bar where they had stopped for drinks after attending the Yankee game when they were assaulted. The assailant approached Joseph first, stabbing him twice in the chest, before turning to Andrew and stabbing him in the throat. Both men died within minutes of the attack. Witnesses say that the assailant, a white male about twenty-five years old, moved quickly. He did not stop to

rob the victims, nor does there seem to be any other motive for the incident. "I was with Joe and Andy all night,"
said their friend Steven Marcomi. "We just stopped in for
a drink or two. I'd never seen the [assailant] in my life. I've
never seen anything like that in my life. It's not like we got
into any fights or anything. I can't imagine why this happened." While motive remains unclear, police say that this
was likely the work of an experienced killer. "Whoever did
this," Lt. John Gallow said to reporters early this morning, "knew exactly what he was doing. He was efficient
and precise." Andrew bled to death on the scene. Joseph's
lungs were punctured when he was stabbed. "Technically,
Joseph drowned in his own blood," said the coroner's
office. "Each stab wound punctured a separate lung.
They quickly filled with blood. The poor kid eventually
drowned." Joseph's mother told this reporter, "I don't
know who could have done such a thing. My boy was such
a sweet boy. He didn't deserve this." Andrew's family was
not available for comment.

Next to a picture of the bar was an artist's sketch of the perpetra-
tor. "Nice picture, Michael. I'm sure your mother's going to be real
proud."

"That shit doesn't even look anything like me." Michael grabbed
the paper away from me to look at his sketch again. It really didn't
look anything like him. It was typical. All artists' sketches did was
build up general suspicion. No matter what the sketch looked like,
everyone knew someone who looked a little bit like it.

"And the quote from his mother. Real fucking precious. Like she
doesn't know why her son was killed." Michael paused for a second,
going over the story in his head again. "But did you see the quote

from the cop? Precise and efficient. I'd like to get that quote on my business cards."

"Did you really have to make things this messy?" I looked again at the bloody picture on the front page and then up at Michael.

"Maybe not, but it was my best move. I had to take both of them out and I had to do it before one A.M. or else I risked them finding out about your guys' jobs and getting all defensive. When I saw them go into the bar, I knew that my best chance was to hit them right when they came out. I figured they'd be buzzed and their reflexes would be numbed."

"That's how you were able to stab the first guy twice before even turning on the second?" Michael was good at what he did. I had to give him that.

"Yeah. That and the fact that the second guy half knew what was going on. An innocent would have run. Instead, this guy stands there frozen. He knows what's happening but can't remember how he's supposed to respond. He's got this dumb look on his face, like 'Am I supposed to run? To fight? To take a shit?' Pffft." Michael made the sound of a deflating balloon. "Too late."

"And then what'd you do?" I asked Michael.

"Slipped away into the cool Bronx night. That's one scary borough, man. I'm telling you, I was the least dangerous looking guy on the street."

I began flipping further through the paper. "Jared's is on page fourteen," Michael said. I turned to the page. There, tucked onto the far right-hand side of the page, was a story about an affluent Westchester couple that left their car running in their garage and died of carbon monoxide poisoning. He was a litigation partner at some big law firm in Manhattan. She had been an advertising executive who gave up her career to take care of the children. The strange part of the story was how both children were found sleeping on the porch in the morning, wrapped in blankets, safe from the fumes. Officials surmised that the parents put their children outside before taking their own lives. No one could fathom why such a seemingly happy couple would want to kill themselves.

"You're a master, Jared. Truly brilliant work," I said as I flipped further into the paper past the article about my friends.

"You're not in there, Joe," Michael said as he continued to watch me flip the pages. "Nothing about your mark at all." Just another body, I thought. Not newsworthy. Just an average woman killed in an average way. Nothing to see here. "You sure you actually remembered to do your mark?" Michael asked.

"Yeah, I remembered. It was easy."

"Yeah, but your kill was probably the most dangerous," Jared said. "Everything was set up for yours. We were just supposed to create noise. You had to take her out, show them that there are consequences." Jared continued driving down I-295, changing lanes and slipping through traffic. "Her husband had to learn a lesson. You don't take out eight of our guys in one year without repercussions."

"I read the preliminaries," I said to Jared. I stared out the window at the faces in the cars that we passed, scanning each one, trying to guess if they were one of us, one of them, or if they were just one of the lucky uninitiated masses. There was no way to tell. We passed a silver Volkswagen Jetta with a cute college-age girl behind the wheel and one of her friends in the passenger seat, passed a big black Escalade driven by a large man with a mustache and a tattoo on his left arm, passed a black couple driving a small red sports car, kept on moving forward, kept on passing people, all potential friends, all potential enemies. All I knew for sure was that I had one more professional killer who had plenty of reason to want me dead.

"What's next on your agenda?" Jared asked me.

"I've got a lecture to do. You guys?"

"A little rest and relaxation for me." Michael smiled. I looked over at Jared, wondering where he was off to next.

"I've got another job to do. It shouldn't be tough. After that, maybe we should try to get together." Jared nodded his head toward the passenger seat. "Where exactly are you headed for your vacation, Michael?"

"You know I'm not supposed to tell you two losers. What if you're caught and tortured, you might give me up." That was protocol. Even meeting for these moments after a job was unorthodox. We were always taught that as few people should know where you are as possible. It was safer that way. Keep moving. Keep quiet. Stay safe. It was boring and lonely as hell. "Besides, you two will probably cramp my style." There was a pause. "But maybe, I might be headed to Saint Martin—the French side. Great sun, great food. My place is big enough for the five of us. Me, you two, and the two girls I'm bringing home each night."

"What do you think, Joe? Saint Martin? Sit in the sun, drink liquor through a straw, stare at the beautiful women cruising the beach?" My eyes met Jared's again in the rearview mirror. He was my oldest friend. We'd known each other since long before we knew what type of life we were destined for. When we were in first grade, we played cops and robbers. We pretended to be firemen, astronauts. This, we never imagined. We never played good and evil. Jared looked a little tired, a little worn down.

"I'm in," I said.

At the airport we went our separate ways again. Michael dropped me off first. He'd drop Jared in a different location and then return the rental car. As they drove away, Michael leaned out of the passenger-side window, cupped his hands around his mouth, and shouted, "Remember, young Jedi, the force will be with you always." I could still hear Michael laughing as I walked through the glass doors into the terminal. From here on out, if the three of us saw each other, we were strangers.

When I got to my terminal, I went to the flight desk and got a seat assignment for a person whose name wasn't mine. I showed them an ID with my picture on it but a stranger's name. Then I boarded a plane to Chicago. It's a shame that it wasn't a longer flight because as soon as I leaned back in my chair, I fell into a deep, dreamless sleep. I didn't budge when we took off. I barely noticed when we landed. It had gotten to the point where the only place I could ever get a deep sleep was on an airplane.

Three

In Chicago, I was supposed to assist in a lecture to some local kids. I knew what to expect. It was more an initiation than a lecture. Each kid would be roughly sixteen years old. They'd still be innocent. They'd still have two years left before their worlds began to collapse around them. They'd have two years to get used to the idea that there were people out there who wanted to kill them. I was invited to these things because I represented death. They didn't know it yet, but I was their future. One of our Intelligence guys would lead the lecture. He would introduce me near the end of his talk. My job was to tell these kids about what I did for a living, to show them what they might one day become. It was kind of like career day for the criminally insane.

The lecture took place in the den of a house in a wealthy Chicago suburb. The kids sat on couches and upholstered dining room chairs that the adults had pulled into the room for the lecture. Everything was set up so that the kids' eyes would be directed toward an empty wall where the television usually was. The man hosting the event had three children, two boys and a girl. The oldest child, one of the boys, would turn sixteen in two months. The father had taken the two younger kids into the city for the day. They'd eventually have to sit through this lecture, too, but not today. Most parents tried to shield their kids from the War for as long they could.

All told, there were eight kids there, all from around Chicago, all within three months of their sixteenth birthday. There were three girls and five boys. Each of the kid's parents had dropped them off for the lecture, kissing them, promising to come get them in roughly four hours and driving off, probably crying as they drove. This was no bar mitzvah or first communion. This wasn't about ceremony. This really was the end of these kids' innocence. None of them really knew what the lecture would be about, but none of them were clueless either. When you grow up in these families, like I did, you can't help but know things.

I sat in the back of the room on one of the chairs. I'd have to watch most of the lecture, only contributing my part at the end. Then the lecturer and I would take questions. We always got a lot of questions. We answered the ones we could. Some questions just went unanswered. The lecturer today was a guy named Matt from Intelligence. I'd never seen him before. I would probably never see him again. There was no rhyme or reason to our pairing. There never was. Matt wore a dark blue, pinstriped suit. His hair was cut short and he wore silver wire-rimmed glasses. He looked like a banker. These kids, they were our investment.

Matt began his lecture. "Hello, everyone. My name is Matt. I'm here to tell you guys a bit about the world and about how you fit into it. I'm not here to lecture you. This is a talk. Feel free to ask questions at any time. I guess this will kind of be like your high school sex-ed classes, only I'm going to tell you some things that you don't already know." That's right, butter them up, I thought. His line got a nervous laugh from the kids. They shot quick glances at each other, trying to figure out if it was okay to laugh. It's okay to laugh, kids, I thought. You might as well laugh now while you still can. Matt continued.

"Before we get started, I think it would be useful if everyone introduced themselves, first names only. Then tell us a little something
about yourself, about clubs you're in, sports, hobbies, favorite band,
whatever." They did this in every lecture that I had attended. I always
thought it was strange because from here on out, so much of their
world would be shrouded in secrecy. Normally, if you get ten of us in
a room together, the idea is to share as little information about each
other as possible. There is safety in silence. This was different. This
was the first time for these kids. It was important for them to know
that they weren't alone. It was important for them to know that there
were others out there, people on their side, people dealing with the
same issues as them, other people who, like them, would go on to lead
lives full of fear and hatred. Matt's eyes turned toward the kid whose
house we were in. "Ryan," he said, as if he were an old friend of the
family, "why don't you start?"

Ryan stood up. He was a big kid. He looked like an athlete. He was
nervous, though. He put one hand in the pocket of his jeans to try to
keep it from shaking. "Hi, my name is Ryan. I'm fifteen, going to be
sixteen in two months. This is my house and I play football." Football. If Matt weren't about to fuck with Ryan's head, Ryan probably
could have been a popular kid. Maybe he could have been homecom-
ing king. Maybe he could have dated a cheerleader. Maybe. The girl
to his left spoke next. "Hi, my name is Charlotte. I just turned sixteen
and I play the violin." Charlotte glanced at the other kids' faces as she
spoke. When she was finished, she quickly turned her gaze back to
her lap. It went on like that for the next fifteen minutes: Rob, the
hockey player; Steve, the science club president; Joanne, the drama
club member. None of these kids knew each other. They had been
handpicked for this very reason. Even if they had friends that were
on our side, they weren't supposed to know it. Jared and I weren't
supposed to know that we were both part of the War. The fact that
we'd found out was just dumb luck.

When the kids were done introducing themselves, Matt went on. "Okay, I know you guys are nervous. You're nervous for two reasons. First, you're nervous because you don't know why you're here. Second, you've got an idea about why you're here and you're nervous that you might be right. You all know that you are different. You know your lives are different from your friends'. You can feel it. I know that you've asked your parents questions over the years that they've refused to answer. Well, first let me assure you that they refused to answer your questions because they were trying to protect you." Matt paused for effect. "I'm here because soon everything is going to change for you. Ignorance will no longer protect you. I'm here to tell you the truth."

The truth? The word bounced in my head. It echoed there for a moment and then died away before I had time to think too hard about it. Matt jumped right in. "How many people here have had a close family member murdered?" Six of the eight kids raised their hands. Matt raised his hand too. I could have but chose not to. "How many of you have had a parent murdered?" Three of the eight. As they raised their hands, the kids looked around the room, the expressions on their faces a mix of fear and amazement. The names, the clubs, the sports, those things didn't help any one of these kids bond. The death, that's what bonds them together, that's what bonds all of us together.

"Strange, don't you think?" Matt nodded. "Well, my job here today is to tell you who killed your parents"—Matt made eye contact with the three kids who had lost parents—"and your relatives"—he lifted his head and gazed across the broader room. At this point, Matt turned on the projector that he had hooked up to his laptop. It projected an image against the blank white wall. All of the kids were now hooked, their eyes fixated on the picture in front of them. In their wildest dreams, this is not what they expected. When I was in their spot, it wasn't what I had expected. I remember how shocked I was.

The picture glowed on the wall. It was a picture of a white man, roughly thirty years old, with blond hair, brushed to the side. He looked like a television star, handsome, strong. The next picture was of a black man, roughly fifty years old, with a white beard and glasses. Matt clicked a button on his keyboard. The next picture was of a dark-haired woman with deep-set eyes and a slightly crooked smile. Another picture, this one of an Indian man wearing a turban, then one of a chubby white man with a crew cut, then one of a young black woman with her hair tied back, a Hispanic woman, a Korean man, another white man, another white woman, a woman wearing a Muslim headscarf, a man with a long beard, a Chinese woman, and on and on. This little slide show lasted nearly twenty minutes. We had video. We had plenty of video, but they'd tested it and the pictures always had more effect. The pictures gave the kids time to ruminate on the faces. I had seen nearly all of these slides before. There were only a few new additions. Each of these people was one of our enemies. We knew it. About half of them had been eliminated already. The rest were still on the list.

When the slide show ended, Matt stood silently. He wasn't going to say anything. He was going to stand there until one of the kids spoke up, even if it took an hour. It never took that long. Rob, the hockey player, raised his hand. "Yes, Rob?" Matt asked.

"So which one did it?"

"Which one did what?" Matt asked. He knew what Rob was asking but he wanted Rob to say the words. He wanted every kid in that room to hear Rob say the words.

"Which one killed my mom?" Rob asked. Then he swallowed so hard I could hear it in the back of the room.

"They all did." Matt turned the lights back on. He walked slowly to the front of the room. We actually knew who had killed Rob's mom. He was still alive. He lived in St. Louis. They chose not to use the pictures of the people who'd actually killed the kids' family members. They didn't just want to show them one killer. They wanted to make these kids hate them all. "They're all complicit. Do you guys know what *complicit* means?" Each of the kids nodded. Smart group. Matt had their full attention. "They all killed them. They worked together. The scary part is that's only a small portion of them. And they're not done. They'll never be done. They'll stop only when we stop them. They are bloodthirsty killers. They are evil. They are the enemy. This is a war. It's been going on for generations. If you're lucky, it will be your generation that ends it." I had heard this part of the speech enough times that it had begun to turn my stomach each time I heard it. The propaganda wasn't my style. I always thought that it was unnecessary. I looked at Rob. He was staring at Matt. He had a slight twitch in his left eye and was flexing and unflexing his right fist. I couldn't help but think to myself, just tell the poor kid who killed his mom and send him on his way. You won't have to tell him which side is good and which is bad. As far as he's concerned, he already knew. Matt continued. "Two years from now, when each of you turns eighteen, you, too, will be a part of this War. There is no way out of it, no escape. These people"—Matt spoke the word *people* with disgust, as if it really shouldn't apply, then continued with more confidence, his voice growing louder with each word—"will come after you too. They want you dead. Make no mistake about it—each of you was born into this world with a special destiny. Each of you can work to make this world a better place. Once you turn eighteen you will be a target. You can be killed, just like your parents or your aunts or uncles were killed. You can be murdered, in cold blood, by the enemy. As Joseph here . . ." Matt pointed to me, acknowledging my presence for the first time. All of the kids turned in their seats to look at me. I simply sat there and nodded. Matt continued. "As Joseph will explain later, there are things that you can do about that. Once you turn eighteen, you can be killed, but you can also act to stop the killing. You can stop the violence. You can get revenge." Now I was interesting. The kids all turned to look at me again. Matt went on unfazed. "There are lots of things you can do to help us defeat the enemy—but more on that later.

"For now, you all deserve to know more about our enemy. They want to kill you simply because of who your parents are. They want to kill you and they want to kill your family. They will stop at nothing to accomplish this. They are corrupt, relentless, and immoral." Matt paused again. "And we must defeat them.

"There have been countless times in history when people have been slow to recognize that evil exists. Each time, people have been passive. They sat around while others died, only acting when it was nearly too late." At this point, a cadence developed in Matt's voice. "Well, I want you all to recognize that evil exists and that you must fight it. We know who they are. We have to fight our enemy head-on." Matt pointed at the pimply-faced kids in the room. "You will fight them head-on. We will attack them and defeat them before the evil grows too large to be defeated. They've already killed members of your family. They will kill again. They'll stop at nothing, unless we stop them. They are filled with hate. You don't have to hate them back. You just need to realize what they are capable of."

With that, Matt turned off the lights again. He turned his computer back on. This time, projected on the wall was the picture of two bloody bodies, covered in white blankets. It looked just like the picture in the *New York Post* I had seen the day before, the picture of Jared's victims. Matt clicked the button on his computer. The new picture was of a car burning, the flames reaching high into the air. I could just barely make out the shape of two charred bodies in the car. Matt clicked the button on his keyboard. The next picture was of an older man, roughly sixty, slumped in a chair. His eyes were glazed over and his mouth hanging open. He was dead. Another atrocity. Matt clicked and clicked. Another murdered man, another murdered woman. And on and on. I remember the first time I saw the slide show. It reminded me of the video I was shown in high school with all the graphic pictures of victims of drunk driving. That movie was supposed to make you afraid to drive drunk. It was supposed to make you afraid. Matt's slide show had a different purpose. It was meant to elicit that other primal emotion—hate. No matter what Matt said, I knew that we could only defeat them if we hated them. Even if the propaganda turned my stomach, I knew that this was true. Sitting in the back of the room watching these kids, I could tell that they were afraid. I could also see that they were beginning to hate. I'll be honest, Maria, at the time, their hate gave me hope.

"This is a lot to take," Matt said, as he flicked through a few more images of strewn, lifeless bodies. Again, we could have shown them video but we had to be careful. Too much too soon wouldn't help these kids turn into fighters. We had to ease them into it. We had two years. "But I have a few more slides to show you. You've seen our enemies. Now . . ." Matt's voice lightened. A smile broke out on his face. He continued. "Let me show you pictures of your friends." Matt clicked on his keyboard and a new image appeared. This picture was brighter than the rest. The room began to glow. The first picture was of a white man. He had an athletic build. He was standing in a large field of grass. He was smiling. Matt moved to the next slide. It showed a blond woman. She was standing in front of a skyscraper on a city street. The next slide was of a black man in scrubs, then an Indian woman working at a computer, then a Hispanic man in a business suit, and on and on. Each slide showed another face, another pose, another race, religion, ethnicity. Each slide showed a new person, each one attractive, attentive, serious yet smiling. These pictures were the same at every lecture I'd attended. These slides were meant to represent hope. Hope for these kids, that they could manage this life, hope that they could survive. Hope because they weren't alone. I remember how much that had meant to me.

When I was a kid, I remember walking into a room full of adults, only to have the room suddenly grow quiet. I knew they had been talking about something, something important, but they left me in the dark. Matt led those kids through a whole cycle of emotions, from fear to anger, from anger to hate, from hate to hope. It was somewhat sanitized, somewhat canned and rehearsed, but it was marketing genius. I knew how to kill people. Matt knew how to convince people to want to kill. I'm pretty sure that there's more blood on his hands than on mine. I remember leaving the meeting when I was sixteen—frothing at the mouth, ready to start killing. The meeting gave me a purpose. I was sixteen. All I wanted was a purpose. Now, I sat watching Matt's little presentation and felt nothing. Now I had my own reasons for hating the enemy. I didn't need the slide show anymore. War will do that to you.

"Any questions?" Matt asked as he flipped the lights back on. He said it just like that, too, like he'd just taught the kids how to operate a washer-dryer. From here, the class could go in two directions, depending on who asked the first question. Ryan raised his hand. It was his house. I knew what he was going to ask before he asked it. I'd heard kids like him lead off with the same question dozens of times before. He wanted to be brave. "Yes, Ryan?"

"When do we get started?" Ryan asked. Only when the words finished coming out of his mouth did Ryan realize how afraid they made him. The words scared the shit out of all of them. There was no answer that Matt could give that wouldn't be too soon. Yet that was the question that was usually asked, burying the other question—the question that we needed to answer—under a heap of peer-pressure-induced bravado. I guess the *when* is the question that's usually asked because when somebody punches you in the nose your first instinct isn't to ask why, it's to feel pain and anger and to want to punch back. Eventually, you'll ask yourself why. The *why* always comes. It's unavoidable. That's why we try to answer that question here, in the first class, because if you give these kids a *why*, they might not try to find their own. We finessed it, though. We tried not to force it because it worked better if they asked first. That way, they felt like it came from them. So we'd only bring it up ourselves at the very end and only if no one asked.

"Joseph?" Matt looked toward me. I wasn't ready. I never was. "Perhaps you can answer that?" Ready or not, I was up. I really only had one job: tell these kids about the rules of engagement. After that, I was just there to answer their questions.

I walked to the front of the room. "You'll get started soon enough, Ryan," I answered him. "In fact, I'm going to tell you guys about all of the rules of this War. Once that's covered, Ryan, your question should be answered." My voice didn't sound like my own. When I talked to these kids, I always thought I sounded like someone else. "The rules are simple. They are simple but they are inflexible and the penalties for breaking these rules are severe. So listen closely."

One of the kids raised her hand. I motioned to her so that she could speak. "How can a war have rules?" she asked. They all looked skeptical. It made sense. They've just spent over two hours being told that their enemy is evil. How their enemy must be defeated at all costs. Now I was going to come in and tell them that there were rules.

I was ready for the question. I'd heard the answer when I was sixteen. Since then, I'd delivered the answer many times. "All wars have rules," I responded. "I know it seems counterintuitive. Why should we follow rules when we're fighting people who killed our families?" The kids nodded along. "The thing is, without rules, there's chaos. In chaos, nobody can win. We follow the rules because the rules will help us win."

"Then why do they follow them?" one of the kids asked.

"For the same reason," I answered. "Because they think that the rules will help them win, but we know better." I did not tell them the real reason why I followed the rules. I followed the rules because they were the only thing keeping me sane. Even if they didn't make sense, at least there were rules. They existed, islands of sanity in this absurd ocean. I continued with my explanation. "Rule number one: No killing innocent bystanders. The large majority of this world does not know that this War is raging on beneath their noses. Those people are to be protected at all costs. No collateral damage. The penalty for killing an innocent bystander is death, whether administered by our side or theirs. No excuses. No extenuating circumstances."

"What if it's an accident?" asked one of the kids.

"There are no accidents," I responded quickly, and then moved on. "Rule number two: No killing anyone under the age of eighteen no matter what side they're on. Until you turn eighteen you're considered an innocent bystander. Therefore, the penalty for killing anyone who is under eighteen, including one of the enemy, is death. The corollary to this rule is that no one, on either side, can play a role in this War until they turn eighteen. So, Ryan"—I addressed him directly for a moment—"you wanted to know when you can get started. Well, you will get started the day you turn eighteen." I paused for a second, debating whether or not to continue, whether or not to pile it on. I decided that I should, that they should hear it. So I added, "You'll get started when you turn eighteen whether you want to or not. Until then, over the next two years, you will be trained. You will be readied for the transition. Your free pass is almost over." Eighteen years wasn't long enough. No amount of time would ever be long enough. The next two years will be hell for these kids. They will have to endure physical training and emotional training. They will be taught how to kill and how to defend themselves from being killed. They'll see things they can't even imagine, things they'll wish they never saw. These kids weren't ready for that yet, but it would come.

"Those are the two key rules. Every other rule flows from those two. There is a third rule that is important for you guys to know." The third rule. I never really thought too much about the third rule. I never really stopped to contemplate the cruel practicality of its punishment. My mistake. "The third rule is necessary because of how the first two rules impact the War. It's really quite simple. You can't have kids until you turn eighteen. Can anyone see why this rule might be necessary?" One of the girls raised her hand. I motioned for her to speak.

"Because if you can have kids before you turn eighteen, no one will ever win the War."

Perceptive. "Why's that?" I asked.

"Well, if you can't kill someone until they turn eighteen, and they keep having children before they turn eighteen, how could you ever stop them? They could just keep growing."

"Exactly. That's why we need the third rule. So, if anyone on either side has a child before they turn eighteen, that child must be turned over to the other side."

"Do they kill them?" the perceptive girl asked.

"No, they don't kill them. We don't kill them. The other side simply adopts them. They raise them as one of their own. So, by violating this rule, instead of increasing the population of our side, you increase the population of theirs. Instead of making our side stronger, you make their side stronger. Eventually, that child will grow up. It will grow up and it will join this War and it will fight. It will grow up to fight its own parents, fight its brothers, fight its sisters." I looked around the room at the shocked faces. It was clear that already they viewed this punishment as more cruel than death. I let it sink in before I went on. "So, those are the rules. That's it. Three rules that you cannot ignore. Three rules that you cannot forget. Three rules that you must obey. Everything else that I tell you today is simply procedure. So, who here has guessed what it is I do for a living?"

A few hands raised and I called on one of them at random. "You kill people."

"That's right," I replied. "I'm a soldier." A soldier. That's what they called us. Me, Michael, Jared, we were soldiers. We were supposed to be proud of the title. I went on to explain to the kids the different roles they might one day grow up into. They didn't have to follow in my footsteps. We organized our side into three basic categories. Which category you joined depended on your desires and your aptitude for any one specific role. Frequently, as people aged, they could shift from one category to another. The first category was the soldiers. I had expressed a desire to be a soldier shortly after I went through my age sixteen information session. I thought it would be cool. Soldiers are the front line in the War. The soldiers are the offense. The soldiers meet the enemy head-on and are responsible for beating them. Like the kid said, we kill people.

Of course, the killing is never as simple as it seems. I couldn't just go out, find the enemy and kill them. A game plan is needed. First you have to know who among the masses is part of the enemy. Figuring that out isn't so easy. They come in all shapes and sizes, all ethnic groups, all religions. It's only if you trace their genealogy back far enough that you'll find they are all related. It was a strategy at one point in this War's history, effectively executed by both sides, to try to hide members by diversifying their gene pools. So what do they have in common? A few genes and a common enemy—me, my friends, my family, these kids. So how do we find them? That's the job of the second group: Intelligence. The Intel group includes guys like Matt. There are lots of different jobs in Intelligence: genealogists, translators, education experts, marketing gurus, military planners, computer experts. The list goes on. The Intel group is the biggest group. They're the ones who tell me, Michael, and Jared who to kill. Sometimes they tell us why. Sometimes that stays secret. They also work on the training and education. They teach us to kill and then they tell us who to practice on.

The third group are the deep cover guys. We simply refer to them as breeders. It's their job to assimilate completely into everyday life, to lay low and to try as hard as they can to raise normal families.

They're the ones who make sure that our ranks are not depleted. The danger for them, of course, is that their defenses will be down, that they will grow soft from years undercover and they will be discovered. If discovered, they'll be killed. Their defenses are limited. Most breeders spend at least some time in another role. They may start as soldiers or in Intelligence. Then they either burn out, or meet someone they want to settle down with. Then they go deep cover.

"So how do you know who to kill?" asked one of the kids.

"I get a message from Intelligence. They let me know who my target is, where my target is, and anything special that I need to be aware of about my target. They also give me a window of time to get the job done, usually a couple of days. Sometimes, if the job is more difficult, a week. So I go to the destination. I have a safe house assigned to me. The safe house is always owned by a person on our side, without children, who will let me stay with them while I complete my job."

"Do they know what you're there to do?"

"They know, but I'm not supposed to give them any details. You'll learn soon that knowledge can be very dangerous."

"What's it like to kill someone?" It didn't feel right telling them the real answer. The real answer was that it was easier than you'd think.

"I don't think of my targets as people. They're simply the enemy. We're the good guys. They're the bad guys." We were nearing the end of the session. The kids' parents would be back to pick them up soon. "A couple more questions."

"But how can you be sure that the person you're supposed to kill is one of them?"

"First, I trust my Intelligence. These guys are good at what they do," I said, motioning to Matt. "But it's not just that. There's something else, something that I can't really describe. You know because they know. When you meet one of them, you can sense it, and so can they. You can feel it. Like I said, it's hard to explain. One day, if you're lucky, you'll know what I'm talking about."

"And what if we're not lucky?" asked one of the kids.

"Then it will be too late." I paused for a moment, unsure if I'd said too much. Another hand went up. It was a girl in the back. To this point, she'd been quiet. I'd almost thought that no one was going to ask the question that Matt and I were waiting for, but if anyone asked it, I knew it would be her. She looked the most afraid, but I knew that was only because she was the only one brave enough not to hide her fear. I pointed to her.

"Why?" she asked, her voice soft but sure.

I knew what she meant but it didn't matter that I knew. I needed everyone else to know too. "Why what?" I prodded her.

She looked around at the others before speaking, almost afraid to ask the question. "Why are they trying to kill us? Why do they hate us? Why do we have to kill them? Why?" Her voice trailed off. She could have kept going. She could have kept asking why this and why that forever but she made herself stop. The room went quiet. All the eyes moved from the girl back to me. Everything depended on my answer.

"Matt has told you that they are evil, but what is evil?" I shrugged. "Sometimes I'm sure I know. Sometimes I have my doubts." I looked at Matt. He was glaring at me nervously, unsure of where I was going with my answer. He didn't have to worry. I'd done this before. "Here's what I do know: they've killed your parents, your brothers, your sisters. If they haven't yet, they're going to try." I paused, purely for effect. "They will kill everyone you've ever loved, and then they will kill you." I stared at the girl even though I wasn't only speaking to her. I was speaking to all of them. "Unless we stop them."

I could have kept going. I could have asked them if that was reason enough. I didn't have to. I could see it in their eyes, even the eyes of the girl who had asked the question. I hadn't actually answered her question. I did better. I'd invalidated it. "Isn't that enough?"

"I've got two more slides to show you guys." We had to ease them into it, but we had to give them a taste too. I motioned toward Matt. He clicked a button on the computer. The close-up of a man's face lit up on the wall. There was nothing extraordinary about the picture. He was a white man, about thirty-five years old. He was stocky and his hair was receding. In the picture he was smiling, but it wasn't a pleasant smile. It was a smile full of malice. Intelligence had picked a good picture for their purposes. "This man's name is Robert Gardner." The kids stared at the face. "When I was twelve years old, this man killed my uncle. I was with him at the time. My uncle had taken me to the mall to pick up a new baseball mitt. We were walking through the mall together and I turned to look at the dogs in the pet store window. When I turned back around my uncle was gone. They came up and grabbed him when I wasn't looking. My parents had to come to the mall and pick me up after I'd searched the mall for my uncle for hours. Nobody told me at the time that even before I gave up my search, they'd found my uncle in the Dumpster behind the food court. The men who kidnapped him had slit his throat from one ear to the other." Nobody in the room made a sound. He was my favorite uncle. I loved him. He was with me one minute and the next minute he was gone and I was alone. I never got to see him again. You don't know what that's like, Maria. Those kids did, though. "When I turned eighteen, they told me what had happened. Then they told me who did it." I looked back at the photo on the wall. Then I turned toward Matt again and nodded. He clicked the button on the computer and another image came up. It was a picture of the same guy. Only this time, he had one eye stuck closed from swelling. His mouth hung down loose on his jaw and his tongue was blue. There was a deep gash on his right cheek. His one open eye was fully dilated but lifeless. "This man's name is Robert Gardner. He murdered my favorite uncle. When I turned eighteen they told me who he was and where he lived." I pointed toward the grotesque picture on the wall. "This is what he looked like when I was through with him. I was eighteen years old and he was the first man I ever killed. After I was through with him, he never had a chance to murder another one of us." I looked around at the room full of kids. They were all staring at the picture of Robert Gardner's beaten, lifeless face. A couple of the kids looked like they were going to be sick. It was to be expected. They'd seen a lot that day. They'd seen more than most people could handle. But it was only a couple. The rest of them looked inspired. I looked at Matt. He was quietly noting each kid's reaction. The inspired were one step closer to becoming killers.

Four

The next morning, I was scheduled to check in with my contact in Intelligence. It was the same procedure every time. Stay at your safe house until your job is done. Wait for the right time. Call Intelligence to get your next assignment. Always call from a landline. Be sure that no one is listening.

I'd call and the woman who answered would sound like the receptionist from any one of a million companies. When she answered the call, I'd ask three successive operators for three different individuals. I would be transferred to the next operator after each request. As far as I could tell, none of the people that I asked to speak with actually existed. It was all just a code. The list of individuals would be given to me at the end of my previous call. I learned early on to memorize the names and never to write them down. If we forgot the names, we'd be cut off from Intelligence and on our own until someone from Intelligence found us. After going through the procedure, I was connected to my contact.

"Hey, Matt," I said when his familiar voice finally picked up the line. There were lots of Intelligence guys named Matt. For a long time, I wasn't sure why this was. I'd find out soon enough.

"How's it going, Joe?" Matt replied. He'd been my contact for over five years. "You teach the kiddies how to survive in the real world?"

"I did what I could."

"You ready for your next job?"

"No," I replied.

Matt started laughing. He thought that I was kidding. He kept talking. "I've got a mark for you in Montreal. This one's important. It's been earmarked especially for you. Apparently, someone upstairs has noticed your work."

"I'm not kidding, Matt," I said. "I'm not ready. I need a break. No more bodies. Not for a couple of days. No more blood. Just a few days and I can come back."

"Seriously?" Five years and I had never asked Matt for a break before. He owed me. "What do you want me to do?"

"Can the Montreal job wait?" I asked.

Matt paused for a minute. I could hear papers shuffling on his end of the line. I didn't have a clue what he was up to. "How long do you need?" he finally asked. Matt was a good guy. He watched out for his operatives. I imagined that this would take some fancy footwork on his part.

"I can call you in five days. I'll get the details from you then."

"Where you going?" Matt asked. I couldn't tell him. I wasn't supposed to be scheduling unapproved time hanging out with other soldiers. It wasn't protocol. It was dangerous.

"Away" was all I said to him. Sandy beaches, warm water, no death.

"Five days," Matt repeated, thinking to himself, trying to figure out how he was going to pull this off. "Don't fuck me here. I'll figure out a way to delay this one for you, but you better be ready to go in five days."

"Thanks, Matt."

"Michael Bullock. Dan Donovan. Pamela O'Donnell." The names

came through the receiver like Matt was speaking in Morse code. I immediately committed each name to memory. "Be careful, Joe."

"Thanks again, Matt." With that, Matt hung up. I booked a flight with my next call. I had no intention of letting him down. The thing is, intentions are a bitch.

Five

Saint Martin wasn't Saint Martin. Saint Martin was a pipe dream. It was a place that Michael had read about in a magazine. We didn't have the money or the initiative to make it to a place like that. One day, maybe. One day, when the forces above us deemed us worthy, maybe we'd get paid enough for a trip like that. For now, for us, Saint Martin had just become a call sign. It was a nickname. When Michael told us to meet in Saint Martin, we knew where to go. It was the same place we'd been going since we were teenagers. Our Saint Martin was the New Jersey Shore.

We'd come in the past during breaks from work. Whenever each of us could find the same free moments, we'd do our best to meet on a skinny little island off the Jersey coast called Long Beach Island. Our stand-in for paradise. It wasn't easy finding the time. It was even harder to get in touch with each other. The opportunities to actually meet were becoming more and more rare. We had to take them when we could even if we all knew that it was dangerous to do a trip like this so close on the heels of the jobs we just pulled only a few hours away in New York. Sometimes you just didn't feel like running anymore.

Long Beach Island wasn't an easy place to get to without a car. I had to fly back into the Philadelphia airport, take a train to Atlantic

City, and then find a cab willing to take on a one-hour fare. I offered to pay the cabbie double since I knew there was no way he was going to get a fare coming back. It was the middle of the day. There wasn't a line of people waiting for cabs so he reluctantly agreed. My cabbie was a large black man with a beard and short cropped hair. There was no shortage of black people in Atlantic City. You could count the number of them at Long Beach Island on one hand. They stood out. That's why I recognized him so easily the next time I saw him.

All I had with me was a backpack with a bathing suit, a beach towel, and a couple of changes of clothes. That and about five hundred dollars in cash. It was late in the season, so the island was starting to empty out. The Jersey Shore works like a faucet. Memorial Day turns it on and the beaches get crowded and stay packed all summer. Labor Day turns it off and all that's left is a trickle, then a drip, then the whole place empties out. It was mid-September. That was always my favorite time at the shore. The water was warm. The air was still hot and the place was quiet.

The cabbie and I didn't talk much during the ride. I'm glad we didn't. It would make the things I would do later much easier. When we got to the bridge that led to the island, he simply said, "Where to?" He had a slight Caribbean accent left over from a youth spent somewhere more exotic than Jersey. I hadn't been in touch with Jared or Michael since they dropped me off at the Philadelphia airport the first time. Still, I knew where to go.

"Beach Haven," I replied to the driver. It was always Beach Haven. It was Michael's preference. More bars in that town than the others. More inebriated women.

"Yes, sir," the driver said. As he drove I opened up my backpack and pulled out my bathing suit. I slipped off my dirty jeans and slipped on the bathing suit in the backseat of the car. The cabbie looked back at me in the rearview mirror and shook his head. I didn't know what he thought I was going to do alone in the back of his cab.

"Just putting my bathing suit on," I said, and he looked away. The sun was shining brightly down on the little island. We drove over the bridge and took a right-hand turn toward Beach Haven. Once we got there, I told him what street to turn down and asked him to drop me off at the beach.

"Thanks, pal," I said, when I got out of the car.

"I'm not your pal," he replied, taking my money and counting it. Great way to start a vacation, I thought. I didn't know the half of it. I stepped out onto the hot pavement but was only two steps from the white sand that led up to the beach. In moments, my toes were digging into the fine, powderlike sand. It was even softer when we were kids, before they started pumping in other sand in the futile attempt to save the island from being washed away forever. I walked up the little path leading to the beach, over the sand dunes. The cabbie stayed and watched me until I crested the little hill. Only then did I hear him pull away.

At the top of the hill, I looked out in front of me. There was the ocean. God, it was beautiful. Every time I saw it, I felt small again. I loved that feeling. The sun beat down on the water and glistened off the waves as they curled in toward the beach. It felt like home. It was only one of two or three places in the world that gave me that feeling.

After watching the water for a few moments, I began to scan the beach for my friends. This is where we met every time—this beach. Either I'd see them or I'd lie down in the sand and wait for them to show up. I didn't see either of them at first. The beach was still relatively crowded, with a towel or blanket every five feet or so. The image looked like it came right out of a 1950s postcard. I took the towel out of my backpack and walked down toward the water. I dropped my towel in the sand about twenty feet from the waterline and lay down. The air was warm. I think I may have fallen asleep. If

I did, I just dreamed of other sandy beaches, because I don't remember anything else. Not until Michael came up and kicked sand into my face, anyway.

"You bastard," I said without opening my eyes, blissfully unaware of the children around me. I sprang to my feet and ran. It took me about half the beach before I caught up to Michael and tackled him into the sand. He tried to avoid it by bobbing and weaving but knew that I had more endurance than he did. Finally, I dove down toward his legs and knocked him over. Then I climbed on his back and pushed his face into the sand. "I was having a perfectly good time until you showed up," I said to him.

"Get off me, fat-ass," he managed to mumble through a mouthful of sand. Then I let him up and he tried to dust as much of the sand off his body as he could. The process was endless. Each wipe left a white residue. "You really know how to say hello to a guy," he complained as he tried to get the sand off his back.

"You started it." I felt like I was twelve years old again.

"All right, fine," Michael replied. "Give me some love." Then he pulled me into a big hug. I could smell the coconut odor from his suntan lotion. "Glad you could make it, Joey. We've come here every day for like three days now."

"Yeah, sorry I couldn't get here sooner," I said. "I guess we're not at this beach."

"Nope. I found us a choice place on the beach down about fifteen blocks."

"Where's Jared?"

"He's back at the house, making drinks, waiting for you to show your lazy ass up." Michael took one long look at me. I stared back. All I saw was my seventeen-year-old friend, even though nearly a decade had passed since we were that age. It was like looking through a time machine. When I looked at Michael, all I saw was an innocent, happy kid—even though he definitely wasn't innocent anymore. "So what'd you want to do?" he finally asked.

"I just want to go home," I replied.

We walked the fifteen blocks on the beach. We were in no rush. That's all I wanted out of the week, no rush. We walked close to the water's edge and each time a wave rushed in, I could feel the coolness engulf my ankles. Michael ogled the women as we walked. He stared at every single woman on that beach. Neither age nor weight held him back. "Don't you have any standards?" I asked him as he stared at a woman who must have been in her late forties as she took off her shorts and lay down on a blanket.

Michael took a step toward me and put his arm around me as we walked. "I see beauty everywhere," he said to me with a grin.

"Right," I replied.

"Come on, man. You have to loosen up a little. What do you think beaches are for, anyway? Ogling and being ogled—that's the whole show, Joe."

"That's it, huh?"

"That's it." Michael laughed. "This is nothing, Joe. Wait until we get to Saint Martin. Those beaches, they're like a three-dimensional porn magazine." This time I laughed. "Paradise," he finished, "Like the garden of Eden, except you don't get booted out because your dick gets hard." He nodded as he spoke. It sounded pretty nice.

We approached the house after about a forty-five-minute walk. I could already feel my skin sizzling beneath the sun and was ready to find some shade. Michael had gotten us a little house right on the beach. It was the top floor of a duplex. As we began to walk up the hill toward the house, I could make out Jared sitting in a chair on the porch reading, his feet up on the table in front of him. "Look what I found," Michael shouted as soon as we were close enough for Jared to hear. Jared waved to us, using his whole arm. I waved back and watched as he put his book down and trekked inside the house.

"Place looks great," I said to Michael.

"I'm glad you think so," Michael replied, "because you owe me seven hundred bucks for the week."

When we made it up to the house, Jared was back outside on the deck. He'd gone inside to grab a blender and some cocktails so that he could mix drinks. The deck was nice. From it, you could see over the sand dunes and watch the waves crash against the sand. Those waves were the only sound that made it up from the beach. The crash. Then silence. Then the slow build toward another crash.

Michael ran to the bathroom as soon as we got back, leaving me and Jared alone on the deck. I hadn't been alone with my oldest friend in a while. "So what's the plan?" I asked.

"Right now? Drink a little. Sit. Watch the water." Jared smiled and picked up a shaker. He had an assortment of liquors and juices in front of him.

"And tonight?" I asked.

"Are you kidding? Michael's been waiting all week for you to show up so that we can hit the bars together. You better not let him down." It was a toss-away line at the time. There was no way that Jared or I could know how badly I would wind up letting Michael down.

"Well, let's pick a mellow place tonight," I replied. "I could use a little rest before things get crazy."

"I think that can be arranged," Jared said. The sun was beginning to drop toward the bay on the other side of the island, creating a glare. Even through the glare, I could see Jared smiling.

"What are you making?" I asked, watching Jared measure and poor and shake.

"Been making 'em for the past two days. If we can't get Michael to the islands, I figured the least we could do is bring a little bit of the islands to Michael."

"What's in it?"

"A little rum, pineapple juice, orange juice, and some coconut cream. Big drink in the islands. You want one?" Jared started pouring the frothy drink into a cup.

"Sounds a little girlie to me. What's it called?"

"A painkiller."

"All right, then," I answered. "Make mine a double."

We drank painkillers and grilled burgers on the deck that night as the sky grew darker above us. Michael gave in and agreed to a relaxed evening after I promised that he would get to pick everything we did the following night. So, on the first night, we picked a small bar on the bay that we knew wouldn't get crowded. When we got to the bar, it was nearly empty. They were playing Jimmy Buffet music, trying to make people forget that they were at a dumpy little bar in New Jersey. We walked in and went straight for the bar. Michael tried ordering a painkiller. The old man behind the bar looked at him like he was from another planet. He settled on a beer.

I grabbed a barstool and sat down. I didn't plan on getting up again until we left. Michael and Jared decided to explore the place before sitting down. They didn't make it back. Instead, they discovered an old bar game tucked away in the back. I knew Jared and Michael well enough to know that, once they found that game, they weren't leaving it until one of them declared himself the champion of the bar. The game seemed simple enough. There was a small golden ring hanging from the ceiling by a string. The ring hung about chest high. About five feet away there was a hook screwed into a post. The object of the game was to hold the ring, place your feet behind the line taped to the floor, and try to swing the ring so that it would catch itself on the hook. It looked easy until you watched people try it. I sat there, with my drink in my hand, and watched as my two friends took turns standing behind the line and swinging the ring. It was unbelievably frustrating and I wasn't even playing. If you aimed the ring right for the hook, it would bounce off the hook and swing back to you. Instead, you had to swing the ring to one side, so that it would pass the hook on the way up and encircle it as it began to swing back toward you.

Frustration has never been a quiet emotion for my friends. Jared and Michael's competition started quietly enough but it didn't take long before the two of them were louder than the music coming over the bar's speakers. I divided my time between watching them and watching the bubbles rise up through my beer. I was perfectly happy just sitting there, continuing down my path toward debilitating drunkenness. I just wanted to let my worries melt away from me. I let my guard down. When I was on my third or fourth drink a woman sat down next to me at the bar. She looked like she was alone. She glanced over at Michael and Jared. They were tough to ignore. They'd always been tough to ignore. She looked at them and laughed and then turned toward me. "Friends of yours?" she asked.

It took me a moment to realize that she was talking to me. When I finally caught on, I tried to play it cool. "What makes you think that?" I asked. The woman was wearing a thin white tank top and a long island-print skirt. She was Asian, probably in her late twenties. She was in fantastic shape. She didn't look like your typical Jersey girl. She didn't look like your typical anything.

"Don't worry. I think they're cute," she said to me, staring at my friends berating each other. "They're not going to kill each other, are they?" I looked over at Jared and Michael. It was nothing I hadn't seen before. I figured my best strategy was to try to ignore them. It was a strategy I'd used plenty of times over the past ten years.

"You here alone?" I asked. It was the alcohol talking, pumping me full of courage that I normally didn't have.

"Maybe," she replied. She had a strange accent. "What would you think of a woman who went to a bar alone?"

"If she looked like you?" I answered. "I'd think she was mysterious. A little pathetic, but definitely mysterious."

"Great. Mysterious and pathetic." She laughed.

"Hell," I replied, "you can't win them all."

We sat for a few moments in silence, watching Jared and Michael argue. "So"—the woman eventually broke the silence—"do you come here often?"

I placed my drink back on the bar. "Are you trying to pick me up?"

"Not yet," she said, smiling. She paused, biting down on the corner of her lower lip. "I should probably get to know you first."

"And then you'll try to pick me up?"

"Maybe, if I like what I hear." She placed her hand on my elbow as she slid herself onto the barstool next to mine. Her skin was rougher than I'd expected but it was still warm, and my skin flared up at her touch. "So, what's your name?"

"Joseph," I replied, and held out my hand to shake hers. It was the first time that I'd used my real name with a woman in ages, maybe since high school. It felt good.

"Catherine," the woman volunteered, and shook my hand.

"Where you from, Catherine?" I asked. "You've got a peculiar accent."

"Yeah, yeah, my accent. There is nowhere in the world where I can go and not have people think that I have an accent." She looked at me, taking in my entire face, looking for something. At the time, I thought that it was good sign. "I grew up in Vietnam but I went to graduate school in London."

"You don't see too many people with that type of pedigree at the Jersey Shore," I offered. She laughed. I liked her laugh.

"What about you? Where are you from?" she asked.

"Right here," I replied, not yet growing uneasy with the questions.

"Really? You're from New Jersey?"

"Well, not New Jersey. I live just outside of Philadelphia," I lied. Lying was easier than the truth.

"So you spend a lot of time around here?" Catherine asked, leaning into me a bit, squeezing her elbows into the sides of her breasts so that they nearly erupted out of the top of her shirt. In an instant, I could feel my pulse in my head. "I'm kind of new to the area," she added. "I just came down from New York. Do you make it up there much?"

"Now and then," I replied. "I have to go there on business sometimes." I knew that I was dangerously close to the truth.

"Really? What do you do?" Catherine asked, still expertly using her cleavage to hypnotize me.

"Shill for the man," I replied, deciding to try to get the subject off of me. "What about you?"

Catherine laughed. "No, really. What do you do? If I'm going to pick you up, I need to know that you've got a stable career." She smiled at me. I never wanted her to stop smiling.

"You don't have to worry about that," I replied. I leaned in toward her. I was drunk and horny and out of sorts.

"I think I'll be the judge of that," she rebuked me. I figured that if I wanted to get in her pants, I needed to come up with a job where I made some money.

"Fine. I'm a financial consultant," I lied. We were taught, during training, to tell people that we worked in professions that wouldn't elicit much of a response. They suggested jobs like product managers for companies that made hangers or salesmen for plastic doorstops. Basically, we were taught to pick jobs that would effectively act as conversation enders. Of course, we were never taught how to do this and get laid at the same time. It really was a flaw in the curriculum.

Her smile broadened. "Is there lots of financial consulting in Philadelphia?"

"Big fish, small pond," I responded.

"Wouldn't you be better off working in New York? That's where all the finance happens, right?" Catherine replied. I began to feel uneasy that she kept bringing up New York. "I mean, you could work downtown and live in Brooklyn. I love Brooklyn." She held the word *Brooklyn* in her mouth for a moment before letting it out. "Have you been to Brooklyn?" That's when the alarms began to go off in my head. My memory ran to the last moments I'd spent in Brooklyn. It was only a week earlier. I saw the face of the woman I'd strangled. I heard the voices of her children. Everything that I had come to the Jersey Shore to forget came rushing back to me. Catherine just sat there, staring at me, watching as the blood began to run out of my face. "Are you okay?" she asked. Her voice was cold. There was no concern in it. I felt dizzy. I needed to change the subject. I took a long swig of beer from the bottle in front of me. I tried to take a couple breaths to regain my composure. My pulse was racing. If I hadn't been drunk or if I wasn't so turned on, or if I hadn't spent the day at the beach trying to forget everything about my life, maybe I would have been able to keep my cool. *Have I been to Brooklyn?*

"No," I answered, trying to buy myself enough time to get my shit together. "Maybe once or twice." I could feel myself speaking quickly, unnaturally. "I don't really remember." I looked over at Catherine, trying to read her response. I was looking for confusion. A normal person would have been confused by my reaction. Instead, she was simply sitting on her stool, that tight little smile still on her lips. I wanted her to stop smiling. Time to pull your shit together, I said to myself. I tried to convince myself to forget everything that I'd been taught about paranoia being your best friend. My best friends were playing ring jockey at the other end of the room. I just wanted to look at this woman and forget everything else. I let my eyes scan Catherine's well-toned body again. She was leaning back in her chair, her eyes fixed on me, sipping her drink through a straw.

"So, you want to try your hand at this ring game?" I offered, knowing that I had to stand up before I fell off my barstool. Before Catherine had time to answer the question, I got up and began walking toward the back of the bar, toward my loud and obnoxious friends. I held out some obscure hope that she would follow me, that we'd play this silly game and I would take her home and that I would eventually wake up in the morning with her toned, naked body next to mine. Somewhere deep in my gut, I knew that wasn't going to happen.

When I made it about halfway between the bar and my friends I stopped and looked back. Catherine was gone. She'd simply disappeared. She had been there thirty seconds ago and now there was no sign of her. My stomach dropped. I tried to wave the feeling in my stomach off as regret but I was lying to myself and I knew it. It wasn't regret. That feeling in my gut was telling me that something was wrong. Too bad I didn't listen.

"All right, Joe," Jared said as I stepped toward my two old friends. "Let's see what you can do." He patted me on the back.

"I think the string's too short," Michael shouted. "Hey, barkeep, what's the deal with this string?" The bartender didn't answer. He just shook his head and looked away. I stepped forward and placed my feet behind the line of tape on the floor.

"Who was the beauty at the bar?" Michael asked. I took the ring in my right hand and stepped back with my left foot, as if I were about to throw a dart. "And where'd she go?" Michael laughed, suspecting that I'd simply blown it with her. He didn't know the half of it. I closed one eye and tried to align the small ring in my hand with the hook attached to the post. The room was spinning, half because of the alcohol and half because I still couldn't get my heart to slow down.

"Just some girl," I replied. I let go of the ring, pushing it slightly off to the side. It swung in a slow arc to my left, swinging back toward the hook as it neared the post. The golden ring flared in the light from the bar as it began to swing back toward us. Then, with a small clink, the ring looped itself around the hook. Michael let out an incomprehensible howl. The string went slack. The ring hung there on the hook screwed into the post. Bull's-eye.

I got up early the next morning. I weathered my headache and decided to watch the sunrise. When I was a kid, I used to get up to watch at least one sunrise each summer. I always liked watching the world wake up. The deck on the beach house was built for it. You could sit there in the morning and watch the sky lighten, hear the seagulls come to life, feel the sun on your skin when it lifted over the horizon, and still be no more than twenty feet from your bed. My plan was to head back to bed once the show was over. I still had some sleeping to do.

By morning, Catherine and the little panic attack that I'd had were nothing but faint memories. I convinced myself that I just needed more time to unwind. Watch the sunrise. Climb back in bed. Sleep until noon. I figured that was all the cure that I needed.

The sky was still a dark purple when I stepped out onto the deck. The wind was blowing off the ocean. It was cold. It may not be darkest right before dawn, but that's definitely when it's the coldest. I went back inside and pulled some sheets off my bed so that I could wrap them around me as I sat and stared at the horizon. Then I started my vigil, wrapped in a blanket, sitting on the deck of that old rental, waiting for the sun to come up.

The sky barely got any brighter before I had company on the porch. "Just like old times," a voice spoke from behind me. I looked back and could see Jared standing behind the screen door. "I thought you might come out here," Jared said.

I shrugged. "What's the good of having a beachfront house if you're not going to get up for the sunrise?"

"Want some company?" Jared asked.

"Just like old times," I replied, and nodded for him to come out.

"So what is it with you and sunrises, Pony Boy?" Jared asked as he sat down in the chair next to me. I laughed. I couldn't even remember how many sunrises Jared had watched with me. He always seemed to be doing it begrudgingly, but he always did it.

"Just something about them," I replied. If I'd had a better answer, I would have used it.

"Someday we'll get Michael to join us for one of these," Jared said.

"Yeah, right. I'd never hear the end of that one." We both laughed. I don't think Michael had ever gotten up that early, not when he wasn't on a job, anyway. Jared and I sat in silence for a few minutes, both watching the water like we expected something to surprise us. The thing with sunrises, though, was that there were no surprises, no matter what else was going on in your life. The sky grew lighter, from a dark purple to a deep red. I could hear the seagulls begin calling out over our heads. I never wondered where they went at night. I was used to things simply disappearing and reappearing.

Eventually, Jared broke the silence. "So, how have you been? It's been a while, you know?"

I knew. "Yeah, it's hard to find time," I answered.

"You ain't kidding." Jared shook his head. "For real, though, are you okay? You don't seem yourself." There was genuine concern in Jared's voice.

"Just tired," I lied. I didn't know why I was lying. I had so few people to confide in to begin with. Lying was just so easy. "I needed a little break, that's all."

"You're getting old before your time," Jared mocked.

"Maybe." I looked over at Jared to see if his face had the same weariness as mine. It did, but he wore his differently. He didn't look beat down like I did. Jared was a machine. "Doesn't all this killing and running, running and killing, ever get to you? Doesn't it just make you tired?"

"I've got moments," Jared said. He was lying to me too. It didn't make him tired. He was trying to make me feel better. It worked. He put his foot up on the deck's railing and leaned back in his chair. "Sometimes it all seems so surreal, you know?" Jared crossed his arms over his chest to fight the chill in the air. "When we were fourteen, did you ever think that we'd be here one day?"

"The Jersey Shore? We were here when we were fourteen," I joked.

Jared didn't even pause to acknowledge my joke. He kept on with his speech. "No, I mean, here, at this place in our lives. Doing what we do."

"No." I shook my head. I was sure of this answer. "I can honestly say that when we were fourteen, I couldn't have imagined that we'd grow up to do what we do. Even if I had, I'm not sure if I would have been too excited by it." I looked out over the beach. The early-morning beachcombers were walking down along the water. A few people had come out with long fishing poles and were casting them into the tide.

"You're lying to yourself, Joe. I know it and you know it. You would have been fucking thrilled. I know I would have been thrilled. When we were fourteen, playing basketball in your driveway, I was sure we'd end up in meaningless, dead-end jobs just like all the other losers from high school. That was if we made out at all, seeing how people in our families were dying around us and no one was willing to tell us why. Don't forget why we became friends in the first place, Joe."

"I remember," I said. It was superstition that led us to each other—not ours, the other kids'. They were convinced that we were bad luck. They wouldn't even talk to us because they thought we had some sort of death jinx.

"My mother, my brother, my uncle, your uncle, your grandparents, your father, your sister. I was pretty sure that everyone I cared about would be dead by the time I was twenty." Jared stood up. "You want a beer? I'm going to get myself a beer." It didn't matter that it was around five in the morning. The beer sounded right. I nodded. Jared went into the kitchen and came back out with two bottles in his hands. He unscrewed the cap from one and handed it to me. Then he unscrewed the cap from the other and took a long swig. I wanted to hear the rest of his speech. I wanted to be convinced. "Instead, look at us now. Our lives have meaning, Joe. Do you know what most people in this world would do to have a little meaning in their lives?" He took a long swig from his beer.

"You know those classes I teach," I said. Jared nodded. I'd told him about them before. Not every soldier taught the classes. They only picked a few of us. Neither Jared nor Michael had ever taught one. "When those kids ask why we fight, we finesse the answer. We tell them what we know works. They don't ask for more than that."

"That's because they don't need a reason, Joe. They've got all the reason they need burning up inside of them. When you've got passion, you don't need reason. It's only when you get old, like us, that you start asking questions. The older you get, the more your passion drains out of you and the more you look for a reason behind everything." Jared took a swig of his beer. "You ever ask one of these old guys that you've stayed with when you were on a job what the War's about?" I shook my head. I'd never thought to ask. I'd heard my share of stories, though. Everybody had. Jared laughed. "They'll go on, man." He shook his head. "They'll tell you stories that'll burn your ear off."

"Do you believe them? The stories they tell?"

Jared thought about it for a minute. "Yeah," he answered. "I figure you don't get to be that old without knowing something."

"So we're the saviors of the world?" I said, half asking, half just letting it float out into the air. "We're the only ones who can stop them?"

"I don't see anyone else trying. Look, Joe, I don't claim to know all the details but I know that the killing and the death are necessary. You know it too." Did I? "Once we win, the world will be better off. We've got a responsibility." Jared believed every word he said. I believed just enough.

"I don't know," I replied, "maybe I'm just running out of hate." I took a swig of beer.

"It's not hate, Joe. Your head is all fucked up." He tapped the lip of his beer against my forehead. "It's just the way it is. Hate is what I felt when I heard that one of those motherfuckers killed my little brother three weeks after his eighteenth birthday. That was hate. Hate was what you felt when you found out that your dad didn't die in a car accident. I remember. I was there. I ran out of hate a long time ago. Hate's got no discipline." If there's one thing Jared had, it was discipline.

"So what is it now?" I asked. "What keeps you going?" I thought that maybe whatever it was that kept Jared going would work for me too.

Jared gave it a quick thought before answering. "I don't know. Knowledge. Purpose. Knowing that I have a cause. Someday we're going to win this War and my grandkids are going to be able to grow up without being afraid and it will be because of you and me."

"So, we kill them because they're evil, just like we were taught when we were kids? That's what you're getting at?"

"Fuck, man. Do you doubt it?" Jared asked me the question and then he stared at me. If he could have found the doubt inside of me, he would have pulled it out and strangled it to death.

"I don't know," I replied. "You really believe that they're evil?"

Jared looked out over the waves breaking on the beach. "Well, it's either them or us."

I was sick of hearing that, Maria. I was sick of hearing that it was either them or us. I was sick of hearing that it was kill or be killed. Even then, even before I met you, that didn't make sense to me anymore. That's not what Jared was saying, though. What Jared was saying, I had to believe. "So that's it? That's your purpose? Them or us? First to kill is the last to survive? I can't find any meaning in that."

"That's not what I said, Joe," Jared replied. His eyes were tight. "Don't twist my words. You asked me if I still believed that they're evil. Yes. Yes, I do. I have no doubt and I have no doubt because there's just too much death for everyone to escape judgment. So it's either them or us, Joe. I'm not saying that it's kill or be killed. I'm saying that either they're evil or we are, because there ain't no way that everyone here is innocent. And I know for damn sure that I'm not evil, Joe. And I know that you're not evil either." He pointed his beer toward me. "I know you. I've known you since before you knew about this War. I'm certain that they're evil because I know that you're not." I had to believe it, Maria. I didn't have any choice. He had to be right. If he was wrong, I was lost. "There's not going to be peace until we win this."

"Or they do," I added.

"Or they do," Jared repeated, nodding. Then we sat in silence again for a long time. We sat and watched the sky go from red to pink. We sat and watched the sunlight begin to reflect off the low-hanging clouds before we could see even a sliver of sun. We sat and watched as the beach started growing crowded with people there just to watch the sun come up, like it did every other day. Then we watched as the sun first peeked over the horizon and slowly rose up into the sky. It always amazed me how fast the sun seemed to move when it just crested the horizon. Jared and I sat together and watched the world change. I looked over at him and knew that he'd only pretended to be doing this for me. He liked watching the new day be born as much as I did. When it was over, when it had officially gone from dawn to morning, Jared stood up. "I'm going back to bed, and I suggest you do the same," he said. "Otherwise Michael's going to drive us crazy tonight."

"Yeah," I replied. "I'm going to follow you in a minute." I wanted another minute to put my thoughts together. "This was good, Jared," I said to him as he pulled the screen door open. "I needed this. Thanks."

"Anytime, Joe," Jared said. His voice was strong. "Sometimes you just need to be reminded, you know? We're doing a good thing, Joe. I know it. You know it too. I know you do. Don't let yourself doubt it. If you start to feel doubt, you have to bury it. When you do what we do, doubt'll get you killed." Jared was serious, as serious as I had ever heard him in my life.

"I know," I replied. He was right. The problem was that burying the doubt wasn't as simple as Jared made it sound.

As we had agreed the day before, Jared and I let Michael plan our evening on the second night. He spent half the day talking about it while all I tried to do was while away the hours on the porch, watching the day go by. I left the house once in the middle of the day to go jump into the ocean and cool down. It felt good to be in the ocean. It felt good to be reminded how small I was.

So that night we headed to the southern end of Beach Haven for dinner. We didn't have reservations, but Michael figured he could get us a table at one of the fancy restaurants on the bay by greasing the hostess. Besides, he liked using his attempted bribe as an opening gambit to try to get the hostess's number. The plan was for an upscale dinner followed by a trip to an overcrowded Beach Haven bar with live music and drunk girls. "College girls," Michael kept intoning, like the words were full of magic. Michael dressed in his summer best, donning a bright red, floral print Hawaiian shirt and a pair of linen pants. He wore enough cologne to subdue an elephant. Michael hadn't grown up with me and Jared. I didn't meet Michael until two weeks after my sixteenth birthday. That was the day of my initiation. That was the day Michael and I sat next to each other while some stranger told us that people wanted to kill us and that, if we didn't want to die, we'd have to kill them first. We went in innocent and came out something completely other than innocent—not experienced, just not innocent anymore. When the class disbanded, each of us was specifically told not to contact or seek out anyone else from the class. It's dangerous, we were told. It could get people killed. Michael didn't care. He found me. He couldn't handle his new knowledge alone. He barely had any family left. He didn't have anyone that could really help him prepare for what was next. Michael needed friends. No rules were going to stop him from finding them. He chose me, whether I wanted to be chosen or not. A couple weeks after Michael found me, I found out that Jared was one of us too.

"You guys ready for a crazy night?" Michael clapped his hands together and began rubbing them like he was trying to stay warm.

"Smells like you are," I responded, laughing.

Jared walked up to Michael, took a big whiff, and looked at him. "You're staying at least ten feet away from me all night."

"This is my lucky cologne," Michael said. "You guys'll see, once the booze starts flowing and the music starts pumping, women will be drawn to this scent."

"Like flies to shit," Jared said. "Can we eat before I get another whiff of Michael and I lose my appetite?" We could walk to the street where all the good restaurants were. We had to cross over the island, but that didn't take long. The island was only three blocks wide. We made our way over to the bay and walked another ten blocks south to get to the restaurant Michael wanted to try. We walked past the amusement park and the water slides and at least three miniature golf courses. Beach Haven was teeming with families, little kids, flashing lights, and ringing bells. The music from the carousel could be heard for blocks. We walked past at least ten kids playing Skee-Ball. The restaurant wasn't right on the strip, so by the time we reached it, the streets had quieted down quite a bit. We could still look behind us and see the lights on the top of the Ferris wheel but the street in front of us was quiet. It was a small street with three or four seafood restaurants facing the bay. Michael made us walk by each restaurant and look inside before picking one. He made his choice based on which hostess he thought was the most attractive. The place he chose was pricy and crowded but Michael was able to get us a table. Sometimes, he just got the job done.

"You get her number too?" I asked after the hostess showed us to our table and started walking away. Michael didn't say anything. He just smiled a big goofy smile.

"I'm not sitting next to Michael," Jared said before we sat down. "I want to be able to smell my food." I don't even think he was kidding anymore. Our table was in the back corner of the restaurant, only a few feet away from the railing separating the restaurant from the bay. From our table, we could sit and eat and look at the reflection of the stars rippling in the water. When the wind shifted just right, the smell of Michael's cologne would be mercifully replaced by the salty smell of the bay. It was just starting to get dark when we ordered our drinks. I was sitting with my back to the wall. Michael was on my left-hand side with his back to the water and facing the entrance of the restaurant. Jared was on my right-hand side, his back to the door, facing the water. I had a straight view of most of the restaurant. While I'd have to strain to see the entrance, I could see all of the seating area and could make out about half of the bar. The room was in high spirits. The light outside was fading quickly. The room was full of the sounds of glasses clinking, silverware rapping against plates, and pointless vacation chatter. We ordered our food—fish, clams, crab claws. We ignored the prices and just let loose. I'm glad we did, since it was the last meal that the three of us would ever have together. Besides, we never did pay the bill.

When we got our drinks, Michael lifted his glass and said, "So, boys, what should we drink to?"

"World peace," I offered, and we all laughed. It was an old joke, older than we were. I'd heard my parents say it. We tried to avoid talking about the War but our conversation kept circling back to it. It always did. Each of us told the others about rumors we'd heard— recent victories, recent defeats, people we knew who'd been promoted up the ranks, people we knew who'd been killed. We didn't talk about why we fought. We'd had that conversation too many times already. It never went anywhere. We'd all heard the theories, some theories more than others. In one, there were originally five groups fighting each other. We were the only two left. In another, we had once been slaves and our enemy the slave masters. When we revolted, we won our freedom and they let us go. The problem was that as soon as we left, they turned around and began enslaving other people. So we came back to fight them once and for all, to end their reign, to keep the world free. That's the version we heard the most—probably because it was the one where we were the most heroic. We all believed that someday we'd be told the whole story. The rumor was that if you rose high enough in the ranks, they told you everything. Sometimes that was the only reason I cared about being promoted.

The food came and we just kept talking. The talk slowly turned from the War to us reminiscing about the good times we'd had when we were young and carefree. Even with the War hanging over our heads, when we were seventeen we felt like we'd be seventeen forever. Those were some of the best times of my life. Then, one at a time, we turned eighteen.

When we were about halfway through our meal, she walked in. Michael had been watching the traffic going in and out of the restaurant since the minute we sat down, hoping he could get two girls' phone numbers before we even got to the bar. He noticed her right away. She was hard to forget. "Hey, your little friend is here," he said to me.

"What are you talking about?" I asked. It took me a few seconds before it dawned on me. Michael was lifting his hand to wave her over to our table when my reflexes kicked in. I grabbed his hand before he was able to get it above his shoulder and slammed it down into the table. It made a loud banging sound against the wood. A few of the people at the surrounding tables turned and glared at us.

"Jesus Christ, what the fuck was that for?" Michael asked, twisting his wrist, checking to see if I had broken something.

"No waving," I ordered. "Answer my question. Who is my little friend?" I didn't dare look for myself.

"That hot Asian woman from the bar last night," Michael replied. "What the fuck's your problem? Did you strike out that bad?"

"Has she seen us?" I asked, keeping my voice quiet. My gut was talking to me again. I was determined to listen to it this time. This was wrong. There were no coincidences, not in our line of work.

"I don't know," Michael answered. His voice dropped, following my lead. "I can't really tell. If she has, she's not acting like she has."

"Act like you haven't seen her," I said under my breath. "Better yet, act like you don't even recognize her." It was another order. I didn't pretend that it wasn't.

"Seriously, Joe, what's going on here?" Jared asked.

I began shaking my head, trying to decipher what this could all mean. "Bad feelings," I replied. "I just got a bad vibe from her, that's all. She was asking me a lot of questions."

"Questions about what?" Jared pressed. It didn't take him long to become deadly serious. It never did.

"About Brooklyn," I replied. The word immediately resonated with both my friends.

"What about Brooklyn?" Jared pressed further. He leaned back in his chair, faking a smile in case people were watching us. We all began acting as casual as possible. Only our words were full of panic. We just had to hope that no one was listening.

"Nothing specific. She was smooth about it. That's what worries me. She kept asking me about how much time I spent in New York and then she just slipped in how much she loved Brooklyn and asked me if I'd ever been there."

"Well, that doesn't tell us much," Michael replied. "Sounds like normal conversation to me."

"Yeah, it sounded that way to me too. But it didn't feel normal." I looked at Michael again. "What's she doing now?" Michael was the only one who could watch her without it being obvious that we'd spotted her.

"She's sitting at the bar. She ordered a drink."

"What's she drinking?" It was an important question. If she was drinking alcohol, then we would know that I was overreacting. If she were on the job, she'd stay sober.

"Clear drink. Regular glass. Lime," Michael replied. "Could be gin or vodka. Could be club soda." Michael knew the score too.

"Why didn't you say something last night?" Jared asked.

"Because last night, it didn't feel right. Tonight, two nights in a row—tonight it feels dangerous. What's she doing, Michael?"

"Not much, just sitting there, nursing her drink. A couple times, though, she's made eye contact with the big black dude in the corner."

"You ever see him before?" I asked Michael.

"Nope. First time. Can you make him out?"

I picked up my beer, pretended to take a sip, and leaned back in my chair to see if I could get a good look at the man standing in the corner. Then I saw him. I recognized him immediately. "We're made," I said.

"What do you mean?" Michael asked. "You know that guy?"

"Yeah, that's my cabbie. He drove me here from Atlantic City. We're made. No doubt about it." I nearly took a real swig of beer. It was a reflex. Instead, I just pressed the bottle to my lips, not letting a drop slip through. Then I placed the beer back on the table. I didn't know what would be in store that night, but I knew that I needed to keep all my faculties. "So, what's our plan?" I asked. Michael and I both looked to Jared. That's how it was. Michael was the party. Jared had the plans. I still haven't figured out what my part was.

"Does she know about us?" Jared asked, motioning to him and Michael.

"Well, if she didn't before, she probably would have guessed by now since we're sitting at the same fucking table." I said. "But, yeah, I told her last night that you guys were my friends."

"We're going to have to split up," Jared said without any hesitation.

"There's another guy at the other end of the bar," Michael interrupted. "He's definitely with her too. Late thirties, white, gray before his time but in pretty good shape, small scar under his left eye." I again took a fake sip from my drink but I couldn't get a good look at the new guy. From what I could see, I didn't recognize him. "Splitting up sounds like a bat-shit stupid idea to me," Michael said. His face betrayed his emotions for the first time since we'd started playing our little game of pretend.

"Easy, Michael," I said. "Let's not give anything away just yet. Why do you think we should split up, Jared?"

"It's the only chance we have here. We can't fight them. We have to run. If we run together we all get caught."

"I don't see why we can't fight them," Michael replied. "We split up and the odds of all three of us making it out are pretty slim." Michael looked at me when he said this. We all figured the same thing. Catherine, or whatever her name was, came looking for me. I was the primary target.

"We can't fight them, Michael," Jared responded. "There are three of them that we know about. There may be more. There are definitely only three of us. Plus, they came here looking for us, so we know that they're going to be armed. Are you armed, Michael?" Jared was just stating the facts.

"I've got my scuba knife," Michael said, resignation creeping into his voice. One knife between us with a two-inch blade, it wasn't enough.

Jared shook his head. "Well, I guarantee you that they've got more than a scuba knife. They're on a hunting expedition. You go looking for elephants, you bring an elephant gun."

"Jared's right," I finally chimed in. It's not what I wanted to say. If I was going to go down, I didn't want to have to do it alone, but Jared was right. The smart move here was to split up and run. Get out of the restaurant, off the island, and as far away as we possibly could. It was becoming clear to me that vacationing so close to our last hits was a mistake. There was no reason to make another one.

"Fine. Let's pick a meeting point, though," Michael conceded. "We need to check in with each other once we've all escaped."

"We'll meet at the Borgata in Atlantic City," Jared said. "If we can get off the island, we can get to AC. Meet at the hundred-dollar blackjack tables at three A.M. Anybody doesn't make it by then, we leave without them. There's only one way off this island. If we're not off by then, it probably means we're not getting off."

"Okay," I said. "Jared leaves first. You get up, go to the bathroom and keep going. They're unlikely to get suspicious until the second person leaves. That'll buy you time to figure out how to get us out of Jersey and as far away from here as possible." Jared nodded. It was almost imperceptible.

"See you guys at three A.M.," he said. With that, without another word, Jared got up, looked me in the eyes for a second, and walked toward the men's room. His eyes were steel. There was no doubt in them. After about two minutes a young guy with dark hair got up from the bar to go to the bathroom.

"There it is," Michael said. "The dark-haired guy there is the fourth. He's going to check on Jared. I think that's all of them." Michael looked at me. "What now?" I knew what he meant. He meant, now that Jared is gone, what's the plan? Running just wasn't Michael's style. He wasn't going to do it unless I told him to.

"I don't know," I said, trying to devise a plan in my head. Jared was the planner. Jared was gone. "We've got to move before the dark-haired guy gets back from the john and lets the rest of them know that Jared isn't in there. We've got to go together or the second person to leave is a sitting duck. And we can't just walk out of this place."

"It's like the end of *Butch Cassidy and the Sundance Kid.*" Michael smiled. I don't know how he did it. Michael had something I never had. "I know what to do. Once we get outside, I'm going left and you go right. But until we get out the front door, follow my lead." I nodded, relieved that Michael was taking the reins. Michael stood up and started walking toward Catherine. I had no idea what he had planned, but I followed him.

"Hey," Michael called out to Catherine before he even reached the bar. "Aren't you the woman who walked out on my friend last night?" He walked right up to her and put his left arm around her waist. "My buddy here's been busted up about it all day." They weren't expecting this. Catherine shot a frightened glance at the gray-haired guy at the other end of the bar. I kept looking toward the bathroom to see when the dark-haired agent would come back.

Catherine tried to keep her cool. She was trying to buy them a second or two to figure out what to do. "Your friend didn't seem that interested last night. Something seemed to get under his collar. Perhaps you'd be up for some fun instead?" Her accent was even thicker than it had been the night before.

"My friend?" Michael asked. Just then I saw the guy with the dark hair coming back from the bathroom. He was walking quickly. What little cover we had left was just about to be blown. I signaled to Michael by giving him a quick nod. "You must be mistaken, baby," he said to Catherine. "My friend's as cool as they come." With that Michael grabbed a beer bottle off the bar and smashed it as hard as he could into Catherine's face. Michael's move was quick and unexpected. I heard a crunch as Catherine's nose collapsed and saw blood shoot out from beneath the beer bottle. Beer bottles don't break when they hit people's heads like they do in the movies. In real life, beer bottles are stronger than most people's skulls. You might as well be hitting someone in the head with a baseball bat. Catherine dropped instantly to the floor. Michael and I ran. In seconds, the two of us were out on the street, running. I went right. Michael went left. Michael's little plan worked perfectly. His attack had accomplished two things. First, it created a diversion. There was enough of a ruckus in the restaurant to buy us a couple moments' head start. Second, it brought their numbers down from four to three. I looked back once after I started running to see if anyone had made it out of the bar yet. The only person that I recognized was Michael, hightailing it in the other direction. He never looked back. One of the waiters from the restaurant ran out in the street and shouted, "Stop them!" but his shout simply added to the chaos. All these people, the regular people, were on vacation. They weren't prepared to play hero. One down, I thought as I ran. Michael had just improved our odds of making it out of this alive.

I knew that the commotion back at the restaurant would only buy us a minute or two. The people who were after us were professionals. Their movements were coordinated. They knew what they were doing. I just wanted to create as much distance between the restaurant and me as possible, so I ran as fast as I could. The island thinned out at its ends. I was close enough to the southern tip of the island that the road I was on simply ended, running straight into the bay. I had to make a left turn and head toward the one road in the middle of the island that kept going south. When I did, I took a second glance back at the scene. I was already over a half mile from the restaurant. Night had fallen. The sky was moonless and the part of the island I was on had grown almost completely dark except for the light on the top of the Ferris wheel. Looking back, the light from the restaurant illuminated the street enough that I could make out a crowd of people milling about the outside. It was utter confusion. I didn't slow my pace as I turned the corner, giving me only a split second to survey the chaos. That split second was enough time for me to see the dark-haired agent, framed by the mass of people behind him, running after me at full speed. He was already only about a quarter of a mile behind me and he was gaining on me.

Once I turned the corner and I knew that I was out of his view, I began looking around for anything that I could use to aid my escape. If the dark-haired agent knew where I was, then there was little question that his friends would know soon too. Up ahead, I spotted a small red bicycle with a basket attached to the front leaning against one of the little houses that lined the road. I reached for it, swung it into the street, threw my legs over the seat, and began to pedal as fast as I could. There was no way that he was going to catch me on foot now. Still, his friends were sure to have a car, so I needed to find a place to hide, and fast.

As I pedaled, the streets grew even darker. The blackness was only intermittently broken up by a random porch light. As the island grew darker it also grew quieter. I was nearing its end where the road just stops. In front of me was the long sandy southern tip of the island. On one side was the ocean; on the other was the bay. There was nothing in between but sand. The farther along you moved the thinner the beach became until there was no sand left and the bay and the ocean became one. I had no time to look back; looking back could get me killed. I just moved forward. I didn't think. It would have been safer to duck into one of the houses, to hide where there were other people. But I wasn't thinking. I was just trying to move and I was moving straight into a dead end where there would be no place for me to hide. Suddenly, out of the darkness, I began to hear the loud revving of a car engine. It was moving fast. It was the only sound that I could hear other than the sound of the crashing waves. I heard the car skid around a turn and knew that it wouldn't be long before they could see me. I just kept pedaling. There was a gate at the end of the road and some Do Not Enter signs. I ditched the bike and jumped over the gate and ran again.

In seconds, I was surrounded on all sides by white sand. I could see the bay on my right side and could hear the waves from the ocean on my left. I took a turn and started running toward the ocean. I thought the sound of the waves might cover the sound of my breathing. The ocean was as black as oil, reflecting back the moonless sky. Looking out into the water, the only lights I could see were the tiny lights of fishing boats drifting miles out over the water. As I neared the edge of the water, the rumbling of the waves got louder. It was high tide and the water here was rougher than anywhere else on the island. I was getting tired but I knew that I'd be caught soon if I slowed down or if I didn't find a place to hide. Only seconds later I heard the roar of the car engine again, skidding to a stop at the end of the road. They were right behind me. I only had a moment to hide or I was as good as dead. My eyes scanned the beach but it was empty. There were a few dunes and some dune grass but nowhere to hide. I looked back again at the pitch black water. The ocean was my only chance. I broke into a run toward the water. I didn't have time to ditch my shirt or my sandals. I simply dove forward as soon as I felt the water brush against my toes. I dove straight into a wave. It tried to push me back but I pulled myself forward through the water. Then I swam. My sandals were lost within the first four strokes. I knew that I could only afford a few full strokes before Catherine's friends made it to the beach. I'd have to stop swimming or they'd see me. Then my only hope would be to quietly drift out to sea.

I took about twelve full strokes, putting a good hundred yards between me and the beach. Then I stopped. I floated in choppy seas, bouncing up and down on the waves. I had gotten out past the breakers so that the waves were breaking between me and the shore. I turned to see if they had made it to the beach yet. Who were these people? I sank down deep into the water, floating with just my eyes and my nose exposed, just enough to see and breathe. The water here was deep. I let my feet dangle straight below me and wasn't able to touch the bottom.

I had stopped swimming just in time. As I turned, I saw the first of them step out of the darkness. It was the dark-haired agent, followed quickly by the cabbie and the guy with the gray hair. They hadn't left anyone behind with Catherine. Nobody chased Michael. I was glad for him. They all carried flashlights. The light from their flashlights made it easier for me to identify each of them on the dark beach. They immediately spread out, shining the flashlights over every sand dune to see if I was cowering behind one. It only took them seconds to realize that I wasn't on the beach. I stayed as still in the water as possible. I could make out from their movements that the guy with the gray hair was the leader. Each of the other two would move to a different part of the beach and then report back to him, letting him know that they hadn't found anything. I watched each flashlight as it danced along the beach. The guy with the gray hair simply stood there, trying to assess the situation.

Then I saw the cabbie walk to the edge of the water and bend down to get a closer look at something. I was too low in the water to see what he had found. After a moment of investigation, he hurried back to the leader. I couldn't hear a thing over the crashing of the waves. All I could do was watch them and try to figure out what they were saying.

The cabbie was now holding something in each of his hands, carrying his flashlight under his armpit. The leader moved the beam of his flashlight toward the item. The cabbie was carrying my sandals. They had washed back up on shore. The leader wasted no time.

"He's in the water," he yelled. I could hear him shouting over the crashing waves. He wanted me to hear him. He wanted me to know that they were onto me. He immediately began moving the beam of his flashlight over the top of the water. As it neared me, I dove down beneath the surface. I must have been in at least fifteen feet of water because even after I dove down, I couldn't touch the bottom. I kept my eyes open under the water. The salt stung but I needed to see. I didn't dare close my eyes. I knew that the water would be dark, but I didn't realize how dark. I felt like I was floating in space, surrounded by nothingness. All I could see around me and below me was darkness. When peering up toward the surface of the water, I thought that I could make out the refraction of the light from the flashlights as they scanned the surface of the water but I wasn't sure. I had to come up for breath but I had to stay hidden. I waited for a wave to pass.

The wave would be my shield. I'd come up for air behind it. I felt a wave move past me like a ghost and then I surfaced quickly, took a another deep breath of air, and resubmerged.

I just floated there, motionless in the darkness. I couldn't see anything but I could hear strange sounds erupting from the black water. There was a constant ringing in my ears, which I assumed was just my ears adjusting to the water pressure. Over the ringing, however, I could hear the sound of the sand moving along the ocean floor with the currents. It sounded like sandpaper rubbing against wood. I could hear the waves breaking along the beach, like thunder in the distance. Then there were other sounds that I didn't recognize, sounds of thumping or thrashing in the darkness not too far away from me. I felt like I was trapped in a nightmare. I tried to ignore the sounds. I tried to keep my eyes on the light moving along the surface of the water so that I could time my breaths. I didn't want to gasp for air when I came up for fear that they might hear me. I waited for another wave that could protect me. Again, I felt it blow by me in the water. I lifted barely more than my mouth out of the water, took another deep breath of air, and sank back down into the abyss.

This went on for another five minutes before the lights abruptly stopped moving. I carefully lifted my head out of the water, wondering what they would do next. I wasn't hopeful that they would give up their search. I knew that they had come too far for that. I wondered how they had found us. I imagine that my cabbie was the one who had alerted the others after picking me up. If that was true, then someone was looking for me. I slowly lifted my head above the water again. I was getting tired from treading water in the waves. The three men huddled up on the beach, planning their next move. All I could hear was the crashing waves.

After a few minutes, the guy with the dark hair and my cabdriver stripped off their shoes and began walking toward the water. They were coming in after me. The leader stayed on the beach. He kept moving the beam from his flashlight over the surface of the water. As his underlings waded into the water, I could see the leader pull a handgun out from the back of his shorts. Now it was just a waiting game.

Once the cabdriver and the dark-haired agent entered the ocean, I knew that I had the advantage over them. I knew where they were. To them, I was still a phantom. As long as I didn't lose sight of them in the darkness, all I had to do was move through the water quietly and stay out of their view. As long as I could stay quiet and keep from being seen, I was safe. It was a strategic mistake on their part. They should have just stayed on the beach. They should have sat on the beach until morning and hoped that I didn't swim off into the night. I'd be a sitting duck in the light.

The dark-haired agent swam off to the right, swimming freestyle with his head out of the water. He stopped every few strokes to look around. I could see the knife he was carrying in his right hand. The cabbie started swimming straight for me. I had gotten lucky. The cabbie didn't appear to be nearly as strong a swimmer as the guy with the dark hair. The cabbie was fresh, though, and I had already been treading water for some time. As the cabbie made his way farther off the beach he became more difficult to see. His dark skin worked as a camouflage against the black water. I did my best to follow his movement through the waves, to catch glimpses when I could of the whites of his eyes. If I lost sight of him, it would be difficult to regain a visual unless he made some sort of commotion. I couldn't see if he was holding a weapon, but I knew that he must be. He wouldn't have come in the water without one.

Avoiding the swimmers would have been easy if the leader hadn't kept moving the beams from his flashlight over the water. He was using all three flashlights. He held two of the flashlights in his left hand, and the other flashlight in his right. So I had to stay quiet, avoid the beams of light, and also keep my eye on the cabdriver all at once.

Every so often, as a beam of light approached me, I would slip quietly under the water and into the darkness. I tried staying submerged for as short an interval as possible because I didn't want to lose sight of the cabbie's eyes. The cabbie would take three strokes and then he would stop and look around him. I didn't want to move too quickly for fear that he might hear me. I just floated, shifting my movement ever so slightly so that I would stay clear of his line of sight.

The cabbie quickly closed to within about twenty feet of me. As he swam, I moved farther off to one side of him. I soon realized that I was actually moving back in toward the beach. A beam of light began to move toward me, so I quietly ducked back underwater. When I pulled my head out of the darkness, only seconds later, I was only about ten feet from the cabbie, floating directly behind him. I wanted to create more distance and began to slowly and quietly swim backward away from his bulking figure. Moving closer into shore was a mistake. I was moving back into the breaking waves. In all my effort to watch the cabbie and the moving lights, I neglected the most powerful thing of all, the ocean. Suddenly, a wave came from out of the blackness. It knocked me over and sucked me down into the depths of the darkness. I completely lost my bearings once I was under the water. The wave flipped me over at least once. For a few seconds at least, I didn't know which direction to go in to get back to the surface. I just struggled against the currents. Finally, I was able to figure out which way was up and pulled my head back up into the night air. I gasped for breath as I surfaced. The cabbie heard me. He quickly turned toward me. I don't think that he was sure of what he heard. He just knew that he heard something. I caught a quick glimpse of the whites of his eyes. I saw confusion in them. I ducked my head back under the water and swam off to one side, trying to lose him again. I took two or three strong pulls with my arms and lifted my head for a breath. That's when another wave came out of the darkness.

I managed to keep my head above it this time, but there was no way to do that and stay hidden. I was giving myself away. My heart started beating fast. I couldn't see the waves until they were nearly on top of me. I tried ducking my head back under the water to hide but I had no breath left. I had to get to the surface of the water. I had to breathe. I pulled my head above the water again and gasped loudly for air.

The cabbie heard my gasp again and this time, he was sure of what it was. He turned toward me in the water. There was about fifteen feet between us. "Got him!" he shouted as loudly as he could manage, his voice full of a hunter's excitement. Within seconds one of the flashlight beams was shining directly on the cabbie while another moved along the surface of the surrounding water, searching for me. The cabbie's eyes became large as he lifted his arms to start swimming toward me. The blade of a knife he was holding in his hand glimmered in the light of the flashlight. I was too out of breath to go back under the water, breathing deeply and trying to get air back in my system before another wave pulled me down. The cabbie just kept coming toward me, swimming in the middle of the beam of light. Just then there was another rumble. It came from directly behind the cabbie. He had swum right into the breakers too. This time, with the light shining on him, I could see the wave. It was moving toward us quickly. The cabbie heard it and turned toward the oncoming wave. It struck him and pulled him under. I was able to duck the wave, having seen it coming. That's when I saw my opening. I had one chance and I wasn't going to miss it. I waited for the cabbie to pull his head back out of the water. I knew he'd be disoriented and out of breath. I took three strong strokes toward him, entering the beam of light from the flashlight for a moment. Then I grabbed him around his neck from behind with my right arm, and dragged him under the water.

It was eerie, being weightless, wrestling in the darkness. All the sounds that I heard earlier were gone, replaced only with the sounds of our own thrashing. I squeezed around the cabbie's neck with my arm, trying to choke him before we both drowned. I pushed everything else from my mind. I forgot where I was. I forgot that I was floating in darkness. I forgot about the waves rolling above us. I concentrated every bit of energy I had into squeezing the life out of the man who had come hunting for me. "It's either us or them," I remembered Jared saying; only, this time it wasn't about right and wrong. I didn't have time for considerations of good and evil. This time it was about survival. It was instinct. At that moment, I knew for sure that I wanted to live even though, for the life of me, I couldn't think of a single reason why. The cabbie was trying to pull my arm away from his neck, so I grabbed my arm with my free hand and pulled it even tighter across his throat. I was sure I had more air in my lungs than the cabbie. I was sure that, if I could keep him underwater, I could outlast him. I could feel him getting weaker with each passing moment. He took his knife and began to stab at my right forearm. I could feel the tip of the knife piercing the skin on my arm. The cabbie couldn't move the knife fast enough through the water to do too much damage. He soon realized that stabbing wasn't working, so he began to saw into the back of my hand with the knife. The pain was intense, the newly opened wound immediately becoming flush with salt water. After only a few strokes over the skin on my hand, I could feel the knife scraping against bone. Unfortunately for the cabbie, the pain helped to keep me focused. As the pain increased, I simply pulled my arm in tighter, knowing that the sooner the cabbie died, the sooner the pain would stop. I closed my eyes as tight as I could and bit down on the inside of my cheek. The sawing became less intense. Then it stopped altogether. The body in my arms went limp under the water. The cabbie was dead.

I let the body go and it began to float away from me in the darkness. In a heartbeat or two, the body vanished in the blackness as if it had never existed. Then everything came back to me and I remembered where I was. I was underwater. I had been underwater for a few minutes now and I needed to breathe. There were still two people above the surface trying to kill me. I was bleeding and tired.

During our struggle, the waves had pushed me and the cabbie even closer to the shoreline. When I kicked my feet to try to swim to the surface, they began knocking against the ocean's sandy bottom. I pushed myself up off the sand and headed toward the water's surface. When my head cracked through the surface, I took a deep gasp of the cool night air. I was spent. I breathed in and then I simply leaned back and floated for a moment in the water. I had floated to within twenty feet of the beach, to within twenty feet of the man on the beach with the gun who wanted to kill me. I couldn't move. After only a second's respite, I felt a hand grab my hair. The hand began pulling me toward the shore. I was glad to get away from the dark water, glad to get away from the waves. Dying on the beach seemed pleasant by comparison.

The dark-haired agent stopped swimming after a few minutes and began walking in the shallow water. I was still too tired to budge. I simply floated on my back as he dragged me along the surface of the water by my hair. It didn't hurt until my body hit the beach. When we got to the beach, he just continued to drag me along the sand by the clump of my hair that he held in his fists. Now there was pain. The pain helped me to regain consciousness. Still, I didn't fight. It was pointless now. I was trying to conserve energy. I was hoping there would be one last chance for survival. I just needed an opening.

Eventually, the dark-haired agent let go of my hair and dropped me back down onto the sand. A moment later, the gray-haired leader was shining a flashlight in my face with one hand and pointing his gun at me with the other. The light from the flashlight was blinding. My eyes had gotten used to the darkness. "Where's Trevor?" I heard a voice behind the light say to me. I assumed Trevor was the cab-driver.

"Shark food," I mumbled.

"Yeah?" the leader spoke, barely acknowledging that his colleague was dead. "Well, you're next." Then I saw a shadow move quickly into the light. It was the heel of a shoe. Before I even had time to process the information, it smashed hard into my nose. I was dazed for a second. They flipped me over. Someone pushed my face into the sand, pulled my hands behind my back, and tethered my wrists together with a plastic ring. This was all done in one motion, in about five seconds. They had done this before.

Once my hands were secured behind my back, the gray-haired man flipped me over again. I spit the sand out of my mouth and tried to get a good look at him. I'd never seen him before, not in person. Maybe I'd seen a picture. I couldn't remember. He glared into my face as if he were trying to read something.

"You killed my wife, you son of bitch." I had seen a picture. It was in the profile of my last hit. I remembered what Jared had told me. I had killed that woman in Brooklyn to send a message to her husband. He was one of their top soldiers. He'd killed eight of our men last year alone—eight that we knew of. My name was about to be added to a very distinguished list.

I began to regain my breath, and with it some of my composure. "How many people have you killed?" I asked him.

He thought for a moment. "More than you." He glared at me, his face full of venom. "I'm sure of that." He gazed down at the gun in his hand. "I don't remember exactly how many." I could see his chest moving up and down as he breathed. His body was full of adrenaline. "Eventually, they all just start to run into one another. I do remember some of them, though." He stared at me with a sick glint in his eye. "And I'm definitely going to remember you." Then he turned to the dark-haired agent, who was standing next to him, dripping wet. "Steve, give me your knife." Steve held the knife out in front of him. The leader took it and handed Steve the gun. Then he turned back to me. "I'd tell you to say your prayers, kid, but five minutes into this, and you won't need me to remind you. Stand up," he ordered. I struggled to my feet. He took a step toward me. I closed my eyes to prepare myself for the pain. I didn't know what he had planned. I only knew that this was going to hurt and that it wasn't going to be quick. I took one last deep breath of air, knowing that it might be the last pain-free breath I ever took. I didn't think about death, just pain. I could feel the ocean breeze brush by my face. I could smell the scent of the salt water blowing in from the sea. Then, from somewhere, wafting through the salty air, I could make out another scent. It was the smell of cheap cologne.

My eyes still closed, I heard a shout come from off in the distance, a maniacal, madman's yell. It got closer with each passing second. I opened my eyes and looked just in time to see Michael flying through the air, his arms stretched out in front of him like Superman in flight. He'd come back for me. I told you he didn't like to run. He tackled the dark-haired agent and wrestled him to the ground. Michael had his scuba knife in his hand. The gray-haired man looked toward them for a second, and as he did, I dug my toes into the sand. When he turned to look back at me, I could see in his eyes that he still meant to kill me, even if it was the last thing he ever did. I was supposed to have sent him a message by killing his wife. Apparently, he had gotten the message. He lunged toward me with the knife. Right at that moment, I kicked up my leg and flung a footful of sand in his face. He flinched back as the sand hit him in both of his eyes. Then, before he could open his eyes again I kicked him as hard as I could in the groin, sending him crouching down on his hands and knees in pain. With my hands tied behind my back, I wasn't able to keep my balance. I fell back into the sand.

Suddenly, the gun went off, a loud bang echoing through the quiet island night. I looked over to see Michael standing over the dark-haired agent's lifeless body. My friend had won. Just then, our last remaining enemy, the leader, leapt on top of me, full of rage. With my hands tied behind my back, I had only my feet to defend myself. I was somehow able to flip him over me once with my legs. In seconds, he was back on top of me, swinging wildly at me with his knife. Michael had the gun now but he couldn't pull the trigger without risking shooting me. Instead, Michael rushed over, grabbed the man with the gray hair by the shoulder, and, using all the strength he could muster, pulled him away from me, gun drawn the whole time. The leader's body twisted as Michael pulled him off me and he swung his right hand around and plunged his knife deep into Michael's abdomen. While the leader's body was turned away from me, I planted a foot in his ribs, sending him sprawling down into the sand. Now that the leader and I were separated, Michael lifted the gun. He aimed. Then he fired, sending the sound of another gunshot crackling through the air, shooting the gray-haired man in the head.

So there we were, a bloody mess, with two dead bodies on the beach and one floating not far off in the water. Our more immediate problem, however, was jammed deep into Michael's stomach. I rolled over toward the dark-haired agent's body, found Michael's scuba knife, and managed to use it to cut through the plastic that had bound my wrists.

Once free, I looked up at Michael to assess the damage. He was still standing there, arm outstretched, gun in his hand. He was breathing heavily and with each breath the handle of the knife bobbed up and down. The knife had pierced through his Hawaiian shirt, pinning it to his side, and the blood was creating a dark circle among the palm trees and red flowers. I looked up at Michael's face. He smiled at me. "And Jared didn't think we could take them."

"We've got to get you to a hospital."

"I think that's a good idea."

"Was their car still parked along the road?"

"Yeah."

"Was it a cab?"

"No." I got up quickly and went over to the body of the gray-haired man. I knew that Steve wouldn't have the keys, since he had been chasing me down the street on foot. I had to hope that the gray-haired man had the car keys, because if the cabbie was carrying them, we were in trouble. I checked the pockets of his shorts and felt a jingle in his right-hand pocket. Bingo. We had our ride.

I had to help Michael to the car. He was losing blood fast. I threw him in the backseat and began to drive. "You know where the hospital is?" I asked Michael, looking at him slumped in the backseat through the rearview mirror. The whole left-hand side of his shirt was now a dark red color.

"I told you we could fight them," Michael slurred. He sounded drunk.

"I'll take that as a no." As I looked back toward the road, I caught a glimpse of myself in the rearview mirror. I was already developing a black eye and there were streams of dried blood coming out of my nose. I looked at my right arm. I could see red marks on my forearm from where the cabbie had stabbed me. Then I looked at the back of my hand. The skin was virtually falling off it. All I could see was a mixture of bone and blood. We were an ugly pair, Michael and I, but at least I knew my wounds would heal.

I pressed down on the gas pedal, moving as fast as I could along the narrow road. I drove toward the only bridge leading off the island. I had to find a hospital.

"Jared's a fucking punk," Michael mumbled from the backseat. "He didn't think we could fight 'em. But we beat the four of them without him."

"Relax, Michael. Don't waste your energy. You're losing blood." I pushed further down on the gas. It wasn't long before we started to hit traffic. I flew past the other cars, passing them on the left and the right. I hit a red light and pulled up to the car next to me. I rolled down the window and yelled over to them. "Hospital!" I shouted. They took one look at my blood-splattered face and yelled back the name of a town just off the island. Manahawkin. I heard the word and ran through the red light. It was about a twenty-minute drive. I didn't know if I had that sort of time. When I got to Manahawkin, I saw signs for the hospital and followed them until I was able to pull up to the emergency room entrance.

"Let's get you inside," I turned and said to Michael.

"No," he said. He had regained some of the life in his eyes. "You can't come in."

"What are you talking about?"

"You go in there with me and neither of us is getting away. Drop me at the door and go."

"I can't leave you. You'll be arrested, at best. I've got to stay with you. You can't protect yourself now. You came back for me. I can't desert you."

"I didn't come back for you." Michael actually strained a smile. I could see a hint of blood on his lips. "I wasn't trying to help you." His voice was weak. Each word was strained. "I get my kicks out of this shit. Go. Go away and try to get in touch with people who can get me out of here. It's what Jared would tell us to do." He was right. It is what Jared would tell us to do. If Michael had listened to Jared, however, I'd be dead.

What he said made sense, though. I told myself that I could help Michael more if I left than I could if I stayed. So that's what I did. I dumped my friend, who had just risked his life to save mine, in the lobby of the hospital with a knife sticking out of his abdomen and I ran. I drove to the highway and headed south toward Atlantic City. I thought about pulling over and calling the Intelligence guys to let them know about Michael's situation, but I knew that it was useless. We weren't even supposed to be there. I didn't have enough clout to get anything done. I got to the casino twenty minutes late. I had pulled over at a rest stop on the highway to try to clean myself up at least enough that they would let me into the casino. I wiped the blood off my face and did my best to bandage my hand. I had to hope Jared hadn't left yet. When I got to the blackjack tables, I saw Jared sitting there, a stack of about a thousand dollars in chips in front of him. He looked almost dapper. As soon as he saw me, he cashed in, tipping the dealer with a hundred-dollar chip.

"You're a fucking mess," he said to me. It was going to take more than one pit stop to make me presentable again. "We've got to get you out of here. You'll attract attention." He quickly began to lead me toward the exit. "You seen Michael?" he asked me. So I started to mumble the whole ordeal to Jared. "Short version," he said to me. So I skipped the story and simply told him that Michael was stuck in the hospital with a knife in his gut and that, if we didn't get him out of there, he'd be found by both the police and our enemies. "Michael will be fine. I'll take care of it," Jared assured me. He placed a hand on my shoulder and pushed me toward the exit.

"What does that mean? What are you going to do?"

"I'm going to make a couple of phone calls. While you two were out playing cops and robbers, I was working on getting us out of here. Sometimes you have to count on our guys being better than theirs. That's the benefit to being the good guys. Here you go, Mr. Robertson." Jared handed me papers from inside his pocket. It was a plane ticket from the Atlantic City Airport to Atlanta. I was traveling as Dennis Robertson. God and Jared only know what had happened to the real Dennis Robertson. "Now lay low until tomorrow. Get to the airport on time. Clean yourself up. I'll work on getting our friend out of trouble."

"He saved my life, Jared." I looked at Jared, trying to impress upon him how important it was that we help Michael.

"I know. But whatever you do, don't go back to that hospital." He shook his head. "Fucking heroes. You're going to get us all killed one day. I'll handle it. Trust me."

I was hoping that I'd see Jared or Michael at the airport—that Jared might have arranged for all of us to leave for different places at the same time. Jared was too smart for that. When I boarded the plane to Atlanta, I boarded alone. When I boarded, I still didn't know what had happened to my friends.

Six

After landing in Atlanta, I rented a car, or should I say Dennis Robertson rented a car, and drove west. I drove aimlessly for a few hours before finding a roadside motel where I could lay low and heal up. The desk clerk didn't even look at me twice when I checked in, despite my bandaged hand and black eye.

Once in my motel room, I slept for nearly thirty straight hours. When I finally woke up, it was morning, a full day later. It was a crazy feeling knowing that I could just miss a day like that. When I woke up, I could hear the couple in the room next to mine fighting. I needed quiet, so I went out for a run. I had new sneakers and new clothes that I purchased at the airport with Dennis Robertson's credit card. I ran for nearly an hour and a half before coming back to the motel. When I came back, I showered. I was running out of ways to delay the inevitable. I picked up the phone. I dialed and waited. The phone rang twice. It was answered by a chipper-sounding woman. "Global Innovation Incorporated. How can we help you?"

"Michael Bullock, please," I responded.

"Please hold."

I waited a few moments before the phone began to ring again. After two rings it was answered by an equally chipper-sounding woman. "Spartan Consultants, how can we help you?"

"Dan Donovan, please," I responded this time.

"Please hold."

Again the waiting. Again the two rings. Again the chipper female receptionist. It wasn't enough that they had us risking our lives but they had to mimic the worst of corporate culture too. "Allies-on-Call. How can we help you?"

"I'd like to speak to Pamela O'Donnell."

"Please hold." This wasn't a prearranged call time. I was pretty sure someone would answer, though. My code would let them know who was calling. My guess was that after the debacle I'd just lived through, they'd be eager to hear from me.

It was only half a ring this time when someone picked up the phone. "Jesus Christ, Joe, what the hell happened?" It was Matt, my contact.

"Have you just been sitting by the phone for the last two days waiting for my call?"

"Basically, yes."

"Don't they let you go home?"

"Not after the shit you pulled. Not when you were supposed to be in Montreal. What the fuck happened, Joe?"

"I don't know. We were ambushed."

"Yeah, so was I. By my bosses. You got me in a shit-storm of trouble."

"Funny. I thought trouble was standing on a beach with your hands tied behind your back with some psychopath explaining how he is about to butcher you. I was pretty sure that was trouble. I guess I was wrong." I wasn't in the mood for any bullshit.

"I'm sorry, man. I know it was bad for you, but I'm just trying to do my job here. The guys that you three took out were some serious characters. They had at least fifty-four kills among the three of them. It's the only thing that kept me from getting demoted." Three of them? They must not have found the cabbie's body yet. Gone and forgotten, just like that.

"Listen; do you know what happened to Michael?"

"No details. They don't share that sort of thing with us, only with his own contact. All I know is that we got him out." I let out a breath of air, a breath that had been knotted up in my lungs ever since I'd dropped Michael off at the hospital.

"So he's okay?"

"As far as I can tell."

"Okay. I need you to do me a favor."

"Listen, Joe, I may be out of favors here." Matt's voice sounded nervous. His nervousness was reasonable. My last favor had gotten us into this mess.

"I need you to get me in contact with him."

"With Michael?" There was a pause on the other end of the line. Matt's voice dropped. "That's impossible. You guys are radioactive right now. The guys upstairs don't want you three near each other. They think it's too dangerous."

"Look, I'm not trying to meet up with him. I just want to talk to him," I argued.

"There's no way. I wouldn't have a clue where to find him and, even if I did, if I passed you that information, I'd have my ass handed to me on a plate." I wasn't in the mood for this. I took the phone and slammed it hard on the desk three times. Someone from one of the other motel rooms shouted at me to keep it down.

"What the fuck is your real name, Matt?" It was breaking protocol to ask. I didn't care.

"You know that I can't tell you that, Joe." I heard his answer and slammed the phone down on the receiver. I stood up and paced around the room for about five minutes trying to calm down. I called back, using the same three names that I had before. I was breaking

more protocol, using the same code twice, but after going through
the motions, Matt picked up again.

"What's your fucking name?" I demanded.

"Pedro. Rondell. Jesus. What difference does it make?" the voice
on the other end of the line shouted. I slammed the phone down on
the receiver again. I waited another five minutes and called for a third
time.

Matt picked up. "You can't call on that code again. If you do, you
won't get through. Calling with the same code again will send red
flags flying all over this place." I knew it would. They monitored the
codes. If a code was used more than once, they checked it in case it
was the other side digging for intelligence. Use a code three times,
and they assume the worst.

"Then tell me your name. We've been working together for five
years. My name is Joseph. My parents' names are James and Joan. It
was a big freaking *J* thing. My older sister's name was Jessica. She was
killed in front of me when I was fourteen. I grew up in a little town
in New Jersey. Just tell me your name." My voice went from yelling
to pleading. I don't know why it became so important to me.

"Fine"— the voice on the other end of the phone began to whisper. "It's Brian. My name is Brian." He was telling the truth. I don't
know how I knew. I just knew.

I almost started laughing out loud. "Your name is Brian and they
make you use Matt. What the hell's the difference?"

"Matt's a rank, a third-tier Intelligence officer. When I get promoted I'll move up to Allen."

"Listen, Brian." I used his real name. It felt liberating. "I really
need to speak to Michael. He saved my life. If it weren't for him, I'd
be buried in a shallow grave right now having my eyeballs picked out
by seagulls. Saving my life got an eight-inch knife punched into his
gut. You want to know what I did then? I ran. I left him alone at the
hospital and ran. I need to make sure that he's okay."

"Jesus, Joe. I'm sorry, but I wouldn't even know where to start."

"Do you know who his contact is?"

"Sure."

"Start there."

There was a heavy sigh on the line. "I'll see what I can do. Call me again tomorrow. Same time. But don't expect miracles."

"I stopped believing in miracles a long time ago, Brian."

"Terry Graham. Annie Campbell. Jack Wilkins." Brian hung up the phone.

I woke up early again the next morning. A good night's sleep had become pretty rare for me over the past two years or so. I usually just chalked it up to anxiety. I had gotten pretty accustomed to it, moving through the day on three or four restless hours of sleep. That morning, I knew that anxiety wasn't the only culprit keeping me awake. It was anxiety mixed with guilt. I got out of bed and headed out for another run, running hard, trying to burn off the stress. When I got home I still had another twenty minutes before I was due to call Brian. I picked up my calling card and dialed the phone anyway.

Eventually, a female voice answered. The voice was no less sing-songy than yesterday. "Hello."

"Hey, Ma, it's me," I responded.

"Joey! It's about time you called me. It's been weeks." I had a clear picture in my head of my mother scampering around in the tiny kitchen of the house that we moved into after my father died, donning her robe, making coffee. I knew she'd be up. My mother never slept past five.

"I know, Ma. I'm sorry. But you know that I'm not allowed to call from the safe houses and sometimes it's just hard to find a secure place to call from."

"I know. I know. Now that everybody's buying cell phones, just a plain old regular phone is so hard to come by." I was happy to have her make up excuses for me. I never would have thought of that one. It must have come to her after hours of rationalizing why I didn't call more often. "How are things, Joey?"

"Things are good, Mom. Same old, same old. How are things with you?"

"Things are okay. Jeffrey passed away." Great, more death. Jeffrey was our cat. He had been at least seventeen years old.

"What happened?" I barely cared. I was just making conversation. After all the death that I'd seen, it was difficult to mourn for a cat, even if it was my own cat. My mom was probably pretty broken up, though. Now the house was completely empty.

"I don't really know. He went out one day and came back all beat up. Part of one ear was missing and he had scratches on his nose and blood all over him. You know Jeffrey, always a fighter. Anyway, he came home, and at his age, it was too much for him. He fell asleep in my lap and never woke up." I could hear her voice beginning to choke up as she spoke.

"Well, at least he made it home. Knowing Jeffrey, whatever he was fighting didn't fare so well."

"Oh, poor Jeffrey," she said in a barely audible sigh. Then she paused, switched gears, and asked in a cheerful voice, "So, how's work?"

"Work is good," I lied. "More of the same." My mother knew what I did for a living, but I never gave her details. It wasn't that I thought it would be dangerous for her to hear. It's just didn't feel right describing to my mother the things that I did.

"You're too modest, Joey. 'More of the same.' And all the while you're out there saving the world."

"I wouldn't say that I'm saving the world, Ma."

"Well, I would," my mother said sternly, rebuking me for my modesty. "But I hope you're finding some time for yourself. I hope you're not working too hard."

"Actually, I just got back from a vacation."

"Really? Where'd you go?"

"I went down to Saint Martin with Jared and Michael," I replied. It was the safe answer. I wished it had been true.

"Really? And how are the boys?"

"They're good, Ma." I checked my watch to see how much time I had before I could call Brian to find out if I was lying.

"That Jared is a fine young man. He's really going to make something of himself. You stick with him, Joey, and you'll go places." My mother loved Jared. She always thought that Michael was a bad influence.

"Anyway, I'm going to have to go, Ma. I have some things to take care of."

"Okay," she said with another sigh. "I know you're an important man."

"Stop with the guilt, Ma. I really got to go."

"I know. I know. But don't make it so long before you call again."

"I won't."

"Promise?"

"I promise."

"Okay. I love you, Joey. And I miss you."

"I love you, too, Ma."

"Stay safe."

"I'll do my best."

"And never forget how proud I am of you. And your father too. Your father would be so proud." Now it was my turn to begin tearing up. The reaction surprised me. I went to say something but the words got caught in my throat. All I got out was a small grunt before shutting up again. I took a deep breath and fought off any real tears.

"You okay, Joey?"

"Fine, Ma," I finally got out. "I really got to go. I love you." Then I hung up and checked my watch. I still had four minutes until I was supposed to make my next call. So for four minutes I just sat there on the edge of the bed, staring down at my empty hands. They were shaking.

When it was time, I picked up the phone and dialed. Terry Graham. Annie Campbell. Jack Wilkins. I went through the process again, past all of the chipper receptionists and waited for the phone to be answered for the fourth time. It rang; each ring seemed to go on forever. Finally, after the sixth ring, someone answered the phone.

"You owe me." It was Brian.

"I guess that means you found him."

"Yeah. But you have to promise me you'll pay your debts before I let you talk to him."

"All right, so what is it that I owe you?"

"Your next job. It's the one in Montreal. I need you to lay low for two more weeks. Just stay where you are."

"Here?" I asked, looking around my dank motel room.

Brian ignored my question. "I'll arrange a flight for you in two weeks. Take the time to get your head on straight. The job in Montreal is an important job. It's a tricky job. You've got to do it right. No mistakes, no drama. You get in, you study the job, you do the job, and you leave."

"That's how I operate."

"Yeah. That's how you used to operate before you attacked a woman in public and left three corpses on a beach."

"They found the cabbie?"

"Yeah, what was left of him. Sharks made off with all the good stuff. Some guy hooked the rest of the body while deep sea fishing yesterday. Betchya that's not the catch he expected." There was a chuckle in Brian's voice. "Anyway, you owe me a clean job. That's all I ask."

"You got it. There's nothing in the world that I want more than to get things back to normal." Brian started laughing. "What's so funny?" I asked.

"Your normal is pretty fucked up. You know that, right?"

"The concept's not lost on me," I replied. Brian proceeded to give me the details of the Montreal job. It was a tricky hit. The guy was a player. He ran with protection. His house was wired to keep people out, to keep me out. I didn't ask who he was or what he did. After what had just happened, I didn't need the motivation. I was to go to Montreal and scout the job for six days. Then I had a couple of days to pull it off. I wasn't to call in again for another ten days unless I needed something. "Try not to call me until you're standing over a body," Brian said.

"Okay," I replied, trying my best to sell the reply. "Now, how do I get in touch with Michael?"

"Stay on the line. I'll patch him through."

"Thanks, Brian."

"Listen, Joe, don't call me Brian. It's Matt. It has to be Matt. Victor Erickson. Leonard Jones. Elizabeth Weissman." There was a click and then dead air on the line. I waited for a few seconds and then there was another click.

"Hello?" Michael's voice came through. He sounded confused.

"Michael? It's Joseph."

"Joe!" Michael sounded genuinely excited. There was no anger or bitterness in his voice. "Look at you, breaking rules. How the hell did you arrange this?"

"I've got friends in high places," I replied. "They didn't tell you that I was trying to reach you?"

"Nope, my connection just told me to stay on the line, so I stayed on the line. How are you? Where are you?"

"Georgia," I replied.

"No shit. Hotlanta. You can have some good times down there." I wasn't really in the mood for good times. "What's up, Joe?" It was like Beach Haven never happened.

"I just wanted to make sure that you were okay. I felt bad about leaving you like that."

"That's pretty sweet of you. Checking up on me." I could deal with the ribbing. Michael paused for a second, considering his own well-being. "I'm good. There were a few scary moments but they all make for a good story now. Right after they stitched me up, a couple of cops came in, dragged me out of bed, threw me in their cruiser, and told me they were taking me in. Real cops too. Real cop car. It was crazy. It turned out they were on our side. Go figure. Who would have thought that? Real cops? Anyway, they told me that they got a phone call from pretty high up in Intel and were ordered to get me somewhere safe, somewhere where they could finish patching me up. You use the same connections to save me that you used to set up this call?"

"No," I replied. I wished I could have said something different. "Digging you out of that hole that I left you in back there was all Jared's doing."

I could feel Michael nodding at the other end of the line. "That guy's really got his shit together. We make a pretty good team, the three of us do. I've got the enthusiasm. Jared's got the plans."

"Yeah," I replied, wondering what it was that I had. Wondering why these guys were still friends with me. Even though I didn't ask the question out loud, Michael sensed it.

"You've got the heart, Joe. You even called to check up on me."

"I'm sorry I left you at the hospital, Michael." I had to apologize. I had to spit the guilt out of my mouth. It was a poison that I'd been holding there for days. I wish I could say that it made me feel better.

"Don't worry about it, Joe. What choice did you have? Staying would have screwed everything up. The cops—those cops who helped me escape—they were only able to lose me because I was alone. Losing both of us would have been tough to cover up. You had to go. Jared would say the same thing."

I didn't care what Jared would have said. "Jared doesn't know everything." I wanted to ask him why he was so much braver than I was. Instead, all I could ask was "Why'd you come back for me?"

"Because I'm stupid. I'm a stupid man who likes a good fight." Michael laughed through the phone.

"Seriously. Why'd you come back for me?"

"We've all got our reasons, Joe." Michael paused for a moment before he answered to make sure that I was serious.

"What does that mean?" I said.

"We've all got our reasons for fighting. I fight for you guys. I fight for my friends."

"You don't wonder about the bigger picture?"

"Sure, I wonder," Michael replied, "but as long as you guys are fighting beside me, it's all secondary. You and Jared saved me when I was a kid. I owe you both."

"Well, if you did owe me anything, the debt's been repaid."

"No, that's a debt that I'll never be able to repay, pal. Don't feel bad, Joe. You did the right thing."

"I'm starting to think that sometimes the 'right thing' is for suckers." There was an awkward pause on the conversation. Michael wouldn't say it, but the pause told me everything I needed to know. Michael agreed with me. "So, you're going to be okay, then?" I asked, breaking the silence.

"Fine. Better than fine. I'm almost back to a hundred percent already. I'm going to have a nasty scar, but what do they say? 'Pain heals. Chicks dig scars. Glory lasts forever.'"

I shook my head in disbelief. "*They* don't say that, Michael. Keanu Reeves said that in *The Replacements*. And that movie was a piece of shit. You do know that you kill people for a living, don't you, Michael?"

"Yeah, so?"

"So maybe you should get some of your own lines."

Michael laughed. "I'll work on it. Next time, we're really making it to Saint Martin," Michael said. "We're going to find some beautiful women, and we're going to have the time of our lives."

"I'm there," I replied. "I just want you to know, Michael, if I'm ever in that situation again, I'm not leaving you behind." I promised myself right then that I would never leave anyone I cared about behind again. That's a promise, Maria.

"I know." Michael's tone was serious, but only for a second. "Jared's going to be pissed, though. Now he's got to deal with two idiots instead of just me. Anyway, I've gotta jet. We'll hook up soon. Stay safe, Joe."

"You too," I replied. Then I hung up the phone. Two weeks later, I was on a flight to Montreal. Saint Martin never happened. I haven't seen or spoken to Michael since that conversation. I'm starting to doubt I ever will.

Seven

It was early in the day when I landed in Montreal. As instructed, I took a cab to a small arcade on St. Catherine Street. I was supposed to pick up the keys to the safe house there. The name of the arcade, Casino Royale, blinked in bright neon lights above the door. I walked in and headed straight to the back of the arcade, past all of the kids with their baggy jeans, past all of the flashing lights, past the bells, the whistles, and the sounds of fake gunfire. I walked to the counter in the back where a couple of teenage employees doled out coins so that the other kids could keep dropping their allowances into the machines. I told the girl working behind the counter that I was there to pick up keys to an apartment and she passed them to me silently. The safe house was going to be empty throughout my stay. My mark was apparently too dangerous to risk anybody's life but mine. If I blew my cover I was a dead man, but this way, the ripples wouldn't stretch out any wider than that. I walked the two miles from the arcade, up a long, store-ridden street, to the safe house.

The safe house was a small, sparse one-bedroom apartment with a balcony overlooking the street below. I checked out the contents of the fridge. I was hungry. Inside was some soda, a block of cheese, and some leftover Chinese food. There was a frozen pizza in the freezer and a wine rack with a few bottles of red wine against the wall. Either my host kept a sparse home or he'd emptied the place out before I got there. I put the frozen pizza in the oven and sat down on the couch. This was going to be a lonely job. There, on the coffee table in front of me, was a thick manila envelope. I had noticed it immediately when I walked in but did my best to ignore it while I got a feel for the place. I simply stared at it for another minute or two until the scent of mediocre frozen pizza began to fill the apartment. Then I tore the envelope open.

My mark was a Canadian scientist turned businessman. Apparently, he ran a large pharmaceutical company. He was loaded. He used his wealth to funnel money to our enemies' operations all over the world. Africa, Asia, Europe, he had money going everywhere. He also developed chemical and biological weapons for use in the War. These weren't the mass-destruction, gas-the-enemy kind of weapons. He developed targeted, precise poisons that were rarely traceable. We knew he did it. We had no idea how many of our people had died, choking on one of his inventions. Dozens? Hundreds? Thousands? Almost anything was possible.

My target generally traveled with two bodyguards. The first bodyguard had been born into the War. He was one of them. He was a trained Ranger in the United States Army. On paper, and in photos, he appeared to be a serious badass. Still, he was fair game. The second bodyguard was a bigger problem. He was a civilian. Everything in the paperwork that I was given said that he was clueless about the War. He'd basically been shanghaied. He thought he was simply being paid to protect a paranoid Canadian businessman. The second bodyguard was formerly of the Australian navy and, being a civilian, was untouchable. It was just like these bastards to use a civilian shield.

My pizza was ready. I found a plate, threw the pizza on it, and began to read about my mark's daily routines. Two days a week, Tuesdays and Thursdays, he taught chemistry classes at McGill University as an adjunct professor. Every Monday, he had lunch in Chinatown with various out-of-town guests. Wednesday afternoons were spent at a strip club on lower St. Laurent Street, again with out-of-town guests. These weren't pleasure trips, they were business meetings. Deals were struck during these meetings. Sometimes the deals involved our War, sometimes they involved other wars. The meetings were closely guarded. Evenings were normally spent at home.

My mark's house was on the other side of Mount Royal. It was a veritable fortress. Only one bodyguard stayed at home with him in the evenings and that job was rotated. The bodyguard would spend the night in a spare bedroom in the house. The next night, the other bodyguard would stay.

I decided that I would start my recon work tomorrow. I would follow the mark for a bit and try to find some chinks in the armor, to see if the bodyguards got lazy. My plan—the only one I could come up with at the time—was to tail him for three days and then develop a better plan. Tomorrow was Wednesday. It looked like the agenda called for strip clubs. I had no idea that you were about to change my life.

I woke up before sunrise the next morning and headed over to my mark's house. It was going to be a full day. I planned on following him from the moment he woke up until he went to sleep. I put a pair of binoculars in my backpack and purchased some more supplies—granola bars, water, etcetera—from a corner store on my way.

The sun was just beginning to rise when I reached the house. I had a floor plan of the house in my bag and when I got there, I pulled it out in hopes of finding a good spot where I could spy on the morning revelry without being noticed. The place was huge. The floor plan didn't do it justice. Every room was gigantic. The front of the house faced the street while the back had a picture-perfect view of the park.

My mark's bedroom was in the back, so I headed into the park. There, I climbed into a tree that still had enough leaves to hide me. I settled myself in the crux of two branches and pointed my binoculars at the bedroom window.

I was a little late. I could just peer through the slats between the vertical blinds in the bedroom. The bed was empty, unmade but empty. I scanned the other windows. None of the other windows opening onto the park had shades. Two windows over from my mark's room was the bodyguards' room. I peered in to see one of the bodyguards doing push-ups on the floor of the bedroom. I stopped counting at eighty-five. After what seemed like about twenty uninterrupted minutes of push-ups, the bodyguard flipped over and began doing sit-ups. This, too, went on for what seemed to be an eternity. Just like it was written in my notes, this bodyguard had a tattoo on his right bicep of the symbol of the Australian navy and a tattoo on his back of a surfer being eaten by a shark. This was the civilian. You're a long way from home, my friend, I thought to myself. I took out a notebook and wrote down the schedule. According to the Intelligence report that I'd received, the two bodyguards alternated nights. So the civilian was scheduled for Tuesday, Thursday, and Saturday of this week and Monday, Wednesday, and Friday of the next. The other nights would be covered by the bodyguard that I could actually do something about. After the sit-ups the Aussie began doing dips, using a chair for leverage.

I scanned the other windows. There was my mark. He was downstairs in the exercise room. He was on the StairMaster and was wearing an earpiece and talking on the phone as he exercised. He was animated as he spoke and it was ruining his rhythm on the machine. A couple of times, I thought he might fall off. My mark was about five eight with dark hair and a beard that was showing early signs of going gray. He wasn't in bad shape for a businessman, but his gut still hung slightly over his exercise shorts. His eyes were a dark brown, bordering on black. I had a visceral reaction to the sight of him. I knew that I wouldn't have second thoughts about taking him out.

I looked over the rest of the house. Next to the exercise room was a den with a purple-felted pool table. The kitchen and a gigantic living room opened onto the backyard. The entire yard was surrounded by a white metal fence. On top of a post at each of the corners of the fence was a video camera. I picked a large piece of bark off the tree I was sitting in and threw it into the backyard. At the instant the piece of bark entered the yard, both of the video cameras turned to follow it until it landed, motionless. Laser motion detectors. I looked back into the bodyguard's room. Just as I'd thought, the movement set off a small alarm in the bodyguard's room and the Aussie turned to look at a computer that was set up on his desk. He saw whatever the cameras saw. I focused my binoculars on the cameras and I wrote down their make and model so that I could research them later.

At seven A.M., the maid showed up, in full maid regalia. She wore a powder blue dress, cropped just below the knees, with a white apron with ruffles on the side. Who still dressed their help like that? This guy was a real piece of work. The maid came in and began cooking breakfast. My mark had bacon, eggs, toast, and melon for breakfast. He sat alone at the table reading the morning paper. The Aussie had eggs, potatoes, melon, and a bowl of granola. He sat alone at the counter. Not a word was spoken by anyone. Then, as the maid began to clean up the kitchen, both men headed back to their respective bathrooms, showered, and got ready for their day. The Aussie wore a dark blue suit with a solid dark-blue tie, typical bodyguard gear. He also wore an earpiece through which he could communicate with the other bodyguard. My mark wore a dark charcoal gray suit, with a yellow shirt and no tie.

At exactly eight A.M., the other bodyguard showed up. He and the Aussie were dressed identically. In their work uniforms, the only way to tell them apart was that the American had darker hair and wore a goatee. The two of them joked around a bit as my mark went back to his bedroom to get his briefcase. I could see them taking turns, talking and laughing. As soon as my mark returned, they were as stoic as statues. At eight-fifteen, the three of them were off. I made my way around to the front of the house to see them pull away in the car. The civilian and my mark sat in the backseat. The other bodyguard drove. I obviously wasn't going to be able to keep up with them in the car. According to the information I'd been given, however, they should be heading to his office for the next few hours. I hailed a cab and followed them downtown.

I spent the next four hours at a café across the street from my mark's office building. I didn't dare go inside. Going inside most likely meant putting my face on camera. I wasn't ready for that. Instead, I just sat across the street in the café, reading the newspaper and watching the door and the garage exit to see when my mark would come out. I learned almost nothing over those four hours.

Finally, at around twelve-thirty, my mark came walking through the door with his bodyguards in tow. I had already gotten the check, so I paid and walked outside. Apparently, they walked to the strip club. I had to assume that this was weather dependent, but it was fine with me. I wanted to stretch my legs. The mark walked with the civilian bodyguard at his side and the American two steps behind them. The bodyguards were very diligent. They could have been trained by the secret service. The bodyguard at the mark's side looked straight ahead, making sure that no one was going to obstruct their path, making sure that nothing was coming straight at them. The bodyguard in the back did continual eye scans of all the other areas, the street, the sidewalks, even the skies. I was walking across the street from them, but even then, I had to make sure that the trailing bodyguard didn't catch me staring at them. I walked casually, making only the random glance over to see if the bodyguards ever slipped, if they ever let their guard down. They didn't.

We walked down René-Lévesque until we reached St. Laurent and then we took a left. They crossed the street and continued to walk on the right side of the street. I stayed on the left. In two more blocks we hit the strip club. The facade was pretty straightforward, blinking neon signs advertising "Live Nude Girls" and "Completely Nude" and "24/7." It was impossible to see inside from the street. There weren't any windows. One door led to a staircase. The stairs led up to the club. A large bouncer stood just inside the door. My mark walked up and shook the bouncer's hand. They spoke for about thirty seconds. The bouncer smiled and laughed and patted my mark on the shoulder. Then my mark slipped him some money and headed up the stairs with the American bodyguard in tow. The Aussie stayed downstairs, standing on the opposite side of the door from the bouncer. They, too, exchanged some words and smiles before getting back to the quiet business of guarding the door.

This was too much. There was no way that I was going to stand here and wait for another three hours. I didn't want to go into the strip club, though. First, if the American bodyguard saw me inside and recognized me from the street, he was sure to get suspicious. Second, the guy in the strip club looking at the other guys in the strip club instead of at the strippers stands out like a sore thumb. I decided just to walk up to the door and get a closer look at the bodyguard. I swear that's all I was doing. I knew that he hadn't eyeballed me yet so I didn't worry too much about being inconspicuous. I walked across the street. Just inside the doorway to the strip club there were some action shots of the strippers in various poses, all completely naked. I was taken aback. You didn't see that sort of thing in the States, not right there on the street like that. I did my best to act casual, looking at the pictures of the girls while also trying to size up the bodyguard. The Aussie had a good four inches on me. He had a friendly face. I asked the bouncer which of the girls was working today. He told me that the pictures were mostly of their night-shift girls, but that the girls who worked during the day were pretty too. I'd played my role so far almost perfectly. That's when you nearly blew my cover.

I saw you walking down the street about half a block before you reached the doorway. I remember first seeing you coming, with the hood to your sweatshirt pulled up, covering your mass of dark curly hair. Your hands were jammed deep inside the pockets of your green sweatshirt. You looked cute. I was getting more of a thrill looking at you all bundled up like that than I did looking at the naked pictures of the strippers on the wall. You must have caught me staring. For a moment, we made eye contact. When we did, the skin around your big blue eyes wrinkled as you broke out into a mischievous grin. I forgot where I was. I forgot what I was doing. I forgot everything for that moment.

"I wouldn't pick that one," you said.

"Excuse me?" I responded. Then I remembered that I was standing in the doorway to a strip club staring at the pictures they had wallpapering the entranceway. Quite a first impression.

"I wouldn't pick that one," you repeated. "You should go to St. Catherine's. That's where all the other American tourists go." You paused and gave me a complete once-over. "Of course, most of them don't go in the middle of the afternoon, alone."

"Oh, me. I wasn't . . ." I had suddenly lost my ability to speak in full sentences. "I wasn't planning on going inside," I finally muttered, realizing only after I said it that standing there on the street gawking at the pictures probably didn't seem much better.

"Whatever. I don't judge," you replied as you walked past me. I watched you as you walked. I did my best to pull myself together before you walked out of my life forever. I had to say something, anything, to get your attention before you were gone.

"Well, why shouldn't I go to this one?" I shouted to your back as you walked away, not ready to let you go just yet.

You stopped and turned back toward me. "I don't know this from experience, but word on the street is that the strippers here have more tits than teeth."

"Oh, is that the word on the street?" I responded.

You turned your back to me again and started walking away for the second time. "That's the word on the street," you yelled without turning back.

"Well, I really wasn't planning on going inside." I was now shouting down the street, trying to make sure that you could hear me. "But after your review, it sounds like it could be pretty interesting as long as I find at least one stripper with more than one tooth."

You heard me. You turned around, still walking away from me, your hands still jammed deeply into the pockets of your sweatshirt, and smiled a world-shattering smile. You lifted one hand in a wave without taking it out of its pocket and yelled back to me. "Good-bye, Perv," you called out. Then you turned away from me for the third time and were gone.

My cover was blown. The Aussie was sure to remember my face now. I had to call it a day, my job barely done. It was worth it. Your smile made it worth it even though I suspected that I'd never see that smile again.

Before heading back to the safe house, I went back over to the other side of Mount Royal to canvas my mark's fortress. I thought that maybe, without professionals there guarding it, I might be able to find some sort of loophole that I could fit through. I investigated the house for a couple of hours, watched the maid move from room to room cleaning the place, watched her leave, and then headed home for the day. My job would start up again tomorrow. It would require extra diligence now. "No more flirting with strangers," I told myself. Just you.

———

My mark taught a class at McGill University the following day. The class was big enough that I figured I could sit in the back of the lecture hall without being noticed. I put on a Montreal Canadiens hat that I had purchased and pulled the brim down low enough that, when looking down at a notebook, my entire face would be hidden. I packed my backpack and headed off to class. I knew that if everything went according to plan, this stakeout should be easy. It was rare that taking notes actually enhanced your disguise.

By the time I reached McGill's campus, it was already brimming with life. There were students everywhere. Thousands of students, most only a few years younger than me, were drifting in and out of buildings, carrying books, wandering from lecture to lecture. I stepped through the gates on University Street and felt, for one of the few times in my life, like a normal person going to my first college lecture. I had my notebook, my backpack, and my pencils. It felt surreal. I felt good. The only difference between me and the other students was that I planned on killing my professor.

I headed over to the lecture hall where my mark would be teaching and waited outside as the students began to shuffle in. I counted the heads as they walked through the doors. The class had over 150 students in it and I assumed at least 75 would attend. I waited until 50 other students entered the classroom and then I walked in. I chose my seat carefully, picking a row two rows in front of the students who were sitting the farthest back. I took a seat just off center, doing everything I could to not stand out. I did a quick visual scan of the lecture hall. It had the capacity to hold about three hundred students, and as I found my way to an empty seat, it quickly filled up to near half capacity. Apparently, my mark's lectures were popular. He was already standing at the podium, rifling through his notes and talking to another member of the faculty. I scanned the room for the bodyguards. It didn't take me long to spot the first one. He was standing in the front of the lecture hall, in one of the corners. No suit today. If he weren't so big, he might have blended in with the students. He was wearing khakis and a blue sweatshirt. He stood with his back to the front wall. From where he was standing, he could quickly survey the entire room. It took me a bit longer to find the Aussie. He was stationed in the back of the room. The positioning was logical. From their vantage points, the two bodyguards could easily catch any suspicious movements and put a stop to them before suspicious became dangerous. Still, I was relieved to know that the Aussie would be staring at the back of my head for the next hour and half. He might remember my face from the day before, but that wasn't going to help him from where he was standing.

I watched the students around me and aped their behavior. When they began to take out their notebooks, I did too. Once everyone had reached into the bags and the collective shuffling of the student body died down, my mark began his lecture. He wore a small microphone that wrapped around his neck, making it possible to hear his voice clearly no matter where you were seated in the lecture hall. The class was a second-year chemistry course entitled "Drugs and Disease."

"Toxicology," he began. "Toxicology is a subject that each and every one of us practices every day. In fact, I shouldn't be so limiting, it's a subject that each of the members of your family, each of your neighbors, nearly everyone on this continent and most of the people on this planet, practice every day. Yes, even your uneducated, out-of-work uncle." There was a sputtering of laughter from the class. "In fact, that uncle, depending upon how much time he spends at his local pub each day, may practice it the most." Again, muffled laughter. "No matter what we do, we are constantly evaluating what we put into our bodies, be it medicine, drugs, alcohol, even food. Why? Because we know that the wrong amount, the wrong dose, can have toxic effects and these toxic effects can lead to myriad results. From euphoria to agonizing pain; from complete but comforting numbness to debilitating disease; from a feeling of raised awareness to death."

He went on. My classmates followed along, clicking away on their keyboards and writing furiously in their notebooks. It didn't take long for the science to be lost on me. Since I was having trouble following the lecture, I began to simply watch my mark to see how he moved, to see how he held himself, to see if there were any idiosyncrasies that I might be able to use to my advantage. To this point, I had paid more attention to the bodyguards than to the man himself. But now, in my disguise, I could sit back and watch the man who had already caused so much death.

He wore a dark suit again, perfectly tailored. Though not tall, he carried himself as if he were the tallest man in the room. His movements were fluid and graceful. He generally spoke with one hand at his side and one on the podium. He moderated his voice to match the lecture. At times, it would rise and he would hold his hands about shoulder length apart, clutching his fists for emphasis. However, during the moments when he truly wanted attention, the volume of his voice would actually lower to just above a whisper and he would stand motionless, holding each syllable for an extra beat. During those times, the students were rapt with attention. The large lecture hall would get so quiet that if a pin dropped I would hear it and the bodyguards would hear it but the students probably wouldn't notice. If circumstances were different, he might have had a lot to offer the world. These students of his, rising and falling on his every word, one of them could cure cancer. It was almost a shame I had to kill him. But he understood the War and still embraced it. He understood the ramifications of his actions. He would have no one to blame for his death but himself.

The class ended with some unpleasantries about an exam and then the students began to shuffle back out of the classroom. I fell in line, put my head down, and walked out with everyone else, being sure that the big Australian did not get a look at my face.

The hallway was crowded, so I simply walked in the direction of the flowing crowd. When I got to a small set of stairs, I turned to take a quick look back. I saw my mark exiting the lecture hall through the same doors that the students had just used. He was in an intense conversation with one of the students. The two bodyguards were walking about two steps behind them. The American kept a stern eye on the student. He looked ready to rip the poor kid's head off if the kid were to make even the slightest awkward move. The student didn't seem to notice. So much for educating the youth. The kid might one day become a brilliant scientist, but he wouldn't have survived one day in my job.

Then I heard your voice. It was coming from across the hallway. I recognized it instantly. For the second day in a row, you nearly blew my cover. It was becoming an annoying little hobby of yours.

"Hey, Perv!" you shouted, stepping toward me, standing on the stairs about three steps above me. As you spoke, you flicked the brim of my hat. Before I even had a chance to look at you again, my reflexes kicked in. I looked back at the big Australian to see if he'd heard you. He had. His head popped up and he began to scan the hallway looking for something, anything. I was certain that he was looking for me, even if he didn't know it. He recognized your voice too. I turned, grabbed you under your armpit, nearly lifting you off the ground, and pulled you down one of the side corridors. I didn't have time to be gentle. I couldn't afford to have the bodyguard recognize me.

"Hey! Hands off!" you shouted, slapping my hand as you found your feet again.

I had to think of something quick, some lie to justify grabbing you like that. "Listen, you can't call me a pervert in front of my professor. He's already got it in for me."

You began to move your arm in circles, looking as if you were testing to see if your shoulder was still firmly implanted in its socket. "Fine, but you could have just asked me to be quiet. You didn't have to grab me like that."

"I'm sorry." The last thing that I wanted to do was hurt you. "It won't happen again," I promised.

"Yeah, it won't happen again. I'm leaving." You threw your backpack over your shoulder and started walking away.

"Wait. Let me do something to make it up to you. Let me buy you a coffee or something," I called out to you as you walked away.

"Really?" You turned back toward me. "I'm supposed to go to get coffee with the strip club guy?"

"I was just looking at the pictures. I'm not used to seeing things like that on the street. Besides, you're one to talk making friends with guys who stand out on the street in front of strip clubs."

"Who said we were friends?" you asked, though you were smiling when you did so. You couldn't help yourself. I love that smile.

"Coffee?" I asked again. You were standing about ten feet from me in the hallway. I forgot all about my mark. I forgot about the bodyguards. My whole world at that moment was you. I had never felt like this before. It happened so quickly.

"You're buying?" you asked.

"Of course," I responded.

So we went for coffee, despite the fact that I didn't drink coffee. I just figured that's what regular people do. I was trying my best to be normal. I wanted to make sure that I didn't scare you away. You led me to a coffee shop just off campus. That was good. It made it less likely that I would suddenly have to hide from my mark's bodyguards. We chatted as we walked. You asked me how my trip to the strip club had gone. Eventually, I think that I convinced you that I hadn't gone inside. It was strange talking to you. You seemed to have no poker face. Everything was out in the open. I wasn't used to that. In my world, everyone is covering up something. Everyone's a liar.

We sat down for coffee, although I ordered hot chocolate, which you made fun of me for, and continued to talk. You pulled the hood of your sweatshirt off and unleashed a wild torrent of dark hair. The crazy mass of curls made you seem even more alive. Twenty minutes into our conversation and I had told you more about my life than I had ever told any woman before. I told you about growing up in New Jersey. I told you what I could about losing my father and my grandparents. I told you about my life, traveling around the world for business.

"You're not a student?" you asked.

"I take classes when I can," I replied, trying to cover my tracks, realizing that being too truthful too soon might scare you away. I turned the questions back on you. How old were you? "I'm a second-year." What were you studying? "Debating between Psychology and Religious Studies. I'm really interested in what makes people tick." What do you do for fun? "Pick up strange Americans in front of strip clubs and start wild, torrid affairs." I nearly choked on my hot chocolate. You just giggled at my reaction. Where did you grow up? "Outside of Toronto in London, Ontario." Family? "Typical cookie-cutter family. I'm an only child." The conversation went on like that as the afternoon slipped away. I completely forgot about the job that I was supposed to be doing. You completely lost track of time too. You suddenly looked at your watch. "Oh, shit, I'm late for class." You jumped up, swung your backpack over one shoulder, and headed for the door.

"When—?" I stood up and started to ask. I shouldn't have been doing this. It was unprofessional. It felt good, though. It felt good to put my life ahead of my job. I was tired of being lonely. I wanted to know what a real life felt like. I wanted to fall for you. Lucky for me, you made it easy.

"Meet me tomorrow night, eight o'clock, in front of the Para-

mount on St. Catherine Street." You shot me one last smile and flew
out the door. Then you were gone again. I knew a lot about you already, but I suddenly realized that I'd never asked you what your
name was.

I spent that night alone at the safe house, heating up frozen food and
poring over my notes from the past few days. I was about a day and a
half behind on my surveillance but I'm not sure if the extra day and
a half would've helped. There didn't appear to be any holes in my
mark's routine. More surveillance would have just led to more frustration. Meanwhile, while trying to develop a plan that wasn't going
to get me killed, I kept getting distracted thinking about you. I spent
random moments trying to remember details from our conversation.
I had to try to chase you from my mind because I was beginning to
drive myself crazy. Eight o'clock tomorrow night, I'd remind myself.
Then I'd tell myself to breathe.

I needed to do some more work before rushing in and trying to
kill the professor if I was going to have any chance of walking away
from the job alive. I started to devise the only plan that I could see
working without getting me killed. It would require a full day of surveillance of my mark's house. I wanted to see when the maid came,
when the maid left, the tasks that she did, and the order in which she
did them. I needed to find out how much time she spent in each room
and when. I needed to find out everything I could about the motion
detecting cameras surrounding the house. I knew their brand and
their model number. I knew that they were state of the art, attracted
to both movement and heat. If there was one thing moving in the
yard or one thing giving off heat, all the cameras would zoom in on
that one thing. If there were multiple variances, like two moving bodies or a moving body and something giving off heat, the cameras

would each zoom in on whatever was happening that was closest to it. It was an intricate system, but it was beatable.

I had to concentrate. It wasn't easy. Eight P.M. It was only about twenty hours away.

As planned, I spent the entire next day casing my mark's home. I noted when people came and went. I wrote down the exact times when the maid went from room to room and how much time she spent in each room. I created a chart noting how often the cameras moved as they picked up various random movements, such as squirrels or falling leaves. I began to develop a plan. I'd need to do another day of surveillance on Monday to confirm a few things. I assumed that the whole weekend was a lost cause. The weekend would likely be patternless and useless to me. I could do some research on these cameras and obtain the equipment that I needed but beyond that, I was going to have to give myself the weekend off. Normally, I'd dread the downtime. This time, there was at least some promise that I wouldn't spend the whole weekend alone.

It felt like the day would never end. At seven o'clock in the evening my mark came home. Only one bodyguard came in with him, the other being dismissed for the day at the front gate. Today's bodyguard was the American, who would be spending the night. It was Friday, they were right on schedule. That was the last note I needed. I marked that down and then I hauled ass back through the park. I needed to get ready to see you.

I got to the theater five minutes early. When I got there, you were already waiting in front of the theater. The sky had grown dark, a deep purple color, but the street and the sidewalk were bright from the lights of the surrounding shops and restaurants. You were standing in front of the theater, looking out at the faces of people as they passed you. I snuck up behind you. I stepped quietly toward your back until my mouth was just a few inches from your ear. "Anything good playing?" I whispered. You didn't jump. You barely reacted. It was as if you'd expected me to come up behind you like that. You simply stood there, your arms crossed, a smile radiating out from the edges of your lips.

"Hello, Perv," you replied, without looking at me, speaking in a whisper, matching my volume and my tone.

"So, are we actually going to see a movie?" I whispered in your ear, not wanting to move my lips any farther from your face, not wanting to move away from the scent of your hair.

"That is why people go to the movies," you responded.

"Okay, then, what are we going to see?"

You turned again and looked up at the marquee. There were about ten movies playing at the theater. The light from the marquee shone down on us. You were glowing in the light. "You pick," you said, spreading your arms out as wide as you could and motioning to the marquee as if to embrace the possibilities.

"Why do I get to pick?"

Without removing your gaze from the listing of movies, you replied, "Because I've already seen them all," as if I had just asked the silliest question in the world.

That night, after the movie, I walked you home. The night had grown cold and you walked with your hood pulled up around your face, just like the first two times that I saw you. It felt good, already having memories of you. It had only been three days and I knew that you would live in my mind forever. The cold didn't bother you much. You teased me about my thin American blood. You talked about the movie, about the things that you saw that you hadn't noticed the first time. You said you liked the movie more the second time. You nearly danced around me as we walked, moving in circles, light on your feet. I barely spoke, already dreading saying good-bye to you. When we finally got to the front of your apartment building, snow had begun to fall. You stepped inside the doorway and slipped your hands inside the back pockets of your jeans. You leaned back against the doorframe and smiled at me. I tried reading the signals. Then I leaned in to kiss you for the first time. We held the kiss for a moment, barely moving, and I lifted a hand and placed it against your cheek. The kiss was sweet and innocent but sensuous. It was an old Hollywood movie kiss. When our lips finally parted, I spoke. "By the way," I said, "what's your name?" Maria. You told me your phone number. Despite the fact that you claimed to be quite fond of the nickname "Perv," I told you my name. Then we said good-bye, seemingly for the night, although I'm not sure that either of us wanted to let the night go yet. I know that I didn't. I watched you until you were safely in your stairwell, moving my eyes away only after I couldn't see you anymore. Then I started the lonely walk home.

When I got back to the safe house, I climbed into bed and, as usual, couldn't sleep. It wasn't anxiety or guilt keeping me awake this time. It was loneliness. I missed you already. Only moments after seeing you disappear behind your apartment door, I missed you. After an agonizing hour or two, armed with your name and your phone number, I picked up the phone and dialed. You answered after only a ring and a half. You weren't sleeping either.

"Maria," I said. It wasn't a question. I knew it was you. I just wanted to say your name.

"Joseph," you replied, saying my whole name.

"Come over," I requested.

"Now?" you asked.

"Now."

"It's too late." You laughed.

"It's never too late," I replied. There was optimism in my voice. I wasn't used to that. I repeated the words just so that I could hear them again, just to make sure I had actually spoken them. "It's never too late."

"We already said good night, Joe. I don't want to ruin a perfect evening." There was something in your voice—a blend of fear and excitement.

"But it wasn't perfect," I replied.

"It wasn't?" You sounded disappointed.

"No," I said again.

"Why not?" you asked.

"Because I'm here and you're there," I answered.

There was a pause on the line. I heard everything I needed to hear in that pause. "I'm afraid, Joe. This is going too fast." I should have told you that I was afraid too. I was afraid that if it didn't go fast enough, I'd lose my chance. Days would go by and I would be gone. I wanted at least this moment—at least this night. Good things can't happen too fast where I come from. They can only happen too slowly, and if they happen too slowly, they are lost.

"Well, if you don't come over here, then I am coming back there."

"You can't come here. I have a roommate."

"Then come here. Be with me. Don't be afraid. Life's too short to be afraid."

Another pause. "Okay," you finally said. "Where are you?" I told you the address of my apartment. "I'll be there in twenty minutes."

I dressed again. Then I sat on the sofa and waited. Despite the cold, I opened a window, hoping that I could hear you as you approached the building. Fifteen minutes went by. I spent those fifteen minutes watching the clock tick time away. Then the buzzer rang. I didn't stop to ask who it was. It had to be you. I pressed the button to let you in. I stood by the door listening to the footsteps in the stairwell as you bounded up the stairs. You moved quickly until you were right outside the apartment door. Then there was that moment. It was that moment when anticipation and reality caught up to each other. It felt like a cosmic event. I could feel you on the other side of the door. You hesitated before knocking. I decided not to wait for you to knock. I wasn't going to give you a moment to doubt yourself. I opened the door and there you were in front of me. You looked scared but excited, excited that you were ignoring your fears, and scared about how excited you were. I waited a moment. Then I grabbed you by the hood of your jacket and pulled you close to me. I kissed you hard on the lips. I still remember how you tasted. You tasted different than you had just hours before. There was a musky flavor on top of the sweetness that I had tasted before. It was the flavor of whiskey. You must have downed a shot before getting the courage up to venture out of your apartment. The flavor was enticing. We moved together as we kissed. You took the lead. Without our lips separating, you led me slowly into the bedroom. You kept your eyes open. We fell onto the bed, clutching each other. I reached down between your legs and pressed my hand into you. You gasped, slightly, quietly. Then you pushed me away from you for a moment.

"It's freezing in here," you said to me. Until that moment, I hadn't even noticed. I had forgotten to close the window.

"Wait here," I said. I looked down at you lying on the bed. Your lips were red and glistening. I could see your chest rise and fall with each hard breath. "Don't move." I ran into the living room to shut the open window. I was back in the bedroom in a moment. You had moved. I should have known better than to believe you'd wait passively. I returned to see that you'd already ventured under the covers. My eyes drifted to the small pile of your clothes sitting next to the bed. I stood in the doorway for a second, dumbstruck, watching the covers move on top of you as you slowly pulled off your final piece of clothing. With that, you dropped a tiny pair of pink underwear on top of the pile of discarded clothing.

Then you smiled. The fear was gone. It had been murdered by excitement and whiskey. "So, you going to come under here and keep me warm or what?" I stepped to the side of the doorway and turned off the bedroom lights. Only the illumination from the window, a mix of soft blue light coming from the moon and the distant streetlights, was left. The soft light made everything glow. It was like a dream. I slowly slipped off my clothes as you watched me. Then I joined you under the covers.

We woke up the next morning curled up in each others' arms. I felt hungover, like I had just awoken from a long slumber, confused as to what had happened the night before. The sun was shining brightly in the window. Your hair was disheveled, your eyes sleepy, but you looked beautiful. I woke up before you. While you were asleep, I lay there, gazing down at you. I wasn't sure what to make of what had happened. You opened your eyes and caught me staring at you. You smiled. I could feel my life changing. For a moment, I was torn. I knew that I couldn't be good for you. I should have chased you from my life right then. It would have been the right thing to do. I should have protected you from me. Instead, looking at you in the bright morning sun, I began to believe that maybe you could save me. I just didn't know what from.

Give it the weekend, I thought.

We each had things to do that day. You had a paper to write. I had a gun to purchase. I think we were both relieved to be apart for a little while, to take stock of things, to try to understand what was happening, but we didn't dare be apart for too long. We agreed to meet again for dinner, near the apartment. It was the first time that I had ever really felt at home in a safe house.

After you left, I went out in search of a pay phone. I could have called from the landline at the safe house, but knowing that you'd be spending more time there, I decided not to take any more chances. I didn't want anyone to be able to trace anything back to you. Finding a working pay phone was a major pain in the ass. I was on a short list of people whose job was made more difficult by the fact that everyone was getting cell phones. Eventually, I found a pay phone. I dialed. After a few rings a woman answered. "Global Solutions. How can I help you?"

"Victor Erickson, please," I replied and was transferred. Leonard Jones, Elizabeth Weissman, and I was finally patched through.

The first words out of Brian's mouth were "Shit, is he dead already?"

"No. I need a gun," I answered.

"In Canada? You're nuts. I thought you weren't going to call me until he was dead."

"Shit happens. Can you help me out here?" I wasn't in the mood for a long discussion. I just wanted to do what I had to do for the day so that I could be with you again.

"You know that we don't like to use guns, right?" This was standard policy. Guns were to be used on a need-only basis. Guns were traceable. Guns aroused suspicion. You strangle someone, knife someone, bash someone's head in with a bat, and people get scared but no one thinks that there's something bigger going on. Hate crime, crime of passion, no way there's an organized war going on where people are killing each other with kitchen knives. Anyway, standard policy or not, for this mission, I needed a gun. I wished I could call Jared. He'd know where to get one, but I'd already cashed all those chips in. I was on my own.

I told Brian what I thought of his policy. "Yeah, well, you want to explain the policy to my mark's bodyguards, because I'm not sure they care. You know, I'd prefer not to die taking this guy out. So can you help me out or not?" In the past, I might have tried to pull this off without the gun. Death just seemed like an especially bad idea at the moment.

"I can't help, but if that's what it's going to take, I can point you toward some people that can. I'd prefer it if you didn't die too. For some silly reason, I've grown fond of your bullshit."

"Yeah, that silly reason's called pity. Who do I need to see?" Brian told me to hold on while he checked some things on his computer. I could hear him clicking away on his keyboard. Then he put me on hold while he made a couple phone calls. I had to drop a few more coins into the phone. Finally, he clicked back on and gave me an address not far from the safe house. I was to go in, ask for Sam, give Sam a password, and then get down to business.

"Brian—" I started before the voice on the other end of the line cut me off.

"Joe, it's Matt. Remember. It has to be Matt."

"Sorry. Matt. I'm curious, is there anywhere you guys don't have connections?" I asked.

"Go everywhere," Brian responded. "You'll find out."

"Thanks, Matt." I tried to clear my mind so that I'd remember the code. Clearing my mind usually wasn't this difficult.

"You got it, Joe. Just don't fuck this one up or it'll be my ass. Carol Ann Hunter. Robert Mussman. Dennis Drazba." Click.

I went to the address that Brian had given me. It was a shop that sold sex toys down near Chinatown. Sex and guns. It was just like being in the States. I thought for a minute that this might be Brian's idea of a joke. I walked into the store, through the aisles of dildos, novelty lingerie, and porn DVDs, and up to the counter. At noon on a Saturday, the store was empty except for a woman standing behind the counter. I walked up.

"Can I help you?" she asked, sounding nothing like the receptionists at Intelligence. Even though she was young, her voice had the raspiness of a longtime smoker. She wore leather pants and a sleeveless, army-green top. She had tattoos running up and down both of her arms, angels and devils in some sort of battle. The devils seemed to be winning on her right arm but the angels had the upper hand on her left.

"I'm here to see Sam," I replied, hoping that this girl was in the loop.

"I'm Sam," she answered. I gave her the password and she told me that she'd been waiting for me. She walked to the front of the shop and locked the door. She flipped the sign on the door to Closed. Then she walked past me again and motioned for me to follow her. We walked up a flight of stairs. We passed a bunch of video booths where you could plunk in a couple of bucks and watch five minutes of porn.

"Wouldn't want to be the guy who has to clean these floors," I joked. Sam glared at me. It dawned on me that she might be the guy who had to clean the floors. Past the video booths was a door labeled Staff Only. We pushed through the door into the stockroom. The stockroom was nearly as big as the floor. It was immediately obvious that they weren't just selling sex toys.

"So, what is it you need?" Sam asked.

"What do you got?" I replied playfully, hardly able to control my good mood. I felt giddy.

Sam wasn't amused. "What do you need?" she repeated.

I finally got the point that this was not time for fun and games. "A handgun. Preferably something powerful but quiet. At least eight rounds before I have to reload."

"Okay." Sam walked over to a shelf about three rows from us, climbed a few steps up a ladder, and opened a big cardboard box. She lifted a few boxes of lubricants out of the box and set them aside. Then she reached deeper into the box for something that was buried beneath the other products and pulled out a small black handgun. "This should do the trick." She handed me the pistol. "Lightweight. Can carry a silencer. Can kill a horse. You'll get twenty-five shots before you need another cartridge, and with a little practice, you can reload a cartridge in about a second and a half." For the first time since I had entered the store, Sam seemed to be enjoying herself. I took the gun in my hand. I held it out in front of me, aiming it. It would do.

Once the sale was completed, I put everything—the gun, the silencer, and three cartridges—in my backpack. Three cartridges, but if I needed more than three shots, then something went drastically wrong. After we got back downstairs, Sam unlocked the front door and reopened the store to other customers. I walked toward the door but stopped before I was halfway there. Sam was on her way back to the counter. I turned toward her. There was a question that had been burning in my brain since I first laid eyes on her. "Sam?" She looked up at me. "I was just wondering. Are you in this for the cash or are you one of us?" It wasn't a question that you were ever supposed to ask. I didn't care. I couldn't help myself.

"I don't know what you're talking about," Sam answered, her voice even, her eyes emotionless. She walked back behind the counter. I turned again and headed toward the door. Before I could open it, Sam spoke again. This time her voice wavered slightly. I turned and looked at her. "I don't know what you're talking about," she repeated, "but I'm rooting for you." Before I walked out the door, I took one last look at the tattoos on her arms. Angels and devils. I wondered which side I was on.

That night we had dinner, our first meal together. You plowed through your food. There was no pretense, no self-consciousness. We shared a bottle of wine. Then we went back to the safe house. We made love on the sofa, not patient enough to make it to the bedroom.

"So, if you're not a student here, what is it that you do?" you asked, propping your head up sideways on your hand, your elbow resting on my chest.

"I can't tell you. I wish I could," I answered. I didn't want to lie to you.

"Is that because you have a wife?" You tried to pretend that you were kidding. I could tell that you weren't.

"No. No wife." You were already the longest relationship I'd ever had. Before this, everything had been a series of one-night stands.

"You promise?"

"I promise."

"A girlfriend?"

"Do you count?" You laughed. "Listen, Maria. Now that there's you, I have two women in my life—you and my mother."

You paused to consider my comment, still trying to figure out my secret. I knew that my secret was safe, too unbelievable, to be guessed. "So, are you sleeping with your mother?" As you laughed I pulled your face toward mine, catching your head in my hands and kissing you again. I knew then that I would never be tired of kissing you. I wanted to stop you from asking any more questions that I couldn't answer. I was hoping the kiss would be answer enough. It wasn't.

You began an inventory. "So, no girlfriend. No wife. Do you work for the government?" I shook my head. "Then what do you have to

hide? Just tell me what you do. I want to *know* you." You kicked me
under the covers.

"I can tell you," I finally answered, "but I'd have to lie. Do you
want me to lie to you?"

You thought about it for a minute, seriously thought about it.
Then you looked me in the eyes. "No. I don't want you to lie to me.
I don't ever want you to lie to me." Then you kissed me. I could feel
the kiss in my toes. The questions stopped for the time being. I knew
that one day I would have to answer them. I thought that on that day,
you would be able to choose whether or not you wanted to stay with
me. I guess sometimes life makes decisions for you.

The next morning, Sunday, you snuck me into one of the school li-
braries. You had some research to do. I took the opportunity to use
one of the library computers to do research too. I looked up security
cameras and took note of everything that I could find—coverage
angles, heat sensors, everything. We spent Sunday afternoon in the
park. I tried to steer us as far from my mark's house as I could. I tried
not to think about tomorrow or the next day or the day after that. We
walked through the park to the top of Mount Royal. We stood there
and looked down on the city, our city. Standing there, that day, Montreal was the most beautiful place I'd ever seen. You stayed over again
that night.

On Monday morning, you left early to go to class. I left early too.
I didn't like how the apartment felt when you weren't there. I spent
the day staking out my mark's home for the final time. Everything ran
like clockwork. My mark woke up at the same time as he had on the
previous two days, dressed at the same time, left for work at the same
time. The extra bodyguard arrived at the same time. The maid arrived at the same time. The maid's daily schedule was the same. She

moved from room to room in the same order every day. First she cleaned the kitchen, then the bathrooms, then she dusted and vacuumed. Once the rooms were clean, she'd go out to the end of the driveway to get the mail. When she returned, she'd change the sheets and do the laundry. It seemed that the expert toxicologist was a bit of a germ freak.

We saw each other again that night. I told you that I thought I was falling in love with you. You told me that I was being a fool, that it was too early for talk like that. What you didn't know was that, if everything went according to plan, I'd be leaving Montreal in two days. I didn't know how to tell you that. So I didn't. All I told you was that I had to work all day Tuesday and that we wouldn't be able to see each other. "Wednesday, then," you said, and kissed me on the cheek.

On Tuesday morning, I woke up early, packed my backpack—a large bottle of water, three power bars, my binoculars, a change of clothes, a ski mask, a pair of black leather gloves, and the gun—and headed toward my mark's house, ready to finish this job.

The plan was simple. Jared always tried to teach me that all good plans are simple. This one was good. The fact that things got so messy wasn't the fault of the plan. Sometimes things just get messy. There were two phases to the plan. First, I needed to get inside the house without being caught on the surveillance cameras. Once inside, I'd hide out until my mark and the American bodyguard returned. Then phase two would begin. I needed to avoid being caught on the surveillance cameras because the first thing the bodyguards did when they returned home was to review that day's video from all four cameras. They'd watch it in high speed and slow it down for anything suspicious. I was sure that if the cameras caught me, not only was the whole plan sunk but I'd be trapped inside the house.

I had learned a few things about the surveillance system through my research. At first I was hoping that the cameras would have an exploitable blind spot, an area in the yard that I could safely move through without being taped, but that was a dead end. Whoever installed the cameras knew what they were doing. I had to find another loophole in the surveillance system. What I came upon was reaction time. The cameras were thorough and they were accurate, but they weren't fast, or at least they weren't so fast I couldn't stay ahead of them. Really it seemed that asking any set of surveillance cameras to be all three, fast, thorough, and accurate, was nearly impossible.

During my stakeouts, I had timed and mapped out the movement of the cameras. Each camera stayed on its target for at least five seconds. When something moved, all cameras that could get a clean visual on the movement would turn toward the movement and focus. The cameras would then stay focused on the moving object until it stopped moving or until something else diverted it. If two things moved in succession in different parts of the yard, the cameras would first focus on the initial moving object for at least five seconds, and then, while one camera stayed locked in on the initial moving object, the other cameras would begin to chase the secondary movement. It often took the cameras as much as two seconds to find and focus in on a moving object. That meant that as long as there was a primary diversion, I could move within certain areas of the yard for eight seconds before being caught on camera. The weekday routine at the house provided me with four usable diversions before my mark made it home at night: First was the arrival of the maid; then the arrival of the second bodyguard; then the departure of my mark and the bodyguards for the day; and, finally, the maid's journey to the end of the driveway to get the mail. Because it would be impossible to make it from the front gate to the front door in under eight seconds, I would need each of those four diversions.

Even sitting here, watching the house, waiting for the right moment to put my plan into action, I couldn't help but think about you. I just wanted to get this done. I wanted to finish this job so I could see you again. I tried not to think about what would happen after that. The only part of my future that I cared about at that moment was the next twenty-four hours, and fourteen of those would be wasted on this son of bitch. It made me hate him even more.

I lifted the binoculars to my eyes and continued making mental notes about the patterns inside the house. Everything seemed to be in perfect order. The mark was exercising in the exercise room, bouncing up and down on a StairMaster while reading the business section of the newspaper. The big Aussie was in the bodyguard's bedroom going through his set of exercises—push-ups, sit-ups, then dips. My timing was perfect; I had a few minutes to get around to the front of the house before the maid arrived. I spent a minute or two stretching; knowing that for much of the rest of the day I was going to have to be completely still, at times in cramped, awkward positions. When I was done stretching, I made my way over to the front of the house and hid behind a bush near the front gate. I waited there for about five minutes before the maid arrived.

The maid, as always, arrived in her own little silver car. She had an electric door opener in her car that opened the front gate. She activated it and pulled into the driveway. The driveway led up a small hill toward the house and then circled around a large fountain. In the middle of the fountain stood an angel, wings spread as if about to take flight, one arm pointed up toward the heavens and the other holding a large scepter that pointed toward the front gate. A stream of water shot out of the end of the scepter as if the scepter were a weapon.

When the maid's car pulled into the driveway, the cameras immediately focused on it. They focused on the car and followed it up the small hill toward the house. I waited as long as I could, allowing the cameras to move farther and farther away from the front gate, away from me. Then I slipped through the gate before it had a chance to close and lock again. Once inside, I had only a few seconds to make it to my first hiding spot. As with much of my life, all I cared about was being invisible. I ducked quickly behind a few bushes planted just inside of the front gate. They'd been planted there to hide the gate's engine from view. I carried my backpack in my hands, quickly crouching down and pressing my back up against the engine. I could still feel the motor purring against my back as the gate finally finished closing. I heard the gate click again as it locked itself back in place. I could feel the engine warming my back. The heat was as important as the bushes. The bushes hid me from the people in the house. The heat hid me from the cameras. The cameras were programmed not to recognize the heat from a few locations. The gate motor was one of them. The areas directly surrounding the house were another. The cameras were programmed that way so that they wouldn't stray toward the gate's engine every time the gate opened or closed. As long as I made no sudden movements, I was safe from the cameras here, all 98.6 degrees of me. The first and easiest leg of phase one of the plan was successful. I was inside the gate. I sat, consciously slowing down my breathing, knowing I would be in that position for a while, preparing for leg two.

Inside I knew that the maid was cooking breakfast for my mark and the big Aussie. In another hour or so, the American bodyguard would show up. Like the maid, he would come in a car equipped with an electric door opener for the gate. He would pull up to the front of the house and park the car before going inside to retrieve my mark and the big Aussie. The three of them would then leave together in the same car.

I heard the car outside the gate before I saw it. Then I felt the motor against my back begin to purr again as the gate began to open. I fixed my eyes on the camera that I was facing, a camera that I could see through the leaves of the bushes but that never pointed itself at me. Once I started moving, there would be no time to look at the cameras again, no time to double-check that the cameras had waited the requisite five seconds before chasing me. I simply watched and waited until the lens of the camera began to follow the bodyguard's car up the hill toward the house. In one more second, I'd have to make my second move. I took off my sneakers and placed them in the backpack I was holding in my lap. It was time to move. I tensed up, got to my feet, and sprinted directly up the center of the driveway. By running in my socks, I made almost no noise. I counted the seconds in my head as I ran. One second. Two seconds. Three seconds. I realized that I hadn't exercised since I was in Georgia. Four seconds. Five seconds. I was going to be cutting this one closer than I'd hoped. Six seconds. I dropped my backpack on the ground. Seven seconds. I was nearing the fountain with the avenging angel. I leapt. I placed one hand on the fountain's concrete ledge and swung my legs over the side. I made a small splash as I entered the water but the sound was easily washed out by the sound of the torrent of water shooting out of the angel's scepter. Without a second's thought, I submerged my whole body in the water with the exception of my mouth and nose, holding them just high enough above the surface of water to breathe.

The water was shockingly cold. My heart rate seemed to double as soon as I hit the water. If my heart was weaker, it might have stopped completely. I stayed as still as possible, doing everything in my power to avoid going into shock from the cold. If everything moved on schedule, I'd only need to be in the water for five to ten minutes, until my mark and the bodyguards left the house. I only hoped to get out before hypothermia began to set in. I stayed as motionless as I could in the cold water, trying to will my body from shivering. I wasn't visible from the house due to the high concrete walls of the fountain. As long as I didn't move, I knew that the cameras wouldn't be attracted to me. The cold water would effectively cover up my thermal signature. As cold as it was, the water was keeping me safe.

As I floated I visualized the next leg. I had thrown my backpack to the right of the fountain, away from the direction that my mark and his bodyguards would drive their car. I lifted an ear out of the water, waiting to hear the car engine rev up again. My body began to become numb in the water. This made lying there less painful but also worried me. I feared that I wouldn't be able to move quickly enough once I got out of the water. I still needed to outrun the cameras. Without generating enough movement to attract the surveillance cameras, I began to massage my legs with my hands, trying to keep the blood flowing through them. After what seemed like an hour, I heard the engine of a car start. I lifted my head farther out of the water, getting both ears above the surface so that I could better position the sound of the car. I listened as the car went down the hill and pulled farther and farther away from the fountain. I heard the electronic gate begin to open and I eyed the one surveillance camera that I had a clear view of. It was pointing toward the bottom of the driveway, aimed directly at the moving car. I climbed over the fountain wall, stumbled toward my backpack, picked it up, and began running toward the front door of the house.

At first, my legs were clumsy and heavy, like I was wearing two concrete blocks for shoes. My mind moved faster than my legs could go and I nearly fell twice. Fortunately, it wasn't a long run. My blood began flowing again, pumping oxygen to my leg muscles. I bounded up the stairs leading to the front porch and then quickly ducked behind a love seat that was set diagonally across one corner of the house's expansive front porch. Once seated, I quickly eyed the camera that I could see from that vantage point. It hadn't chased me, still pointing toward the front gate, toward the sight of the last moving object. Slowly, so as not to attract the attention of the surveillance cameras, but as quickly as I could, I stripped off my wet clothes and replaced them with dry ones: a dry sweatshirt, sweatpants, socks. I put my sneakers back on. I pulled the ski mask over my head in an effort to warm myself back up. Then I pulled my knees up and hugged them against my chest and waited. I was close enough to the house now that the surveillance cameras wouldn't be attracted to my body heat. It was approximately an hour and a half since I had first reached the house. I would be crouched in a ball in the corner of the porch for another two and a half hours, before I had a chance to make another move.

Two and a half hours. For those two and a half hours, every movement I made, I made as slowly and deliberately as I could. I took a few drinks of water, ate a power bar, and waited. Waiting had always seemed to be eighty percent of my job—waiting for planes; waiting for buses; waiting for orders; waiting for the right moments to act; waiting for the right time to kill—but rarely had the waiting been so literal. I counted the seconds. I watched the cars that drove by on the street. I tested to see how long I could hold my breath. I ran over the plan again and again in my mind. I thought about you. I thought about what it would be like trying to say good-bye to you. I tried to stop thinking about you. It didn't work.

The time passed. Eventually I heard the knob on the front door begin to rattle. The maid had finished dusting and vacuuming and cleaning the bathrooms and was now about to venture out to get the mail. The door opened and she stepped outside. She didn't even glance in my direction. She simply wiped her hands on her apron and started walking down the driveway. I watched her as she walked, watched the surveillance cameras follow her down the hill, and then, once she reached the other side of the water fountain, I stood up with my backpack, walked quickly to the front door, opened it, and stepped inside. I left my wet clothes on the porch. I wouldn't need them again.

Once inside, I made my way downstairs to the exercise room. The maid always cleaned the exercise room right after breakfast. She had no need to visit it again. There were no linens to change there. I'd be safe. Once in the room, I ducked into the closet and sat on the floor.

I took the gun out of my backpack, attached the silencer, checked to make sure that it was loaded, and then placed it back in my lap. I drank some more water and ate my second power bar. I congratulated myself. I was still cold and a bit tired, but the plan was working perfectly. It was time to wait again. It would be another nine hours before phase two of my plan went into action.

Eventually, I fell asleep. I don't know how long I was out for. Falling asleep wasn't part of the plan. The five minutes lying in the cold water must have taken more out of me than I'd expected. When I woke up, I was slouched down in the dark corner of the closet, leaning against the walls. I opened my eyes and lifted my head. There was a spot on my shoulder from where I'd been drooling in my sleep. The air in the closet was extremely warm. I don't remember what I was dreaming about but I woke up with a crick in my neck and a raging hard-on. Falling asleep like that had been dangerous. I could have snored. I could have flinched, banging against the wall. I could have mumbled or screamed in my sleep. It was that type of recklessness, those small mistakes, that got people killed. If they had found me, asleep in the closet, with a gun in my lap, it would not have ended well; not for me, anyway.

I was lucky. Everything was okay. I hadn't screamed or snored. I checked my watch. It was five-thirty in the evening. I had gotten away with napping. The sleeping was dangerous but it probably did me good. I just wanted to get it all over with. I checked the gun again. I stopped and listened. I held my breath for a moment, trying to make as little noise as possible so I could hear any other movements in the house. There were sounds of footsteps on the floor above me. They were faint but I could hear them. The maid was still at work. Had the footsteps been the American bodyguard's or those of the mark, they would have been louder.

I visualized the rest of the plan again in my head. I'd wait in the closet until my mark and the bodyguard got home. I'd have to act sometime between their arrival and when they armed the night sensor. They generally armed the sensor right before going to sleep. The night sensor would set off an alarm if it detected any movement. They would effectively trap me in the closet. I'd have to get upstairs before the bodyguard turned it on. The bedrooms were on the third floor. That's where the hits would go down. At the top of the stairs, the library was on the left and the bedrooms were on the right. The plan was to take the bodyguard out first. That's why I needed a gun. I'd kill the bodyguard on the way in so that I wouldn't have to worry about him on the way out. It should have been easy enough—open the door to the bodyguard's bedroom before he suspects anything, pop two shots into him, and then move on to the true target.

At around seven-thirty, right on schedule, my mark and the body-guard got home. From my spot in the closet, all I could hear was the sound of footsteps on the floor directly above me. I couldn't hear voices. I could, however, make out three distinct sets of footsteps. Not long after the footsteps became a trio, they were reduced to a duet when the maid went home. As long as I could hear the footsteps directly above me, I could track what rooms my targets were in, and by looking at my watch and checking their usual schedule, I could track what each person was doing. The mark was like a robot. He didn't deviate from his nightly schedule at all. The bodyguard's schedule was less fixed. He went upstairs once to check the surveillance video but other than that, I was able to follow his footsteps and feel safe. Just in case something showed up on the surveillance cameras, I readied myself for a sweep of the house. I sat with my back upright, pushed up against the back wall of the closet, and pointed the gun at the closet door, ready to pull the trigger. The sweep never came. When my mark went into his office after dinner, the bodyguard simply went to the den to watch television.

Finally, at around ten P.M., both sets of footsteps disappeared up the stairs. With that, it was time for me to put phase two into action. I ate the last power bar and drank the rest of the water. I pulled the ski mask out of the backpack and slid it back over my face. The mask was for the getaway. After the job was done, I intended to walk right out the front door, surveillance cameras be damned.

I slung the backpack over my shoulders and quietly pushed the closet door open. The exercise room was nearly as dark as the closet. I tried to remember where all the equipment was located so that I wouldn't trip over anything. I could see just enough to make my way through the shadows. Slowly, I walked toward the stairs leading up to the second floor and climbed. At the top of the stairs, I turned, holding the gun out in front of me with two hands. I had never been formally trained to handle a gun so I moved like I had seen actors in television crime dramas move, turning the corners of the dark house quickly with my arms outstretched, leading with the gun.

When I came to the base of the second flight of stairs, I could see the light coming out of the spaces beneath the two bedroom doors, cutting into the darkness. My targets were still awake. I listened. I couldn't hear any sound coming from my mark's room. I could hear the bodyguard playing some sort of video game on his computer. There were sounds of screeching tires, gunshots, and general mayhem. The real mayhem was going to be quiet by comparison.

I made my way up the stairs. I walked with my back against the wall and kept my eyes on the bedroom doors. If someone came out now, I was ready to shoot on sight. The doors didn't budge. I made it to the top of the staircase without incident and was able to duck back into the shadows. Not a single stair squeaked. My targets stayed in their rooms. As I reached the top of the stairs, the sounds coming from the bodyguard's bedroom grew louder. When I got to his door, I reached out and touched it, the same way I would have if I were testing to see if there was a fire in the other room. It was a reflex. The door was cold.

I took a deep breath. I held the gun in my right hand and reached for the doorknob with my left. I twisted the doorknob. Two shots—that's all it was supposed to take. I pushed the door open. As it swung, it let out a faint squeak. I stepped through the door and aimed my gun at the bodyguard. Somehow, over all the noise coming from his computer, he had heard the door. He reacted quickly. He looked at me, then the gun. His eyes grew wide with fear. He dove off his chair, trying to reach a safe place behind the bed. I fired. My aim was good. If he hadn't dived so quickly, I would have hit him right in the chest. If he hadn't heard the door squeak that one shot would have probably killed him. Instead of hitting him in the chest, the bullet lodged in his shoulder. Even with the silencer, the gunshot was loud. I got a little flustered and fired again quickly, aiming for the widest part of him and shooting him in the stomach. As the bullet entered his gut, the bodyguard let out a grunt. He fell to the floor, already bleeding heavily from his stomach. Then he made another move. He lunged for the bedside table. He kept his gun there. I'd seen the bodyguards put their guns there. I took aim again. This time I aimed for his head. I just wanted to take one more shot and end it. I wanted to take one more shot and move on to the man that I was supposed to be killing. I had to hope that he hadn't noticed the gunshots, that they were lost amidst the sounds of the video game. I lined the handgun's sight up with the bodyguard's hair but his hair was wrong. His hair wasn't supposed to look like that. His hair was blond. It should have been brown. It was the wrong bodyguard. I wasn't about to kill one of the enemy. I was about to kill an innocent man.

I took my finger off the trigger. I looked down at the trail of blood on the carpet that the Aussie left as he crawled. I froze for a second.

I felt like I was seeing a stranger's blood for the first time, like his blood was a different color than all those people I'd killed before. My stomach turned. I started to sweat. The Aussie took another lurch forward toward the nightstand. He reached up to open the drawer. His hand neared his gun. Instinctively, I took a step toward him and kicked him in the stomach as hard as I could. I kicked him right where I had shot him. He cried out in pain and doubled over before he could reach his gun. I pulled my foot back. It was covered in blood. I leaned in closer to the Aussie, holding the gun inches from his head, and spoke to him in a whisper. "You're not the one," I said to him, my voice full of anger. The bodyguard didn't move. I walked over and shut the bedroom door so that I could think.

The bodyguard simply stared at me, dumbfounded. I could see the fear in his eyes. I had just shot him twice and then told him he wasn't the one. He must have thought I was insane. He opened his mouth and a single word came out. "What?" he asked.

I lifted up the ski mask so that my mouth was no longer covered. "You're not the one," I repeated. "But if you keep fighting me, I'll blow your fucking brains out." That registered. The bodyguard turned over, sprawling his legs out in front of him, and leaned his back against the bed. He looked down at the two new holes that I had created in his body. Blood was pumping slowly out of the hole in his shoulder, dripping down his chest and getting caught in the ribbing of his white tank top. The blood there was nothing compared to the blood coming out of his stomach. He held his hand over the hole. His hands were huge, at least twice the size of mine, but his giant hand didn't come close to covering the ring of blood that was growing out of his stomach. The stain on his shirt was already as large as a globe. He studied his wounds for a second. Then he looked back up at me, standing over him with a gun. He started to cry. "Shut up," I said to him, wanting to punch him in the face just for being there. "You weren't supposed to be here," I mumbled under my breath. He couldn't hear me over his own sobbing. My mind raced. My mark was twenty feet away. I could go over there and plant two bullets in his head and be done with this in less than thirty seconds. I looked down at the Aussie again. His sobbing had stopped. He was staring up at me, trying to look at my eyes through the ski mask. His face now was a mix of confusion and anger. If I left the Aussie alive, I knew that he'd go for his gun. He'd try to be a hero. Leaving him alive was not an option. I couldn't kill him either. I wasn't a murderer. I was a soldier. I decided that I had to save him. I couldn't have innocent blood on my hands. I just couldn't. Fuck it, I thought. Fuck the mark.

"I'm not going to kill you," I said to the bodyguard, speaking barely above a whisper. "I'm going to get you out of this house and I am going to save you. But if your boss sees us or hears us or calls the police, I am going to kill you both. Do you understand?" The Aussie nodded. The anger began to drain from his face. All that was left was confusion. I'd just shot him and now I was trying to save him. There was no way for him to understand. Still, if I was going to save him, I had to act quickly.

"Can you walk?" I asked him. Without saying a word, the Aussie grabbed the post on the corner of the bed and tried to stand up. He made his first effort using his left arm, the one with the hole in the shoulder. The attempt didn't take. When he tried to pull himself up, his bloody hand slipped and he fell face-first onto the floor, his nose pushed into the carpet. I stepped forward and rolled him over. "Can I trust you?" I asked, looking in his eyes for the answer.

"Yeah," he said, his voice twinged with an Australian accent. The confusion was gone from his face. All that was left now was fear. I still didn't trust him. What I trusted was that fear. I had seen enough of that in my life to know that I could depend on it.

I took his good arm and wrapped it around my shoulders. I stood up, propping the Aussie against me and pulling him to his feet. I wrapped my other arm, the one holding the gun, around his waist to help his balance. "We're going downstairs," I told him. He nodded again. We took two steps toward the door. The Aussie was already weak. He dragged his feet with each step, barely lifting them off the ground. "Stronger," I said to him as we reached the door. Before opening the door, I turned to the bodyguard. "The motion detectors. Do you have control over them or does he?" With his free hand, the Aussie pointed to his chest. "And they're not on?" I asked. He shook his head. It was clear now. We were on the same team. We had the same goal.

I opened the door and we stepped through it. The Aussie was walking more confidently now, getting used to standing on his feet. He continued to press his good hand against the hole in his stomach, applying pressure to try to lessen the bleeding. We took a step toward the stairs. Then I heard something coming from the mark's bedroom. A rustle of movement and then a voice. "Close your goddamn door, jackass!" the boss shouted from his room. I swung my foot back and kicked the Aussie's door closed. I listened. Nothing else. The boss didn't suspect anything.

When we got to the top of the staircase, I looked down at the stairs. The Aussie wasn't going to make it down the stairs under his own strength. I turned my face toward his. Our noses were no more than an inch apart. He was breathing heavily and his eyes were beginning to glaze over. "I'm going to carry you down," I said to him. He nodded. Then, in one quick motion, I bent my knees and threw his body over my shoulders. He was heavy. I started down the stairs, trying to walk quietly without losing my balance. About halfway down I began to feel the Aussie's blood seep through the back of my mask. It was warm and sticky.

When we made it to the bottom of the stairs, I propped the Aussie up against the wall near the front door. He was still conscious. I pulled my face close to his. "The gate. How do I open the gate?"

His voice came out in a lisp. He sounded weak. "There's a button.

On the inside. Next to the gate." Of course, it was easy to walk out, just not easy to walk in.

"Wait here," I said to the Aussie, and began to turn away.

"Don't," he said, more loudly than I would have liked.

I turned and looked at him. He wasn't asking me not to leave him. He was asking me not to kill his boss. I wanted to tell him that his boss deserved to die. I wanted to tell him that his boss used him. I wanted to tell him that he was a stupid piece of shit who didn't know anything. I didn't. There was no time.

"Don't worry," I said to him. "I'm not going to kill him. Not tonight." That's all I could get out. I should have killed him. It would have been easy, easier than it ever would be again. It would have been quick. I wasn't thinking straight. If I couldn't save the Aussie, I was going to have innocent blood on my hands. My stomach was churning. It had held together until I hit the bottom of the staircase but now it let loose. I stepped away from the Aussie into the darkness and bounded into the closest bathroom. I lunged forward and vomited in the sink. I had never thrown up on a job before. I had nearly thrown up after my second kill, a thirty-three-year-old man, an instructor. He trained their killers. I slit his throat with a knife while he was trying to get into his car. It was messy. Blood spurted everywhere. That's when I started strangling people. It was usually more of a struggle, but it was much cleaner. I wiped the remaining chunks of vomit from my lips and flicked them into the sink. That was done.

I walked out of the bathroom and headed toward a phone. I picked up the phone and turned it on without thinking. I was lucky that the boss wasn't on the line. I got a dial tone. I dialed 911 and hoped that this was the appropriate number in Canada. I quickly got an operator. She said something in French and then, in English, said, "Nine one one. How can we help you?"

"A man's been shot. He's on the corner of Maplewood and Spring Grove. Send an ambulance."

"Okay, monsieur," the operator spoke in an official tone. "We would like more detail. Can you stay on the line?"

"No." I hung up the phone and headed back toward the front door. The Aussie was right where I had left him but his head was dangling loosely on his neck. His eyes were closed. He was out cold. Still, I could see his chest moving slightly up and down as he breathed. I stepped forward and slapped him as hard as I could. His eyes shot open and were, for a second, full of life. "Stay awake," I ordered. Then I swung his good arm over my shoulder again and headed out the front door.

We didn't have much time. We had to manage the driveway, the front gate, and another couple of blocks before we got to the corner where I had directed the ambulance. If we were too late, they would assume it was a prank. We had to move. I turned toward the Aussie. "Speed. We need speed." He was struggling but still attentive. He nodded and our pace quickened. With effort, we made it down the driveway, through the gate, and along the street. We left a trail of blood behind us as we walked. After about ten minutes, we had gone all of about half a mile. When we turned the last corner, I could see the flashing lights from the ambulance. The ambulance wasn't alone. There were cops there too. That was more than I'd bargained for. It was the end of the road for me.

I took the Aussie's arm off of my shoulder. I tried to steady him by placing one of my hands on his still good shoulder. I stepped behind him. "Walk," I said, and I gave him a firm push with my free hand, the one in which I held the gun. He took two weak steps forward and fell to the ground. Then he got on his hands and knees and began to crawl toward the blinking lights. He looked like a cartoon of a thirsty man crawling through the desert toward water. He made it about two more feet and then he collapsed under his own weight again. He rolled over on the sidewalk and looked back at me, tears flowing from his eyes. If I left now, he was going to die in the street, thirty feet from help.

I stepped forward, picked the Aussie up again, and threw him over my shoulder. I pulled the ski mask back down over my mouth and walked toward the ambulance, holding the gun out in front of me.

The paramedics and the police were chatting away, assuming by now that the call had been a prank. The first paramedic noticed me when I was only about twenty feet away. As soon as his eyes fixed on me, I aimed the gun directly at him. He froze. He didn't say a word. He was paralyzed with fear. Even at that distance, I could feel his fear. I must have looked like the grim reaper, walking the streets at night, dressed all in black, a ski mask covering my face, a gun stretched out in front of me and a corpse draped over my shoulders. At about ten feet, the cop and the paramedic who had been chatting away finally noticed me too. The cop went for his gun. He was out of practice, his movements were clumsy and slow. "Don't even think about it." I shouted. "Anyone pulls a gun, and people die. Lots of people." The cop took his hand away from his belt. I yelled at his partner to stand next to him. I wanted everyone with guns to be standing where I could see them. The partner, who looked to be about fifteen years old, quickly obliged.

I bent down and placed the Aussie on the ground without taking my eyes off the cops. The Aussie made an audible gasp when he hit the ground. By now he was completely covered in blood, but he was still conscious. I looked at the paramedics. "Take him to the hospital. Fix him," I ordered. They didn't move. I took two steps backward. "Now!" I shouted. Their daze broken, they went into action. They pulled the cot off the ambulance, got the Aussie on the cot, and loaded him inside. They moved quickly and with purpose, suddenly realizing that the faster they moved, the faster they would get away from the psychopath with the gun. The cops watched with envy.

As soon as the ambulance drove away, I knew that the paramedics would be radioing for backup. Within minutes, the area would be inundated with cops. This wasn't protocol. I wasn't trained for this. I looked at the two cops in front of me. They were as white as ghosts, scared shitless. They were probably even more scared than I was. "You saw me save that man, right?" I yelled. I was standing close to them. I probably didn't need to yell anymore. They nodded in unison. "I don't want to kill anyone," I yelled again. They shook their heads in agreement. "I'm going to run away," I said. They nodded again. "But if I hear a single gunshot, I'm coming back and there will be hell to pay." More nodding. I turned and ran. There was no plan anymore. I just ran as fast as I could. I ran for the park. There were no gunshots. Soon, the sounds of sirens began to pierce the night air. I threw the ski mask away. I kept running. I needed to get back to the safe house. Until I changed clothes I knew that I wasn't safe. That was the fastest I ever ran, probably the fastest I ever will run. I didn't slow down. I burned off the fear as I ran. It was just after midnight when I made it back to the safe house.

When I got back inside, I stripped off my clothes and got in the shower. It took me a long time to scrub the blood off the back of my neck.

The rest of that evening went by in a blur. Even thinking back on it now, I only remember disparate moments and nothing in between. I don't remember how I got from place to place. In my memory, I simply drifted from one place to the next as if in a dream. I do remember calling Intelligence and talking to Brian. At first he was pissed off that I had blown the hit. That changed, however, when he realized what a mess I was. I treated the call with Brian as a confessional. I cried, blabbering. "I almost killed someone," I muttered through trembling lips, repeating the phrase over and over again. Brian just sat there and listened, waiting for the purge to end. When it did, Brian simply responded, "Just get out of the city. Hell, get out of the country. Do it tonight. Find a place to lay low in Vermont. Just get out. Call me in three days." Then he gave me the code. I broke protocol and wrote the names down. I was worried that my head was too messed up to remember them. Stephen Alexander. Eleanor Pearson. Rodney Grant.

Next, I did the one thing that you are never supposed to do. I did the unthinkable. I went to the hospital to see my victim. I knew that I couldn't move forward, couldn't leave this city, and could never face you again unless I knew that he was going to be okay. I wasn't a murderer. You wouldn't have fallen in love with a murderer. You were too good for that.

Sneaking into the hospital was easy, even in the middle of the night, even to visit a man who had just been shot. The hospital staff's job was to keep people healthy, not to run surveillance for them. I went into the Aussie's room and sat down in a chair across from the bed. I didn't dare turn the lights on. The big Aussie was asleep. He had an IV sticking in his arm. His shoulder was bandaged. His stomach was covered by the sheets, but it had to have been bandaged pretty heavily too. The bandages covered the stitches that closed the holes that I had made only a few hours earlier. He was attached to a heart monitor. The heart monitor let out rhythmic beeping sounds. It was soothing. I nearly nodded off in the chair. I remember wondering if my heart would ever beat that evenly again. I doubted that it would. The Aussie woke up after about fifteen minutes. He turned his head and looked at me, slouching in a chair in the darkness. He looked in my eyes and recognized me. "It's you," he said. I nodded. He knew I was the guy who had shot him. "In front of the strip club?" he asked. He remembered that too. I nodded again. Then he asked, "Why?"

I wanted to answer him. I wanted to tell him about the godforsaken War that I was trapped in. I wanted to tell him that he was actually the lucky one and that I was the unlucky one—that I would gladly take two bullets to be in his shoes. I wanted to explain to him that I was a good person. Even more than that, I wanted him to assure me that he knew that I was a good person. But there never seemed to be enough time for anything. "It was a mistake," I told him. I don't think he would have understood anything else. Then I got up to leave.

I had one more stop to make before leaving Montreal. It was about three in the morning when I finally made it to your apartment. I woke up your roommate when I hit the buzzer but you didn't mind. When I got up to your apartment, you pulled me into your room and, before I could speak, kissed me deeply. "I have to leave," I told you once you released me from our kiss. My entire body shaking as I spoke.

"Why? What happened?" you asked, your voice full of concern. You were worried about me. No one had worried about me like that since I was a child.

"Nothing. I have to leave. Business. Some crazy stuff happened with my business." I couldn't control the shaking.

You took my hands in yours to steady the shaking. "Are you okay?"

I looked you in the eyes. They were strong. "I'll be all right," I finally responded. "But I have to go." Each word was painful. "I'll call you as soon as I can." I felt like I was being punched in the stomach with each sentence. "And I'll come back soon. I promise."

"Okay," you replied. "It's okay." You rubbed your hands on mine to soothe me.

I leaned in toward your face and we kissed. I prayed that it wouldn't be for the last time. "I love you," I whispered.

"I love you too," you whispered back.

I took a cab to the airport and from there I rented a car. I drove through dawn. I saw the sunrise out of my car window. I crossed the border sometime in the morning. I listened to French talk radio during the drive. I don't understand a word of French. For some reason, the sound just soothed my nerves. Eventually, I stopped at a small roadside motel in Vermont. The parking lot was full of cars with ski racks and skis. Vacationers. I stumbled into my room and dropped onto the bed. Over the next twelve hours, I may or may not have slept—I can't be sure—but I know that I didn't move, not once. I just lay there, slowly trying to forget everything about my life except for you.

Eight

At about noon on Thursday I got up and went for a run. I had neglected to exercise during my time in Montreal and it almost cost me. I ran ten miles. When I got back to the motel, I did sit-ups and push-ups until I nearly collapsed from exhaustion. I was hoping that the exercise would help to calm my nerves. It didn't. I felt trapped in the little snowbound motel. I felt like I was about to spontaneously combust. Even if I got in my car and drove, I had nowhere to go.

The first day went by and I didn't call you. I wanted to. I even picked up the phone and started to dial countless times, but I couldn't. I didn't know what I could say to you without lying. I had promised not to lie to you so I didn't call.

I spent most of the rest of the day watching television. I drove to a nearby pizza place for lunch and dinner. That night my insomnia returned. I tossed and turned. I decided that your voice was the only thing that was going to keep me from going insane. I called you at two o'clock in the morning. I was trying to fend off madness.

The phone rang three times before you picked up. You had been asleep. It made me jealous that you could sleep while my agonizing over you kept me awake. Your voice was quiet. It had that husky quality that it often has first thing in the morning. "Hello," you said. I almost hung up the phone. I was suddenly afraid to speak. "Hello?" you repeated. "Joseph?" When you said my name the spell was broken. It gave me courage.

"Hey, Maria," I answered.

"What time is it?"

"It's late. Really late. I'm sorry for waking you up. I just wanted to hear your voice. I'll let you go back to sleep."

"No. Don't go," you replied. "Where are you?"

"I'm in the States. I'm stuck in a motel for a few days but I'm hoping that I can come back to Montreal soon." There was silence on the other end of the line. I wasn't sure if you were nodding off. "Do you think you can wait for me?" I asked.

"I wait for no man," you replied with a laugh. You were slowly waking up. "So you better come back here soon." Your voice made me feel better, like I belonged to the world.

"I'll come back as soon as I can," I replied, "but I'm going to have to go now and I'm not going to be able to call you for a couple of days."

"Why can't you talk to me, Joe?" you asked. I could hear the disappointment in your voice.

"When I get back, if you'll still have me, I'll tell you everything," I replied. I'd have to lay my cards on the table at some point. You deserved as much.

"You promise?"

"I promise," I replied. "Go back to sleep."

"Joseph?"

"Yes?"

"I love you." The words were like a shot of morphine, a cure-all for all my pain.

"I love you too," I answered.

"I'll wait for you, for as long as you need me to." Then you hung up. After our conversation, I slept.

I exercised again the next day, going through the same routine. Friday afternoon I drove to the nearest bar. It was half roadhouse, half Swiss ski chalet. I sat alone at the bar and drank a couple of beers. I was just biding my time until that evening, when it would be safe to call Intel again. I threw the beers back and ordered a cheeseburger. The place began to get crowded as early-season skiers started coming in off the slopes. Soon the place was alive with people who didn't seem to have a care in the world. That's when I had to leave. I knew I didn't belong there anymore.

I drove back to the motel. As soon as I go into the room, I picked up the phone to dial up Intelligence. I was looking forward to hearing Brian's voice even if he was going to yell at me. I took out the piece of paper that I had written the code for this call on. I went through each of the operators. Stephen Alexander. Eleanor Pearson. Rodney Grant. Finally, it was time to be transferred to a real person. I was ready to do everything that I could to convince Brian to send me back to Montreal, ostensibly to finish the job, but really so that I could see you again.

"Hello, Joseph," the voice, a deep, gravelly man's voice, said. I had never heard the voice before. "This is Allen." Allen? Who the hell was Allen? I looked back down at the piece of paper on which I had written the names—Stephen Alexander. Eleanor Pearson. Rodney Grant—just like I had said.

"What?" I said. What I meant to say was "What the hell is going on?" but only the first word made it out of my mouth.

"My name is Allen." Allen? What happened to Brian? I was confused.

"Where's Matt?" I asked, careful not to let on that I knew Brian's real name.

"Matt's been transferred. It was decided that the two of you no longer made for a productive working relationship. You'll be working with me now." Allen used the same tone with me that you'd use on a misbehaving five-year-old.

"That doesn't work for me," I replied. I did my best to sound strong, even though I felt as weak as I'd ever felt before. "Did Matt ask to be transferred?"

"No, he did not. In fact, Matt put up a pretty big fight. Apparently, he liked working with you. That may have been the problem. Let's just say that we weren't happy with how things were advancing with you. First there was the incident in Long Beach Island, where you were fraternizing with other soldiers without permission. Then you fuck up this hit in Montreal. It was decided that you needed to work with someone else—someone with a little more experience."

"I don't get any say in this? I want to speak to Matt." My voice was trembling. I could barely control my anger.

"I don't care who you *want* to speak with. You're going to speak with me, and only me, from here on out." Allen's voice was even and monotone.

"Fuck you," I said, holding the phone an inch from my mouth. Nothing like this had ever happened to me before. I wanted it fixed. "I'm only working with Matt. Get Matt on the line, or I don't do anything." I kept trying to sound tough, but it was all bluster. I was scared. Brian was my only real connection to the world. My mother was clueless. I couldn't get in touch with Jared and Michael without Brian's help. Without Brian, I was simply adrift, alone. I didn't know what this Allen character would be like, but I already knew that I didn't like him.

Allen responded to my impertinence with some righteous anger of his own. "Fuck me? Fuck me? Who the fuck do you think you are?" Despite the words, his voice was still calm. "You think you're somebody? You're nobody. You think you can make demands? You can't ask for shit. We've got real men out there who have been doing what you do for decades. We have men out there who have dozens of kills under their belt. We've got men out there who have earned their stripes. You? You get sent to fucking Montreal in a rental car and fuck up a job because a guy's got a couple of bodyguards? Who the fuck do you think you are? I'd like you to tell me who you think you are because I know who you are. You're nobody. You're a fucking pawn. Do you play chess, Joey?" I wanted to reach through the phone and wring his throat. "Do you?"

"I know how to play, yeah," I responded. Even in my own head, my voice began to sound like the voice of a petulant child.

"Good. Then you know what your job is as a pawn. It's your job to get pushed around. You're the first one to get pushed into danger, and if we have the option to trade you for one of their pieces, and it looks like it will help the cause, so be it. You don't get to make decisions about what happens to you. You move when we tell you to move. You kill when we tell you to kill. And if you survive, then maybe someday, just like the measly little pawn that you are, if you get pushed forward far enough, then you might turn into something useful. Then you can make demands. Until then, you little punk, you simply need to shut up."

My anger nearly boiled over. "If I'm the fucking pawn, then what are you, you bastard? You sit there doing nothing. You jabber on the phone all day. What the fuck are you?" I asked, seething.

Allen spoke slowly when he answered, careful to enunciate every syllable. "I'm the pinky on the hand of the man who moves the pawn." He didn't sound proud. He was just stating a fact.

I had nothing. I didn't know how to fight the faceless voice on the other side of a phone. He had my life at his fingertips. It was the fourth rule. The one we didn't teach the kiddies. Rule number one: No killing of innocent bystanders. Rule number two: No killing of anyone under eighteen. Rule number three: Babies born to babies get traded to the other side. Rule number four, the unspoken rule: Bite the hand of the man and he'll bite you back, only he'll bite you twice as hard. "Okay," I finally relented. "I'm sorry. No more requests that I'm not entitled to." The words pained me as I said them, but if I wanted to get back to Montreal, I'd somehow have to get in this guy's good graces.

"That's better," Allen said. "See, not so hard."

"So what do you have in store for me, because I'm ready to go back to Montreal to finish the job." I didn't have high hopes that he was going to send me back.

"No one's going to be finishing that job anytime soon, kid. You fucked it up too good already. I've got another job for you."

"Define *soon*," I said without thinking.

"You still don't understand, do you, kid? I don't have to define anything for you. You've got to earn respect and right now you're running at a deficit. Soon is soon. Weeks, maybe months. We'll send someone back there when the job's ready to be done and not before that. If you impress me on this next job, maybe we'll send you. Maybe we won't." I felt like a marionette, pull the strings and I'd dance. Weeks, maybe months. I had promised you that I'd be back sooner than that. What could I do?

I relented. "Okay. What do you have for me?"

"Naples, Florida. The safe house will be ready in three days. Your host will pick you up at the airport then, and no sooner. Take the first flight that day out of Boston. Your host will know what you look like. The details of your job will be there when you arrive."

"What do I do for the next three days?" I asked. I didn't expect him to care.

"You stay out of trouble, stay out of Canada, and don't bother me." Before I could say another word, Allen gave me the code—Jimmy Lane, Sharon Bench, Clifford Locklear. Then he hung up.

Nine

I spent the next two days the same way as I had spent the previous two. I'd exercise, watch bad television, go to the bar for some drinks and some food, and not sleep. I couldn't get you out of my mind, not even for a moment—not that I tried. Each day dragged on endlessly. I considered going back to see you but I worried about what would happen if I got caught. If I got caught now, I'd probably never see you again. I decided that calling would be too painful. To hear your voice when I had no idea when I would see you again was too much. It wouldn't be fair to you. That's what I told myself, anyway. So I worked through each minute of each day, watching the clock, wishing that I could simply push the hands of the clock forward to make time move faster. Your last words to me echoed through my head: "I'll wait for you, for as long as you need me to." After two more agonizing days, I drove to Boston to catch a plane to Florida.

I landed in the Fort Myers airport outside of Naples in the middle of the day. The crowd at the airport was sparse. There were a few grandparents there to greet their grandchildren but that was pretty much it. I stepped off the plane with my backpack. The backpack was lighter than usual because I had actually checked a bag this time, a small duffel bag that I could have carried on if it weren't for its contents. I wasn't ready to give up the gun yet. The way things were going, I thought that I might need it.

I slung my backpack over one shoulder and had begun to walk toward the baggage claim when a broad, silver-haired man with a wide smile walked up to me. He extended his hand. "Joe?" he asked me as he presented himself. I nodded and shook his hand. His smile widened. His handshake was firm and deliberate, like the handshake of a man who had spent a lot of time shaking hands. I thought that maybe he had once been a salesman or a politician. He was wearing aviator glasses with clear lenses. His face was friendly and earnest. He looked way too honest to have been a politician. "Name's Dan," he said. "I think you're staying with me for the next couple of days."

"Pleased to meet you, Dan," I replied, speaking much more formally than I normally would, inadvertently aping Dan. "I appreciate you coming to pick me up."

"Of course. Of course. It's an honor, really. I just want to pitch in where I can." He nodded his head as he spoke. "You ready to go?"

"Actually, I have to get my bag."

"I didn't think that you boys checked bags. I thought you traveled as light as possible." As he spoke, he turned and starting walking toward the baggage claim.

"Usually I do, Dan. I just didn't want to carry everything on the plane today."

Dan smiled and put his hand on my shoulder. "I don't blame you, kid. I don't blame you. I can't stand fighting for space in the overhead compartment." We got to the baggage claim area and stood behind the women and children.

"You been here long, Dan?" I asked, as we stood there, waiting for the buzzer to sound that would announce the arrival of the luggage from my flight.

"Just about an hour," he replied.

"An hour? Was my flight delayed?" I asked. I knew that it hadn't been.

"No, sir. Right on time. But I didn't want to keep a working boy like you waiting. Besides, I like coming here, watching the action, seeing the people coming and going." I don't think I'd ever met a man like Dan before. I looked over at him. He stood there, never taking his eyes off the baggage carousel even though there were no bags on it yet and it wasn't moving.

"Well, again, I appreciate it."

After we retrieved my bag, we walked to Dan's car in the parking lot. Dan drove the car that I expected him to drive, a large white sedan, and for some reason, that made me happy. As Dan drove us into town, I peppered him with questions, trying to decode him. He was retired and, after a short stint in the navy, had indeed spent much of his life working as a salesman. He sold whiskey and cocktail napkins to bars in New York, New Jersey, and Pennsylvania. He was excited to hear that I was from New Jersey too. He told me that nearly half the people in this part of Florida were from either New York or New Jersey. He had been a "working man"—those were the words he used to describe my job—in his earlier years too. Back in his day, he informed me, the soldiers worked and kept day jobs too. Traveling around as a salesman was good cover. He'd do his routes, make his sales, and once or twice a year duty would call, as he put it. I asked him how many people he had killed during his days as a "working man." He said that he hadn't kept track, that the numbers didn't matter anyway and that he wouldn't be proud of the number even if he knew it. He was just proud that he had been able to do his part during his time. Now he was proud to be helping me, proud that he still had something to give to the cause. Oddly, he made me feel proud too. I had almost forgotten what that felt like.

I asked him about his family. He told me that he didn't have any family left. His parents both made it to the end, dying of natural causes well into their eighties. He'd had a wife once and a daughter. Both had been killed. His wife was a civilian before he married her but that didn't stop them. She was murdered eight years into their marriage when their daughter was just three years old. It was a sloppy job, he said. She was killed in their home one day while he was out running errands. He was pretty sure they were looking for him. When he got home that day, there was blood everywhere, blood in multiple rooms. She must have put up one hell of a fight, he said. He found her body sprawled across the dining room table. They had stayed and watched her die before laying her on the table and leaving. His daughter was home the whole time. When he got home, she was hiding in the bedroom closet. He couldn't be sure if she ran there or if they put her there. She never said. She never spoke about what she saw that day, not once. She never talked about what she saw them do to her mother but as soon as she was old enough, she threw herself into the War. We have to teach some people to hate. Others learn it all on their own. She became a high-level Intelligence officer, one of the youngest in history. She rose through the ranks quickly because of how aggressive she was. That aggressiveness made her a prime target. She was murdered just two weeks shy of her twenty-eighth birthday. "Look, Joe, I don't like 'em and I'm proud that I've done my part in the fight against 'em," Dan said to me as he drove, "but too much hate will ruin you. My poor little girl, I don't know if she had more than a couple of happy days in her life after seeing what happened to her mother. I've always felt guilty about that." We were silent for a few moments. "Enough about me, son. What about you?" he said, slapping the top of my knee.

I didn't expect to tell him much. What was there to tell? Once I started speaking, though, it was hard to stop. I told him about growing up in New Jersey, about my family members who had been killed in the War. I told him about my job, about what being a "working man" entailed nowadays. He was thrilled to hear the War stories. He wanted to know as many details as possible. He seemed to think that my life was extremely exciting. To him I *was* James Bond, no matter what that bastard Allen had said about me being a pawn. I told him about how my two best friends were "working men" too. I loved using the phrase in front of Dan. It made me feel honest. I told him all about my adventures at the Jersey Shore, embellishing the story in some places. Dan ate every bit of it up. The only thing I didn't tell him about was Montreal. I didn't tell him about you.

After about an hour on the road, we pulled into a little retirement community just outside downtown Naples called Crystal Ponds. We drove slowly through the neighborhood. Everybody we passed waved to Dan and Dan waved back to everyone. All of the lawns were superbly manicured and there was a flagpole adorned with a waving American flag in every yard. After making a couple of slow turns we pulled to the end of a cul-de-sac and into Dan's driveway. Dan's house was a small white ranch sitting in front of a tiny pond. "We're home, kid," Dan said to me after pulling into the garage and turning off the car engine. "Go inside and grab yourself a drink. I'm going to get the mail." Then Dan hopped out of the driver's seat and began sauntering down the driveway toward the mailbox.

I walked into the little house and was immediately hit by the rush of cool air from the air-conditioning inside. The first room that I stepped into was the kitchen. Not wanting to disappoint Dan, I decided to take him up on his offer and help myself to a drink. I walked over to the refrigerator and opened it. Everything in the fridge was newly stocked. There were two full six packs of beer, an unopened loaf of bread, an unopened orange juice, an unopened package of hot dogs, and on and on. Dan had done some shopping in anticipation of my visit. God knows what he ate when I wasn't there. I reached into the fridge and pulled out a bottle of beer. I twisted off the cap and threw it in the garbage under the sink. That's when Dan walked in. He spotted me with the beer in my hand and asked, "Mind if I join you?"

"Be my guest," I replied. I turned back toward the fridge and pulled out another bottle. Then we sat at the kitchen counter together and drank our beer in comfortable silence. "So, Dan, I believe you have a package for me," I said to him, midway through our beer.

"Yes, sir," Dan replied. "Wait here." Dan walked off into another room and returned with a familiar, sealed manila envelope. "I suppose you're going to want some time alone to go over that?" Dan asked as he handed me the package.

"I think that'd be best," I replied, feeling the weight of the package in my hand. It was light—that tended to mean that the job was supposed to be pretty easy.

"My office is just down the hall." Dan pointed in the direction from which he had come with the envelope. "I won't bother you while you're working. Just let me know if you need anything."

"Thanks, Dan." I took the package and began walking down the hall toward the office.

"You going to be up for some dinner tonight?" Dan asked as I walked away, eager for the company.

"You name it, Dan, and I'm up for it," I replied. I was eager for the company too. I turned into Dan's office and closed the door behind me.

Dan's office was just a small room with a sofa and a desk. Above the desk were bookshelves containing a few books and a bunch of pictures. I stared at the pictures for a while. It was obvious that every picture was of Dan's family. In some, the colors were fading into a sepia tone. One was in black and white. Not a single picture could have been less than thirty years old. It was like Dan's life had stopped then. There was one of Dan and his dad. Dan had to have been about eight years old but he looked exactly the same. In the picture, Dan was holding a fish that he had just caught up to the camera. His father was squatting down behind him with a wide grin on his face. There was a picture of Dan and his wife at their wedding, decked out to the nines. Dan's wife was gorgeous. She looked a little bit like you, only taller. I imagined for a moment what you'd look like in a wedding dress. There was a black-and-white picture of two people that, from the looks of them, must have been Dan's mother and father looking young, smiling, standing in front of a small box with a roof that I could only assume was their first home. Then there was the picture that stopped me cold. It was a picture of Dan and his wife, standing next to each other, Dan's arm draped around his wife's shoulder. His wife was holding their baby girl in her arms. In the picture, Dan and his wife were gazing directly at the camera, but the little girl, who couldn't have been more than six months old, was staring up, smiling at her father. Finally, there was the newest picture, still probably at least thirty years old, but the one whose color had faded the least. It was a picture of Dan's daughter, as a teenager, standing in a white, puffy prom dress next to a pimply faced boy in a tuxedo. In this picture, Dan's daughter was smiling. This must have been one of her few happy days. As I stared at the picture, Dan's voice echoed in my head, reminding me, "Too much hate will ruin you." "But not enough and the world falls into chaos," I whispered to myself. I sat down at the desk, opened up the envelope, and began to study the next man whose life I was supposed to end.

My target's name was Jimon Matsudo but he just went by the name "Jim." He was born in Hawaii to Japanese immigrants and fought for the United States in the Korean and Vietnam Wars. He was a logistics expert who had, throughout his career, planned multiple deadly and strategic operations for the United States Army. He had also, separately, planned multiple deadly and strategic operations against us. He retired from the U.S. Army as a major general. As far as our Intelligence could tell, he stopped actively planning operations against us at about the same time. To this day, however, he continued training their logistic experts. In fact, most of their top guys had been trained directly by Mr. Matsudo. It was impossible to gauge exactly how much damage he had caused in his lifetime, either directly or through his pupils, but taking Mr. Matsudo out would apparently be an enormous blow to their operations. According to my paperwork, this was a key strategic strike. Even so, Mr. Matsudo apparently kept a low profile, with little evidence of protection. It looked to me like the job would be relatively easy. Then I got to the end of the report, the part that contained the information I needed to actually find my target. That's when I found out that my target lived in a small, quiet, unguarded retirement community in Naples called Crystal Ponds. That bastard Allen had me killing one of my host's neighbors. Brian never would have pulled a bullshit move like that. I couldn't help but think that this was a test.

That night, after I had reviewed my target's file and slipped the envelope into one of the drawers in Dan's desk, Dan and I headed out for dinner. Instead of driving toward the fancy part of Naples, we drove in the other direction. We went to some backwoods joint that served ribs and catfish in the front and had live country music in the back by the bar. Dan told me that he couldn't stand the pretentious new restaurants downtown. The ribs were great, drowned in a spicy barbecue sauce. Dan and I threw back a few more beers while we ate. The more Dan had to drink the more interested he became in my job. To Dan, I really was a hero. I was the avenger of his wife and daughter. I'll have to be honest, I ate it up. After the verbal beat-down that Allen had given me on the phone, it felt good to be told that I was somebody; that there was a good reason why I didn't have a life. It felt good to be told that the trade-offs that I'd made weren't a complete waste.

We went to the bar for a few more drinks after dinner. "So, what else do you have to do to get your job down here done?" he asked me in between beers.

"I'll go out tomorrow to do some reconnaissance, check out the target's patterns and tendencies, try to figure out the best time and place to make my move. To be honest, this job looks pretty easy. I don't think there should be too much trouble." The quicker the job was done, the quicker I might be able to get back to Montreal, I hoped.

"Reconnaissance, huh? Back in my day, you were just given a name. You'd go out and find the bastard and do the job. Bang, bang, two in the head behind the shed, that sort of thing."

"Yeah, well, they don't make them like you anymore, Dan," I replied. I couldn't help but think about how much Dan would like Michael.

"Nah. It's just more complicated now," Dan said. "You kids have it a lot harder than we had it in my day. I don't think I'd last twenty minutes on the job today. God bless you." Dan lifted his bottle of beer toward me in a toast. "So, who's the bastard?" Dan asked.

"Excuse me?"

"Who's the bastard that you're going to kill?" he asked again, more loudly than I would have liked.

"I really don't think I can tell you that," I whispered back to him. I could immediately see the disappointment in his eyes. "It's too dangerous."

"What, I buy you dinner, buy you beers, welcome you into my home, and you still don't think you can trust me?" Dan was kidding. He knew the rules. Still, he would have loved for me to answer him.

"It's not that," I replied. "It's not that I don't trust you. It's that the information is dangerous. The more people who have it, the more dangerous it becomes, for you and for me." I swallowed hard. "That's what they taught me."

"I know. I know. Fucking protocol, right?" Dan said, slapping me on the back. "Play it by the book, kid. Make me proud." Dan paused for a moment, trying to think of something else to say, trying to think of something else that mattered. Dan threw back the rest of his beer. When he was done he slammed his hand back down on the bar. "Barkeep," he shouted, "two scotches, neat. The cheapest single malt you got." The bartender came over and poured us two half full glasses of scotch. Dan lifted his glass toward me and made a toast. It sounded like an old toast, like Dan had lifted a glass to it many times before. "To breaking the bastards' backs before they break ours," Dan said.

I was game. "To remembering what it is we're fighting for," I countered. Dan was pleased, finding a drunken man's wisdom in my words.

Dan put his hand over my glass to make sure that I didn't drink before he was finished. "I got one more, one more." Dan lifted his glass in the air again and looked me in the eyes. "To not drinking alone." Then Dan took his hand off my glass and we both threw our heads back and swallowed our drinks whole. The cheap shit burned and the burn felt good. After that, we paid our tab and headed home.

We were both still a little drunk when we got back to the house. There was no way that Dan should have been driving, but that didn't seem to faze him any. I was feeling pretty good. Then I remembered what Jared had told me back at the beach. He told me that these old guys would tell stories that would burn your ear off. I had to imagine that Dan was pretty high up in the ranks when he retired. I wondered if he knew something.

"I think I'm going to call it a night there, kiddo," Dan said to me as we walked into the kitchen from the garage.

"Wait," I said, not sure where I was going with this. "I've got a question for you, Dan," I said.

Dan looked at me. I could see the old soldier in him now. He wasn't dead. It wasn't too long ago. "Shoot," he directed me.

"You were in the War a long time." Dan nodded. "So did they ever tell you what the whole thing was about?"

"The War?" Dan asked.

"Yeah," I said, though I almost told him to forget it. Maybe I didn't want to know. What if knowing made things worse? I'd watched my family die in the name of this War. I'd killed in the name of this War. What if it wasn't worth it? Dan looked as if he had suddenly become sober.

"Sit down," Dan said, pointing to the small table in the corner of his kitchen. I walked over, pulled out a chair, and sat down. Instead of walking to me, Dan walked to the refrigerator. He opened the door and took out another two bottles of beer. He twisted off the caps, placed a beer in front of me, and then sat in the chair on the other side of the table.

He took a long swig from his beer. "What do you know?" he asked me.

"I've heard stories," I answered.

"What stories have you heard?" he asked. I wanted him to just tell me the truth. I didn't want to play games anymore.

I cleared my throat. "The one I've heard the most is that hundreds of years ago, we were slaves. They were the slave masters. But we revolted and after years of battle, we won. So they told us we were free and we left. But as we left, we got word that they'd already begun enslaving other people. Our leaders stood up and said that we couldn't let them do that. We knew what it was like to be slaves and we couldn't let it happen to other people, especially other people who were basically just taking our place, people who would be free if it wasn't for us. So we went back to fight them for everyone's freedom and that was the beginning of the War." I looked up at Dan. I tried to figure out what was going on in his head but I was too drunk. I couldn't read him. "So as long as we fight them, the innocent people stay free."

Dan leaned back in his chair. He took another slug from his beer. I could see that it was already nearly half finished. "I don't have anything to add to that," he said, putting the beer down on the table.

"So you're telling me that everything I just said is totally accurate?" I asked.

"As far as I know," Dan said. He was holding something back now. I could tell.

"I also heard that there used to be five groups fighting and that we're the only two groups left," I said.

Dan looked uneasy. "I think there's a kernel of truth to each of the stories."

He was bullshitting me. I didn't expect that from Dan. "How is that possible, Dan? How is it possible that we started fighting them because we were slaves AND that there were originally five groups fighting each other? How can there be a kernel of truth to both of those stories? Do you even know the truth, Dan? Because if you don't, just tell me." I waited for his answer. He sat there in silence for some time. Then he stood up.

"Wait here," he said to me. He walked away from the table and into his office. I stayed in my chair. I could hear him rummaging through the closet of his office, lifting boxes down from the top shelf. About five minutes later, he returned holding a picture in his hand.

"You see this?" he said to me, handing me the picture. It was an old picture of a young Dan shaking hands with a tall, dark-haired man with a mustache. Dan couldn't have been more than thirty years old. The man with the mustache had to have been in his fifties. "Do you know who that is?" Dan asked me. I shook my head. I had never seen the man before. "That's General Corbin," Dan said, "General William Corbin. Of course, 'general' wasn't a real title in the War, everyone just called him General Corbin or just the General. He was the head of North American operations when I was working. The man was a genius. A lot of the methods and protocol that you use today were his design. He turned the War around for us in North America." I looked at the picture again. It was hard to imagine the man in the picture doing all that. "And you've never heard of him?"

"No," I answered.

Dan shook his head and laughed. "What do they teach you kids nowadays? Anyway, there's a reason why I'm telling you all this. After my twentieth kill, and twenty was a lot back then, mind you, I was invited to have dinner with the General." Dan had told me that he hadn't kept track of how many people he'd killed. He obviously knew more than he let on. Dan pointed his finger at the picture on the table. "That picture was taken during that dinner." I could feel myself sobering up as Dan spoke. "I was a cocky kid back then, kind of like you." It was clear that Dan meant it as a compliment. "So at that dinner, I asked the General the same question you just asked me. Which one of the stories was true? And you know what he told me?" I shook my head. "He told me that he didn't know either. He told me that he didn't want to know. It wasn't important to him. What was important was that each soldier picks the story that inspires them the most and believes that story."

I hated that answer. "And you were okay with that?" I asked.

"Hell, no," Dan said, shaking his head. "But the General also told me this." Dan's voice suddenly grew quiet. "He told me that in the last two hundred years, we've reached peace agreements with the other side on three separate occasions after long, drawn-out talks." Dan held three fingers out in front of him for emphasis. "Everything was worked out, agreed to. War's over."

I'd never heard this story before. "What happened?" I asked.

"Each time, they went back on their word." Dan's voice was deadly serious now, like he hadn't had a drop to drink all night. "Each time, they reneged. Each time, they tried to take advantage of the fact that we were willing to negotiate. Each time, good people died. No matter how much we give them, Joe, they want more." Dan finished off the beer that was in front of him. "So the General told me that we weren't going to negotiate anymore. Now, if you want me to tell you why the War started, Joe, you're out of luck. That information is above my pay grade. But if you want to ask me why we're still fighting, then there's your answer." I sat there in utter silence. "Can I go to bed now?" Dan asked me after waiting to see if I was going to say anything.

"Yeah," I answered him. My head was spinning.

Dan got up from the table and walked toward his bedroom. "See you in the morning, son," Dan said before closing his bedroom door behind him. I had barely touched the beer that Dan had placed in front of me when he started his story. Now I lifted it up and downed the whole thing. Then I went to the refrigerator and got another.

I called you that night at two in the morning, drunk. You were half asleep when you answered. I told you I was in Florida on business. You sounded jealous and told me that it was cold in Montreal. After I spoke to you, I went to bed. In the morning, Jim Matsuda awaited.

The next day, I went to do my due diligence on Jim. I got up early and went for a run around Dan's neighborhood. It was my normal routine—get up early and run. Usually, I'd be running through desolate streets during the early-morning hours. Not at Crystal Ponds. The folks at Crystal Ponds got up early. Old, gray-haired people were already out on their morning strolls. I passed house after house of old men working in their garages, fixing fishing poles, or painting mailboxes that had just been painted months earlier. Everybody waved. Everybody smiled. The sun was bright and the land flat and it felt good to be outside in shorts, working up a sweat. I deliberately made two passes by Jim's residence. On my first pass, the place seemed empty. As I approached his house for the second time, however, a small Japanese man with glasses and a graying goatee was standing out on the front lawn in his bathrobe and slippers. It was Jim. He looked like he had come out to get the morning paper but had stopped at the end of his lawn, still a few feet from the paper. He was standing there, holding a mug of coffee, gazing off into the distance. His robe was undone in the front and underneath he wore light blue boxer shorts and a white T-shirt. He must have heard me running because he turned his head toward me when I was about half a block away. When he saw me, he lifted his hand in a wave. I tried to act casual. I waved back just like I had waved to everyone else that I had passed. Mr. Matsuda's eyes followed me as I ran. As I neared him, reaching a point no more than three feet from the man I was planning to kill in the very near future, he made eye contact with me. There was recognition in his look, like he had come out that morning just to wait for me to run by. That look frightened me. I began to think that maybe this new Allen character at Intel was more careless than I'd thought. Maybe Jim Matsuda had been tipped off that I was coming. I tried to ignore the ideas in my head. I told myself that if Jim knew that I was coming for him, he wouldn't be standing outside in barely more than a bathrobe and slippers. Everybody waves here, I thought. Everybody. He's no different. I broke off eye contact with him. He had still been staring into my eyes. Then I looked down at my feet and ran past him.

From what I saw that morning, my job should have been easy. Mr. Matsuda had no security. Not only that, but he seemed to have no concern for his own safety. I decided to tail my target for a day anyway. I couldn't afford to blow another job. Beware the easy target—another lesson from early on in our training days.

I spent the rest of the day following Mr. Matsuda. Dan lent me his car. I stayed just far enough away to not be seen by Mr. Matsuda again. I was afraid that he might recognize me. I was afraid that he might recognize Dan's car. It all seemed unnecessary, though. Mr. Matsuda simply went about his day's business. It was a day full of nothing. No danger. No urgency. No fear. Mr. Matsuda's life seemed ordinary—terribly, frighteningly ordinary. We went to the grocery store. We stopped at the pharmacy. We stopped for gas and he got out of the car to wash his windshield. We stopped at a local diner for lunch. Jim had a tuna melt. I had a cheeseburger. We went back to Crystal Ponds for a bit, dropping in on a few friends. We stopped at the bank. There was an ATM machine outside but Jim didn't use it. Instead, he walked inside, flirted with the tellers, deposited some checks, and took out some cash. Then we headed home. I could have easily taken him out at any point during the day. At around six o'clock, I decided I had seen enough. I wasn't learning anything. There wasn't anything to learn. I headed back to Dan's. That's where things got complicated.

When I got back to Dan's house, Dan was sitting in a chair, facing the front door. His face was blank, expressionless. The chair he was sitting in was out of place. He had moved the chair that way, facing the door, so that he could sit in it and wait for me to come in. God only knows how long he'd been waiting. In his lap, Dan held the manila envelope containing the details about my mission. He must have found it in the desk and taken it. I stepped into the silence. Neither of us said a word for a moment. Dan just sat there staring at me like you'd stare at an animal at the zoo. Eventually, I broke the still-ness. "You know you weren't supposed to look at that, Dan," I said, reproaching the old man as if he were a misbehaving child. It didn't feel right but that's what I did. "It's not safe."

"I know," he replied to me, his voice warbled and weakened by the phlegm in his throat. He held the envelope out to me. "Take it. I've seen enough." I took the envelope from him and placed it under my arm.

"What did you see?" I asked. The man in the chair in front of me was a deflated version of the one who had picked me up at the airport the other day. Dan looked smaller.

"I didn't want to cause trouble." Dan spoke softly, speaking as much to the air as he was to me. The sun was setting around us and the rich colors of dusk were seeping through the windows. "It's just that the days here, they all run into each other. I wanted to feel like part of the action again. I wanted to remember what it felt like."

"What did you see, Dan?" I asked, looking down at the opened envelope, trying to see if the papers were organized as I had left them. "What were you doing?"

"They killed my daughter, Joe. They killed my wife and my daugh-ter." Dan looked up at me, his eyes swollen but dry. Dan had cried all his tears ages ago. He kept looking at the envelope out of the corner of his eye. "I wanted to know who it was. I just wanted to know who the big shot was that they sent a professional killer down here to kill. I wanted to see the name of man you were going to end and I wanted it to feel good. I wanted it to feel like revenge." He spoke the last few sentences through clenched teeth.

"So you looked in the envelope?" I asked, knowing full well there wasn't any doubt.

Dan nodded. He unclenched his teeth. "I just wanted to feel good again."

"So you looked in the envelope and now what do you feel?" I was mad. He'd had no right.

"I knew that it couldn't bring my wife and my daughter back to life, but I thought that maybe it could do it for me."

"Do what for you?"

"Bring me back to life, Joe. I wanted it to remind me what it was like to be alive." Dan began wringing his hands together in his lap.

"So what did it do, Dan?" My anger passed quickly. "It's just a name, Dan. He's one of them. I'll take him out. The world will be a better place for it and you'll have done your part. Isn't that something? Didn't you tell me last night that there was no negotiating with them?"

"You don't get it, Joe. I don't care about doing my part anymore."

"Then what's the problem?" I asked. I probably should have figured it out, but reading people was never my forte.

"He's my best friend, Joe." Dan took off his glasses and rubbed his eyes. "He's one of the few friends I have left. And you're going to kill him." If he'd had any tears left, I think he would have cried.

"Jim Matsuda?" They were friends. Fuck Allen. Fuck him, that bastard.

"Yeah," Dan responded. "It started as an old military thing. Army versus navy. But when you get to be our age, all the bullshit fades away and you just see each other as old soldiers. We bonded over that. I guess we have more in common than I realized." Dan looked down at the floor. "Honestly, I don't know what I'm going to do without him."

"I didn't know, Dan," I said, not that it mattered.

"He fought for this country in two wars, you know. Two wars. I fought in one of those wars. He and I, we were on the same side, fighting those bastards together"—Dan smiled a little as he spoke—"fighting against the bad guys on the same team, defending our families together. That's how we bonded—old war stories." Dan began to shake his head. "I thought I knew him."

"What do you want me to do, Dan?" I didn't know what I could do. I couldn't take myself off the job. Dan knew that. But if Dan had asked me to, I would have tried.

"He defended our country, Joe. *Our* country. I play poker at his house. He's been in here, in my home, standing right where you're standing. I've shared my scotch with the guy. I celebrated my seventieth birthday with him. He's a good man. How can he be the bad guy?" He didn't expect me to answer.

"What do you want me to do, Dan? Tell me what you want me to do."

"This War has taken a lot from me, kid." Dan closed his eyes and shook his head again. I thought he was going to rub the skin off his hands the way he was wringing them together.

I got down on one knee in front of him. I pried his hands apart and held each one of his hands in one of mine. Once Dan opened his eyes again and looked at me, I asked again, "What do you want me to do?" Whatever he said in that moment, I would have done it, no matter what the cost. I just wanted someone that I trusted to tell me what to do. I didn't want to have to make the decisions. "What do you want me to do, Dan?"

"Your job, Joe. Do your job." He didn't look at me when he answered. Instead, he just stared at the floor. Once the room grew quiet again, Dan got up out of the chair, grabbed a beer from the refrigerator, and walked into his bedroom. He closed the door behind him without saying another word.

I considered going right over to Jim's immediately after my conversation with Dan and getting the whole damn thing over with, but then

I thought better of it. I had to stay disciplined. I had to stay under control. I had to stick to the plan. I couldn't afford any mistakes.

Dan didn't come out of his room in the morning, at least not at first. I got up early and went for another run. This time, I steered clear of Jim's place. I kept my head down and kept my waving and my hellos to a minimum. The web was already tangled enough. I didn't want to risk making it any messier. When I got back to the safe house, I showered. When I got out of the shower, Dan was standing in the kitchen. "Morning, Dan," I said to him.

"Morning, Joe." Dan stirred his cup of coffee in his hand. "You didn't go out last night, did you?"

"No," I replied. "I thought about it, but decided not to. I decided it would be smarter to stick with the plan."

"You're probably right." There was no emotion in Dan's voice. It was flat, monotone. "So when are you going to do the job?"

"This evening. As soon as it gets dark." I didn't ask him again what he wanted me to do. He'd had his chance. The fates were sealed. He knew it too.

"Okay." Dan nodded. "You know, he knows you're here," Dan said. Somehow, I wasn't surprised. "How so?" I asked.

"I mean, he doesn't know who you are or why you're here, but I told him that I was going to have a visitor."

"Okay. That's good to know." It really was useful information.

"He was happy for me." Dan swallowed his last gulp of coffee and put the mug in the sink. "He was happy that I was having visitors." He had aged ten years overnight. When I first saw Dan at the airport, I could tell that he was old, but he looked old and sturdy. Now he looked frail.

"Does he have any reason to suspect that you're on the other side or that you know who he is?"

"No."

"Then everything should be fine." I felt horrible using the word *fine*. Nothing was fine. Nothing ever was fine. I could count the hours in my life that had been fine on one hand.

"Right," Dan responded. "I'm going to be out all day. I probably won't see you until this evening. You'll be okay without the car?"

"Yeah, Dan. I'll be fine." There was that word again. Dan took the keys off the hook on the wall and walked toward the door that led to the garage. The same door I had first entered two days earlier. "And, Dan . . ." He turned to me as I spoke, but I didn't know what I wanted to say. All that came out was "Be okay."

At some point during the day, I walked to the hardware store and bought a length of rope with cash. On the way home I picked up a sandwich. I spent the rest of the day sitting on Dan's porch, staring at the pond in his backyard. It wasn't crystal. It was more of a murky green color. When the sun began to drop below the rooftops of the surrounding houses, I walked into my room and got ready. I put on a pair of long pants and a light, long-sleeve T-shirt. I was trying to leave as little skin open to scratching as possible. I couldn't dress too warmly for fear that I'd arouse suspicion. I packed my backpack with the rope, a pair of gloves, and some Wet-Naps in case I needed to clean anything up once the job was done. I left everything else—the rest of my clothes, the ski mask, the gun. I wouldn't need those. This job would be hard for all the wrong reasons. Once the sun had completely disappeared from the sky and the incessant chirping and croaking that haunted the Florida night began, I stepped outside of Dan's house and began my walk across Crystal Ponds to Jim Matsuda's.

By the time I got near Mr. Matsuda's house, the sky was dark and colorless. I didn't have much of a plan. Frankly, I didn't think I'd need one. I stopped on the street in front of his house at roughly the same spot where he and I had made eye contact the morning before. I stood there and peered inside his windows. The lights inside his small house were on, and I could see a shadow moving inside. If he wasn't alone I'd have to come back later. If he was alone, I figured the whole job would be finished within the next half hour. Finish this awful job, I thought, and I could head back to you. One step at a time, Joe, one step at a time.

Unfortunately, from where I was standing on the street, I couldn't really make out whether or not Jim had company. After about ten minutes I got sick of waiting and decided to go ahead with the plan anyway. I could always abort and regroup if need be. So I stepped forward, walking up the gravel path that Jim had leading to his front door. The plan, if you could call it that, was to knock on the door, tell a few lies, get inside, and then wring the life out of him. After that, I'd clean up and go home. War hero or not, for my purposes he was just an old man.

I walked lightly along the path to the door, not because I was afraid that Jim would see me but because I didn't want to attract the attention of his neighbors. The whole neighborhood was quiet; the only sound came from the crickets and frogs. I stepped up to Jim's door and rang the bell. I could hear some noises coming from inside. I could hear people talking. Then, Jim clicked off the television and the only sound that was left was that of a small, elderly man shuffling toward the door.

Jim answered the door wearing a pair of light blue pants and a striped polo shirt. He wore the same slippers that I had seen on him the day before. He pulled the door wide open without first checking to see who it was. He sized me up quickly upon opening the door and then asked, "Can I help you?"

"I'm not intruding or interrupting anything, am I?" I said, trying to peer inside the house to be sure that Jim was alone.

"No. No. Not at all. I was just catching up on some television. What can I do for you, young man?"

"You're Jim Matsuda, right?" He nodded. "My name is Joe. I'm staying over at Dan's place for a few days."

"Yes. Yes. Dan told me that he was going to have a visitor. Pleased to meet you, Joe." Jim held out his hand for me to shake. I had never killed a man after shaking his hand. I looked down at Jim's extended hand for a moment and paused. Then, not wanting to draw suspicion, I shook it.

"Pleasure's all mine, Mr. Matsuda. Mind if I come in?"

"Of course, of course. Where are my manners? Please." Mr. Matsuda extended his arm into the apartment, welcoming me. After I stepped inside, he closed the door behind me and shut out the rest of the world. Mr. Matsuda had all of the windows closed and was blasting the central air-conditioning. Unless someone was standing right outside the front door, no one would hear a sound. Mr. Matsuda's impeccable manners doomed him from the start. "So, how do you know Dan?" Mr. Matsuda asked as he led me toward the sitting room in his house.

"Old family friend," I replied. I didn't even consider it to be a lie.

"Well, it's nice to see Dan have visitors. It seems that fortune hasn't dealt him the easiest hand." Don't remind me, I thought. "It's nice to know that there are still people out there in the world thinking about him. Sometimes, it feels like we're in our own little world down here, floating off into space. It's only when we have family or friends, young people like you coming for a visit, that we're reminded that we're still attached to reality. Can I get you something to drink?"

"A glass of water would be great." Jim stepped into the kitchen and I could hear him opening up a shelf to get a glass for me. While he was gone, I did a quick study of the sitting room to see if there was anything inside that Jim could use as a weapon. The most lethal thing in the room appeared to be a lamp. I wasn't worried. The room had two exits, one into the kitchen and the other into a hallway that must have led toward the bathroom and bedrooms. Jim wouldn't have anyplace to run. There was a window facing the backyard, but the blinds were drawn.

In only a couple of minutes, Jim came back holding two glasses of water, each with two floating ice cubes inside. He handed me a glass. "Would you like to sit down?" Jim asked, motioning toward one of the sofa seats along the wall in the room.

"No, thanks," I replied. "I'm fine standing for now."

"Do you mind if I sit?" Jim asked. "Old legs."

"Be my guest," I replied. Jim walked over and eased himself down in a chair. As long as he didn't have a gun hidden between the cushions, he couldn't be in a worse position. "You said before that you thought Dan's had it kind of rough. How about yourself?" I asked. I don't know why I was bothering with the small talk.

Jim sat and thought for a moment before speaking. When he answered, he stared into my eyes with the same prescient look that he had given me the morning before. "The fortunes, I believe, have been a bit kinder to me. I never married or had any children, but I've lived an eventful life. Even now, I keep busy." I bet you do, I thought. "I do some military consulting here and there. But still, getting old is never easy for anyone. I've been in three wars, young man, and I daresay that getting old is the hardest thing I've ever done."

Jim leveled his gaze at me and it sent a chill through my body. "So, Joe, to what do I owe this little visit of yours?"

"Three wars?" I asked. "Dan told me that you were a veteran of two wars."

"Well, until recently, I suppose, Dan only knew about two of the wars." Jim swirled the ice in his glass and then took another drink. "But there are three: Korea, Vietnam, and this godforsaken War that you and I are fighting in now. Three wars, over fifty years, and I still don't have one damn clue why we fought any of them." He knew. I could feel sweat beginning to seep out of my pores. I held my glass of water down in front of my face and swirled the water, trying to see if I could see anything inside. Jim laughed at me. "Don't worry. There's nothing in your water. Although, I do have to say, you've been doing a pretty careless job."

My emotions quickly ran from fear of being poisoned to embarrassment. "How long have you known?" I asked.

"I've known that Dan was one of you for years. But I also knew that he wasn't causing us any harm. He hadn't done anything to us since we had his daughter killed. That's when they retired him, whether or not he wanted to retire. And I like him. He's a good friend." There was something in his words that disgusted me. It was a reflex.

"Did you have something to do with his daughter's death?"

"No. That happened long before I met Dan. Since meeting him, I've heard the stories, though. She, apparently, was a pistol. I really don't think we had much of an option."

"You don't think you had an option about killing your friend's daughter?"

For the first time, Jim's tone was less than pleasant. "I told you, Joe. I had nothing to do with it. But this is war and ugly things happen during wars. There's little that you or I can do about it."

"Well, you could always end the War."

"My God, son. You still think that you're the good guys and we're the bad guys? The same way I was taught to think about you when I was young, over half a century ago. The same way that I was told to think about the Chinese and the North Vietnamese. Good guys and bad guys. Cops and robbers. Cowboys and Indians. They're all children's games, Joe."

I was in no mood for a lecture. Jared's words echoed through my head. It's either them or us. Either Jim's evil, or I am. "You do realize that I'm going to kill you?" I was hoping that this sentence would end the lecture.

"I've had my suspicions ever since I heard that Dan was going to have a guest. A visitor that I have never heard of. A man whose background Dan couldn't explain. That's why I went outside yesterday to watch you run by, after your first pass by my house. I thought you might be the young man sent to do me in."

"So are you going to fight me?"

"Is there any sense in fighting?" Jim finished off his water and placed his glass on the coffee table. The liquid was thicker than I had thought at first. He'd given me water. He was drinking vodka.

"No. There's no sense in fighting. You're not trained for this."

"Don't be silly, Joe. I've been training for this day my entire life."

"So you plan on putting up a fight?"

Jim laughed. "I haven't been training to fight, Joe. I've been training to die. Three wars, countless deaths. Some at my hands, some in my arms. I've seen enough."

So had I. I took my backpack off. I reached in and pulled out the gloves and placed them on my hands. Then I pulled out the rope, which I had tied into a cinch with a loop. The cinch could be tightened but it couldn't be loosened without untying the knot. The loop was large enough to fit a man's head through, along with some extra space, in case he struggled. I walked over and stood behind the chair in which Jim was sitting. I slipped the noose around his neck. "I do worry what this will do to Dan," Jim said. Those were his last words.

"That's not what I'd be worried about if I were you," I whispered in his ear and tightened the noose around his neck. As the life wrenched out of Jim's body, he struggled, but there was no clawing or hitting. There was no attempt to reach out and pry the rope away from his neck. Instead, Jim struggled against his own will to survive. His reflexes kept kicking in and he would start to lift his hands up toward the rope wrapped around his neck but then he would fight his own reflexes, stopping his hand in midair before it had a chance to reach the rope. His face started to glisten with sweat as he struggled. During the final few moments, his eyes began to bulge and his entire body jolted in such a strong spasm that he almost flew out of the chair. Eventually his body weakened, his arms dropped listlessly to his sides, and his will slipped out of his body. The moment before his life left him, his mouth opened as if he were trying to say something, but with no air going in or out of his throat, no sound came out either. Then his eyes glazed over and he was gone. Once I was sure he was dead, I untied the knot and slipped the rope back off his neck. I had to move in close to untie the rope. When I did I could see the blood on his neck from where the rope had burned through his skin. Even without his wanting it to, his body had put up a hell of a fight. It always does.

I left Jim's lifeless body sitting in the chair. I couldn't help but wonder how long it would be before anyone missed him, before anyone realized he was dead. I poured the rest of my water into the sink. I cleaned my cup off with the Wet-Naps that I had brought. I placed the slightly bloody rope back in the backpack and headed for the door. After closing the door behind me, I took off my gloves and placed them into my backpack as well. The rest of it should have been simply making it back to Dan's house without being noticed. Killing someone shouldn't be that easy.

I really didn't expect to see Dan when I got back to his house. I wouldn't have been surprised if he somehow managed to avoid me until I left. I wouldn't have blamed him. It came as a bit of a shock, then, when I walked through the door and Dan was sitting at his kitchen counter, nursing another beer. He looked up at me when I walked in. He had gotten some of his strength back. The eyes weren't nearly as heavy as they had been the day before. I didn't say anything. He had to break the silence. He took a swig of his beer. "So, is it done?"

"Yeah," I replied. I walked passed him and into my room, where I dropped off my backpack. I didn't want there to be a chance that Dan might see some of the evidence. Then I came back out into the kitchen.

"You want a beer?" Dan asked me when I got back out.

"Sure," I responded. I took a seat in the stool next to Dan's. Dan got up and went to the refrigerator and pulled me out a bottle of beer. I noticed when he opened the refrigerator door that there was only one beer left. This meant that he had saved the last beer for me. It also meant that he'd had a lot to drink in the last twenty-four hours.

He handed me the bottle and I immediately began to drink from it. I didn't even want the beer. Drinking after a job seemed disrespectful to me. But as long as I had the beer bottle to my lips, I had an excuse not to talk.

So we sat next to each other in silence. It was the loudest silence I'd ever experienced. Eventually we both finished off our beers. When the bottles were empty, Dan turned to me. "I'm going to go to bed," he said. "It's been a long day." I nodded and watched him as he walked toward his bedroom door.

Right before he closed the door behind him, I finally mustered up the courage to speak. "He wanted to die, Dan," I said. "He was waiting for me." Dan looked at me and nodded to let me know that he understood. Then he closed the door. I'm glad that I said something. I wish it had been enough.

I sat at the counter for another twenty minutes or so before I decided to go to sleep myself. I don't remember what I thought about for those twenty minutes. Before walking back to my bedroom, I turned off all the lights. The darkness felt good. When I got to the bed, I stripped down to my boxers and climbed in. I usually showered after a job, but I didn't need to this time. I just lay in the darkness and closed my eyes.

———

I awoke to the sound of a bang. A loud, horrible bang. I remember shooting up in bed, sitting up straight, my heart racing, short of breath, before I could even remember what it was that had startled me. Then I remembered. The bang. I jumped out of bed and ran over to the dresser. I pulled open the top drawer and peered inside. My gun, it was still there. I pulled it out of the drawer and carried it with me as I moved through the house. The bang. Had they found out? Had they come back for vengeance already? I moved through the house without turning the lights on. If there was anyone in there, I'd get the jump on them. I moved quickly, holding the gun up near my head so that I could aim and fire it quickly if I needed to. The gun was starting to feel dangerously comfortable in my hands. The living room was empty, as was the kitchen. I noticed a light coming from Dan's room. I moved more slowly and quietly as I approached. I turned the doorknob to his bedroom and swung open the door. His bedroom was empty, his bed unmade. There were six or seven empty beer bottles sitting on top of his nightstand. The light was coming from the crack below the door that led to his bathroom. "Dan?" I shouted. There was no response, no movement whatsoever. I held the gun out in front of me and pushed open the bathroom door.

The white linoleum was covered in blood. It was splattered all over the tiles on the wall. It had already begun to drip toward the floor, creating long red stripes against the white wall. Dan's body was slumped against the wall, his head slacked and his jaw hanging open. The back of his head was missing. In his hand was an old revolver. I looked down at the gun. There were still five bullets left. The only one that was missing was the one that had traveled through Dan's mouth, out the back of his head, and into the wall.

I had no time for sympathy or anger or whatever other emotion I was supposed to have at that moment, looking down on Dan's wasted body. I had to get out of there. I had to move fast. Anyone could have heard that gunshot and called the police. The police could already be on their way. Dan's suicide would be easy enough to cover, but they'd eventually find Jim's body too. I had to leave, and I had to cover my tracks. I ran back into my bedroom and grabbed my backpack and my duffel bag. I'd be leaving on foot, so I would have liked to carry as little as possible. I took the gloves back out of the backpack and slipped them back onto my hands. I pulled the rope that I had used to strangle Jim out of the backpack as well. Then I dropped the backpack and the duffel bag near the back door and went back into the bathroom where Dan's body was lying. I knelt down beside his body, careful not to step in any of the blood that had seeped down to the floor. I didn't want to leave any suspicious shoe prints. I took the gun out of Dan's hand. I took both his hands in mine and began to wring them around the rope that I had used to kill his best friend. I rubbed until there was visible rope burn on his hands. "Sorry to tarnish your good name, Dan, but you didn't exactly leave me with much choice," I said to what was left of Dan's head. Some of the fiber from the rope and possibly even some of Jim's blood should have gotten on Dan's hands to match the rope burn. When I was done with that, I put the gun back in Dan's hand. I took the rope and placed it on Dan's nightstand, near the incriminating, empty bottles of beer. Then I grabbed my things and ran out the back door.

Crystal Ponds didn't afford much cover. The palm trees and low bushes wouldn't have worked in a ten-year-old's game of hide-and-seek. They surely didn't provide cover for a full grown man. Instead, I slipped from house to house, hiding along the unlit outside walls of homes, trying not to walk past any windows. Eventually, I got out of the neighborhood and onto the highway. Next to the highway there was a long stretch of barren woodland. It would provide me with enough cover to get away from Crystal Ponds.

I was just hoping to make it downtown before it started to get light out. There I could find some shelter in the crowds. Maybe I could even find a place to stay and rest for a couple of hours. A couple of hours, then I wanted to get the hell out of Dodge. On my way downtown, I passed a brand new condo development. There were only a couple of finished units, but one of them had a sign out front labeling it an open house. I decided to see if there was any truth in advertising and was lucky enough to find that the sliding glass door in the back had been left unlocked. I slipped inside, thinking that I could lay low in there for a few hours while the heat died down. I'd attract a lot less attention walking around with my duffel bag in the daytime than I would at four in the morning.

The little model home was fully furnished. There were even some cookies and bottled water in the refrigerator. I drank two bottles and tossed the empties in the garbage under the sink. I didn't turn on any lights or any of the appliances, but I did set the alarm clock in the bedroom for six-thirty. It was three o'clock in the morning when I climbed into the bed. Three hours of sleep would have done me well. Unfortunately, when I lay down, it was like uncorking a bottle. All the emotion that I had suppressed upon seeing Dan's body slumped on the floor slowly came to me. I ached, but I don't know if I was feeling anger or grief. I wanted to be mad at Dan, mad that he couldn't have waited one more day and let me leave with a clear conscience. But what I felt was grief, grief for this poor old bastard who'd had every last thing in his life taken away from him. What had I done? First I had almost killed a civilian in Montreal and now this. I tried thinking of you, to see if it could clear my head, but the image of Dan's body slumped on the floor, streams of his own blood trickling down the wall around him, kept returning. I thought about the pictures on Dan's bookshelf, souvenirs of a life gone horribly wrong.

"I'm sorry, Dan," I whispered into the darkness. I hoped somehow that he could hear me. I closed my eyes but didn't sleep. I just lay there for three hours, wishing time away. I thought about Dan's first toast, when he took me out drinking, "To breaking the bastards' backs before they break ours." I guess the order didn't really matter, did it, Dan? A broken back is still a broken back.

I got out of bed at six, a half hour before the alarm was set to go off. There was simply no sense in my lying in bed anymore. I searched the house for a phone. They had one phone set up, hanging on the wall near the kitchen. I picked it up and got a dial tone. I dialed the number for Intel. Jimmy Lane, Sharon Bench, Clifford Locklear. I was patched through to Allen.

"Don't say anything to me unless the job is done," Allen said as soon as he picked up the phone. So much for hellos.

"The job's done, but there were complications," I replied.

"You're the fucking king of complications." Allen was on a roll. "Is he dead?"

"My target?" I asked

"Yes," Allen replied.

"Yeah, he's dead."

"Well, then, that doesn't sound that complicated. That actually sounds pretty simple." God, I hated him.

"He's not the only person who's dead. My host is dead too. He shot himself in the head."

"Well, it serves your host right for fraternizing with the enemy." Allen knew. The bastard knew. People knowing more than me was quickly becoming an unpleasant trend. "So how did you handle it?" Allen asked. It was a test.

"I planted the evidence of the murder on my host. I tried to make it look like a murder-suicide." That's what the papers would say, and the police, "murder-suicide." In the end they'd be right; they'd just have the labels backward.

"Good work, kid. Very clever. Maybe I'll make something of you yet."

"Anyway, I need to get out of town. I did your job. I'm ready to go back to Montreal."

"I'll send you back to Montreal, kid, but it's going to take some time. Rent a car. Start heading north. I have a few jobs that I want you to do along the way." I wanted to argue, but I remembered how far that had gotten me last time. Allen gave me the next code: "Mary Joyce. Kevin Fitzgibbon. Richard Klinker." Then he hung up.

Ten

Allen's few jobs took me the better part of three weeks and totaled four more bodies. After only two of the killings, I was begging off the job. I told him that I couldn't do it anymore. I asked him if I could teach a class instead, that I was willing to work doing other things. He told me that I wouldn't be teaching any classes anytime soon, that I had get my head back on straight before they'd let me influence the next generation again. "We need men teaching tomorrow's men," I believe he told me. "Right now, you're not man enough for that job." So he kept me killing instead. I was man enough for that.

First there was a thirty-five-year-old man in Georgia. He was a recently retired assassin for their side. He had just settled down with his new wife and was ready to start a family. His new wife wasn't born into the War. She married into it. Allen gave me the "option" of taking her out as well. I declined.

The second killing was a woman in Tennessee. She was just a dispatcher. I asked Allen why we were bothering killing dispatchers. He told me only that this was war and that she worked for the other side and that we wanted everyone who worked for the other side to tremble in fear at the thought of us. "Until they are defeated, every last one of them is a target. They kill ours and we have to strike back." I assume this meant that one of our dispatchers, one of the joyful-sounding women who shuttled me from place to place when I was calling Intelligence, had been murdered. It seemed a horrible waste to me, on our side and theirs.

The third was a twenty-one-year-old black kid in Washington, D.C. He was poor. He lived in a tenement house in Southeast D.C. with his entire family. He put up a hell of a fight. It took me two days in a hotel room to recover. I had a small knife wound as well as scratches and bruises all over my body. He'd begun killing for them when he was eighteen and had already amassed a portfolio of murders. He was vicious. Once he knew he wasn't going to survive, he did his best to take me out with him. Before he died, I asked him why he did it. Why he fought for people who clearly hadn't given him anything. His response was "They give me hope." Those were his last words.

On my second day recovering in the hotel, while still trying to clean my wounds and recuperate, I got a phone call. When the phone in my hotel room rang, I wasn't sure I should answer it. I didn't get phone calls. No one was supposed to know where I was. Allen knew but there was no way he was going to break protocol like that. But it kept ringing. A wrong number would have hung up. On the seventh or eighth ring, I picked up the phone.

"Joe," an old familiar voice echoed out of the receiver, "for a second there I didn't think you were going to answer."

"Jared," I replied, "you have no idea how good it is to hear from you. How did you find me?"

"Forget that," Jared answered. "Look, I'm in D.C. Do you have any plans tonight?" Plans? What sort of plans would I have?

"Well, I was going to order room service and maybe watch a movie on pay-per-view," I said.

Jared laughed. "Any way you can cancel those plans and meet me for a drink?" Nothing could have stopped me. I was at one of the lowest points I'd ever been. It was like somehow Jared knew that. It was like he knew just when to reach out to me. Jared suggested that we meet at some old bar in Georgetown. The place was a little out of the way, he said, but that was the draw. It would be quiet. We could talk.

Jared was already sitting in a booth in the back corner of the bar when I walked into the place. It was dark inside. The floor, the bar, and the booths were all made from an old, dark wood. Frank Sinatra was playing on the jukebox. I didn't need Jared to wave me over to him. I saw him right away. I knew which booth he'd be in, the one farthest away from all the bar's other patrons. There were maybe half a dozen other people in the place and they were all sitting at the bar watching a basketball game. I walked past them toward Jared's booth. When he saw me approaching, he got up and gave me a hug. I still wasn't walking right from my last job. It would take some time for the bruises to heal. "You all right?" Jared asked me as we sat down.

"Yeah," I answered. "Just recovering from a tough job."

"I heard," Jared said.

"Really?" It was an odd thing for Jared to say. We weren't supposed to know about other people's jobs. We were only supposed to concentrate on our own.

"What can I say? I've got good connections." Jared motioned for the waitress. He hadn't ordered anything yet. She came by to take our order. I kept trying to process what Jared had just told me. Jared ordered a Manhattan. I followed his lead and ordered a scotch on the rocks since, apparently, we were drinking. I waited for the waitress to walk away before saying anything else.

"Is that why you're here?" I asked, suddenly confused. "Did they send you here?"

Jared's eyes glistened in the dim light of the bar. He smiled. "Don't sound so paranoid, Joe," he answered. "I'm here because I wanted to come here. I'm here because I was worried about you. I wanted to see you." I was happy to hear it. I was happy to spend even a few minutes with someone I could trust. The waitress came by with our drinks.

"I'm sorry," I said. "I didn't mean to imply anything, Jared. It's great to see you." I considered lifting my glass in a toast but then I remembered the last night I went out drinking with Dan and thought better of it. "It's just been a tough couple weeks."

"I know," Jared said. "I've been keeping tabs on you since LBI. I know about Montreal. I know about Naples. It's been a tough row."

"How do you know all this?" I asked. "I thought we weren't supposed to know things about each other. I had to pull teeth just to be able to talk to Michael on the phone after LBI."

Jared smiled again. His smile was big enough that even through the darkness I could see the shine on his teeth. "I've been promoted, Joe. I don't just take orders anymore."

"Wow," I answered. "I had no idea." I turned toward the bar and put my hand up to hail the waitress. "Can I get two shots of tequila?" I called out to her when she was halfway to our booth. "Promoted? That's crazy." I have to admit I was a bit jealous. It didn't seem right that Jared would be promoted before me. We grew up together. We went through training together. I did everything I'd been told. The waitress came by with our tequila shots. I lifted mine, ghosts be damned. "Congrats," I said.

"Thanks, man," Jared answered as we clicked glasses. Then we each threw back our shot in a quick gulp.

"So what do they have you doing?" I asked.

"I'm a Fixer," he said to me. I had heard of the role. I'd never met a Fixer before. It was still a frontline position, still a soldier's position, but you weren't just killing anymore. Beyond that, I didn't really know what a Fixer did.

"Okay," I answered him, leaning against the back of the booth, "you're a Fixer." My jealousy was beginning to wane. Slowly, I was becoming happy for my friend.

"You don't know what a Fixer does, do you?" Jared laughed.

"Not a fucking clue," I answered, shaking my head and taking another sip of my scotch.

"It's pretty simple. I'm assigned a list of soldiers and I'm supposed to help them get out of any trouble they get themselves in."

"So you don't have to kill people anymore?" I asked.

Jared laughed again. "You really think it's possible to get other soldiers out of trouble without killing people?" I didn't know. Maybe it was possible. Jared wouldn't have wanted to give up the killing, though, even if he could have.

"Well, congrats again. That's crazy." I shook my head in disbelief. I should have seen it coming. Jared was the best. He was the most disciplined. He was the most reliable. "You really deserved it," I said. "But still, how do you know all that shit about me?"

Jared looked at me. He took a sip of his drink. He knew that it would be hard for me to accept the next thing he said. "I've been assigned to you."

I laughed. I didn't know how else to react. When the laughter stopped, I looked at Jared again. "What the hell does that mean?" The string of Sinatra from the jukebox ended. An Otis Redding song began to play.

"It means that when you get into trouble, I'm supposed to help you out of it."

"So are you here on official business or are you here because you wanted to see me?"

"Both," Jared answered without any hesitation.

"So what type of trouble am I supposed to be in?" I asked him.

"People are just worried about you," Jared answered. I wondered who these people were who cared so much. It didn't feel to me like anybody cared.

"Why are they worried about me?" I asked.

"Because you've had a string of bad luck," Jared answered. A string of bad luck didn't really seem to cover it. I didn't say anything in response. I just sat there. "Look, Joe, don't be mad at me. I really want to help you. I really want you to be happy for me."

"I'm sorry," I said for already the second time that night. "But how do you expect to help me get out of a string of bad luck?"

Jared put his empty glass on the table. He motioned to the waitress to bring us two more drinks. "They offered me the Montreal job." He was staring down at his hands now. "They didn't think that it would be good for you after what happened last time. They wanted me to finish it." I could barely believe my ears. "I refused. I know that job's important to you. I told them that I'd talk to you. I told them that you just needed a morale boost." The waitress dropped the new drinks off at our table. I drank half of mine in one gulp. "Listen, Joe"—Jared leaned across the table toward me—"you've got a future here. Don't take me coming here the wrong way. They don't waste our energy on lost causes. Everybody believes that you've got a really bright future. I may have been fast-tracked, but a lot of people think you're the one with real potential. I hear about it all the time. They say you've got a fire that most people just don't have."

I let my muscles relax. "If they're so high on me, why'd they move Brian off my case?" I used the name Brian with Jared. I knew I could trust him.

"That wasn't a punishment, Joe," Jared said. "I know your new Intel contact probably told you that it was but that's just because he's a hard-ass. Brian was taken off your case because the guys upstairs are afraid that they can't trust him."

"What? Do they think he's a spy?"

Jared shook his head. "Nobody knows anything for sure," Jared answered. "So the less said about it, the better. Just know that it wasn't punishment. In fact, the guy that you've got now is the real deal, even if he is a hard-ass. They assigned you to him on purpose. He's got a reputation for moving people up the ranks quickly. It's hell dealing with him, but he gets the job done."

"What are you telling me, Jared?"

Jared's voice suddenly got very serious. "I'm telling you that nobody blames you for what happened in Montreal. In fact, a lot of people were pretty impressed that you saved that guy. I'm telling you that nobody expects you to just be an ordinary soldier for much longer. I'm telling you to keep your chin up and get your job done and things are going to start looking up for you pretty quickly."

"That's your pep talk?" I was finally able to smile at Jared again.

"That's what I have," he answered.

"So how come you get promoted while me and Michael are still out here busting our humps?"

Jared laughed. "I got promoted ahead of Michael because Michael, God love him, is a fuckup. He's good at killing but it's a savant's gift. He's already where he needs to be. He's already where he's got the most to offer. I got promoted ahead of you because you need to get your head on straight. Once you do that, you'll be watching me in your rearview mirror." Jared took a sip of his drink. Now it was his turn to get jealous. "You should hear the way they talk about you, Joe. They believe in you more than you believe in yourself." I wanted to ask Jared why. I wanted to ask him exactly what he'd heard. I didn't have the guts.

"So are you happy for me, or what?" Jared asked.

"Come on," I answered. "You know I am."

"Being assigned to you meant a lot to me, Joe, and not just because we're good friends. It meant a lot to me because of what I think we can achieve together. I really think that we can make a difference." I know he meant it. "Do you remember that one kill that they let us do as a team?" Jared asked me. I remembered. The two of us hit a safe house with four people inside. Two of them were there to do a job the next day. They never got the chance. "We were like fucking dancers, man. It was a thing of beauty." It really was. I nodded in agreement.

"So what do you need me to do?" I asked.

"Just listen to Allen," Jared said. "Accept your destiny. Know I've got your back. And don't fuck up." He laughed. I laughed too. We ordered another round of drinks. I made a promise to myself to start getting rededicated in the morning. I figured I owed that much to Jared.

"So what's after Fixer?" I asked.

"After that, I'll be in charge of a unit. I'll start working with Intelligence on strategy." Jared grinned. He was in his element. I wasn't sure they were right about me, but Jared was definitely going somewhere.

"Do they really talk about me like that?" I asked.

"Yeah," Jared said, nodding. "And you know what? I've known you for a long time, Joe, and I don't blame them. All you need is a little discipline. I know I wouldn't want to have to fight against you."

The next morning, I got my orders for my final kill before being told I could go back to Montreal. The final kill was a black woman in Boston. She was an MIT student. She was a target based solely on her potential. "Cut them off at the root," Allen said. "Take them out before they can do any real damage to us."

That was it. For three weeks, I barely slept, bathed in death and blood. Finally, after the fourth killing, Allen told me he thought I was ready to go back to Montreal. He gave me a week to do the hit, told me not to screw it up this time. He told me not to even call him when the job was done. He'd know. He had his ways. "After that," he said, "you've earned yourself some time. Do whatever you want for two weeks. I don't care what you do, so long as you don't cause any trouble. Call me in three weeks. Be ready to work again. And, kid?"

"Yeah?" I replied. I was worn down, nearly worn through. Not even Jared's pep talk had been able to pick me up for more than a day. The only thing that had kept me moving over the past three weeks was the thought of getting back to Montreal to be with you.

"You've done a good job. Paul Acker. Herman Taylor. Preston Stokes." Then Allen hung up.

During my three weeks on the road, I wanted to call you, but couldn't. It was all too much to take. After Dan, all the killing felt worse. Good and evil. I had a harder time believing it with every additional body. I tried using Jared's mantra to keep me going. "Either they're evil or we are. And I know for damn sure that I'm not evil." But with each passing day, I became less and less certain that we weren't all evil, on both sides. Now the only thing that I had to hold on to was the fact that you loved me and the hope that you were still waiting for me.

I was giddy after Allen told me I was finally headed back to Montreal. Finally, I had the courage to call you again. You answered with a quick hello. "Maria?" I said when you answered the phone. Just hearing your voice gave me hope. Hope for what, I couldn't be sure.

"Joe?" you replied. "Is that you? Where have you been? Why haven't you called?"

"I'm sorry," I replied, hoping it was enough of an answer to all your questions for now. "I've been meaning to call but I couldn't. I'll explain it all to you when I get back to Montreal."

"You're coming back?" you responded.

"Yeah. I'll be there tomorrow. Assuming you still want me to come back."

You started crying. I had never heard you cry before. Hearing it over the phone was heartbreaking. I wanted to be able to comfort you. "I told you that I'd wait for you. Come quickly," you replied.

"I'll see you tomorrow," I finally said.

"Tomorrow," you echoed. We hung up without either of us saying "I love you" for the first time since we'd first said it. At that moment, the word *tomorrow* meant the same thing. Nothing else needed to be said.

Eleven

They didn't assign me a safe house this time. The job was deemed too dangerous, especially after I messed it up the last time. I should have been insulted, but I considered it a blessing. Ever since Naples the safe houses had become a burden. I'd find myself staring at my hosts, wondering why, if they were so excited about the War, they weren't fighting it themselves. Maybe then they'd see things differently. It's not easy to hold a pom-pom in one hand and a gun in the other. In the heat of battle, if given the choice, most people drop the pom-pom.

Instead of the safe house, I was given a new identity and told to check into a hotel. When I got to Montreal, I decided that the hotel could wait. They thought I was in Montreal to do a job. I knew better. I headed straight to your apartment. I left the rental car illegally parked around the corner from your place. What the hell did I care? It wasn't my car. It wasn't my money that'd be paying the parking tickets. Hell, the car wasn't even under my name. I parked the car and walked to your building. My heart was beating so fast, I could feel the blood moving in my veins. I got to your door and leaned on the buzzer. I wasn't going to let go until somebody let me inside. The drone of the buzzer was strangely soothing. Then I heard your voice. "Hello?" It was music.

"Maria, it's me," I spoke into the intercom—whispered, really—unable to fill my lungs with air. You didn't say anything. You simply hit the button to let me in. I heard the lock on the door click and I went inside. I started up the stairs. Everything I had done in the past month, everything I had gone through, all rushed back to me as I walked up the first flight. I felt dizzy and light-headed. I told myself that there was no future after this moment. There was no past before it. This moment was life. You, standing behind the door waiting for me. Me, climbing the stairs toward you. It was all worth it for this moment. I tried to forget my promise to tell you everything. That didn't matter right now. I simply tried to remember your face, your lips. Once up the three flights of stairs, I lifted my knuckles to knock on your door. You pulled it open before my fist could reach the surface. You must have been waiting there, listening to my footsteps.

You opened the door. You were wearing a skirt and a black sweater. I had never seen you wear a skirt before. You looked so feminine. I tried to drink in your image. My eyes traveled down your body, lingering on your legs. I couldn't help but linger there, on your bare skin. I stepped inside the doorway. I lifted my head and finally looked at your face. You had tried to pull your wild hair back into a ponytail but strands of curly hair had escaped and hung down, framing your face. You looked anxious. "Hello, Maria," I said. I had yet to really catch my breath. I could barely make the words escape my lips. You grabbed my shirt collar and pulled my face toward yours. We kissed. You kissed me with your eyes open. I followed your lead and stared into your eyes as we kissed. They were bottomless.

"Hello, Joe," you said as we parted lips for a moment. Then, I closed my eyes, pulled you back toward me, and kissed you even more deeply. I could feel the edges of your lips curl up as I pushed my lips into yours. Then you put one hand on my chest and pushed me away from you, but only a few inches away, creating just enough space between us so that you could bend down. You began to unbuckle my belt. I swung my hand back and pushed the door closed behind me. Then, suddenly, you dropped down in front of me, squatting, your knees spread open just enough for me to catch a glimpse of your sheer black underwear as your skirt rode slightly up your thighs. You pulled my shirt up and began to kiss my stomach. You ran your tongue gently over my skin. Then you began to unbutton my pants.

"Your roommate?" I whispered, hating myself for the words as I spoke them.

"She's gone." You looked up at me, your blue eyes full of mischief. Thank God, I thought, believing in God again for the first time since I was a child. You tossed my belt over your shoulder, flinging it aimlessly across the room. Then you pulled down the zipper of my pants and pulled them down, along with my boxers, with one firm tug. I looked down again. I glanced past the darkness between your spread legs again and watched your lips as you took me, already hard, into your mouth. I didn't have the will to stop you. I felt guilty. I thought I should have stopped you and told you that everything about my life was a lie, but I was powerless as you moved your lips over me. You began stroking me with your tongue. I know now what you were doing. You were claiming me. You were making sure that I would never leave again. You were using every tool at your disposal for that purpose. It was all unnecessary. I was already yours. I had been from the first moment I saw you. Nothing would change that. I had already promised myself that I would never leave you again. I would never put you through that again. I would never put myself through that again.

"Stop," I pleaded, barely believing the words that were coming out of my mouth. If I hadn't stopped you, it would have all been over way too soon.

"I don't have to," you replied, looking up at me. I felt guilty. I didn't deserve this. After what I'd done, I didn't deserve this.

"I want you," I said, pulling you up toward me and kissing your moist lips. Then I placed one arm behind your shoulders and reached down, sliding my other arm behind your knees and pulling you up into my arms, cradling you and carrying you into the bedroom. I was determined to regain some control but you were even more determined to conquer me. We fell onto the bed. I tried to climb on top of you. I tried to slide between your legs. You outmaneuvered me. You climbed on top of me, straddling me, moving. In the rush you had left your underwear on, simply tugging it to the side once it got in the way. You placed your hands on my chest, your arms pushing your nipples closer to my mouth. I took your breasts in my hands. I ran my lips and my tongue over your nipples. You gasped. Then you pushed my head back down to the bed. You moved up and down on top of me, staring into my eyes as your pace quickened. My eyes wandered over your body. I tried to look you in the eyes but I couldn't help letting my eyes drift over your skin. Your skin was pale but flawless. Your breathing quickened. You leaned back, arching your back, placing a hand behind you for balance. There you were, all of you, naked before me. If your plan was to claim ownership of me, if your plan was to forever brand me as yours, it would have worked, if I hadn't already been branded. Then it ended, my own spasm sending you into yours, our bodies clenched together. You collapsed on top of me, both of our bodies glistening with sweat.

We didn't speak. I pulled you closer to me, holding your naked body against mine and wondering if this would be it, if this would be the last time you wanted me. With every passing moment I grew more and more certain that I would tell you my secrets and you'd run. All the while, you were lying there, afraid that once you told me your secret I would run from you. In the end, our secrets didn't push us apart. They bound us together.

For that one night, neither of us had the courage to talk. We pretended everything was normal. We got out of bed only to eat. Eventually, we wore each other out. You fell asleep first. I could feel your heartbeat on my skin as you slept. Lying next to you, feeling the heat of your body against mine, I closed my eyes and slept too.

The following morning, I remember waking up with my eyes still closed. I just lay there for a few minutes. I didn't want to be awake. I didn't want the morning to come. With the morning came the payment of debts unpaid, the revealing of truths unspoken. I could hear you next to me. You were awake. I glanced through partially closed eyelids. You were sitting up in bed, the sheets wrapped around under your armpits for warmth. I could see fear in your face—fear and determination. Slowly, I opened my eyes.

You didn't waste any time. "We have things to talk about," you said to me as soon as you saw that I was awake. You looked nervous. I watched your eyes dance between my face and the ceiling.

"I know," I answered. "I promised you that I was going to tell you everything." My words drifted off. I couldn't think of what to say next so I just stopped talking. There was silence.

"But?" you prodded.

"But nothing," I replied. "If you really want to know, then I'm going to tell you." I froze again.

"Of course I want to know," you replied. "You go off for weeks. You barely call. You don't tell me what it is that you're doing. You barely even tell me where you are. When you do call, you call in the middle of the night. I *need* to know, Joe." You were on the edge of tears. I could see the need in your eyes. It was tangible. I didn't know where to start. I thought about all the classes I'd been to. I thought about how the Intel guys would show the kids those slides. First, they showed the kids pictures of their enemies. Then they'd show the pictures of the bodies—bodies on top of bodies. Finally, they showed them pictures of their allies. They had a system. That system worked.

But you were different. All these kids in these classes, every one of them, grew up suspicious. The world around them didn't make sense until someone showed up with slides and explanations. To them, the War actually made everything make more sense. Your world already made sense. The only thing in your world that didn't make sense was me.

"What are you afraid of?" you asked, sensing my fear.

So much, I thought. "I'm afraid that you won't believe me" is what I settled on.

You wanted to help me. You wanted to believe me. I've always heard that monsters are scarier when you don't see them. That the monster you imagine is usually scarier than the truth. What happens when that's not the case? What happens when the monster is more horrible than you could possibly imagine? "What if I promise to believe you?" you said, as if such a promise were even possible.

"I'm afraid that might be worse," I replied. My mouth was dry. I tried to look at you for courage but it only made things harder. This War had taken a lot from me. I didn't want it to take you too.

"You have to tell me," you demanded, tears beginning to well up in your eyes.

"I know," I answered. I had run out of excuses. The rest of my life hinged on that moment. There was nothing left to do but step into the abyss. I leapt. "Everything I'm about to say to you is going to sound absurd." You opened your mouth to speak, to give me confidence, to make more promises you had no business making. I lifted my hand to stop you before you could start. "Everything I'm about to say to you is going to sound absurd. I believe that by now, you trust me, so I don't imagine that you'll think I'm lying. Instead you'll probably think I'm crazy." I looked up at you. You were staring at me with incredulous eyes. "First, let me promise you that I am not crazy. Though, by the time I'm finished, you may wish that I was." I kept watching your face, trying to read your reactions. This was how I

shadowy giants. Jessica leapt at one of them. He caught her. She just started yelling, 'Run, Joe, run.' So I ran. I didn't look back. I could hear Jessica screaming as the man dragged her back into the house but I didn't look back. I spent that night cowering in the woods. I remember shivering all night but I don't remember if it was cold or not. I didn't go home until morning. When I got home, my mother was there. My sister was gone. She died because she agreed to come babysit for me. My mother should have known better. They couldn't kill me anyway."

"Why not?" you asked.

"Because I wasn't eighteen."

"I don't understand," you said.

"I know." How could you understand? "I'll explain." Slides of the enemy, in every lesson I ever sat through, that was what came next. Talk to them about death and then show them the killers. "There's a group of people out there and they are trying to kill me, my family, and my friends." Your face changed again. This time, after the confusion turned to fear, the fear turned to disbelief.

"Why?" you asked.

I only had one response, even if I didn't fully believe it anymore. "Because they're evil," I answered. Forget all the other stories. Forget the story about the slave rebellion. Forget the story about the five armies. Forget the broken peace treaties. I had to convince you that my enemy was evil so that you wouldn't run from me when I told you all the things I'd done.

You responded with the appropriate disbelief. "So you're telling me there's a group of these evil people out there that are murdering your family and your friends and no one notices?"

"A lot of people notice," I answered. "But everything is covered up. And it's not just my family and friends. It's more than that. It's a lot more. Do you know how many deaths are attributed to accidents in the United States each year?" You shook your head. "Over a hundred thousand." I knew the numbers. We all knew the numbers. "People aren't that accident prone. Most of those deaths aren't accidents."

"What are you telling me?" you asked. You weren't sure if you believed me.

"It's a war," I answered.

You understood now. For the first time, you understood. I could see it in your eyes. "So what do you do?"

"I fight them," I responded.

"What do you mean, *you* fight them?" you asked.

"I seek them out. I find them and I make sure that they can't kill people anymore. I make sure they can never again do what they did to my sister."

"You kill them?" There was no color left in your face.

"If I have to," I responded.

"How often do you have to?"

I didn't want to answer this question but I had promised. "A lot. It's a war, Maria."

"Are there others?" I chuckled at this question. You would only ask it if you thought that maybe I was crazy, a lone vigilante fighting an imaginary enemy.

"Thousands of others," I answered. I had no idea what the actual number was. Hundreds? Thousands? Hundreds of thousands? They never told me. Maybe Jared knew.

"But what are you fighting for?" you asked. By this point, you were barely able to speak.

"My sister," I answered, hoping that, after everything I'd just told you, this would resonate.

"Okay," you responded. "That's why you're fighting. Why is everyone else fighting?" I had never been asked that question before.

"Because everyone has a story like that, Maria. My friend Jared watched them strangle his older brother to death. My friend Michael never even knew his parents. He was raised by one of his aunts. Everyone has a reason to fight."

"But that doesn't make any sense, Joe. It had to have started somewhere. People don't have wars for no reason. You have to be fighting over something. Power? Land? Money? Something." There was pity in your eyes. Hiding behind the fear was pity. The pity made me angry. It made me feel like a fool.

I thought about telling you the stories then. I thought about telling you about the slave rebellion and how we fought to keep the rest of the world free. I thought about telling you about the broken peace treaties, but I knew that it wouldn't make a difference. Even if these stories were true, they weren't your stories. You can't understand until you have a reason of your own to fight. We all want to know the history. We all want to know that we're the good guys. But history only gets you so far. So I answered as best I could. "Survival" was all I could come up with.

"That doesn't make any sense, Joe." There were tears in your eyes.

"You just don't understand," I replied. "Your family wasn't killed. How could you understand?"

You began to cry. "You can't have a war for survival, Joe. It doesn't make any sense. If you're both just trying to survive, all you have to do is stop fighting."

"If only it were that easy, Maria."

"So when does it stop, then?" you asked. You knew the answer without me saying a word. You began to cry. The tears flowed freely down your cheeks. "Does it ever end?"

I didn't answer you. I was growing weary of answering questions that I didn't know the answer to.

"How many?" you asked, the flow of tears waning. You wanted to know how many people I had killed. I wasn't going to answer that question either.

"As many as I've had to," I answered.

"How many?" you asked with more force. I just shook my head. You saw that you weren't going to get anything more from me.

"What am I supposed to do?" You looked up at me, your blue eyes as large as moons.

"Trust me," I pleaded, kneeling down in front of you. "I'm a good person, Maria. Trust me." Even as I said the words I knew that you had no reason to trust me. If it weren't for your own secrets, I'm convinced that you would have run. I wouldn't have blamed you for running.

"And what about me?" you asked.

"If you stay with me, you become part of this. There are certain rules that will protect you, at least in the beginning."

"Rules?" you asked.

"Yeah," I responded, realizing how ridiculous it sounded. "It's like how I told you that they couldn't kill me when they came for my sister because I wasn't eighteen. That's one of the rules." As I spoke, I didn't realize how important the rules would become. "Another rule is that they can't kill innocent bystanders. So they can't touch you, not unless we become a family. If that happens, I'll protect you." I should have told you to run. I should have begged you to stay as far away from me as possible. If I were brave, I would have left you. Instead, I muttered, "I can't ask you to stay. All I can do is promise that I will do everything I can to protect you."

There was a long stretch of painful silence. My whole body ached. It was your turn to speak. You took my hands in yours. You turned my hands over so that you could look at my palms. "You kill people. You kill people with these hands." It was my turn to cry. I buried my face into your shoulder and wept.

You must have thought about leaving me. You would have been crazy not to. Still, I could tell that you weren't trying to break me down with your questions. You were just trying to fully assess the situation. Do you stay with a man you now know to be a killer or do you run? Eventually my own crying stopped. "Do you trust me?" I asked with as much strength as I could muster.

"I don't think I have any choice," you replied.

Now it was my turn to be confused. "What do you mean?"

"I'm pregnant."

In the end it is our secrets that bind us.

"What?" I stood up again, in shock.

"I'm pregnant, Joe."

"How?" I was fishing for words.

"You know how, Joe." Your reply was curt. I wasn't reacting like you wanted me to. I just told you that I end lives. Now you were telling me that you were going to be the source of one and I was acting like a jackass.

"What about birth control?"

"What about it, Joe? This may be the wrong time to bring it up for the first time." Your voice was becoming angry.

"You're in college. What type of college student isn't on the pill?" It was a stupid comment, but without it, we wouldn't have realized the mess that we were in.

"Yes, I am in university, Joe. But I'm not on the pill."

"Why not?"

"I'm seventeen, Joe," you replied.

My thoughts raced. Seventeen? How could you be seventeen? I began to do the math in my head. Seventeen plus nine months. What was seventeen plus nine months?

"But you said you were a sophomore."

"I told you that I was in second year at university. That's all you ever asked me. You never asked me how old I was. I graduated from high school early. I was advanced." You were shouting. "I was seventeen, in university and lonely, and then I met you. I've always been different, Joe. I was different from my classmates in high school. I was different from my classmates at university. Then I met you and you were different too. We were different together." You were pleading with me now. All I could do was keep trying to do the math in my head. Seventeen plus nine months, what was seventeen plus nine months?

"When's your birthday?"

"What difference does that make?" You had gone from being angry at my response to confused.

I looked at you. My look must have frightened you, because you flinched. "When is your birthday?" I repeated.

"I turned seventeen two months ago." Two months ago. What did that mean? My mind was racing.

"How far along are you?" I asked. It was a stupid question. My brain wasn't functioning properly.

"What do you think, Joe?" you answered.

It was a month ago. I put it together. It was a month ago when we spent the weekend together. You were due in eight months. You'd be two months short of your eighteenth birthday. There was no getting around it. There was no way to stretch things out for an extra two months. I froze.

"Joe?" you shouted, trying to get my attention as I stared off into nowhere. I looked at you. You looked as if you were about to cry again. "Are you happy?"

I couldn't answer your question yet. "Do you know what you're going to do?"

"What do you mean?"

I should have been more tactful. I wasn't. I didn't think we had time. "Are you going to keep it?"

You began to cry again. Your tears made it clear that I was going to be a father. I was going to be the father of a child born to a woman under the age of eighteen. My child was going to be my enemy. That's what the rules said.

I went over to try to hold you, to try to comfort you so that I could explain my reaction. I tried to hug you and you slapped me across my face. It stung. There simply wasn't any time for pain. I reached out and grabbed you again, fighting through your flailing arms until your body was pressed against mine.

"I'm sorry. I'm sorry. I'm sorry," I chanted. I kept repeating the words. They were a mantra. I said them until you stopped struggling and your body went limp in my arms. The secret that I had just revealed to you was already beginning to fade into the background. I couldn't let it fade away. I couldn't let you forget about the War, about my part in the War. I couldn't let you forget any of that because now there was more to tell. You asked me why I fought. I couldn't answer you, not in a way that would make you understand. But now there was a new reason to fight. "Of course I'm happy," I said to you, trying to soothe you, "but you're a child. You're only seventeen. Are you sure you know what you're doing?"

"A child, Joe? Fuck you. You haven't treated me like a child up until now. You weren't treating me like a child last night. Maybe now's a bad time to start treating me like a fucking child." Seventeen. Jesus Christ. I looked at you. You were right. If either of us was acting like a child it was me.

"I'm sorry," I begged again. "I'm sorry for calling you a child. I'm sorry for how I reacted. I'm sorry for everything. I was just surprised. You caught me off guard." You sobbed into my shirt. It became damp and stuck to my skin. I decided to say whatever it was that I thought you'd want me to say. "I'll be happy to have a child with you. I am happy." I was still in too much shock to sound convincing. I knew it. You drank it in, though, wanting so badly to be convinced. "I want my child to be your child, but I have one more thing that I need to tell you." I held you away from me so that I could look into your eyes as I spoke. You were beginning to calm down, my words finally equaling what you had hoped to hear.

"I don't think I can take anything else," you replied, more prescient than you could even know.

"I'm sorry. But there is one more thing." Seventeen? I was only sixteen when this War was dropped on top of me. It seemed so young and so long ago. I lived through it, though. You were stronger than me. I told you about the rules again, the rules that I had always viewed as a safe harbor against the madness of this War. Now those same rules seemed beyond cruel. Rule number one: No killing innocent bystanders. Rule number two: No killing anyone under the age of eighteen. All that was left was to explain to you the third rule. Children born to those under the age of eighteen had to be handed over to the other side. You gasped when I told you, quickly grasping the idea. "I would tell you to run but they'd find you," I said. It was true. Running without me was no longer an option. "They'd find you and they'd take our child. If you're with me I can protect you."

"There has to be another way."

"No. There's not. If we are going to have this baby, these are the rules." You shook your head in disbelief. I wish I had better answers. Better answers didn't exist.

"So what do we do? I'm not giving this baby up, Joe." Your voice sounded stubborn and strong, stronger than I would have imagined possible at that moment.

I wasn't about to give our baby up, either, Maria. "We run," I said to you. "We run." Not yet, but soon.

The rest of the day went by in a blur. Both of us were exhausted. We were emotionally spent. We passed the day trying to absorb the new twists in our lives. We both knew that nothing would ever be the same. Every so often you would ask me a question or I would ask you one, trying to clarify some details, trying to clear up uncertainties, just trying to get to know each other. It was hard to believe that we'd only actually spent five days together.

"So, have you been to the doctor?" I remember asking.

"Why? Are you doubting that I'm pregnant?" You smiled again. "Are you still trying to get out of this?"

"No. No. No. Trust me. I just want to make sure you're taking proper care of yourself. I just want to make sure that you're taking proper care of my child."

"This is Canada," you replied. "Of course I've been to the doctor."

"So when are you due?" I began counting on my fingers.

"July," you said before I had a chance to finish counting.

"July," I replied, and smiled.

"What about my family?" you asked at one point. I barely ever heard you talk about your family. I mythologized them in my head. They were normal. They'd produced you.

"If people think they know anything, their lives will be turned upside down. They're innocent bystanders, so they can't be physically hurt, but there are a lot of ways that people can mess with you without physically hurting you."

"So I can't even reach out to them? I can't tell them where I am?"

"Well, there are ways. We'll be able to let them know that we're safe, maybe even send them pictures. But we won't be able to see them." You looked worried.

"Ever?" There was strength in your voice again. I could tell that you were already willing to make any sacrifice to protect our child.

"One day, after we get away, both sides will forget about us. They'll write us off. Then we can visit your family." Maybe, I thought. Maybe we'll be able to escape. "I want to meet them." I smiled, trying to cheer you up. "I'm sure they'll want to meet their grandchild."

"They're not going to understand," you said. Your voice was sad. I wanted to say something wise to make you feel better. I didn't say anything.

"So what are you, some kind of genius?" I asked.

"No," you replied. "I was homeschooled. My parents always kept me ahead of the other kids. I sit in classes now and I'm amazed at how smart the other students are."

"But you're two years younger than they are."

"So, what does age have to do with anything?"

"Why don't you just admit that you're really fucking smart?" I asked.

"Nice language, Joe."

"Maybe if I was homeschooled, too, I'd speak more better," I teased.

"Shut up," you said. You picked up a pillow and threw it at my head.

"I'm excited. My kid has like a fifty/fifty chance of being a genius," I replied after dodging the pillow. For the first time all day, you smiled.

"Does everyone have to kill people?" you asked. It was a fair question. You wanted to know if I'd volunteered for this job.

"No. There are lots of different jobs."

"So how did you end up with the one you have?"

"Aptitude testing," I replied.

"You're shitting me."

"I wish I was, but I'm not. I could have been sent to Intelligence, genealogy, a bunch of other jobs. But they analyze how you react during your initial training. After analyzing my reaction, they gave me a test and the test said that I'd make a good assassin." I looked at you. You didn't like it when I used that word. "I'll be honest, though. When I was seventeen, eighteen, I would have volunteered for this job. I was so angry with them."

"And now?" you asked.

"Now I wish my hands were clean. But I'm still angry."

"At them?" you asked.

"Yeah," I replied, "at the people who murdered my family."

"Do you think I'm a bad person?" I asked after building up the courage.

"No," you replied. I breathed a sigh of relief. "But I don't know you." I looked at you. You did know me. You just didn't know it. You already knew me better than anyone else in the world. I couldn't explain that to you, though. I'd have to show it to you. It would take time. "I love you, but I don't know you." Love was good. It had gotten us this far. "And I think that what you've done is wrong, no matter how you try to justify it." I accepted this. You hadn't lived my life. "And I'm a little scared of you. And I want you to stop killing."

"Fair enough," I replied. I couldn't ask for much more than that. I'd lived with fear my whole life. It was only natural that you'd be afraid, too, after what I had told you. I wish you weren't afraid of me, but time would take care of that. You didn't think I was a bad person. That was enough for me for now.

"So will you?"

"Will I what?"

"Stop killing."

"Yes, I will," I replied, "if they'll let me."

"Where are we going to go?" you asked. I hadn't thought about it. We were going to try to find a place where they wouldn't think to look for us.

"I don't know. South?"

"Why south?"

"I'll take you someplace warm," I replied.

"If we go someplace warm, what will I need you for?" you replied. Our first night together already seemed like a long time ago. I stared off into the distance, remembering the look on your face when you asked me to get under the covers with you. "What are you thinking about, Joe?" you asked.

"You," I answered, and left it at that.

Outside the window, day was slipping into evening. "So when do we leave?" you asked.

"Soon," I replied. "I have to take care of one thing. It will buy us some time. Then we can leave." You didn't ask any questions. I think you knew what I had to do. You had asked me to stop killing. I promised you that I would. I planned on keeping that promise but I couldn't yet. I needed to do one more job to buy us enough time to escape. For that, I needed to do some planning.

That evening, when we had run out of questions to ask each other, I checked into a hotel under the assumed name that Allen had given me. It was suddenly important that everything look as normal as possible. I was sure that they'd be tracking me, checking to make sure that I was up to the task this time. I remembered what Jared had told me, that they had big plans for me, but I knew that I couldn't be too careful. In my whole career, I had only blown one hit, but that one was enough. Plus, I was already a day behind. They had expected me to check into the hotel the night before. From here on out, my every move had to be by the book. Check into the hotel. Do the job. Then we would have a two-week head start. It would be two weeks before they expected me to call in again. We could get halfway around the world in two weeks. For all I knew, that's what it was going to take to get away.

I picked the hotel at random, eventually checking into a place in the old city that used to be a bank. As if to drive home the point that I was being monitored, I received a package in my hotel room only three hours after I'd checked in. They must have been monitoring the credit cards they'd given me because I was sure that I wasn't being followed. The package contained an updated status report on my target. There wasn't much in it that was new, two days a week teaching classes, one day at the strip club, lunch one day in Chinatown. The big Aussie had quit the job after getting out of the hospital. As far as they could tell, he'd fully recovered and gone back to Australia. My mark had hired a new bodyguard to replace him. This time the second bodyguard was one of them. Last time I had spent a week developing a plan that didn't work. Now I had two days to put together a new plan and I had to factor in the probability that the mark and his employees would be on high alert. There had been a killer in his house, only feet from his bedroom door, and he knew it. There's no way that didn't stick with a guy. No matter how I sliced it, this job was going to be a bitch. But this was it—the last job that I'd ever do. Get in, get out, and run. Then I'd be free. Then we'd be free to be together.

I took out my notes from the last job. I wanted to see if I could find any openings that I had failed to notice last time. His home was out. There's no way that they hadn't beefed up security since my last attempt. Besides, I'd feel like a fool screwing up the same job, the same way, twice. I had to find another location. There was too much security in the strip club. I thought about the university, but I worried that this was too close to you. I hoped that no one knew you even existed and planned on keeping it that way. Plus, there were too many eyes on campus, too many young, alert people who could ruin things. I needed to get my mark as isolated as possible. I needed to start with a smaller crowd.

There was only one option left, the Chinese restaurant where he went for lunch once a week. It was a small place, maybe twenty tables. They had two small rooms off to the sides, which were separated from the general dining area by wooden beads. My mark and his business partners always took one of these rooms. The bodyguards approached the lunch the same way every time. They split up. One ate with the mark, sitting next to him. The other ate alone in the general dining area, keeping an eye on the restaurant. The situation was far from ideal, but it was the best of the bad options. So the venue was settled. Now I needed a plan.

Poison? It would be poetic justice to kill him with one of his own poisons. The idea was too complicated, though. How could I poison him without running the risk of poisoning the other people at the table? I kept bumping into the same fact. Killing people was easy. Killing the one you wanted to kill was hard.

I began asking myself what Michael would do. I couldn't help but shake the feeling that I had simply overplanned my first attempt. I'd tried it Jared's way. I just wasn't up to Jared's standards. He was the one who'd gotten promoted. So what would Michael do? He'd probably walk in, pull out his gun, take out the bodyguard in the dining room, walk into the side room, plug the other bodyguard, plug the mark, and walk out as if he owned the place. That was just Michael's style. It went against everything we were taught. But my mark knew everything we were taught. He was taught it too. I would have to be careful not to shoot any bystanders and I'd have to work quickly. I'd have to get out of there before anyone else in the restaurant had a chance to realize what was going on. It was risky, but I was going to have to start getting used to risky.

Lunch in Chinatown was the next day. I tried to concentrate on the job. It wasn't easy.

The next morning I got up early and headed over to my mark's house. I had decided that I should follow them throughout the day, all the way up until they went for lunch. I wanted to make sure I had a few hours to watch the new bodyguard. I needed to have his image imprinted in my brain. I needed my aim to be true this time. I couldn't afford to have any doubts when the hit went down.

The new bodyguard had spent the night at my mark's house. He was blond with sharp blue eyes. He was smaller than the Aussie, but there was something about him that made me nervous. He looked a little crazy. He was, at most, five foot seven. He lacked the spectacular build the other bodyguards had. Intel hadn't given me much information about him other than that he was one of them and that he'd been hospitalized multiple times, at least three of which were for gunshot wounds. So I knew ahead of time that he was a tough person to kill.

As I followed my mark, it dawned on me that this was my last hit, my last job. After this, I'd never have to hear Allen's voice again. I could go wherever I wanted to. I could take you and run to anywhere in the world. We could have a child that wouldn't have to worry about death and murder and war. We'd be free. The whole idea began to scare the shit out of me. What scared me wasn't the running. It was what would happen after the running. I began to doubt myself in ways that I couldn't explain to you then. Suddenly, the idea of becoming a father was terrifying. All I knew how to do, all anyone had ever taught me to do, was one thing. Killing, up to that moment, had been my entire life. I took a deep breath to try to calm my nerves. I felt the weight of the gun in my backpack and found it comforting.

I followed my mark and his men downtown and watched them as they headed into the same office building I had staked out only a few weeks earlier. Just like last time, I went to the café across the street to watch the building entrance and wait. I remembered that the last time I'd sat in that café I was bored, counting down every moment as it passed. This time, I sat there terrified, wishing that time would slow down so that I'd have a few extra moments to pull myself together. The questions in my head wouldn't stop. I looked across the street again and watched the motionless door. I prayed that it would never open. I placed my backpack in my lap. I slipped my hand inside it so that I could feel the weight of the gun in my palm. I thought back to the moment, only a few months earlier, when I was sitting in the parking lot of that mall in New Jersey waiting for Jared and Michael to come and pick me up. I remembered watching the people go in and out, being envious of their lives. I looked at them and saw no fear. They came to the mall on the weekend to buy a few things and then head back to their suburban homes to watch television and wait until Monday morning, when they would wake up and shuttle off to jobs they hated. I envied their lives, their "normal" lives—their pointless, tedious, normal lives. Is that what I was destined for? And what about Michael and Jared? What about the others on my side? What about the children that I'd taught? I remembered what Jared had told me only a few nights earlier. They believed in me more than I believed in myself. Could I just give this War up? Give up the only fight I'd been raised to care about? Was I ready for any of this? I caressed the handle of the gun. Maybe I liked killing. Maybe I had seen so much death that it was the only thing that made me feel comfortable. I tried to chase these ideas from my head.

I nursed my drink, watching the front door of the office building, waiting for them to come out, waiting for my destiny to come out that door and head down the street toward Chinatown. I was afraid. I had never felt that type of fear before. Not even when I was kneeling on that beach in New Jersey, my hands tied behind my back, a gun pointed in my face, did I experience fear like this. The fear I felt on that beach was simple. I was afraid to die, but it was only for me. All I had to lose was my own pitiful life. But from now on, if I fail, I fail you and I fail our child. Up until that moment, I had been a soldier in a war that was bigger than me. I was a pawn. I knew it. My only responsibility was death. Even if I failed, it led to death. A successful job meant they died, a failed job meant I did. Now I was responsible for life too. It was terrifying. Right then, sitting alone in that café, the butt of that gun resting in my hand, I had to remind myself that that my only skill in the world was still going to serve me well, at least one more time.

After a few hours, my mark and his entourage came out of the building, the new bodyguard in front, my mark in the middle, the American behind them. The new bodyguard's eyes scanned the street as he moved. For a second he looked in my direction. I felt his stare in my gut. The three of them left the building and started down the street. It was time to move. Suddenly, the doubt was gone. The fear was gone. I was on the job for the last time. I'd have time for doubts again when I was done.

I didn't follow them to the restaurant, fearing that I'd be spotted. I knew where they were going. All I had to do was figure out which of the two bodyguards was sitting in the general dining area and which of the two private rooms my mark was in. Then I'd walk through the door, stroll casually up to the first bodyguard, shoot him at close range, walk into the private room, shoot the second body-guard, and then shoot my mark. Then I'd walk out of the restaurant through the kitchen and disappear forever. If I was successful, it would be a job to brag to people about, though I knew that my days of bragging were over. After this job was done, I knew that I'd never see Michael or Jared again. I couldn't put them in that position. I couldn't ask them to ignore the rules for me.

As I walked to the restaurant, I continued to visualize the event. I tried to look at all the angles, tried to make sure there was nothing that I was overlooking. I assumed that no one in the kitchen was going to try to stop me. It was a safe assumption. I'd have a gun in my hand that I'd proved I was willing to use. I tried to picture it in every sce-nario. First, my mark would be in the room to the right. Second, in the room to the left. I tried imagining how the job would go with each bodyguard in the different positions. I hoped that the new guy would be in the general dining area. I wanted to get him out of the way first.

When I got to the end of the block, I peeked around the corner to see if I could locate the entourage. The three of them were standing outside the restaurant waiting. The new bodyguard was taking a long, deep drag off a cigarette. He didn't open his mouth after inhaling, instead blowing two long streams of smoke out of his nostrils. I turned back behind the building, leaning against the wall to make sure that they couldn't see me. I listened but none of them spoke. I kept looking around me, knowing that I would have to move if I thought I saw my mark's business associates coming. I got lucky. They came from the opposite direction. I heard my mark greet them. I recognized his voice instantly from the lecture. There was a general greeting, followed by some introductions. There was no discussion of business outside—that would be taken care of inside the restau-rant. I knew what these men were here for. They were buying weap-ons. I just didn't know for what war. I didn't really care.

I wanted to get a good look at the buyers before they went inside.

I needed to be sure I could differentiate them from my targets. I stepped forward for a second and casually looked both ways along the street, pretending that I was looking for someone. As I did I glanced over the faces of the buyers. There were four of them. They were wearing similar outfits. Each had on black slacks, a dark shirt, and a bright tie. They each wore a black leather jacket in lieu of a suit jacket. All had dark hair. They looked like brothers. Once I caught a quick glimpse of them, I stepped back into the shadows. Mistaken identity wouldn't be a problem. My only worry now was that they'd be armed. If any one of them had a gun and decided to play hero, I was in deep shit. I wasn't Dirty Harry. A gunfight wasn't something that I was prepared for.

I stood there for a few moments, my back leaning against the brick wall behind me, and listened, waiting to hear them go inside. I wanted to see them being seated so that I knew which side of the restaurant they'd be on. The left side would be easier, as it provided faster access to the kitchen, but either would do. It was only important that I knew. After walking in and shooting someone in the head, walking to the wrong private room would be a disaster. I waited until I heard the last footsteps on the stairs leading up to the restaurant's front door, then I turned the corner and peered inside through the front windows. The restaurant was rather small. The building itself was bright red, with a dragon carved into the archway above the door. The entire front of the building had waist-high windows that opened up onto the street on the hotter days of summer. I looked through those windows and watched as they showed my mark to his table. I was in luck. The new bodyguard entered the building last. As the last in, he'd be sitting in the general seating area. While the larger party was being escorted to the private room on the left side of the restaurant (luck appeared to be on my side), another waitress motioned the blue-eyed bodyguard to an empty table in the back right-hand corner of the main dining area. He nodded and took his seat.

I could have still called it off. We could have run. I could have skipped the hit and gone back to get you and we could have left that afternoon. We'd still have a little bit of a head start. It would probably take them a day or two before they realized that I wasn't going to do the job. It would take a day or two before the manhunt started. We could get pretty far in two days. We could have flown to Europe or Asia. We could have gone to visit the big Aussie back in his hometown. The world was small. A day or two might have been enough time to run and hide, but our trail would be fresh. Our scent would still have been on everything we touched. It didn't matter where we could get to because they could get there just as quick. We needed more time. We needed time not just to run away but to get lost.

I took a deep breath. One job. That was it. I took the gun out of my backpack and placed it in my jacket pocket. I slung the backpack over my shoulder. The backpack now contained the other two magazines for my gun, three passports in three different names, and a few hundred dollars in cash. I was ready to leave this job and be gone forever. I hoped it wouldn't come to that, but I was prepared. I stuck my hand in my coat pocket and wrapped my fingers around the gun. I slipped my index finger over the trigger and caressed it lightly. The silencer was still on the muzzle. I had never removed it. The safety was off. It was time to go.

I walked straight toward the restaurant's front door. I walked up the steps, pulled open the door, and walked toward the hostess. As I walked, I stared straight ahead, but out of the corner of my eye, I watched the blue-eyed bodyguard. He was watching me too. I took two steps toward the hostess. She smiled at me and was about to ask me how large my party would be. Before she could get the words out, however, I saw the bodyguard move. He gently took his napkin off his lap, and folded it on the plate in front of him. It was odd. Why would he take the time to fold his napkin? I stepped quickly past the hostess. I saw the confusion on her face. I took a few large steps toward the new bodyguard. By then he was on his feet. He had an object in his left hand. I stepped closer to him. He began to move his left hand toward me. I made it to about ten feet from him before I pulled the gun from my jacket pocket. I moved quickly, quicker than he did. I lifted my gun toward him and fired. One shot. I hit him in the head. Not between the eyes, but in the head nonetheless. He had gotten his arm about three quarters of the way toward me. Some blood squirted on the wall behind him and he fell to the ground.

No one in the restaurant moved. The hostess, sensing that something was wrong as soon as I walked past her, stifled a scream. Other than that, the place was a museum, a funeral home. I'd expected everything to move slowly. I'd expected time to slow down. I'd expected to see everything in slow motion. For a few moments, it was like that. Once I pulled the trigger the first time, however, everything went into hyperspeed.

I walked immediately across the restaurant, toward the private dining area. No one in the restaurant moved. I tried to stay focused. All the images outside the small tunnel of my vision became blurry. I walked holding the gun out in front of me. I pushed the hanging beads in the doorway aside with my left hand and stepped toward the long rectangular table. All six of the diners looked up at me. My mark and his bodyguard were seated against the wall facing me. The four buyers were in chairs with their backs to me, but they turned to look at me when I entered. I didn't bother to make eye contact. I lifted the gun again and fired one shot directly into the chest of the American bodyguard. He looked at me for a second and then looked down at his chest, confused. Then I turned toward my mark. I aimed my gun at his head and fired. Then I fired again. Then again. I don't remember how many times I pulled the trigger. The first two shots went into his head. After that, I just riddled the bullets into him. With each shot his body jerked and each time his body moved I lost confidence that he was actually dead. Everything hinged on his being dead. By the time I was done pulling the trigger, I could have killed five of him.

Just then I heard a loud popping sound coming from behind me. It broke my trance and I stopped firing. I looked around the table. The American was just sitting there, his eyes glazed over, not moving. My mark was hunched over in his chair, his face nearly touching his plate. All the planning and work that went into the first attempt on his life and now he was dead just like that. It really had been that simple. Then I looked over the stern, ugly faces of the buyers. They looked stoic. They weren't about to involve themselves in someone else's battles. One reached down for his spoon and continued eating his soup.

I heard another pop from behind me and suddenly felt a searing, burning sensation in the back of my left leg. I turned and looked back through the beaded curtain. There was the blue-eyed bodyguard, standing, holding his gun out in front of him. Half his face was covered in blood. He kept one eye closed to avoid getting blood in it. He stumbled forward and pulled the trigger again. This time the bullet buzzed by my head and entered the wall behind me. I heard someone scream and saw a few people run toward the front door. The bodyguard lifted the gun again, but before he could pull the trigger, I pushed my way through the beads and headed toward the kitchen. Until I took my first step, I had forgotten about the pain in my leg, but as I walked the leg screamed out in agony. I had been shot in the back of my thigh, luckily a few inches above my knee. I made my way toward the kitchen as fast as I could. I heard another popping sound and a whizzing by my ear. I had to get out of there.

I walked quickly through the kitchen, holding the gun up by my head. The kitchen staff stayed out of my way. I limped toward the back door. I exited the building near the Dumpsters in the back. It smelled like rotting meat. The scent from the garbage combined with the searing pain in my leg almost made me sick. I swallowed hard. I had to keep moving. I had to get away from the scene. I made it about half a block down the back alley when I heard the kitchen door open behind me. I looked back and there was the blue-eyed bodyguard stumbling toward me like a zombie from a low-budget horror movie. He was a walking nightmare. I could see where I had shot him, grazing the top of his head and blowing off a piece of his skull. It wasn't a direct hit. He lifted his gun toward me and fired again. The bullet whizzed by me and I heard glass shatter. The bodyguard's aim was gone. He was losing blood, getting weaker. His one closed eye must have been wreaking havoc on his depth perception. Still, throw enough darts with your eyes closed and you're bound to hit the bull's-eye eventually. I wasn't going to stand around and let him use me for target practice.

I tried to run around the next corner and disappear, but I couldn't push off with my left leg. Instead I wobbled toward the turn, the walking nightmare following close behind me. Despite his injury, his legs were in better shape than mine. I turned the corner before he got too close to me. Then I waited.

I could hear him walking, both his feet dragging along the ground like a drunk's. I looked down at my jeans. Everything below my knee on the back of my left leg was a dark purple. Fuck, I thought. This wasn't good. The monster stepped closer to the corner. He came relentlessly. If he'd had any sense, he would have taken another route, or he just would have given up and tried to save himself. He came nonetheless. His left hand, extended with his gun out in front of him, crossed the edge of the building first. I reached out with my hand and grabbed his wrist. I pulled his hand, holding the gun, far above our heads to keep him from being able to point the gun at me. The motion ended up pulling his body toward mine. Our chests collided and our faces were now only inches apart. He was weak.

I looked directly into his eyes and saw death. How many times had

I seen that before? He returned my gaze. Only God knows what he saw. Then he spoke. "They brought me here to kill you," he said to me, the blood pouring down his face. As he spoke blood ran into his mouth and collected in the corner of his lips. The thickness of the blood muffled his words, making him sound as if he were half under-water. He stared directly into my eyes. "They brought me here to kill you. They knew you'd come back. They knew." With each word, I could feel more strength slip from his body. I lifted my gun and pointed it into his chest. Even in his weakened state he wouldn't take his eyes off mine. I jammed the muzzle of the gun into his ribs. I'm sure he felt it, but he continued to stare at me coldly. "They brought me here to kill you," he repeated again, spraying blood on me as he spoke. I pulled the trigger, sending a bullet into his heart. He gasped one more time after I fired. Suddenly, we were no longer struggling. My hand was still wrapped tightly around his wrist and I was holding him up. I had seen death before and his was imminent. I kept holding him up. I decided to let him die on his feet. With his last gasp of life, he looked at me again. His eyes were now confused, as if he couldn't understand what was happening, as if he'd completely forgotten who I was. Then his body shuddered and he was gone.

I dropped his body in the alley. I reached down, and with the only clean patch of his shirt that I could find, I wiped the blood from my face. The struggle over, the pain in my leg returned with a vengeance. I had to get back to the hotel. I had to fix myself up as much as pos-sible. I had to find you and then we had to leave. It all seemed so urgent now. I should have gotten you ready before this. I should have told you to wait at the hotel. The blue-eyed bodyguard's words kept echoing in my mind. "They knew you'd come back. They knew." I could hear him speaking them again and again through his blood-stained lips. They know, I thought. They always fucking know. If we were going to get away, we had to give ourselves as much time as possible. We'd run and hide and run and hide until our trail was untraceable. It was the only way.

I took my gun and put it back in my backpack. I looked back at my leg again. I could see the hole in my jeans where the bullet had gone through. There was nothing in the front. The bullet was still lodged in my leg. I'd have to get back to the hotel, clean out the wound, and pressurize it to stop the bleeding. I was pretty sure I'd be okay. There was pain, but I didn't think that the bullet had hit any bone. It was simply lodged in my muscle. Clean the wound, make sure it doesn't get infected, stop the bleeding, and I'd be fine. That and a half a bottle of painkillers would do the trick.

I limped out into the street, gazing at myself in the reflection in the window of a nearby building to make sure that I looked presentable. From the knee up I looked fine. My skin was a bit shiny from sweat, but there was nothing too extreme to give me away. I hadn't heard a single siren yet. Any moment, I expected to hear the roar of police cars racing down the street. The sound didn't come. It didn't make sense to me, but I wasn't about to question my luck. I'd read later that the buyers, who were themselves armed to the teeth, had warned the entire restaurant not to call the police. They did not want to find themselves mixed up with Canadian officials. They stayed in the restaurant for another fifteen minutes, guns drawn, sitting across from two corpses, and finished their meal. When they finally left, they told everyone in the restaurant to wait twenty minutes before calling the police. They said that they'd find anyone who disobeyed. They asked for twenty minutes, they got ten. Those ten minutes probably saved my life.

My leg ached with each step. I bit down on my bottom lip and kept moving. The inevitable sirens, those that I wouldn't hear until I was half a block from my hotel, inspired me to keep moving. My hotel was only about ten blocks from the restaurant, maybe half a mile. The walk took me nearly twenty minutes. As I neared the hotel, I heard sirens for the first time. They'd be a few minutes too late to catch anyone and twenty minutes too late to save anyone. When I reached the hotel, I gritted my teeth and did my best to walk through the lobby without a limp. I went immediately over to the elevator and pushed the "up" button. The waiting there, watching the numbers above the elevator drop ever so slowly as the elevator car approached the lobby, was the most painful moment of all. I turned my body so that no one could see the back of my bloodstained jeans. After about thirty seconds, the bell went off and I stepped inside the elevator. Once inside, I slammed on the button to close the doors.

When the doors opened again, I stumbled out and headed toward my room. I took out the key card and opened my door, nearly falling over as I pushed my way inside. I fell to the floor and immediately stripped off my jeans. The blood on the jeans had begun to coagulate so I had to actually rip the jeans off my leg. It would have been fine except for the fact that the bullet hole had started to scab over, so when I pulled off the jeans, I pulled off the scab as well. The blood, which had slowed down, began to flow freely again. I went into the bathroom and turned on the hot water in the shower. I stepped into the water, as hot as it would go, and began to scrub the wound with soap. I'd have to make do with the limited resources that I had. After scrubbing out the wound, I walked over to the minibar. I left the water running in the shower. I opened up the minibar and grabbed every miniature bottle of liquor they had and dragged them back into the shower. I lay down in the tub on my stomach, letting the hot water splash against my back, and, one by one, I opened up the bottles of vodka, scotch, and gin and poured them into the hole in the back of my leg. Each successive bottle stung a little less. When the alcohol was gone, I scrubbed the wound again with soap and water. It continued to bleed. I got out of the shower and dried myself off. I took an old T-shirt and I wrapped it around my leg, tying it tightly over the bullet hole to stop the bleeding. Once that was done, I grabbed a bottle of painkillers and downed a handful. Eventually that would dull the pain, although I'd need something stronger if I really wanted to forget it.

What was there left to do? I sat down in a chair, naked except for the T-shirt tied around my leg, and took a moment to rest. "They brought me here to kill you. They knew you'd come back. They knew." What the fuck did that mean? My mind raced. I wanted to sleep. I wanted to lie down and sleep. I wanted to forget the faces of the dead. It wasn't going to happen. Not then, not ever. We had to move. I picked up the phone and dialed your number. It rang twice. You picked up.

"Maria. It's me. We have to go."

"I know." Your voice sounded sad, resigned, but there was no urgency. I needed urgency.

"No, Maria. You don't know. We have to go now."

"Now?"

"Yes."

"Why? What happened? Why now?"

"Just trust me. We have to go now. Come to my hotel. Bring everything you think you'll need but no more than what you can carry."

"This is crazy, Joe. We can't go now. We can't just get up and go like that!" It was crazy. You had no idea how crazy. I didn't even know how crazy.

"We don't have a choice, Maria." I tried to keep my voice calm but stern. I should have prepared you better for this. But it didn't matter. No matter how well I prepared you, you wouldn't have been ready. After telling you where I was, I got dressed. I left the T-shirt tied around my leg, although I was pretty sure that the bleeding had stopped. I threw everything I owned in a bag. I called down to the front desk and told them that I would be out of town for a few days but that I would keep paying for the room and that I would like them to hold it. They were happy to oblige. Almost exactly nineteen minutes after I had hung up on you, there was a knock on my door.

We took a bus to Boston. You slept most of the way, your head leaning up against my chest. As requested, you had packed light, carrying only a couple changes of clothes and a toiletry bag. I stared down at your face as you slept, your head bobbing up and down as the bus bounced over the bumps in the road. You slept through the bumps like they were nothing. I had to protect you. I didn't want to be the worst thing that ever happened to you. My hope was that one day you'd think that meeting me was a blessing. Every morning I wake up with that same hope.

We didn't have any trouble at the border. I warned you that I was traveling with a fake passport and under a fake name. The lying didn't faze you. That boded well for our future.

When we got to Boston we rented a car. We'd drive the rest of the way. We were headed to New Jersey. I thought we'd be safe there. I didn't call my mother to warn her that we were coming. After this trip, I knew that it was doubtful that I'd ever see my mother again. Before that happened, I wanted her to meet the mother of her grandchild. For one moment, I just wanted us to feel like a regular family.

Throughout the car ride from Boston to New Jersey, you were quiet. The only question you asked during the entire trip was "Are you sure you can do this, Joe?"

"Do what?" I asked, trying to figure out what you were talking about.

"Are you sure you can leave the War behind?"

I thought about it. I thought about what the War meant to me. I thought about the family of mine that they'd killed. I thought about my father and my sister. I thought about what Jared had said about my future. I thought about the friends I was leaving behind. I knew I'd never find friends like that again. "I'm sure," I answered.

"How can you be sure?" you asked, sensing my thoughts, knowing that I hadn't given up on the War.

I looked at you. I looked down at your stomach, still hiding the secret that would change my life forever. "I had a good reason to fight. Now I have a better reason to run."

Twelve

It was dark by the time we reached my mother's house in northern New Jersey. We had been on the road for nearly five hours. I wasn't comfortable speeding. The guys at Intel would be able to track us to Boston, where we rented the car using one of the fake IDs that they had given me. My hope was that eventually, as long as we spent cash and stayed out of trouble, they'd lose our trail. It was still two weeks before I was supposed to check in. We were supposed to have those weeks to lose ourselves among the masses.

I pulled into the driveway of my mother's little house and killed the lights. You were asleep when I pulled up. You'd been sleeping a lot. Thus far, it was really the only sign that you were pregnant. I knew my mother hadn't heard us pull up because I didn't see her peer out of the kitchen window the way she did whenever she had visitors. This was going to be a surprise. I looked at you, asleep in the passenger seat, and realized that this was going to be a series of surprises. I thought about how long it had been since I'd actually seen my mother. Three years? Five years? When was the last time I'd seen her? I couldn't even remember. I looked at the house. I had so many memories of that house—some good, some awful.

I leaned over and shook you awake. "We're here."

You woke up slowly and gazed out the windows, turning your head to get a sense of your surroundings. All you could really see from the car were trees and forest. "This is New Jersey?"

"Yeah," I whispered, leaning over to kiss your forehead. I was happy—as happy as I could be under the circumstances. Happy to be home, happy to be bringing you home with me. "It's not all toxic waste dumps and highways."

"It's beautiful," you said. You opened the door and stepped out of the car. The air was brisk but still much warmer than in Montreal. It smelled like pine trees and burning wood. Mom had a fire going inside. You couldn't see another house from the driveway, just woods. "You grew up here?"

"For most of my childhood, yeah. We moved into this house after Dad died. This was supposed to be our little hiding spot. We probably should have moved after they killed my sister but I think my mom just thought, Fuck it. If they wanted to come get her, let them come. They never came back. My friend Jared lived only ten minutes from here and my friend Michael lived a couple towns over. I met them when I lived in this house, so not all the memories are bad. Where they grew up, it's a little more civilized."

"This is where they killed your sister?" I nodded. You began hugging yourself and rubbing your arms to fight the cold.

I slammed the car door behind me, as I had every evening coming home as a teenager. It was a signal that my mother and I had. We were supposed to make noise when we came home because they would never make noise. You flinched when the door slammed. The cool night air had been so peaceful. "Sorry about that."

"That's okay," you replied.

After slamming the door closed, I stood there for a few seconds, peering into the kitchen window, waiting. As if on cue, my mother's face appeared. She pushed aside the curtains and looked down at us. She looked old—old and tired. I waved into the window as she looked down. When she realized who it was her face began to beam. Then it disappeared again. I knew she'd be making one last mad dash around the house to straighten up. She'd want it to look good for guests. We were probably the first guests she'd had in years. "Let's go," I finally said to you. You started walking down the thin stone path toward the front door. "Not that way," I called out to you as you walked. "We're family. We go in through the side door." I led you around the side of the house toward the door that went directly into the kitchen. You huddled behind me as I knocked on the door, hiding yourself from my mother's view until I was able to make a proper introduction.

My mother was at the door in a flash, pulling it open and grabbing me in a giant hug before we even had a chance to say hello. After a minute, she finally eased up on her grasp of me but she didn't let go. As she held on to me she said, "This is such a wonderful surprise. Just wonderful."

"Good to see you, too, Ma," I said as she finally let me go.

"Now come inside. It's cold out," my mother ordered. That's when I stepped aside to give her a view of you. "And who is this?" my mother asked me with a triumphant smile on her face.

"Mother," I went forward with the formal introduction, "this is my girlfriend, Maria. Maria, this is my overbearing mother." My mother gave me a playful slap across my arm.

You reached your hand out, expecting my mother to shake it, but in seconds she was all over you with a hug nearly as long as the one she'd given me. I looked over my mother's shoulder at your face as she hugged you. You were in a daze. I had told you so much about the horrors in my life that my mother must have seemed an anachronism.

When my mother finally let you go, she took two steps back and looked you up and down as if eyeing a piece of artwork. "Well, aren't you the cutest little thing?" she said. "Well, Maria, you can call me Joan. It's wonderful to meet you." You didn't reply, still dazed from the welcome. "Now, let's get both of you inside before we all freeze to death." Then my mother ushered us inside. I limped up the steps.

"Oh my, Joseph, are you okay?" my mother shouted when she noticed the limp. The wound was healing well but it still hurt. The pain had dulled but spread over my entire leg.

"Just a small work injury," I replied. She took that as a signal to let it drop for now.

The place was exactly as I had remembered it. The spatulas were even in the same place. My mother led us through the kitchen and straight into the tiny living room. She sat you down right in front of the fire, trying to warm you up. I hadn't brought a girl home since I was seventeen. I really didn't know how my mother was going to react. I sat down in the love seat opposite my mother, who sat in the middle of the couch. We were each, at most, five feet from each other. My mother looked us both over again in silence, as if trying to paint the picture with her mind. Eventually she spoke. "So, to what do I owe this visit?" She looked at you when she asked the question. You looked at me. Perhaps we should have prepared for the questions in the car. I hoped she didn't think we'd come to announce an engagement.

"I got a couple of weeks' vacation, Ma. Maria and I decided to take it together." You looked relieved when I spoke, relieved that you didn't have to talk yet. "I wanted her to meet you." I knew that this last part would make my mother happy and hoped, in vain, that it would stop the questions for a little while.

"Where did you guys drive from?" Again, my mother looked at you when she asked the question. Again, I answered the question anyway.

"We drove from Boston after taking a bus from Montreal. Maria's a college student in Montreal." The conversation was a little dance with neither you nor my mother knowing exactly what you were allowed to say. My mother handled it by asking questions. You handled it by shutting up completely.

"Really? A college girl? That's wonderful. We could use a little education around here. And what are you studying, dear?" You looked up at me to make sure that you could safely answer this question. I nodded to you to let you know that it was safe to speak.

"I'm still trying to decide between Psychology and Religion," you replied.

My mother nodded. "Aren't we all," my mother replied with a laugh. "Well, those sound like wonderful choices. Montreal? Are you Canadian?"

"I'm going to grab us some food, Ma," I interrupted. "You got anything in the fridge?"

"Oh, my, where are my manners?" My mother started to stand up. "You guys have been traveling all day. I should have offered you something."

"Sit down, Ma," I said. "I know my way around our kitchen. You stay and keep Maria company. By the time I get back, I'm sure you'll know more about her than I do. You hungry, Maria?"

"Starving," you replied, dropping your guard when you spoke to me. We'd stopped to grab a snack in Connecticut on the way down but hadn't had a real meal all day.

"You want anything, Ma?"

"Well, I'm not about to let my son and his girlfriend eat alone." My mother's voice sounded ecstatic just to be saying the word *girlfriend*. I almost thought she was going to trill her *r*'s. I made my way into the kitchen and left you and my mother to your own devices. My mother knew the game. She wasn't going to say anything controversial. She'd leave all that for conversations with me later. I just wanted you two to talk. I wanted you to get to know each other. I knew that these fleeting moments would likely be the only time the two of you would ever get to spend with each other. Despite everything that happened, I still treasure those moments.

The refrigerator was predictably empty. My mother had virtually given up eating about the same time that we moved into this place. The cupboard, however, had enough for me to throw a meal together. I could hear you and my mother, mostly my mother, chatting away in the other room as I put on a pot of spaghetti. The house was warm. It was cozy. I set the table so that we could all eat together in the kitchen. The kitchen table was pushed up against the wall so, without moving it, there was only room for three people. That was plenty for that evening. I set it up so that you would sit on one side of me and my mother would sit on the other. As the pasta cooked, I opened up a can of crushed tomatoes and took out some seasoning to make some sauce. "Do you have any wine for the spaghetti sauce, Ma?" I shouted from the kitchen, interrupting whatever topic the two of you had moved on to.

"Sure," my mother replied. She got up from the couch and walked into the kitchen. She grabbed a bottle of wine from her little wine rack. "We'll have to open a new bottle, but I don't think we'll have a better occasion for that anyway." She handed me the bottle and came over and kissed me on the cheek. "She seems lovely," my mother said to me in a whisper. "You've outdone yourself."

"I know," I replied.

Then my mother gave me a look. It was just a quick glance but I knew that it meant that she wanted to talk to me later, alone. "Why is this the first I'm hearing of her?" she asked me with a smile. I simply shrugged and lifted my eyebrows in response. She'd have more questions later. I wanted her to get to know you a little bit before I had to answer them. It had taken me all of ten minutes to fall for you. I figured that it shouldn't take my mother more than an hour.

I uncorked the wine and poured a full glass into my spaghetti sauce. My mother went back into the living room and the two of you continued to chat. You never told me what you talked about while I was cooking. The entire subject of my mother eventually became taboo. When I called the two of you in for dinner, you were happy. You glanced at me before sitting down at the dinner table and your eyes twinkled.

"Look at my son, the chef," my mother purred as she sat down. "It didn't take you long to domesticate this one, did it, Maria?"

"Don't look at me," you replied, staring down at the food. "This is the first time he's ever cooked for me."

"How shameful, Joey. Didn't I teach you how to properly treat a woman?"

"Sit. Eat. Let's see if it's edible before we start complaining that I don't cook enough." Just as I sat down at the table my mother got up. She stood up from her chair and ran over to one of the cabinets to retrieve three wineglasses.

"Before we eat," she spoke as she came back over to the table, "a toast." She filled each of the wineglasses with what was left in the bottle of wine I had used to make the spaghetti sauce. "I guess I'll have to make up for my son's bad manners." This was the happiest I could ever remember my mother. At least I gave her this moment. She lifted her glass. "To my son, who I don't see nearly enough, and to his new friend, who I hope to see more of." All three of us clinked our wine-filled glasses together. "Anything to add, Joey?" My mother looked at me. I have no idea what she expected me to say.

"To not drinking alone," I added, barely remembering where I had heard the toast before.

"Very classy," my mother scolded me, but we all clinked our glasses together again. My mother and I each lifted the glass to our lips. You slipped yours back onto the table. My mother noticed. There was never any chance that she wouldn't. "You're not drinking, sweetie?"

"I'm not much of a drinker, Joan," you responded.

"Well, just a sip, dear. It's not a real toast if you don't have a sip," my mother pressed on. She watched you carefully.

"That's birthday wishes and fortune cookies, Mom," I butted in, eyeing my mother to let her know to drop the subject. "It's been a long day. Let's eat." I forked some of the spaghetti onto each of our plates. I started with equal portions. My mother didn't finish hers. I had seconds. You had thirds. I was amazed by how much you could eat already.

We chatted through dinner. My mother asked us how long we were planning on staying. We hadn't even discussed this yet. I told her that we were staying for two nights. That just sounded right. There were a few things that I wanted to show you in town before we left. I didn't think two days was too long. We'd still have ten days to make our run for it. Then my mother asked us where we were going on our vacation. Again, I didn't know. You looked at me when she asked this as if you were wondering yourself. Even if I knew where we were going, I wouldn't have told my mother. I wouldn't tell any-one. The fewer people who knew the better, for them and for us. South, I said. Maybe we'd go to Graceland, I said. You seemed to be enamored with that idea.

"Well, don't let him make you stay at any of the cheap hotels, dear," my mother said to you, reaching across the dinner table and placing her hand over yours. "He's got to learn a little class someday."

"Yes, ma'am," you replied with a giggle. I hoped you remembered that this wasn't a vacation—that we had to stay diligent. For now, I let it go.

When we were done eating, you helped my mother clear the table. Both of you insisted that, since I had cooked, I got to relax during the cleanup. Once the kitchen was back in order, you told me that you were tired and ready to go to bed. My mother showed you to my sister's old room. My mother hadn't touched it since my sister died. Pictures of her and her friends from high school still sat in frames on the bookshelves. A few pictures of her with her college friends were hung with thumbtacks on the wall above her desk. Her high school French award was still prominently displayed as if she'd won it yesterday. I carried your bag up the stairs and dropped it off in the room. "So I guess I'm alone in here tonight, huh?" you asked me as you placed your nearly empty duffel bag at the foot of the bed.

"I think so. My mom's a little old-fashioned," I replied. "Are you going to be all right?"

"I'll be fine. It's so peaceful here." You stood up on the tips of your toes to give me a small kiss on the lips. "Your mother's sweet."

"Yeah, to you," I teased. "Now that you're going to bed, you're leaving me alone to face the inquisition."

"So we're staying here two days?"

"Yeah, that sounds about right."

"And then we're going to Graceland?"

"We'll see."

When I got back downstairs, my mother was waiting for my return.

"She's lovely," my mother said to me before I reached the bottom of the stairs.

"You don't know the half of it," I replied with a smirk. I was a little boy again, showing my mother the gem that I'd found in the woods.

"How long have you two been together?" She was trying to gauge how serious this was. She should have known simply by the fact that I'd brought you home.

"Long enough to know that I never want to be with anybody else."

"Well." My mother paused, taken aback by my response. Then she sat back down on the couch. I sat across from her. "How long has that been?" She smiled again.

"A few months, but it seems like longer. We hit it off instantly."

"She's young, Joe. She's young to be making this type of commitment." I thought she was trying to protect me.

"She's young in some ways. She's not so young in a lot of others. She's smarter than me. Sometimes it feels like she's older than I am."

"How old is she?"

"She's a sophomore in college, Mom. That's not that young," I used the same half-truth that you had used on me. My mother had put me on the defensive. Something seemed off.

"Is she one of us?" Finally, she asked the question that I was sure she was dying to ask from the moment she first laid eyes on you.

"No, Mom. She's not. She's just a person. She's not one of us. She's not one of them."

"Does she know about things?" She meant the War, though my mother would never use the word.

"Yes."

"So you told her?" My mother stared momentarily out the window into the dark night. She didn't expect me to answer the question again. "Well, I guess there's no going back now, then, is there?"

"I told you, Mom. She's it for me. Even if I could go back, I wouldn't." I wanted her to be happy for me.

"It's a hard life you're leading her into, Joe," she said. She looked sad. My mother was a living embodiment of just how hard that life could be. I imagine that she was thinking about my father, about my sister, about her parents. All of them died violently, all before their time, leaving her to grow old alone, hiding in a small house in the corner of the world.

"Would you have given any of it up, Mom?" I asked.

"What do you mean?"

"Would you have traded your life for an ordinary life, knowing that you'd never get to spend time with Dad, never would have had known Jessica, never would have had me?"

She looked aghast that I would even ask the question. "Of course not." Some strength was returning to my mother's voice. "It's a hard life, sure, but for us, it's a just life and worth the sacrifice. You know that."

"Well, then, be happy for me, Mom." I stood up and walked over, taking a seat next to her on the couch. I put my arm around her shoulder. "The world's not perfect, Ma, but it's better for me when Maria's around."

"Then I'm happy for you," my mother said. I could tell that there was some truth in what she was saying but it was only a partial truth. "I'm just worried about her."

"I think she knows what she's getting herself into, Mom." I didn't believe the words even as they left my mouth.

"Let's hope so," she replied. Then she turned to me, her eyes glistening as if she were holding back tears. She hugged me again. The hug at the door was for the past, this one was for the future.

"Listen, Mom," I finally said, breaking away from her grasp. "I'm going to show Maria around tomorrow, maybe take her up to Rocky Point. Besides, I need to get some sleep. I'm exhausted." I stood up and limped toward the stairs. My leg was throbbing.

"Okay, Joe," my mother replied. She never asked for more information about my injury. She knew not to ask me about the details of my job. "Good night," she said, not budging as I slowly made my way to the stairs. When I was about to place a foot on the first step, she called out to me. "Joseph?" I could tell from the tone of her voice that there was something she'd been waiting to say, something she'd been holding back.

I turned around. She was sitting on the couch, her hands folded in her lap. She looked nervous. "Yeah, Mom?" I asked.

"She's pregnant." I don't know how she knew. She just knew.

"I know, Mom." I stood for a second at the bottom of the steps debating whether I should say anything else. I decided against it. Then I limped up the stairs and went to bed.

———

I woke up in the morning to the scent of frying bacon wafting up from the kitchen. I felt like it was Saturday morning and I was twelve again. I climbed out of bed. The leg felt better. It still hurt but it felt better. I grabbed painkillers from my bag and swallowed a few without water. I got up, got dressed, and began to head downstairs. On my way, I knocked on your door to see if you were awake yet. I didn't hear anything, so I thought I'd let you sleep. I walked down the stairs alone. The walk down the stairs was twice as painful as the walk up had been, but there wasn't much to do now but grit my teeth and bear it.

I was surprised, upon reaching the bottom of the stairs, to hear your voice echoing out of the kitchen. Apparently, you were already awake and bonding with my mother. Now that my mother knew that you were pregnant, the bonding frightened me. I don't know why. It was a classic case of paranoia. I should have remembered to trust it.

My mother had you hard at work, mixing pancake batter as she flipped the bacon in the frying pan with a fork. You both looked happy, free of worries. At least for the time being, I decided to join in the fun. I smiled and sat down at the kitchen table.

"Nice to see that my mom is already teaching you how to domesticate yourself."

"Morning, Joseph," my mother turned and said to me as I stared at you, hard at work. It was the first time I'd ever seen you cook. You looked dangerous.

"Forget that college education, forget working, all you need to know how to do in this man's world is cook and clean, right, Ma?" You shot me a dirty look. My mother walked over and slapped me on the shoulder with a dish towel. "How long have you two been up?"

"I got up early to run to the store to make sure I had some food for breakfast. When I got home, Maria was already awake. She was kind enough to offer to help me cook." My mother wore an apron as she cooked. She looked like a Bisquick ad from the fifties.

I walked over to the frying pan and picked out a piece of bacon with my hands, reaching in quickly to try to avoid being burnt by the bubbling grease. "Can't you wait ten minutes?" my mother cried out as I popped the sizzling bacon into my mouth.

"I could wait three days," I replied, "but I'd rather not." You hadn't said anything yet. "Has my mother been treating you okay?" I finally asked you, only half teasing.

"It's been really nice," you said, your tone much more serious than I expected. You almost sounded sad. Someday maybe you'll tell me what you were thinking about.

We sat around the table together and ate breakfast. Once again, my mother barely ate and you ate twice as much as I did. The conversation over breakfast moved from one inconsequential subject to another, each of us hoarding our own secrets. Mostly we discussed our plans for the day. I told my mother how we had a few errands to run and then I was planning on taking you up to the top of Rocky Point, an old rock ridge above town where Jared, Michael, and I used to camp when we were kids. You seemed genuinely excited to see some of my history firsthand.

"You sure that's a good idea," my mother chimed in, "considering"— and then there was a pause. The pause spoke volumes. It said quite clearly, "Maria's condition." Eventually, however, my mother finished by saying, "Considering your leg."

"We'll be fine, Ma," I responded. "The fresh air and exercise will be good for both of us." I placed my hand on top of yours on the table. It just felt good to touch you.

Soon the food was gone. Shortly after that, you and I climbed into the car and headed into town. We left our things upstairs, knowing we'd be back in only a few hours. My mother stayed at the house, alone.

The first thing that we had to do was gather supplies for when we left New Jersey. We went to a bank and I used the cash machine to take out four hundred dollars, the maximum amount that the machine would let me take out in a day. The account was my spending account. I had the ATM card and the pin number but the account wasn't in my name and I didn't have any control over it. The actual account was controlled by headquarters. I'd go to get money and money would be there. We were told not to spend extravagantly. If we did, we'd be cut off. That's all I knew. Along with the ATM card, I had five different credit cards, each under a different name. I never saw a single credit card bill. They went straight to headquarters. Again, I never had a problem using any one of them. The rules were the same as the ATM card. Do your job and keep a low profile. We couldn't live like James Bond. Allen made that clear enough, but we never had to worry about money. It was something that I had always taken for granted, but I wouldn't be able to do so much longer. The plan was to take out four hundred dollars every three days until we had over sixteen hundred in cash. We'd do all our spending on the credit cards, buying supplies that we could use while on the run. I hoped that the spending wouldn't raise any red flags. After all, I was supposed to be on vacation. After two weeks, we'd throw everything away, abandon it all. The free ride would be over, because as long as we used their ATM card and their credit cards, they'd know where we were. As long as we kept using their money, we couldn't be free.

After the bank, we headed to the grocery store. We shopped like we were going on a camping trip: no perishables; lots of things that we could prepare easily; lots of things we could eat without cooking; lots of bottled water. We bought granola bars, beef jerky, ramen noodles. I also picked up enough prenatal vitamins to get us through your entire pregnancy. Now was the time to spend.

We filled up most of the trunk with our supplies from the grocery store. Then we headed down the highway to a camping supply store. We brought two sleeping bags, two flashlights, a first-aid kit, and a tent.

The shopping took up the rest of the morning and started to eat into our afternoon. Still, I wanted to show you around before we left so that you could see the world I knew when I was still innocent. I wanted you to see the best of me. I parked the car at the end of a small cul-de-sac. We cut through the backyard of an old house and hiked through the woods for a bit. I checked to make sure that you were doing okay, but it quickly became clear that my leg was holding us back more than your condition. You were full of energy. We crossed a small stream and gradually started making our way uphill. Nothing had changed. It was like the forest had been frozen in time. I had changed. My world had changed. The forest hadn't. As we headed deeper into the woods, the trees grew taller and farther apart. The woods opened up, only the random beam of sunlight finding its way through the forest canopy. "It's beautiful," you said as we hiked up the ever steepening slope.

"You haven't seen anything yet," I replied. My leg throbbed with each step but it was worth the pain. After covering in thirty minutes what used to take me fifteen, we reached the base of the rock. From its base, the rock shot straight up, nearly a hundred and fifty feet. You craned your neck and looked straight up to the top as it jutted just above the top of the tree line.

"Wow," you said when we reached the rock, holding the word in your mouth. You walked up and touched the rock, feeling its texture. "This is amazing. How high is it?"

"Almost a hundred and fifty feet," I replied. "We used to climb it growing up."

"Really?" you asked, surprised you didn't know this about me already.

"Yeah." I remembered the first time I climbed it like it was yesterday. Jared had read all the books and had done all the prep work, so he volunteered to man the rope during the first climb. It fell to me and Michael to see who got to climb up first. I offered to shoot for it. Michael wouldn't have it. "It's your rock, Joe. You brought us here. You go first." The first climb took over two hours. I made my way up slowly, dangling a hundred feet from the ground, holding on to tiny rock ledges. Jared and Michael yelled out the whole time, encouraging me upward. We were still more than a year away from our eighteenth birthdays. The world was still simple.

"So how do we get to the top?" you said. There was mischief in your eyes that I hadn't seen since the first weekend we met.

"There's a path around the side. It's pretty steep. Do you think you're up for it?"

"You think you can hold me back, Gimpy?"

We hiked on. My leg burned. A few times you had to turn around and reach your hand out to help me. I tried not to pull too hard on your hand, worried what it might do. Eventually, we made it to the top together. From the top, it felt like we could see half of New Jersey spread out beneath us. We walked up to the edge and sat down, dangling our legs over the hundred-and-fifty-foot drop, the tops of the trees barely reaching our feet. You leaned against me and rested your head on my shoulder.

"How long have you been coming up here?"

"Since I was seven. I'd come up here whenever I wanted to get away. After my father died, I came up here all the time. I'd ride my bike over from our new house. When me and Michael and Jared found out about the War, all of us came here. When we came here, it was just us. No War. No death."

"Sounds nice."

"It was."

We spent another twenty minutes just gazing out over the world, watching the little matchbox cars move along the street, watching the miniature people move about their yards. We sat up there, your head resting on my shoulder, looking at the world we weren't a part of anymore. As the afternoon wore on, it started to get cold and we decided that we had to head back.

We pulled up to the house in the early evening. When we walked inside, I went up and gave my mother a hug. She hugged me back, but her heart wasn't in it. Something was wrong. I ignored it. I didn't want to get into it with her. We walked into the living room. You sat down on the couch and I turned on the TV. I excused myself so that I could go to the upstairs bathroom and check on the hole in my leg. I went into the bathroom and pulled off my jeans. I stared at my leg in the full-length mirror in the wall. There was no blood and no pus. It seemed to be healing well.

I was in the bathroom for maybe five minutes when there was a knock at the door. "Who is it?" I asked.

"It's your mother, Joseph. We need to talk."

"Hold on a minute. Let me get my pants on." I pulled my jeans back on and opened the door. My mother was standing there, not more than three inches from the door. Her eyes were full of tears and her upper lip was trembling. Everything was crashing down. Time froze.

"She's seventeen, Joseph," my mother said through trembling lips. The last time I saw her cry like that was when Jessica was killed.

"How do you know?" I responded, trying to stay calm.

"Her passport," my mother responded coldly.

"You looked through her things?"

"I had to, Joseph. I knew something wasn't right. I was just trying to look out for you. She's seventeen years old, Joseph. You know what that means!"

"Keep your voice down, Mother. She's downstairs."

"She's asleep. She's asleep on our couch, Joseph. She's seventeen, she's pregnant, and she's asleep on our couch!"

"I didn't know until it was too late, Mom," I said to her.

"You knew?" My mother's face turned ugly. I'd never seen her that way before. "She's a child, Joseph. You slept with that poor child and now you're going to ruin both your lives."

"She's no more a child than I am."

"Then you're both children—spoiled children who are throwing away your lives!"

"Listen, Mother, I didn't know," I repeated.

"She can't have that baby." The words came out cold and bitter.

"She's going to have it."

"You're going to let her have it?" She gasped.

"We're going to have it together. It's what we both want." I meant it when I said it.

"And what do you plan on doing? You know the rules!"

I got quiet. I wanted her to calm down. I hoped that if I stayed calm she would calm down. "We're going to run, Mother. That's why we came here. I wanted to introduce you to the mother of your grandchild and then I wanted to say good-bye." I wanted to cry but I promised myself that, if my mother didn't cry, I wouldn't either.

"Are you sure you know what you're doing, Joseph? If you run . . ." She couldn't finish the sentence. Her lips continued to tremble. "If you run, you'll be giving up everything. You'll be giving up on everything that your father fought for, everything that your grandfather fought for! You'll be giving up your future. You'll be giving up on everything that you've been fighting for!" Her voice got louder as she spoke.

"And what are we fighting for exactly, Mom?" I asked. "You tell me."

She just stood there aghast. I looked into her eyes and didn't recognize her.

"I'm sorry, Mother, but we've made our decision." I stepped past her, into the hallway.

"I don't think you've thought this through, young man," my mother called out to my back as I walked away from her. I turned toward her and gave her a look that was meant to tell her that I had thought it through and that she couldn't stop me. "Your father would be very disappointed in you," she said to me as I stood there staring at her. It was like she had just slapped me the face.

I stayed calm. My voice was soft. "It was nice seeing you, Mom. Maria and I will spend one more night. I'll let you sleep on all of this. If your opinions on the matter haven't changed by tomorrow, we'll leave in the morning." Then I walked down the stairs. I wanted to be near you. I had a sudden urge to protect you.

When you woke up, I suggested that we go out for dinner. You thought it was strange but said okay. During dinner, I ate slowly. You ate a lot. As I'd hoped, my mother was already locked away in her bedroom by the time we got home. The lights in her bedroom were off. I knew she wasn't asleep.

When we got upstairs, we kissed good night and you headed toward my sister's old room to sleep. "Maria? Can you do me a favor?" I asked as you walked away from me.

"Sure, Joe. What do you want?" you asked, a little confused.

"Lock your door tonight."

"Why?" you asked, confused.

"Just in case," I replied. "Do you mind sleeping with the door locked tonight?"

"You're scaring me, Joe. Is something wrong?"

"Maria, please. Just lock the door. I'm sure everything will be fine by morning."

"Okay," you said, afraid to ask any more questions.

I went to my room and lay down in bed. For the longest time, I simply lay there. Thoughts ran through my head but none of them were coherent. I just kept hearing voices. *And what do you plan on doing? You know the rules, young man! Either they're evil or we are. But what are you fighting for? I'm pregnant, Joe. Who the fuck do you think you are? You think you're somebody? You're nobody. They knew. She can't have that baby. Good guys and bad guys. Cops and robbers. Cowboys and Indians. They're all children's games, Joe. I came here to kill you. They killed my daughter, Joe. They killed my wife and my daughter. Your father would be very disappointed in you. I haven't been training to fight, Joe. I've been training to die. She's seventeen, Joseph. I'm seventeen.* Then, interrupting the voices, I heard someone crying. At first I thought it was just another sound trapped inside my head. Just another voice, only one that wasn't even able to make out words. But as the crying persisted, I began to slip back into consciousness. Someone was actually crying. Not in my head, in real life.

I leapt out of bed, rushing toward the door. My immediate thoughts were that my mother had gotten to you, that she had done something to you. I couldn't imagine what she would have done to you. I thought that maybe she woke you up. Maybe she woke you up to lecture you about how you were ruining my life. I regretted not telling you everything. I should have told you what my mother knew and how she reacted.

When I got outside my door, I saw that your door was still closed. The lights in your room were still off. The sounds of sobbing were coming from downstairs. I could tell by the sound that it was my mother. I hoped beyond hope that she had accepted my decision—that she was crying because she knew that she would never see me again.

All the lights in the living room were on. I walked down the stairs. My mother was sitting on the couch sobbing, the cordless phone in her lap.

"What's the matter, Mom?" I asked. I would have assumed the worst if I could have imagined what the worst was.

My mother simply shook her head in response. She couldn't get enough breath between sobs to speak.

"What happened, Mother?"

Finally, the sobbing slowed down and she was able to speak. "I'm sorry, Joseph," was all she could get out before she broke into another series of deep sobs.

"Sorry for what, Ma?" My eyes moved from my mother's crying face to the phone in her hand. "What did you do?"

She stopped crying. It was as if she was suddenly possessed by an entirely different person.

"I did what I had to do, Joseph," she said, trying to keep her voice as strong as possible.

"What did you do, Ma?" I asked again, pleading this time.

"I told them, Joseph." She held the phone up in her fist. "I did what you should have done already. I did what you were too weak to do. I told them. I did what I had to."

"You realize what that means, Mom!" I screamed at her. She simply turned her head and looked away. "They're going to come after me! They are going to come after me and Maria and our child!"

"I did what I had to, Joseph," she said again, unwilling to turn to look at me.

"You did what you had to? That child is your grandchild!"

"Don't you say those words!" she shouted back, lifting a finger toward me but still unwilling to make eye contact.

"That child is your grandchild!" I repeated, louder so that the words would ring in her ears long after we had gone. "Your grandchild!"

Finally, she turned toward me, her eyes large and red. "That child is no such thing. It is not my grandchild. THAT CHILD IS ONE OF THEM!" I looked into my mother's eyes. The woman I knew was gone.

I had wasted enough time already. I turned and ran back upstairs and began banging on your door with my fist. "Maria! Maria! Wake up! Get your things together! We have to leave! We have to leave now!" It was the second fire drill I'd put you through in three days. It wouldn't be the last. You opened up the door. "Get your things together. We have to leave now," I said to you, lowering my voice. You simply nodded in response. You were ready to run. You were already growing accustomed to it. You started to pack. I ran into my bedroom and threw everything I owned back into my bag—everything but the gun. The gun I took out of the bag and tucked into the back of my pants.

When we got to the bottom of the stairs, my mother was still sitting on the couch, the phone still clutched in her hands. The tendons on her hands bulged out as if she would die if she let go of the phone. She looked up when we got to the bottom of the stairs. I looked into my mother's eyes one last time. She was my mother again. Whatever creature had possessed her was gone. Too bad it was too late. People were coming for us. We had to go.

We headed for the door. You were about to turn to say something to my mother but I gave you a slight push on your shoulder to keep you moving toward the door. You took the hint and continued on. You never asked what had happened. I assumed that you had figured it out. As I was about to walk out the door, my mother finally stood up from the couch, tears flowing freely from her face.

"I love you, Mom. I always will," I said before stepping out the kitchen door. She nodded in response. We threw our bags in the backseat of the car and leapt into the front. I turned the ignition and we skidded out of the driveway. As we left, I took one look back at the old house. My mother was standing at the window, crying, her one hand lifted above her shoulder. She was waving good-bye.

Thirteen

We made it out of town without incident. I took as many side roads as possible, changing direction frequently and watching every car we passed. I kept one eye on the road and one on the rearview mirror to make sure we weren't being followed. Every time I saw the brake lights of a car that had just driven by us, I flinched, thinking it could be turning around. I had no idea how much information my mother had given them. I didn't know what was compromised. I had to assume that they knew your name now. I had to assume they knew what car we were driving. I figured that we had, at most, an hour to put some distance between us and my old hometown. After that, I had no plan. Considering the situation, it wasn't worth thinking more than an hour ahead.

You sat in silence for some time, watching me, watching me check the mirrors, watching me think. You didn't interrupt until I began to calm down. "What happened?" you finally asked. After being pulled out of bed in a strange house, in the middle of the night, and told to pack up your things before being dragged into a car and driven to God knows where, you still waited over an hour to question me. You were getting good at the game. Knowing when to ask questions and knowing when to simply move was the first key to survival. Shortly before you asked your question we turned onto open highway. It was closing in on two in the morning. The road was mostly empty. It looked like we'd gotten away, for now.

"They're onto us," I replied. I looked out over the road in front of us. I didn't tell you anything you didn't already know.

"What does that mean?" you asked after thinking for a few moments.

"It means they know. They know about you. They know about our kid. They know we're on the run."

"No, Joe. What does that *mean*?" you repeated. "For us?" I looked over at you. You didn't look scared, just nervous. I put my hand on your leg and rubbed it gently.

"It doesn't really change much. We were going to have to hide eventually. Now we just have to do it sooner." You nodded. You looked strong. You looked much stronger than I felt. But here we were, on the open highway, no one telling us where to go; no more people lining up to die. We were on our own for as long as we didn't get ourselves killed. "This is Route Eighty," I told you as we drove, looking out across the highway. "It starts in New Jersey, right off the George Washington Bridge, which goes into New York," I continued.

"I know about the George Washington Bridge. I'm Canadian, not retarded," you replied.

"Okay. Point noted. Anyway, this road goes all the way from the George Washington Bridge to the Golden Gate Bridge. New York to San Francisco, straight across the country. And tonight it's ours." You placed your hand on top of the hand that I had yet to remove from your leg.

"So where are we going?"

"I was thinking Chicago." If we drove straight through we could get to Chicago in about twelve hours. We could have been there by tomorrow afternoon. I didn't think we should hit a city, any city, that quickly, though. My mother's call would set the alarm bells off. For the first day after the alarm bells went off, things would be awfully thick. People would really be on the lookout for us. As time wore on, other things would come up and we'd be pushed to the back-burner, at least by those that didn't have a personal interest in catching us.

"Why Chicago?"

"I don't know." I shrugged. "I've never been to Chicago." That was true, but it was only half the reason why I chose Chicago. The real reason was because I had never done a job in Chicago.

"Chicago it is," you replied.

"Chicago," I repeated, nodding. It sounded right. "I think we should get a couple of hours of sleep tonight. I'm going to drive for another two hours, get us pretty far into Pennsylvania. Maybe there we can find a good place to rest until morning. Until then, you can sleep while I drive."

"I really don't think that's going to happen, Joe," you said. "Not tonight." Apparently you looked stronger than you felt too.

We drove on, passing the Delaware Water Gap and moving into Pennsylvania. As we drove past the Water Gap, I remembered how my grandfather used to bring me down there when I was a little kid. We'd leave from home early on Sunday mornings, before the sun came up, so that we could go down to the Water Gap and release homing pigeons that he kept as pets. We'd drive down, the pigeons cooing in their cages in the back of my grandfather's station wagon. We'd pull the car down near the river. We'd get out of the car. My grandfather would pull the cages from the back of the station wagon. Then we'd sit and wait for a few moments. As we waited, I could hear the pigeons rustling with excitement. They knew the drill. They knew that they would soon be free, free to fly. My grandfather was a pretty stoic guy. Thinking back on it now, I can't even remember the sound of his voice. I can't remember ever hearing him speak. I remember driving down to the Water Gap to release those pigeons, though.

Soon the cages would begin rocking as if they were alive. My grandfather would want to wait until the pigeons were at peak excitement before opening the door to their cages. The more excited they were, the faster they'd fly. Once the cages began to rustle with enough excitement, we'd open them up and the pigeons would fly out. They'd fly straight up in the air. Then they would make one giant turn as a group, twisting toward the heavens, trying to get their bearings. They'd shoot up until they were little more than specks in the early-morning sky. Then they'd flap their wings and fly away. It would all happen in a flash and then they'd be gone. Once we couldn't see any of the pigeons anymore, my grandfather and I would load the cages back into the station wagon, climb back into the front of the car, and head back toward the highway. On the way home, we'd stop for breakfast and I'd gorge myself on pancakes and bacon, dumping syrup on everything on my plate. My grandfather always ordered scrambled eggs, extra dry. I can't remember his voice but I can remember what he ate. Memories are funny that way. When we were done eating, we'd get back in the station wagon and drive home.

The trip home, including breakfast, would take me and my grandfather about two hours. In two hours we drove probably about fifty miles. When we got home, we'd go to the backyard. There were two lawn chairs in the backyard that my grandfather kept facing the pigeon coop he'd built. We'd sit in them and wait. It would still be early, so the morning dew on the grass in the backyard would just have started to dry off. We'd take our seats and my grandfather would take out his watch and his clipboard and we'd wait. The way I remember it, we never waited long. Soon, one by one, the pigeons that not long before had been so eager to break free of their cages and fly away would return. One by one, they'd land by the pigeon coop and walk back into their cages. They could have flown anywhere. Yet here they were, diving out of the sky, returning to the little coop my grandfather had built in his backyard. My grandfather knew each bird on sight. As they returned, he'd mark each of their times down on the pages on his clipboard so he could compare the times to previous weeks. He'd smile when one of his favorites was the first to make it back. He'd worry when it would take any particular bird longer than he expected. In the end, they always made it back. My grandfather never lost a pigeon. They'd struggle through winds, through rain, through whatever obstacles got in their way. Once each bird had made it back into the coop, my grandfather would walk up to it, close the door, and snap the lock shut. When I was a kid I always wondered why those pigeons worked so hard just to be locked up in their cages again. Driving out of New Jersey with you on that night, I finally felt like I knew.

In minutes, you and I were through the Water Gap, leaving New Jersey behind us forever. We pushed on into Pennsylvania and the farther we drove, the more rural our surroundings became. We were surrounded by trees. The two-lane highway seemed to stretch on in front of us forever. We'd drive mile after mile and it didn't feel like we'd gotten anywhere. We kept moving, pushing forward. I drove within a few miles per hour of the speed limit, not wanting to attract any attention. Every so often a truck would drive past us or we'd see the headlights of one headed back the way we'd just come. Mostly, however, there were just trees.

I tried to keep hard to our schedule. Discipline. That's what we'd need. Always stick to the plan. Always be ready to change plans on a moment's notice. At three-thirty A.M. I took an exit off the highway leading to a small town somewhere in Pennsylvania. The idea was to get the car off the road somewhere, pull out our sleeping bags, and see if we could get in a few real hours of rest before the sun came up. The night was pretty clear. It was chilly, but not too cold. We wouldn't need to pitch the tent. We made one pit stop on our way into deeper country when we passed an old gas station. There were three beat-up cars sitting on cinder blocks next to the garage. I pulled into the parking lot and stopped the car.

"What are we stopping here for?" you asked. You hadn't slept. I thought you would, despite your fears. You didn't. I motioned toward the beat-up old cars parked at the edge of the property. "We're going to steal a car?" you asked. "We're going to steal one of those?" you asked incredulously.

"Not the cars, babe," I responded. "You steal a car and people come looking for it." I dug through my duffel bag that was in the backseat of the car until I found my pocket knife. "We're just going to take the license plates." The people looking for us knew the car that we were driving. They knew the make, the model, and, most likely, the license number. I unscrewed the Pennsylvania plates from one of the cars. Then I took the rear plate off a second car and screwed it onto the front of the first so that it wouldn't be too obvious that the plates had been stolen. The odds of anyone at the shop noticing that two of their old junks now had the same license number were pretty slim. It was obvious that no one had worked on these cars in years. I took our Massachusetts plates and threw them in the trunk. Then I screwed on the new plates. We were now in disguise.

We drove on. I turned onto every smaller road that I could until we were on a long, barely paved road, running between a small forest and a cornfield. When there was a large enough clearing in the trees to fit the car through, I pulled the little rental car into the woods. I got us as far from the road as I could before putting the car back in park. We were only about thirty feet from the road. The gray car would be visible from the street in the daytime, but in the dark of the night, we were pretty well hidden. We were home for the night.

I got our new sleeping bags out of the trunk. "We should have brought pillows," you said after seeing me carry the sleeping bags into a small open spot in the woods.

"Well, you can't think of everything," I replied. You took two sweaters out of your duffel bag and wrapped them in the plastic bags we had gotten while shopping the day before.

"Pillows," you said to me, throwing me one of the sweater-filled bags. We laid our sleeping bags out on the ground and climbed in. We were about three feet apart. I had placed my duffel bag next to me. Inside the duffel bag, on top of all the other items, was the gun, just in case. I placed my pillow under the sleeping bag, placed my head down on top of it, and closed my eyes. Sleep would be hard to come by that night, but I knew we needed it.

"Joe?" you said, lying on your side and propping your head up on your arm. I opened my eyes again.

"We're going to need to sleep, Maria," I said. "We have to try, anyway."

"One quick question," you said. Then you continued, before I could argue or dissent. "What happens now?"

"What do you mean?" I replied.

"I know that we run and we hide, but what do they do?"

"They look for us."

"How? Has this ever happened before?"

"This specifically?" I wondered out loud, glancing down at your stomach. "I don't know. I'm sure it has. I've never heard any stories, though, never heard any details." You looked relieved. The relief didn't last. "I do know about one time when somebody went on the run, though. Guy's name was Sam. Sam Powell. He was one of them. He was a hit man for their side. Anyway, during the course of one of his jobs, something went wrong. He'd gone to a restaurant on Long Island. He was supposed to kill the cook. He waited out back, in the parking lot behind the place, after it had closed down for the night. He'd scoped the joint out over a couple of nights before that and on each of those nights the cook came out back with these big bags of garbage and tossed them into the Dumpsters they had at the back of the parking lot. So he'd be carrying these two heavy bags of garbage across the empty parking lot, alone, in the middle of the night. He'd be totally defenseless. Nobody knows what they had on this guy, the cook. I never heard who he was or why they'd be after him. Just because, I guess.

"So that night, it was really dark. And this Sam Powell guy stationed himself behind the Dumpster with a knife. He was planning on waiting until the cook came out and, just as he was about to toss the first bag into the garbage, at that point when he was most vulnerable, Sam was planning on popping out and sticking the guy. Sam was, apparently, an old pro at this. One jab was all it was going to take. So Sam waited and listened and when he heard the right sounds, the sounds he'd heard the two nights before, the sound of the cook bending over to try to toss this bag of garbage into the Dumpster, Sam popped out and knifed the guy right in the throat. The guy was dead in less than a minute. The problem was that it wasn't the cook. For some reason, that night, one of the dishwashers was the one put on garbage duty. He had the same build as the cook, but he was just some poor immigrant dishwasher. And he was a civilian.

"Now, protocol dictates that, when you kill a civilian, you're supposed to turn yourself in. You turn yourself in to your own side. They can then either turn you over to the other side, which never happens, or they can carry out the execution themselves." You flinched at this, apparently not a fan of capital punishment. "So there's Sam. He just knifed some poor bastard in the throat and now he's supposed to sacrifice himself on the pillar of justice. He's supposed to give up his life for the cause. Instead, he runs. It's the only time I've ever heard of it happening." I had been speaking for a good five minutes when I looked up at you. You looked horrified. Those people that say that imagining a monster is scarier than actually seeing a monster, I don't think that they've ever actually seen a monster. Children are afraid of the dark because they don't know any better. If they were smart, they'd be afraid of the light.

"So what happened?" you asked. The expression on your face almost made me stop, but you needed to know the truth. If we were going to make it on this run, you needed to know what we were running from.

I went on. "The Long Island police were clueless about the murder. Just another random act of violence. It never gets solved. A Mexican gets stabbed in the back of a restaurant. There are no clues, no motives. The story comes and goes. But it didn't take long for us to realize what happened. The cook knew right away. The other side knew that Sam was on that job and that Sam had disappeared. So word gets out. I'm sure that both sides put some official people on the case. They probably had to for appearances, if nothing else. But that's not the problem. The problem for Sam is that when the call goes out, Sam is cut loose. No one on his side is allowed to protect him anymore. Not only that, but they have to release all the information they have about him. They literally send out packets on the guy. The packets have his picture in it. It lists all of his known aliases. And there's more. I know because I got one of Sam's packets. Like I said, I'm sure some people are officially put on the case, but a bunch of other guys are sent the packet. And in the packet, it lists every job Sam's ever done. Every man or woman he's ever killed is on there. Every death he's ever been involved with. And they send this packet out to everyone who's got an interest in the information. I had never heard of Sam Powell before I got that packet. But it turns out, Sam Powell took part in my father's murder. He murdered a lot of people. I wasn't even the only one who got that packet because of my dad. Everyone who was close to my father got it. Now, Sam's list of jobs was pretty long. So there's a lot of people out there with this information. They know what he looks like. They know where he's lived. They know a lot about him. They all get this packet that basically says, you try to get him and we won't try to stop you. And everyone who got one of those packets has reasons to want to get him.

"Sam was a real professional. I don't say that with admiration. It's just a fact. He lasted six days. His body was mailed back to his family from Holland. I don't know any of the details, but I know that the funeral was closed-casket."

"Did you go after him?"

"No. I had work to do." I paused. "I never thought of myself as a vigilante."

"So what does that mean for us?"

"First think of every sin you've ever committed. Think of every person you've ever wronged. Now imagine that all of those people are given the chance to get back at you for those sins, guilt free, repercussion free. You with me so far?" You nodded. "Now pretend that what you did to them was unforgivable."

I looked into your eyes. You were frightened. That was good. Fear would serve us well. "They're going to come after us. They're going to come after us and they are going to try to kill me. They are going to try to kill me and they are going to try to steal our child. To be honest, I don't know what happens to you."

"Who are they?" you asked, but what you meant was "How long is your list, Joe?"

"I don't know who they are," I replied, "but there are a lot of them. Don't trust anyone, Maria."

We both stayed awake for some time after our conversation, listening to the chirping crickets, listening for any strange sounds that might come out of the woods. Eventually, we fell asleep.

———

The next morning we had breakfast out of the trunk, dry cereal and water. I didn't bring up money to you yet. I didn't want to pile the problems on you. You'd digested enough already. It wasn't going to be long, however, before money was a problem. We had less than five hundred dollars between us. I had the credit cards, but I didn't dare try to use them. From that point on, we were off the grid. It'd been seven hours since we left my house. In seven hours we could have been anywhere between Montreal, Cleveland, and Richmond, Virginia. It was a big circle. We were going to need money, though, and a doctor to monitor your condition. Eventually, I was going to have to find work. It was that or stealing, but I'd never thought of myself as a thief.

We were about nine hours from Chicago, but I didn't want to get there for another two days. Once in Chicago, maybe I could find a job. Maybe there we could find a cheap apartment. Maybe there we could settle down for a bit. It sounded nice, but it was a lot of maybes.

For the next two days, the idea was simply to avoid cities and lay low. I didn't want you to have to spend too long in any one stretch in the car. It wasn't healthy. I'd started to notice your changes. You needed a lot more sleep. Your appetite was voracious. The way you'd been eating, we'd eat our way through the supplies we'd brought in two days. We'd do some meals on the road. We'd only go to places far off the highway, though. The highway was dangerous. People would be traveling to try to find us. We wanted to stay away from those people. You tried to hide it from me, but I could tell that you were nauseous. You weren't throwing up, but I would catch you clutching your stomach with a pained look on your face. I assumed this all was normal. I hoped it all was normal.

That first day was pleasantly uneventful. So was that night. We ate breakfast at some little diner in some corn-fed town in the middle of the state. We hit the highway again for a few hours, heading west. The highway made me nervous. I felt a lot better when we were off the road. We stopped in at a gas station and I bought a detailed map of the state. The gas prices were going to eat into our cash pretty quickly, but we didn't have much of a choice. If we had to, we could have tried to siphon some from another car at night. It would be safer later. For now, we just needed to stay invisible.

You slept during most of the car ride. We stopped once during the day. I passed the map to you and you devoured it. You marked every exit. You announced every sight that we passed, whether we could see it from the road or not. I told you that I thought we should get some exercise, so you led us off the highway to some state park you found on the map. We did a two-mile hike around a creek. It was good to stretch our legs. My wound was healing well. The two miles knocked you out again. Once back in the car, you were asleep in minutes, the map unfolded in your lap.

I counted every hour that we went unnoticed. Every one was another hour closer to our being forgotten. It wasn't about distance, just time. That afternoon we crossed into Ohio. We took another random exit in Ohio to find a cheap place for dinner. The money was quickly dwindling. The night was clear again, so we found another deserted place on the side of a back road to sleep. I watched you as you slept that night. I felt so guilty. You were seventeen, pregnant, and homeless. We were floating on the edges of civilization, hoping no one would find us. One day I'll bring you back to civilization. I just don't know when.

That night, we made love for the first time since we'd told each other our secrets. You climbed into my sleeping bag with me. It was so much warmer with both of us inside one bag. We clumsily undressed each other from the waist down, leaving our sweatshirts on to fight off the cold night air. We kissed. The sleeping bag fit snug around us with both of us inside it. Our movements were restricted but we could move enough. We moved slowly, carefully. It was different. We were different people now. Before we were innocent people playing a dangerous game. Now we were dangerous people, doing the most innocent, primal thing we could imagine. Near the end, you bit down on your lip and your body shuddered but you didn't make a sound. The whole sleeping bag shook with you. When we were done you cried.

The next day was more of the same. We were plodding through a twelve-hour drive, trying to stretch it into three days without actually stopping anywhere. You found another place on the map where we could kill some time. It was a lighthouse on Lake Erie. We spent a few hours in the park around the lighthouse. We had lunch out of the trunk of the car again. You deserved better than that but you never complained.

I bought a newspaper at one of our stops. I scanned the headlines and police blotter for anything that might be interesting, anything that might give me a hint as to what was going on in my old world. Things were quiet. I checked the weather. The forecast that night was for rain. With the rain, the creatures began to crawl up from the mud.

The rain began in the late afternoon. Even before it began, we spotted the tall, dark clouds as they rolled toward us from across the plains. The air became thick and damp. Shortly after that the dark clouds covered the sky, blocking out the sun. It became dark. The air turned cold and the wind began to blow. The trees around us rustled in the wind. Then the rain came, hard and fast.

When we spotted the rain clouds moving toward us, you begged me to pull over. You said that you wanted to feel the storm approach. So I pulled over to the side of the road and we sat on the hood of the car as the clouds rolled toward us. We felt the mist and the wind. Just before the rain began to fall, I asked you, "Is that enough?" You said yes and we ran back into the car. Our clothes were damp from the mist and I turned on the car and turned up the heat to try to help dry us out. The rain pounded on the car. We could barely hear each other speak over the thumping of raindrops. We just sat there for a few moments, waiting for the rain to ease up enough so that I could see out the windshield.

"It doesn't rain like this where I'm from," you said.

"We should find a place to get some dinner," I said once I was able to pull back on the road. The rain was still pouring out of the sky. With each swipe of the wipers, I would have just enough time to catch a glimpse of the road before the world would disappear again in the flood.

"Where are we going to sleep tonight?" you asked while watching the sky fall down on top of us.

"Let's worry about eating first. Then we'll worry about where we're going to sleep," I replied.

I couldn't push the car much above ten miles per hour because of the rain. We passed other cars that had simply pulled over, planning on waiting the storm out. I might have done the same if it looked like the storm was ever going to end. We eventually found a small diner just off the side of the road. I pulled the car into the parking lot and parked just to one side of the diner. "Why are we parking here, Joe?" you asked. "There's a parking space right up front." I'd pulled our car to the side in order to hide it from people driving by, even on the little back road we were on. I didn't want to leave anything to chance. But I didn't have the heart to tell you that. So I backed the car up and parked it out front.

We took two stools at the counter. You wanted to eat at the counter. There were plenty of free booths. You said that you didn't understand how anyone could come into this kind of place and not sit at the counter. You talked like you were on vacation seeing sights. We sat on the big, plush, red stools, our backs to the door, facing the kitchen. One of the two cooks working the diner came up to us and took our order. He was straight out of central casting, a chunky man, mid-fifties, wearing a white apron covered in grease stains. I ordered a Coke. You ordered a black-and-white milkshake. They didn't have milkshakes. You changed your order to a chocolate milk. Sometimes I forgot how young you were.

I ordered a cheeseburger and fries. You ordered a grilled cheese sandwich with tomato soup. You slid your hand onto my back and began to move it in small circles around my shoulder blades. I think that you could sense that I was feeling tense, despite not knowing why. I didn't even know why. It was just a general sense of unease. Things had been going too smoothly. Your touch calmed me down for the time being.

About halfway through our meal, the door opened. When it did, I could feel the wind from outside rustle through the entire restaurant. It whistled as it came through the door. I could hear the rain pounding on the pavement outside. It was loud and persistent. Some kid walked in with the wind. He quickly closed the door behind him, shutting us off again from the ugly weather. He was a gangly kid, tall and skinny. He had on a pair of jeans and was wearing a now sopping-wet hooded sweatshirt. It wasn't ideal rain gear. He had a backpack draped over one shoulder. He took a seat on a stool two stools down from you. When he sat down, he slipped his other arm into the second strap of the backpack. It sagged on his shoulders. He ordered a Coke and grabbed a menu. He looked to me like he was about fifteen. Truth was, he was at least a year older than you. His skin was almost as greasy as his hair. He had acne on his chin and his forehead. After he ordered his food, he began swiveling himself in circles on his stool. This lasted for all of about two minutes before the cook came back out. He scowled at the kid. "It's a stool, kid, not a fucking merry-go-round."

The kid stopped. "Sorry," he said. I almost felt bad for him. He immediately turned his attention to his Coke. He began busying himself by playing with the straw.

Suddenly, you broke my focus. "So where are we going to sleep tonight?" you asked again. The rain hadn't let up one bit. It banged and blew against the diner windows.

"I already told you, Maria. I don't know."

"We could stay at a hotel." There was just a hint of hope in your voice.

I shook my head. "We've got to save our money, Maria. It's running short already, with the food and the gas. We need something for when we get to Chicago. It's easier being homeless out here than it will be there." My own words depressed me.

"What if we found something real cheap?" you asked. Yeah, that's just what I wanted, to bring my pregnant, seventeen-year-old girlfriend to a cheap motel in backwoods Ohio. I suddenly felt like everything Allen said about me was true.

"Maybe," I said. I just wanted to end the conversation. I had eaten about half my burger. You pounded through your soup and sandwich. "You want the rest of mine?" I asked, motioning toward my half-empty plate.

"You're such a gentleman," you said, your voice dripping with sarcasm.

"You want it or not?" I replied.

"Sure," you said. I pushed the plate in front of you.

I needed a moment alone. "I'm going to run to the bathroom," I said. "I'll be right back." I eyed the kid again before I left. There was something about him. I could tell that he felt my eyes on him but he didn't look over at me. I figured I wouldn't be gone long enough for there to be any trouble. I went into the bathroom and closed the door behind me. The bathroom was tiny. There was a toilet on one side with a sink and mirror on the other. It was only slightly larger than an airplane bathroom. I stood up and ran the cold water in the sink.

I took a few handfuls of the cold water and splashed them into my face. I stared at my own image in the mirror. I looked old. Compared to that kid out in the diner, I looked ancient.

I don't remember how long I had been gone. I had lost track of time. It couldn't have been more than five minutes. But it was too long. It was a mistake. The kid had moved. The kid, a human bundle of twitches and nerves, had moved to the stool next to you. The two of you were talking. I wanted to scold you. I wanted to walk right up to you and tell you that you shouldn't talk to strangers. He was probably just hitting on you. God knows I would if I were him. Still, I had a sinking feeling that this was going to end in violence.

Despite my premonition, I wore my best face. I walked back to my stool and sat down. You turned to me once I was back in my stool. "Joe," you said, "this is Eric. He heard us talking and told me that he knows of a nice, cheap place where we can stay tonight."

I reached out, offering to shake the kid's hand. "Nice to meet you, Eric." Then I watched for his reaction. He paused, looking down at my hand. He hesitated, not knowing what to do. It was only for a split second, but he definitely hesitated. He didn't want to touch me. He was one of them. There was no doubt about it. He was one of them and he knew who I was. It only took him a split second to regain his confidence, but in that split second, he had given everything away.

"Hey" was all he said in response as I shook his hand. I hated the kid, real hatred. I hated that he had been talking to you. I hated that he had come here looking for us. I hated that I was going to have to kill him.

"So, you know of a good place where we can crash tonight?" I asked him, staring into his eyes as I spoke, testing to see if he could hold my gaze.

"Yeah," he replied, quickly staring back down at his soda. "I know a guy who has an extra room at his place. He's been trying to rent it out but hasn't had any luck. Anyway, I'm sure he'd let you guys stay there for twenty bucks."

You looked at me, your eyes heavy with expectation. I could almost read the thoughts in your big blue eyes. A bed, that's all you wanted. "Well, the price is right," I said. I knew it would make you happy. At this point, even ten minutes of happiness was worth it. God only knew how many more chances we'd get to make each other happy. "How do we find this place?"

The kid sat there, chewing on the end of his straw, letting it dangle out of his mouth like toothpick. He hadn't really thought this out. "You guys could follow me. I'll lead you there and then I'll tell my buddy about the deal I struck up with you." He smiled. His smile was genuine. He liked his plan.

"What's your friend's name?" I asked.

"Pete," he replied without missing a beat. The whole thing fell in place for him quickly. He was young but he wasn't stupid.

"And what's in it for you?" I asked. I gave him a hard look. I wanted to scare him. I wanted him to back away and run. I wanted him to abandon his plan before it even got started. I was giving him an out. At the time, it was more than I thought he deserved. I was doing it for you, not for him.

"Joe," you interrupted, not understanding what I was doing. "That's not very nice." You tried to sound like you were just teasing me, but I knew that you were pissed off. You thought that I was going to ruin things for us.

"No. No. That's all right," the kid spoke up in my defense. "I'm just trying to help a couple people out." This time, he returned my gaze. He gave me a cold, hard stare, or as much of one as he could muster. As he stared at me, I saw in him something that I recognized. I recognized that fearlessness, that unbridled anger. "It's friendly country around here," he continued. I don't know what the kid was thinking. Did he think he could outdraw me? Did he think this was the Old West? "Sometimes the hospitality just takes a while to get used to." He turned to you and gave you a big smile. You returned his smile—that made me hate him even more.

"Well, I guess we can't pass up on hospitality like that," I said. You turned around in your stool and gave me a quick hug. I hoped it wasn't the last. The kid didn't scare me. You scared me. I didn't know how you were going to react. Still, I tried. I gave the kid his out. He didn't take it. His loss. It was nearing nine o'clock in the evening. You and I had been sitting at that counter for nearly two hours. "I guess we'll settle up and go." I looked down at the plate in front of you. You had burned through my burger and the rest of my fries. "You done with your meal, Eric?"

"Yeah," he replied. "I just have to get the check."

"Don't worry about it," I said. "You found us a place to stay. The least we could do is buy you dinner." I motioned for the cook to bring me our check and Eric's too. You seemed proud that I had suddenly recovered my manners. I didn't have the heart to tell you that none of it mattered. I wasn't being generous. I just figured that we'd have all of Eric's money by the time the night was through anyway. Robbing generally wasn't my style, but we needed the money. If I was going to have to take the kid out, there was no sense in letting his money go to waste.

"Thanks a lot, Joe," the kid said. "I appreciate it." I took both checks, left a couple of bucks on the counter, and paid at the cash register. I nodded at the kid again. This time I avoided eye contact. I didn't want to remember his face later. I wanted to forget what I was about to do even before I did it. It was time to venture back out into the storm.

We rushed out into the rain. I made sure that the kid ran to his car before we did. I didn't dare let either of us turn our backs to him. The kid had conveniently parked right next to us. Right out front. He was driving a little beat-up red car. The fenders were rusting. The car was probably only about seven years old, but someone had beaten the hell out of it. The kid probably bought it for a couple hundred bucks. The car had Ohio plates. Ohio plates was a good sign. Maybe he'd lucked upon us. Maybe he wasn't actually chasing us. Even so, if he'd found us, then other people, people with more experience, could definitely find us too.

Before he ducked his head into his car, the kid stood up and yelled back to us, "It's just a couple of turns. I'll drive slow so that you can keep up." I waved in response as we stood under the awning of the little tin-roofed restaurant. What was he trying to do? Was he trying to lead us into an ambush? Or was he simply trying to take us out into a field where he thought he could get the jump on us? I couldn't figure out his angle. Maybe he didn't have an angle. Maybe he was just winging it. It didn't matter. He was all but dead anyway. Under different circumstances, I might have liked this kid. He had more heart than brains.

It took the kid three tries before his engine turned over. Once he had his engine running and had turned his headlights on, we ran to our car. You jumped in the passenger side and I slid in behind the wheel. I turned the keys in the ignition, flared on the lights, and pulled behind the kid as he drove out of the parking lot. I didn't say anything to you as we eased out into the rain-soaked road. The kid, good to his word, drove slowly so that we could follow him. I didn't even look at you as we made our first turn, right behind the kid. Every second, the world around us became more desolate. I could feel your eyes burning on me as I drove. I didn't dare turn toward you. I wasn't ready to face you yet.

"What's wrong, Joe?" you finally asked.

"You're not suspicious?" You should have been suspicious. If we were going to survive another two weeks, you needed to be suspicious.

"Suspicious of what?" you asked, incredulous.

"You're not the least bit suspicious?" I repeated, this time with more force.

"Of him? Of Eric? He's a kid, Joe. He's like nineteen." You fought my anger with your own.

"Well, that would make him two years older than you."

"Fuck you, Joe," you answered. I tried to keep my cool.

"It's not an insult. I was about his age when I made my first kill. He's one of them. The kid is one of them."

"What the fuck does that mean? He's trying to help us out, Joe." I just shook my head. "How do you know that he's one of them?"

"I just know it. He didn't want to shake my hand. He hesitated."

"I don't believe it." You stared out through the rain. You didn't want to believe it.

"Yeah, well, watch." I suddenly cut the wheel to the left, veering off the road onto a small dirt path. "If he didn't have any angle, do you think he'd follow us?"

"What are you doing, Joe?" you yelled. You turned in your seat to look back at the road, to watch the kid's headlights, to see if the kid was going to turn around and follow us.

"Are you going to believe me if he follows us?"

"Stop it, Joe!" you shouted. I drove up the path about five hundred yards and pulled the car off to the side of the dirt path.

"Are you going to believe me if he follows us?" I turned and asked again, staring at you. "Why would he follow us if he wasn't one of them?" You stared back at the road, watching the kid's headlights. He had stopped his car on the road. The car wasn't moving. He was assessing the situation. I looked at you. Your lips began to move. Even though no sound came out of your mouth, I could read your lips. You were saying over and over again, "Don't come. Don't come. Don't come." I knew that it was useless. I reached into the backseat of the car and grabbed my duffel bag. I took the gun out of the duffel bag.

"What are you doing, Joe? What are you going to do?"

"He's one of them, Maria. He's one of them and he knows where we are. If we don't get rid of him, then the whole world is going to be all over us. He's got his out. If he doesn't follow us he's free. If he follows us, we don't have much choice." Your eyes kept darting between the gun and the kid's car. Suddenly the kid jerked his car into reverse. He was coming to get us.

"There's always a choice, Joe," you said. It was a last-ditch effort.

"That's a cliché, Maria. Sometimes other people make your choices for you. Sometimes you never get a chance." I looked at you. I wanted you to know that this wasn't something I wanted to do. It was something I had to do. You weren't buying it.

"What if you're wrong? What if he's just being nice?" you asked. The kid slowly pulled his car up the little dirt path on which we'd parked. He stopped his car about fifteen feet behind us. Once he stopped his car, he flicked on his brights. The light was blinding. It was his first professional move. He could see us now and we couldn't see him.

"Buckle your seat belt," I ordered.

"What?"

"Buckle your seat belt," I replied. I buckled mine as if to show you how to do it, keeping the gun in my right hand as I did so. When you saw me do it, I think you realized I was serious, so you quickly buckled yours too. As soon as I heard your seat belt click into place, I put the car in reverse. Fifteen feet. In the mud. I had to hope it was enough room. Once locked into reverse, I slammed on the gas. The wheels turned in the mud a few times before catching a grip. Then, suddenly, the car jerked backward. I steered it straight into the light. We were moving at a pretty good clip by the time we rammed into the front of the kid's car. I hoped it was fast enough. The kid's car skidded backward in the mud. The front end of the car smashed in like a soda can. One of the headlights cracked and went out. The other simply dimmed, now shining crookedly off to the side, sending a glimmer of light across the rain-swept field.

I opened my car door and stepped out into the rain. I walked right over to the kid's car and pulled open the driver's side door. The impact was enough. His air bag had deployed. The kid was sitting in the front seat, still dazed from the impact of the air bag. A small trickle of blood leaked out of his lower lip. He didn't have his seat belt on. His backpack sat on the seat next to him, partially unzipped. He had been reaching for the backpack prior to the crash. He looked at me when I pulled the door open. His eyes looked lost. He wasn't able to focus them yet. I wasted no time. I grabbed him by the shoulder and pulled him out of his car. I dragged him into the light radiating from his car's one working headlight and threw him down in the mud. Then I went back to his car. I didn't take my eyes off him. I pulled his backpack out and threw it down in the mud next to him. I stood over him, the light from the one working headlight shining on us like a spotlight. The rain cut through the light, throwing off shadows like a million tiny daggers. I pointed the gun down at the kid. He climbed to his knees and stared at me. He was finally coming to. His eyes refocused. He finally realized what was about to happen.

At first he didn't look at me. He just stared at the barrel of the gun. I knew his face but I couldn't figure out why. Then he looked up at me. He didn't flinch. He looked right into my eyes. I couldn't see fear; not yet, anyway. All I could see was hate and pain. The look on his face was the same as the looks on the faces of every sixteen-year-old kid I had ever taught about the War. It was the same face those kids wore when we first showed them that slide show of death and destruction. The fact that he was staring at his own death didn't change a thing.

I heard a car door slam. I knew that you'd gotten out of the car. I didn't know if you were running away or coming toward us. I didn't look up. I didn't take my eyes off the kid. I didn't want to face you, not until I had done what I had to do. I knew that if you ran away, you'd come back. I didn't know how you'd react if you stayed.

"Who are you?" I asked. It was killing me. Why did I recognize this kid?

"Fuck you," he responded, staring at the gun as he spoke. I had no problem with that response. I respected it. Still, it wasn't helpful. I planted my left leg in the mud and kicked the kid as hard as I could in the gut. I heard a gasp when I did so but it didn't come from the kid. You'd stayed. I would have rather done this without you, but you were going to have to be introduced to violence sometime.

The kid had keeled over in the mud after I kicked him. He gasped for air, swallowing rain as he did so. That started a coughing fit. I waited from him to finish. When he did, he climbed back onto his knees defiantly.

"Who are you?" I asked again, leaning toward the kid, speaking more softly this time. He just glared at me. His eyes repeated his earlier words, but this time he saved his breath. "What? You think you're some sort of cowboy?" I yelled at him. "You thought you could lead us out here and you and I would have some sort of duel? Twelve paces at midnight? Is that what you thought? You're a fool, kid. You're going to die a fool." The kid looked ashamed but he still didn't look scared. I stood up straight again and pointed the gun at the kid's head. I'd make it quick. "It didn't have to be this way, kid. You could have just left us alone. You could have run away. You could have kept driving. I wish you had." I tensed my trigger finger, and started to pull. As if he'd rehearsed for this moment, the kid turned his head to the side so that the bullet wouldn't enter through his face.

"What are you doing, Joe?" Your voice suddenly cut through the sound of the beating rain. You thought that I'd been posturing. You thought it was a bluff, that I was acting. You didn't know that I didn't bluff. I wasn't planning on gambling with our lives. I eased up on the trigger. The kid looked up at you, through the falling rain. I didn't dare look at you. I kept my eyes on the kid. "What are you doing?"

"He's one of them, Maria." I aimed the gun again. I didn't want you to talk me out of it. Killing him was the smart play.

"He's just a kid, Joe!" You were shouting. Your voice was laced with panic.

"No, he's not," I replied. I looked at the kid again as I spoke. "He's a soldier. And he's a liability." The kid glared up at me through the corner of his eyes as I spoke. Finally, there was something in his face besides hate. It was pride.

You suddenly turned to the kid and shouted, "Tell him! Tell him you don't know what he's talking about!" You were now pleading with both of us to simply stop it. Stop the madness. It was beyond us. The kid and I were in it together.

"Go ahead, kid. Tell me you don't know what I'm talking about," I said to the kid. He shot me the glare again. I kept the gun pointed at his head and walked over to his backpack, lying in the mud, sopping up the rain. I picked up the backpack and reached inside. Just as I'd expected, the backpack was full of papers. Under the papers was a gun. I took the gun out and threw it away. I simply tossed it off the side. It quickly disappeared into the blackness. I couldn't even hear it land over the sound of the rain. It was as if nothing existed in the world outside of this small triangle of light given off by the car's smashed-in headlights. Like the gun, the rest of the world had disappeared.

I threw the backpack, now free of weapons, down on the ground next to the kid. "Show her what's in the backpack, Eric." He looked up at me. He didn't move. I mustered up my meanest voice. "I know you're a proud kid and you ain't afraid of dying, but I'm not above killing you slowly. So show her what's in the fucking backpack." Finally, the kid reached over to the backpack. He unzipped it, reached inside, took out a large stack of papers, and flipped them into the mud. There were pages and pages of printed material. Paragraph after paragraph full of details. From where we were standing, we couldn't read the words. I didn't need to. I knew what they said. I had seen this before. Along with the printed pages were pictures. Even from where you and I were standing, the pictures were clear. There were five or six pictures of me. Pictures with a goatee, pictures clean shaven, older pictures, and one picture that had to have been taken within the past three months. There was a picture of our car. The one we were standing behind. The picture clearly showed the Massachusetts license plates that we had ditched back in Pennsylvania. Then, to round it off, there were two pictures of you. The first appeared to be a blow-up of the picture from your college ID. You couldn't have been more than fifteen years old. You looked fifteen. You had grown up a lot in two years. The second was a more recent picture of you, standing in front of a lake next to an older man. The older man's arm was wrapped around your shoulders. It must have been your father. Whoever had gotten that picture got it from your family. They had been to your parents' home. I could hear the pace of your breathing increase as you stared at the pictures as they crinkled in the rain.

Suddenly, the kid spoke. "Your child doesn't belong with him, Maria," he said to you. He spoke directly to you. "Your child is one of us. Your child can have a chance to do something good for the world."

Hearing his words, you began to cry. You placed your hand over your stomach, as if to protect your baby. You leaned over, placing your other hand on the dented trunk of our car. You sobbed, stopping momentarily to try to catch your breath. Then your words came out. Angry words directed at the kid. "What did we ever do to you?" you cried out. "Why can't you just leave us alone?" You sobbed again, bending over. When you caught your breath again, you repeated more quietly, "Why can't you just leave us alone?" Then, looking down at the kid, kneeling in the rain, covered in mud, as if the question could end it all, you said again, "What did we ever do to you?"

"That bastard," the kid replied, pointing at me, having the audacity to point at me while I aimed a loaded gun at his head, "that bastard killed my older brother." He spoke to you as if I weren't even there. "He came into my house"—the kid's voice rose in anger—"when I was thirteen years old. He came into my house when my brother and I were home alone. He grabbed me first because my brother was upstairs. He grabbed me and he tied my hands and feet together and he put masking tape over my mouth. Then he went upstairs and I listened as he strangled my big brother to death." The kid kept pointing at me as he spoke. "That's what he fucking did to me." That's why the kid had gotten the package. That's why I recognized the kid. His brother was my third job. He lived in Cincinnati, a good three hours from where we were. I don't remember why he was a target.

You didn't respond. It was all too much. I began to worry about the baby. I had to end it. The kid kept going, "Your baby, Maria, your baby can be better than that." I'd heard enough. It was my baby too. I hauled off and kicked the kid in the face. His body jerked to the side and he fell face-first into the mud. Slowly, he struggled back up onto his hands and knees. I hated him at that moment. He was trying to convince you to leave me. He didn't even care if he died.

"Because you're not a killer?" I finally yelled at him. He was just like me when I was his age.

He lifted up his head, and for the first time in minutes, he looked at me again. His eyes were filled with scorn, his voice filled with hate. "I'm not like you," he said. "I'm righteous." I pulled the trigger. The shot rang out through the night air as if it would echo for days. The kid's head jerked back. Then his body fell forward into the mud, motionless. I immediately regretted it. For the first time I could remember, I felt remorse.

You screamed. Then you ran off into the darkness. You made it maybe twenty feet before falling to the ground. I could hear a retching sound coming from the darkness as you threw up into the mud. I started to walk after you. I stepped out of the beam of light. Once out of the light, the darkness wasn't so complete. Though they were still difficult to see, I could make out outlines, shapes, and shadows in the grayness surrounding us. I could see your form, hunched over on the ground. I stepped closer to you. Suddenly you stood up and turned around. You extended your arms out toward me. At first I thought you were going to reach out to hug me. Then I realized that you had stumbled upon the kid's gun.

You held the gun in front of you. You aimed the gun directly at my chest. I stopped walking. I didn't dare move any closer to you. I wasn't sure what you were capable of at that moment. You were still crying. You didn't want me near you. "Why did you do it, Joe?" you cried. Your hair, straightened by the rain, hung over your shoulders. Your wet clothes clung to you.

"I had to, Maria." You let out an audible cry when I spoke. "I know you think I had a choice, but I didn't. It doesn't stop with him, Maria. If we let him go, he tells everyone where we are. He tells everyone where we are and it's over. We're trapped."

My logic didn't mean anything to you. Killing still didn't make sense to you. "You promised me you'd stop killing, Joe." I had. I'd meant it when I said it. That was four corpses ago.

"I didn't want to kill him, Maria." I went to take another step toward you.

"Don't, Joe." You lifted the gun, changing your aim from my chest to my head. "Don't come near me, Joe."

"Please, Maria. Please come back to the car. You're sopping wet. You're cold. We need to get you into some dry clothes. We need to get you warm. This isn't good for the baby."

"Don't, Joe."

"Please, Maria. Come back now. Get warm. Get dry. If you want to leave me in the morning, I'll take you anywhere you want to go." You reluctantly dropped your arm down to your side. You didn't walk toward me. You walked past me toward the car. I followed a few steps behind you. Before you climbed into the backseat of the car, you took one last look at the kid's body, sprawled out, lying facedown in the mud. Then you threw his gun back into the darkness.

I went back to the kid's body. I picked him up and carried him to his car. I opened the back door and laid his body down on the backseat. I took off my jacket and my shirt and used my shirt to wipe the mud off the kid's face. The bullet had gone in and out through the sides of his head. His face was untouched. Once I had gotten the mud off his face, I reached into the front of the car and turned off the one working headlight. I put my jacket back on, leaving my shirt in the mud next to the car. "I'm sorry, kid," I said to his lifeless body. "I'm sorry about your brother too." Then I closed the car door, leaving the kid's body sheltered from the rain in the backseat, and walked back to our car. On the way, I picked up the papers and the pictures that were strewn on the ground. I left the backpack. I left the money. I didn't feel right taking it anymore even though we needed it. I left everything that couldn't incriminate us. I threw the papers and the pictures in our now dented trunk, not wanting to leave evidence lying there in the mud. The damage to our car was minimal, little enough that it shouldn't arouse suspicion. They had pictures of our car, though. We'd have to trade it soon.

You didn't speak to me for the next three days, but you didn't leave me either.

Fourteen

We made it all the way to Charleston, South Carolina, the day after I killed the kid in Ohio. I drove through the night. You eventually fell asleep in the backseat of the car. I knew as soon as we met the kid that Chicago was no longer an option. We'd left New Jersey and pretty much driven in a straight line leading directly to Chicago. Once they found the kid's body, it wouldn't take them long to guess where we were headed. We had to change course.

I had never been to Charleston. That was the draw. I'd never done a job there, never taught a class. I'd driven past it but never stopped. As far as I knew, no one in Charleston had a reason to want me dead. If they were to find us in Charleston, they'd have to come looking for us. I hoped it was a big enough city that I could find a job and we could still disappear.

We made it to Charleston with about two hundred dollars and a smashed-up car. We still had some food left, but that was starting to run low too. We needed to find a new car. We needed to figure out a way to make some money. I was willing to work but my list of marketable skills was painfully deficient. I wasn't about to start killing people for money. It wasn't right. Besides, I'd made a promise to you. We'd need a place to stay. I'd need to be able to clean myself up if I expected to find any sort of work. But I was afraid to stay in any one place for too long. I decided on a three-night rule. We wouldn't stay at any one place for more than three nights. We'd keep moving. It was all I could think of for us to do. We couldn't keep changing cities, not without cash. I would have let you in on my plans but you weren't talking to me. I figured you needed time. I think seeing what you saw in Ohio finally drove everything home for you. This was real. We spent the first night in a cheap motel about forty miles outside of Charleston. We went into the city during the day, trying to scope it out and see if I could find work.

During our second day in Charleston, you finally spoke to me again. "What do you think happened to him?" you asked me. We were sitting on a bench in the Waterfront Park. I was flipping through the help-wanted ads in one of the free local papers. You had a blank expression on your face. At first I was afraid to say anything. I simply looked at you, scared that anything I might say would make you stop talking again. You stared off into the ocean. "I mean, what do you think happened to his body?" There wasn't sadness in your voice anymore, just curiosity.

"If his parents and friends haven't realized that he's missing yet, they will soon. They'll send people out looking for him. Eventually, someone will stumble upon the body. The police will be called in. With no suspects and no motive, they'll just write it off as another unsolved murder, a random act of violence. His parents, his family, they'll know the truth." A cool wind blew in from the ocean. It smelled of rotting fish.

"And they'll have lost another son," you said, looking at me, searching for any remorse.

"Yeah," I said, the guilt that I'd felt after shooting the kid coming back. The guilt felt good. The guilt was beginning to make me feel human.

"And that's why we're in Charleston and not Chicago?"

"And that's why we're in Charleston and not Chicago," I confirmed.

You didn't ask any more questions, not yet. You'd done enough talking for the time being.

After two nights in a motel, we spent two nights sleeping in the car. We tried to keep the car off any main roads. I still hadn't figured out how to get a new car. Our supplies were running low and so was our cash. Four days in Charleston and I hadn't found work yet. But it was four days without incident. That was progress in my book. Four days in Charleston. We would make it almost four months. Maybe the next place we'll make it five months, then six, and then, eventually they'll forget us and we'll be able to settle down.

The job search was painful. I'd known it would be. I had no papers, let alone skills. The only thing I had going for me was the fact that I was willing to work cheap. I knew I had to start somewhere. Even in the War, I'd started at the bottom. So every day I pounded the pavement, walking into places unsolicited and asking for work or answering ads in the papers for unskilled labor. I wasn't having any luck. They'd look me over, a twenty-five-year-old guy with no history, no backstory, and every one of them balked. I can't say that I blame them. I reeked of trouble. I could smell it on myself.

I'd always known that starting a new life wasn't going to be easy. I just hadn't expected every single person that I met to remind me of that. After three days we agreed that you should start looking for work too. I wasn't too happy about having you out in the world alone, but we needed the cash and you seemed a lot more innocent than I did. You were still less than two months pregnant. You weren't showing yet. We both knew that changes were going to start happening quick, though. I couldn't ask you to sleep in the car much longer. It was uncomfortable enough as it was. As your stomach grew, it would only get worse. We needed to find you a bed, even if it was a different bed every few nights.

After you'd spent a couple days looking for jobs, we decided to rent a room at a hotel outside the city. There was a local bus stop outside. The hotel wasn't extravagant by any standards, but it was still a hit to our dwindling supply of money. The money was running short but we needed the hotel room. You needed to rest. I needed to shower.

You were already in the hotel room when I got home from another day of rejection. I remember putting the key in the door, hearing nothing but silence from inside. I remember thinking that you must still be out, braving the rejection better than I was.

I turned the knob on the door and pushed my way inside. You were sitting upright on the edge of the bed. Your hands were in your lap and you were staring at the wall. The television was off. You didn't budge when I opened the door. You could have been a mannequin, based on how much you moved. I stepped beside you so that I could get a look at what you were staring at. Behind the television set, above the dresser, was a mirror. You were staring at yourself in the mirror.

"You okay?" I asked.

"No," you replied, your voice flat, your eyes still dry.

"What happened?" I asked. You took your eyes off your reflection and moved them onto me.

"I don't know if I can do this, Joe."

"What happened?" I asked again.

"Who is that, Joe?" you asked, pointing toward your reflection in the mirror.

"That's Maria," I responded, taking your face in my hands and kissing you on your forehead. "That's Maria. That will always be Maria."

"Then why do I call myself by another name when I meet strangers?" you asked. We had agreed to start using pseudonyms. It was safer.

"The name you call yourself doesn't change who you are."

"But I don't recognize myself, either, Joe. It's not just the name. I walk down the street and people look at me and they don't see me. They see someone else." I knew you were telling the truth. I'd been living with that for most of my life. There were only a handful of people in the world who looked at me and saw *me*. Everyone else saw a mirage, an illusion. Your life had become that way now too. It hurt me to see it, but to the world, your identity had to be a secret now. To me, you'll always be Maria.

"They don't know you, Maria. It doesn't matter what they see."

"It matters to me, Joe. Because I'm afraid that one day, I'm going to forget who I am and I'm just going to see what they see."

"What happened? What triggered this?"

"I was in a store today, a clothing store downtown." Your eyes darted around the room as you spoke, as if you were afraid someone was watching us. "I decided to apply for a job, to see if maybe they could use another salesgirl. The woman I went to speak with was an older woman. She started asking me some questions, you know, basic job questions about my experience and stuff. Then she looked at me. She took a long, hard look at me. It made me so nervous. I just kept thinking to myself, does she know who I am? Then she smiled and I got so scared." You looked up at me, your eyes pleading with me to make it stop. Your voice trembled. "Then she said to me, 'You look so familiar, darling. Why do you look so familiar?' And all I could think was, this woman wants to steal my baby." Your whole body started to tremble now. "I can't do this, Joe. I can't live like this. That poor kid in Ohio. He seemed so nice. He was so nice to me. He was so nice to me and all along he just wanted to steal my baby. And now he's dead and I see him in every face that I meet and I don't feel guilty, I just feel afraid."

I stood up. "It's the paranoia, Maria," I told you. "It's healthy. I have it too. One of the first things they taught me is that only the paranoid survive. It's that fear that will guard you. You learn to live with it." I walked over to the bathroom to wash my face. I walked over to the bathroom to wash the sins off my skin.

"Everything they taught you is insane, Joe!" you yelled at me so that you could be heard over the running water.

I walked back out of the bathroom. I walked over to you and kissed you on the cheek. "Everything but that," I said softly.

The next day, I found a job.

I found an advertisement in the paper for a carpenter's helper. It was the eighth ad that I'd answered that morning. The guy who answered my call was gruff and to the point. He liked the fact that I spoke English. He asked me if I had my own tools. I told him that I didn't but that I was willing to buy them. The job paid ten dollars an hour.

"When do I start?" I asked.

"Six A.M. tomorrow morning," he answered, giving me the address where I needed to go.

Paying for the tools was pretty much going to wipe out the rest of our savings, but they were an investment. There was no way that I could turn down work. Ten dollars an hour. It would take me two days just to make enough money to pay for the tools I had to buy. But after all we'd been through already, ten dollars an hour sounded like a fortune.

As instructed, I showed up on the site the next day with a brand new tool belt, new hammer, new tape measure, and new cat's claw. When I went to the store to buy the stuff, I had to ask the guy working there what a cat's claw was. He showed me an item that looked like a miniature crowbar. "It helps you to pull out nails. You hammer this end under the nail, pull the other end like a lever, and the nail comes out."

"Fine," I said, just wanting to get out of there. "I'll take it." After spending the money, I knew that we'd be back sleeping in the car for the next couple of days. I'd get paid at the end of the week. One week, and I'd earn almost as much money as we had started with, only this time it would be our money, money we earned. It felt like the start of something. It felt like the start of a normal life.

The job was pretty simple. We were tearing a house down and building a new one on top of the old one's foundation. It was just two of us, just me and Frank. I showed up at the site twenty minutes early on the first day. When I got to the site, I backed the car into a parking space so Frank wouldn't see the smashed-in trunk. Then I sat on the hood and waited. The air was cool and damp but I could tell it was going to be a hot day. It was quiet. Then I heard a car pull up.

Frank was about forty years old. He drove a white pickup truck with some rust on the sides. He had a red beard, trimmed short, but covering much of the front of his neck. He wore jeans and a T-shirt. He didn't bother to look at me when he first arrived. He simply went to the back of the truck and climbed into the truck bed. I walked over. "Take these three barrels," he said, motioning toward three white buckets, "and carry them over toward the house." I grabbed the first barrel. It was heavy. I looked inside. It was full of nails. I carried it over toward the old house and found some dry ground to place it on. Then I went back to the truck. I looked in the next barrel. It was full of nails that were about 50 percent larger than those in the first bucket. "No slacking on my time." The man peered at me when I got back to the truck. "You can carry both barrels at once. We've got a lot to do today." I grabbed the next two barrels by their handles. The third barrel was more of the same, full of nails, this time even smaller than those in the first bucket. I dropped the two buckets off next to the first and returned to the truck bed. "All right, now help me get this thing down," he said, motioning toward a gas-powered generator that was sitting in the truck bed. He pushed it off the truck and I grabbed it by one end. He grabbed the other and we walked it down toward where I had left the buckets of nails.

Once we'd set the generator down on level ground, Frank stood up. "Name's Frank," he said, extending his hand toward me without taking his eyes off the house.

I grabbed his hand firmly and shook it. "I'm Jeff," I responded. I had been using Jeff since I'd arrived. I liked still having the *J* in my name. It made me feel like I wasn't completely forgetting my family.

"Well, Jeff, you showed up on time, that's something. You look strong and I see you got yourself some shiny new tools." Frank looked down at my tool belt and laughed to himself. "So you work and I'll pay for that work and we'll see how long this thing lasts."

"So what's the job?" I asked, eager to get started.

"You're looking at it," Frank said, motioning toward the house. "We tear the old house down and build a new one on top of it. We're going to expand the foundation a bit, but mostly, we're just building up."

"Is it just the two of us?" I asked.

"Yup," Frank answered.

The air grew hot that first day. I don't know if I'd ever sweated so much in my life. By noon, I had worked harder, physically, than I had ever worked in my life. At first it was just hammering, knocking the old boards of wood off the frame of the house. My right forearm was sore from the hammering. Even when I stopped, I could still feel the bones in my forearm vibrating. But by noon I'd already made over fifty bucks.

At about five-thirty, Frank turned to me and said, "Help me get this shit back on the truck." I helped him carry the generator, some tools, and the buckets of nails back to the truck and load it onto the truck bed. By six o'clock, everything was packed up again. You couldn't even tell that we had been there, except that the house that had stood there this morning was now barely more than a skeleton. Before Frank drove away, he turned to me and said, "So you going to be here in the morning?" I think he could see how exhausted I was.

"Six o'clock?" I asked.

"Six o'clock," Frank responded, nodding his head and driving away.

That night, you told me that you wanted to cook dinner for me, a real man's dinner, you said. I appreciated the thought but we were sleeping in the car. We didn't have the money to go out, so instead you made us peanut butter and jelly sandwiches and we had a picnic on the hood of the car. You told me that you were proud of me, though, and that was good enough for me.

All I did that first week was work and sleep. On Friday, I got paid. Frank had no problem paying in cash. "It's your money," he said to me. "You earned it. Whether you want to give any to the government is none of my business." I let him think that I was only interested in skipping out on taxes. I never told him the real reason I needed to be paid under the table. After I got paid, we moved out of the car and started staying in motels again. The timing was good. Your back was beginning to hurt and I was glad to get you into a real bed.

———

The following week, you found a job too. You'd been spending a lot of time at the local bookstore, reading. After four days there, they asked you if you wanted to work the register part-time. It didn't pay much but the job wasn't too taxing for you and meant an extra $150 a week for us. With our combined incomes, we were able to start saving some money. I wanted a buffer. We needed the buffer because there was no way to know when we were going to have to run again. It was bound to happen. It was just a matter of time.

As the days went by, Frank started to trust me more and started to give me work that was more demanding than knocking down walls and carrying buckets of nails. Slowly, I started to learn things from him, practical things. First, Frank had me simply measuring and cutting wood. He'd hand me a sheet of paper with a bunch of measurements on it. Six ten-foot two-by-fours. Eight eighteen-foot two-by-twelves. I sat on the pile of wood with a tape measure and pencil, marking the wood and cutting it down with the buzz saw. I tried to remember everything Frank told me, not caring what other information it was going to dislodge from my memory.

"The buzz-saw blade is about an eighth of an inch wide," Frank told me on that second week before he trusted me to start cutting the valuable lumber. "You can't make a cut without taking into account the size of the blade. Once you cut, that eighth of an inch is gone. It's sawdust. You cut, you take wood away, there's no getting around it." He took the buzz saw in his hand to demonstrate, lining the blade up along the outside of the pencil line that he'd drawn. "So when you saw," Frank yelled over the grinding of the circular blade, "you have to cut to the outside of the line or you'll be cutting the wood too short." He sawed through the wood so I could see the eighth of an inch that simply vanished. "Don't cut the wood too short. It's expensive." After cutting the wood, I'd haul it down toward the base of the house. I spent days just cutting and hauling lumber.

Each week grew easier than the last. My body started to acclimate to the heat. I was less tired at night. I realized that I could ease the soreness in my forearm by gripping the hammer less tightly. Days went on. Your job at the bookstore was going well. We tried to remember to switch motels every three nights. Sometimes, we let a night or two slide. Things seemed to be going well. One night, when I got home to our motel room, you handed me something in a brown paper bag. It was this journal. You asked me to write for you. You said that you wanted to understand me. I remember looking at you with well-earned skepticism. My life was a secret. That's how it had always been. That's how it was supposed to be. Still, you made me promise you that I'd try.

Two nights later, after you had fallen asleep, I opened the journal and wrote about the woman I had strangled in Brooklyn. It was easier to write than I'd thought it would be. It helped that I felt like I was writing about someone else's life.

The days quickly turned into weeks and then the weeks into months. The days were all the same. The only thing that marked the passage of time was the changing motels and you. Your stomach grew with each passing day. Your body changed. We did our best to keep our guard up. It wasn't always easy. Sometimes, we had to remind ourselves that nothing had changed. People were still out there looking for us. It couldn't be this easy. I knew it. Even you knew it. Still, it was often all too easy to forget that we were still running. Sometimes, I only remembered in my sleep. I had dreams, but in my dreams I was never running. I was always the one doing the chasing and the people I was chasing were running for their lives. When I had those dreams, I would wake up in a cold sweat. When I woke up like that, I'd write in this journal for you. I was purging.

You brought a book home from the bookstore that explained what you were going through, what our baby was going through, on a week-by-week basis. We couldn't afford to take you to the doctor, so we relied on the book. We learned that your blood volume had increased by 50 percent, a fact that just floored me. We made it through morning sickness. Your skin broke out but then cleared up again. Your clothes stopped fitting. We'd have to get you new ones. It was going to eat further into our limited budget. Meanwhile, the baby was growing. It was developing a skeleton, a brain, its own heartbeat. It was becoming a person. Soon we'd be able to feel the baby move. It made everything else so easy to forget.

After about two months of working, I paid to have the trunk of the rental car fixed. We could have tried to trade it in, but without papers, it would have been tough. This way saved us money to boot. They hammered the dents out of the trunk and repainted it to cover the scratches. When they were done, it looked almost new.

I'd started getting into a routine at work. Frank began to loosen up. He taught me so much. He taught me how to measure out and hammer in the studs for the walls in the proper intervals. He taught me where to place my foot when I was angling nails down into the studs in order to keep them flush. We worked together sometimes, making

sure the frame of the house was level, pulling and pushing and hammering it into place. I learned some lessons more quickly than others.
Frank taught me how to hammer a warped piece of wood until it was
flush with a straight piece. You simply lined the boards up together
and drove a nail diagonally into the warped piece, hammering the
nail through until the warped piece straightened out. Once the nail
went through the warped piece and entered the second board, each
swing of the hammer would straighten the warped board out. Soon,
the two pieces would be forced flush. Sometimes it took more than
one nail. If you did it right, though, when you were done, you could
barely see where one board ended and the other began.

It didn't always appear to work. One afternoon, I was working
with two boards and I just couldn't get them to go flush. "Hey, Frank.
What do you do when the boards won't go flush even after you've put
in a couple of nails?" Frank looked at me. He didn't say a word. He
took his hammer and dropped it into the leather loop at the bottom
of his tool belt. Then he walked over to me. He took my own hammer out of my hands. He held it in his hand, measuring the weight.
Then he raised the head of the hammer and he swung the hammer
down four times, two times on each of the nails that I had tried to use
to make the wood flush. In four swings, Frank had done what I
couldn't do in twenty. He handed the hammer back to me. I looked
down at the two pieces of wood, now a single solid block.

"Sometimes," Frank said as he walked away from me without
bothering to turn his head, "there are no tricks. Sometimes, you just
have to swing harder."

After we'd been in Charleston for a little more than three months, I
turned twenty-six. If you'd asked me when I was twenty if I'd live to

see twenty-six, I would have laughed at you. Now, not only had I made it, but I was going to be a father. You took me to the movies to celebrate. It was the best birthday I ever had.

One week after my twenty-sixth birthday, I came home from work to find you locked in the bathroom of our motel room. You were just short of twenty weeks pregnant. I banged on the bathroom door but you wouldn't open it. I yelled through the door, asking you what was wrong. You could barely get out the words. You told me that you were cramping and bleeding. I could hear the panic in your voice. As soon as you told me what was happening, I ran to the book. I grabbed it and looked up your symptoms. It wasn't normal, not at this stage of a pregnancy. You weren't supposed to be bleeding now. The book that had given us so much good news over the past four plus months now told me to take you straight to the hospital. I yelled for you to come out so that I could drive you to the emergency room. I didn't have to say it twice.

Fifteen

The motel that we were staying at wasn't far from the hospital. You gave me directions as I drove. You had memorized the route. I don't know when. I wonder if you'd done that for all the motels that we stayed at without telling me. Other than giving me directions, you didn't speak. You didn't even answer me when I asked you how you were doing. Instead of saying anything, you just shot me a look. That look was answer enough for me. I didn't ask again.

The emergency room was already crowded when we got there. The woman behind the counter gave us paperwork to fill out. I handed it to you. There was no way that I could fill it out. I could barely see straight. I stood up and paced, every few minutes walking up to the nurse who had given us the paperwork to ask her when we'd get to see a doctor. "Everyone is waiting" was the only answer she'd give me. I didn't care about everyone. I only cared about you. Your cramping had slowed down but hadn't stopped. There was nowhere for you to go to check if you were still bleeding. I was about to go say something when they called your name and told you that there was a doctor ready to examine you. You had given them your real name. I'm sure you didn't even think about it. I couldn't blame you even though I knew it was a mistake. At a moment like that, it's hard to prioritize your fears.

We walked through the waiting room doors to the inside of the emergency room. It looked like an infirmary inside. The fluorescent lights were unforgiving in their starkness. I could hear them buzzing beneath the nurse's chatter and the cries of the patients. The patients were lined up along both walls, lying on cots, with makeshift curtains the only thing separating one person from the next. We followed a nurse down the aisle in the middle of the room until we got to your cot. She asked you to take off your clothes and put on a hospital gown. I pulled the curtain around us and helped you undress. That's when I saw the blood. Your underwear was drenched. It was a dark crimson color. Your hands were shaking as you bent down to take them off. I reached down to help you. Where the hell was the doctor?

We got you changed and up on the cot. Minutes later a doctor came in. He didn't look much older than me. He asked us why we were there. You spoke to him calmly. You told him your symptoms.

"Have you been seeing a doctor?" he asked.

"No," you replied, shaking your head. I looked down at my hands, feeling impotent. We had talked about getting you to the doctor's but I didn't think we could afford it. We needed to save money. I knew that there were going to be emergencies. This just wasn't the type of emergency that I was accustomed to.

"We're going to have to run some tests," the doctor said, before pulling the curtain aside and walking away again.

"You gave them your real name," I said to you without thinking, once the doctor stepped away.

"Don't do this to me now, Joe," you answered. I let it go. I figured that we could worry about it later. I could only hope that we'd still have something to worry about.

The doctor came back with a nurse. They took some of your blood. He had you spread you legs so that he could examine you. I looked the other way when he did. Then another nurse wheeled in a machine that looked like a television set on wheels. I had seen it in the movies before. It was an ultrasound machine. I turned away again. I didn't want to look at the screen in case something was wrong. The doctor began to run a scanner over your stomach. "Let's see what's going on here," he said.

Then we waited. We waited for what seemed like forever, though it was probably only a minute or two. "What's happening, Doctor?" you finally asked.

The doctor didn't answer for a moment. He just kept moving the scanner in his hand over your stomach and watching the screen. "There it is," he finally said. I looked up. I couldn't help it. I needed to see, even if I didn't want to. "You said that you're almost five months pregnant?" the doctor asked.

"Yes," you answered, on the verge of tears. "Is everything okay?"

"Well," the doctor said, "you see that movement on the screen?" I looked at the screen. I could see it. It was a tiny flicker. I could feel my own pulse increase. "That's your child's heart beating." I looked over at you. You couldn't take your eyes off the screen. I looked at the screen again too. There was the flicker again, beating steadily. I could feel my own heart race until my heart and the baby's heart seemed to be beating at the exact same pace.

"Is everything okay?" you asked the doctor again.

"The heartbeat looks good," the doctor answered, "but I want to get the results of some of the tests we're running and I want to monitor you for a bit. We're going to move you upstairs."

"We don't have insurance," I said to the doctor. He knew what I meant. He knew that I meant we couldn't pay for anything.

"I'll let the people upstairs worry about that," the doctor answered before walking away. They wheeled you to the elevator without making you get out of your cot. I walked beside you, holding your hand. We passed other people in the emergency room, coughing and screaming and crying out for painkillers. Then we got to the elevator, the doors shut behind us, and all was quiet.

When we got upstairs, they wheeled you into your own room. There was another bed in the room but it was empty. A whole team of people began attending to you. Nurses came in and hooked you up to a couple of machines. There was a heart monitor and an IV and some other machines whose purpose was beyond me. No matter how many times we asked, no one would tell us if everything was normal. No one would tell us anything. I sat down in the chair next to your bed. "Everything is going to be okay," I said to you.

"You don't know that," you replied. "Don't you dare say that to me unless you know that it's true." So I stopped talking again and waited. At one point they came in and did more tests. I lost track of everything they did to you. I wanted to see that flicker again. I wanted to make sure that it was still there. That flicker had instantly become my whole life.

Soon the testing stopped, though they kept you hooked up to a couple machines. Maybe an hour later, another doctor came in. This one was older. He wore regular clothes beneath his white robe. He looked me up and down over his glasses as soon as he walked into the room. He was carrying his clipboard in front of him. I didn't trust how he looked at me. I immediately thought that he was one of them. The only reason that I didn't do anything about it was because he was our only hope. We needed him to save our child. After that, all bets were off.

"Can I talk to you *alone*, Ms. _____?" The doctor spoke your last name, your real last name. The suspicion inside me grew even stronger. You looked at me. You didn't want me to leave. I could see it in your face. You didn't have to worry. There was no way I was going anywhere.

"He can stay," you answered.

"I'd really prefer to speak with you alone, Ms. _____." He said your name again.

"No." Your answer was firm. "He stays."

"Okay," the doctor finally relented. "I've got a few questions for you and there are a few things that I can tell you." He looked down at the chart in his hands. "The good news is that your baby's heartbeat is strong and everything seems to be progressing fine. The baby is a good size and appears to be growing at the proper rate. Everything with the fetus looks good."

I could hear you breathe a partial sigh of relief. You still had questions. "Then what's happening?" you asked.

The doctor put the chart under his armpit so that he could talk to you directly. "The bleeding and the cramping are from a condition called placental abruption." I tried to commit every word to memory thinking that, if I knew what the problem was, I could help fix it. "That means that at some point during your pregnancy, your placenta partially separated from the wall of your uterus and blood has collected between the placenta and the uterus."

"Is it dangerous?" you asked. You were ahead of me with every question, asking it even before I could properly process my thoughts.

"It can be," the doctor answered. "You can lose a lot of blood and that can be dangerous for you and for the baby. It can also cause premature labor, which, this early in your pregnancy, would not be a good thing, since your baby is not viable yet."

You looked over at me. You were scared. I gave you my hand and you clutched it tightly. "Why is this happening?" you asked. You were looking right at me, as if I could answer you, but you knew that I didn't have any answers.

"That's what I wanted to talk to you alone about," the doctor answered. "For someone like you, in their first pregnancy, who doesn't smoke or do drugs, the cause is usually some sort of trauma." The doctor glared at me again. It was the same look he had given me when he first walked through the door, the look that made me think that he was one of them. I knew now that he wasn't one of them. He had other reasons for glaring at me.

"Are you accusing me of hitting Maria?" I asked him, knowing full well what he was implying.

"No one is accusing anyone of anything," the doctor answered. "It's just that in cases where there are no other obvious causes of trauma, spousal abuse is not an infrequent cause." The doctor looked at you again. "We just like to be sure," he said.

"Joe's not like that," you replied, shaking your head. "He's not violent like that." You meant it. I guess it was true. I wasn't violent *like that*. A wave of guilt rushed over me before I even knew the extent of things that I had to feel guilty about.

"Okay," the doctor said. "Can you think of any other trauma that you might have had?" He looked down and made a few marks on the sheet on his clipboard.

I could think of one. I wish that I couldn't. "We were rear-ended," I said to the doctor. It was a half-truth. The truth was so much uglier. I thought back to the image of that boy's body lying in the mud in front of his wrecked car, the rain falling down and splashing in the puddles around him. "But that was months ago," I finished.

"Well, that could do it," the doctor said, making another note on your chart. He turned toward you again. "Do you have a history of high blood pressure in your family, Maria?" he asked. You shook your head. "Because your blood pressure is extremely high. The car accident you were in could have caused the abruption and you may not have had any symptoms until now because it was suddenly exacerbated by your high blood pressure. Have you been under a lot of stress recently?" the doctor asked. I looked at you. You didn't even know how to answer his question. Stress didn't begin to describe what you were under, Maria. It didn't matter that we hadn't run into any trouble in months.

"Some," you offered as a compromise between the truth and a boldfaced lie.

The doctor nodded. "I'm going to keep you on fluids for a couple more hours," the doctor said. "The bleeding has seemed to calm down but we'll want to monitor that as well. There's not much else we can do at this point. I'm going to prescribe you some medication for your high blood pressure. That might help. Beyond that, you need to do whatever you can to eliminate your stress." The doctor looked at me again as if I were the cause of all your stress. I suppose, this time, he was right. "You should probably also try to stay off your feet as much as possible. I realize that bed rest at this early stage in your pregnancy probably isn't possible, but whatever you can do might help. Either way, no strenuous activity."

I wanted to ask him what we should do if that wasn't possible. What should we do if we had to physically run for our lives? What if, no matter what we did to avoid stress, we knew full well that stress was going to find us? I wanted workable answers to questions that I didn't even have the courage to ask. "That's it?" was the only question I could think of.

"That's it," the doctor answered. "Do those things—and hope for the best." He looked at us again from over his clipboard and smiled. "The good news is that the heartbeat is strong. The baby is strong." He paused. "Did they tell you the baby's gender after they did the ultrasound downstairs?"

"No," I answered, finally getting the words out before you.

"We can't always tell this early but we got a pretty clear picture this time. Would you like to know the baby's gender?" he asked you.

We looked at each other. I let you answer. "Do you think the baby's going to be okay, Doctor?"

"I can't make any promises," the doctor said. "Pregnancy is always touch and go. The odds of you making it full term aren't very high. But your baby looks strong. It's trying. It only needs to make it another couple months to be viable."

"Then I want to know," you answered him.

"Your baby is a boy," the doctor said. It's a boy, Maria. We're having a baby boy. I wanted to be excited but the risks suddenly seemed almost unbearable. *Placental abruption.* I had another name for my growing list of enemies. I couldn't forget our other enemies, though. They were still out there. They were still looking for us. So tell me how I'm supposed to relieve your stress and keep you from doing anything strenuous. How am I supposed to figure out how to do the impossible?

Sixteen

We should have left Charleston as soon as we got home from the hospital. We should have come back to the motel, gathered up our things, and left town forever. That would have been the smart thing to do. You gave them your real name. I should have made us run right away but I was afraid. I was afraid of what might happen if I made you run again. Fear had been my ally for so long, I didn't know how to act once it became our enemy. Fear equalled stress. No one knew that better than me. I lost focus. I was afraid of what fear might do to our son. I just wanted you to be able to relax. I wanted everything to be calm. I wanted our son to be safe. So I tried to act like everything was fine. Everything wasn't fine. You had given the hospital your real name. I knew deep down that now it was only a matter of time.

It's only been five days since we left the hospital. So much has changed already. We made it almost four months in Charleston before we had to run. Maybe we'll make it even longer this time. I try to stay positive for you. I keep writing in this journal because I can tell it things that I'm afraid to tell you. I can tell it how scared I am right now. One day I'll give you this journal but I want our son to be born first. I want to know that he's safe first. Until then, all I want to do is protect the two of you. There are things you should know about

Charleston, about how we left Charleston. There are details that I kept from you because I didn't understand them. I still don't.

After we got home from the hospital, I knew something was going to happen. I just didn't know what and I didn't know when, so I waited like a fool. It could have been worse. If we hadn't gotten that phone call, we might not have even made it out of our motel room.

I woke up that night before the phone even rang. I can't explain why. Something was wrong. I could feel it. I might have started ignoring some of my instincts but they weren't dead yet. My body was drenched in sweat. My heart was racing. I tried to catch my breath. I could feel you move beneath the covers next to me. You moved a lot in your sleep now, trying to find a comfortable way to lie despite your ever-growing stomach. I took a few long breaths. You didn't wake up. Not yet. I glanced over at the window, trying to remember what woke me up. Our blinds were drawn. A pair of ugly yellow drapes covered the window overlooking the motel parking lot. I began to think that someone must be out there. Someone must be waiting just outside our window. I must have heard them and that had to have been what woke me up. I thought about walking over to the window to look but I didn't want to wake you. I couldn't afford to frighten you unless I was certain we were in danger. Besides, if they were outside, it was already too late.

So I just lay there, paralyzed by some sort of irrational fear that turned out to be all too rational. I could feel a large weight pushing me down onto the bed. I lay there and waited for something to happen. I glanced over at the clock beside the bed. It was two-thirty in the morning. The room was dark. All I could see was the light creeping in from the crack just below the curtains. My eyes scanned the ceiling and the walls. I watched a cockroach run from one end of the ceiling to the other. I couldn't see any signs that something was wrong. It was just my instincts running amok.

I heard a clicking sound come from the phone before it started ringing. It was just the slightest noise but I heard it. Then the phone rang. I leapt across the bed and reached for the receiver. I picked up the phone before the second ring. I had no idea what to expect. All I wanted was answers. I held the receiver to my ear and sat straight up in bed. You barely budged.

"Hello?" I whispered.

The voice on the other end was muffled but it spoke with urgency. "You've got to get out." There was something that I remembered about the voice, something that I recognized. It was a voice that I'd heard on the phone before.

"Who is this?" I asked.

"Joe," he replied, "you've got to get out of there." It clicked when he said my name.

"Brian?"

"Don't say my name, Joe. Don't worry about who I am or why I'm calling. Just go. Go now." I could hear the fear in his voice. It was real.

"What's going on?" I asked, confused. I was sure it was Brian. I just didn't understand why he was calling me. I'd been cut loose.

"They know," Brian replied. "They know where you are, Joe. They know everything. You don't have any time. You've got to get out of there." His voice quivered. It finally sank in that he was trying to help me.

"Where can I go?" I asked, hoping that Brian would have more answers, that he would have some sort of plan. I was hoping Brian would tell me what to do and where to go just like he used to back when things were simpler.

"I can't help you, Joe. If they even find out I called you, I'm a dead man. Just go. Please go. I can't talk anymore. Just go and don't look back."

"What do they know?" I asked, trying to get as much useful information as I could before he hung up.

"Everything, Joe. They know where you work. They know what

car you drive. They know everything and they're coming. You're not safe. They're coming for you right now." I wanted to ask more. I opened my mouth but before I could say anything else I heard a clicking sound and then a dial tone. Brian had hung up. Either that or somebody had disconnected us.

I held the phone to my ear for a few more seconds, listening to the drone. It was time to run again, only this time the stakes were raised. This time, our son's life was on the line too. I looked down at your body as you slept. I didn't want to wake you up. I didn't want to make you run again. But I knew that the only thing riskier than running was standing still.

I stood up quickly. I grabbed a duffel bag and began throwing everything I thought we might need inside of it. I went into the bathroom and reached under the sink and grabbed the cash that we had stashed there. We had been able to save up some money over the past few months. We spent a lot of our savings on your blood pressure medication. There wasn't a whole lot of money left but I had to hope that it was enough to help us get away. I opened a drawer, pulling out clothes and throwing them in the duffel bag too. Then I grabbed the gun. I held it in my hand for a second. I hadn't held it since I shot that kid in Ohio. The gun felt good in my hand. Whatever the reason, the weight of it in my hand calmed me down.

I didn't turn the lights on in case we were being watched. They could have been waiting outside. For all I knew, the flicker of the lights was the trigger that would set their whole plan into action. I wanted to be ready first. I wasn't trying to be quiet. You were going to have to wake up anyway—better to do it with noise than by me shaking you awake. When your eyes finally blinked open you were staring at me holding the gun.

"What's going on?" you asked, squinting at me through the darkness.

"We're leaving," I replied.

"What?" you asked.

"We're leaving. Now," I replied.

"We can't, Joe. It's too dangerous." You looked down at your stom-ach.

I grabbed a handful of your clothes from the dresser and threw them on the bed next to you. "Get dressed," I pleaded. "Please."

"We can't do this, Joe. It's too dangerous." You placed a whole hand over your belly as if trying to protect it. "We have to be careful."

I walked over to the window. I lifted the curtains slightly and peered outside. I couldn't see anything. The parking lot was still. Nothing was moving. Everything was where it should be. I tried to glance at the outside of our motel room door. The angle was difficult, but it didn't appear that anyone was out there waiting for us. Maybe Brian was wrong or maybe it was a trap.

"I got a phone call," I said to you. "It was a warning."

"From who?" you asked.

"A friend," I replied. I had to believe that Brian was a friend. I had to trust someone. "Please put on your sneakers."

"I thought that you were cut loose. I thought that you didn't have any friends anymore."

"Me too" was the only answer I could give you. You sat on the edge of the bed and started to slip your sneakers onto your feet.

"I can't run, Joe. You know that." I knew. No strenuous activity. We'd have to get out without making you run.

"We're escaping, Maria. I'm not asking you to run."

"Do we even know who we're escaping from?" you asked.

I didn't. Brian could have had inside information or he could have heard rumors coming from the other side. We didn't have time to try to figure it out. "Yeah," I answered, "whoever is chasing us."

I looked around the room for anything else we might need. I packed our money and about half of your clothes. I went to the closet and grabbed my tool belt and my tools. I threw them in the duffel bag with our clothes and zipped it up. I felt the weight of the duffel bag. It would have been easier if you could carry it, but it was too heavy. I couldn't ask you to do that. I slung the bag over my shoulder. Then I checked to make sure the gun was loaded. "We need to get to the car," I said to you. You nodded. "I'm not sure it's safe out there." The doctor had told me to try to limit your stress. Some things are easier said than done.

I held the gun in my right hand and guided you behind me with my left. I opened our motel room door, half expecting all hell to break loose when I did. Nothing happened. The door creaked open. Once the door stopped moving and the creaking sound stopped, it was replaced only by the hollow sounds of night. The moon was about a quarter full but the parking lot outside of the motel was lit brightly from a streetlight. Beyond that, the night was full of shadows.

"It looks safe," I whispered over my shoulder without looking at you. "Are you okay?"

"I'm trying," you answered as honestly as you could.

"Here are the car keys," I said to you, handing the keys behind me. I felt your hand reach out to take them. Your hand was warm. "Stay behind me until we get to the bottom of the stairs. Once we get to the bottom of the stairs, duck down and head for the car. I'll follow you. I'll protect you." We walked slowly together. Once we got to the bottom of the stairs, you dropped your head beneath your shoulders and made a dash for the car. All I could think was, *not too fast, Maria.* You squatted down by the passenger side door of the car and unlocked it. I walked quickly after you, trying to look everywhere all at once as I ran. All I saw was more of the same, more of nothing. By that point, the nothingness was what began scaring me the most. I threw the duffel bag in the backseat and climbed into the car.

You handed me the car keys. I slid them into the ignition and turned the key. The engine revved up.

I pulled the car out of the parking lot. My mind raced, trying to make some sense of things. I knew that getting away wasn't going to be this easy. I knew it.

"Now what?" you asked me. "Do we just try to drive away?" I could see in your eyes that you were beginning to question whether or not we even really needed to run away.

I weighed our options in my mind. Brian's words echoed in my head. *They know what car you drive.* Eventually we'd have to get rid of the car, but not yet. Our first goal was to get out of town. "That's one option," I answered you. "But they know what car we're driving."

"Well, do we have any other options?" you asked

"I don't know." I didn't even know where I was driving. I just kept moving forward, turning deeper and deeper into nowhere. The night was still and peaceful. Nothing was moving but us. I drove along the empty, tree-lined street, making turn after turn, and we saw nothing.

"Let's just drive," you said. "Let's just get on the highway and go. So they know our car. So what? There's nobody here, Joe." I could see the shadow of each passing tree float over your face as we moved forward, casting your face in alternate strips of dark and light. "How are they going to find us when they're not even here?"

"Maybe you're right," I said. It was a relief to even think. Just drive away. "We can abandon the car later. We can get lost again." I turned the car around another corner, heading us back toward the long two-lane highway running away from Charleston, away from our new life. All I had to do was get on that highway and step on the gas. For one sweet moment it all seemed so simple.

Then we heard a crash. It came out of nowhere, echoing through the still night air like thunder. "What the hell was that?" you shouted, turning in your seat, unaware of what direction the sound had come from. It sounded almost like an explosion. It came from the highway, the highway that we were headed toward.

"I don't know," I said, slowing the car down so that we could listen better. Seconds after the crash there was the sound of an engine revving, then tires screeching on pavement. It was coming from the highway. The sound started getting louder. Whatever it was, whoever it was, they were headed in our direction. Without stopping the car, I flicked off the car's headlights. We were driving in darkness. The sound kept coming. It was close now. I yanked the steering wheel to the right and pulled the car off the side of the road, barely squeezing between two trees. Right as I turned the car off, a car sped past us down the road. I watched it in the rearview mirror. It flew by in a blur. Only a split second after that, another car followed, chasing after the first. The second car's front fender was smashed in. It had hit something. God only knows what. We sat in silence for a few moments before I dared start the car again. Neither of us took a breath.

"Do you think they were looking for us?" you asked. I started the car again, flicking the headlights on. Then I pulled the car back up onto the now empty road.

"Does anything else make any sense?" I answered you. You shook your head. You knew the truth. They were out there. They were close. And they were after us.

"What do we do now?" you asked, the fear that was absent almost moments ago now creeping into your voice.

"That doesn't change anything. We already knew they were here." I slowly sped up the car. We were heading for the highway. When we made it to the turn, I looked down the dark highway. It was long and straight and empty. The end of it simply disappeared into the darkness. I pulled our car out onto the highway. All I wanted to do was drive. I stepped on the gas but it only lasted a short moment.

"Holy shit!" you shouted. "What is that?" I saw it too. I barely caught a glimpse of it at the very edge of the light from our headlights. There was something moving off the side of the road. Whatever it was, it didn't look human. For the second time in minutes, I pulled the car over to the side of the road and switched off the headlights.

"Stay here," I said to you. You didn't listen. By the time I got out of the car, you were already standing outside. The air was warm. There was a pungent smell in the air that I recognized but couldn't place. I pulled the gun from my belt and began walking toward whatever it was that was moving by the side of the road. You walked closely behind me. I could almost feel your body against mine. I could feel your breath on my neck. Before I saw anything, I felt you gasp behind me.

"Oh, my God!" you yelled. I looked ahead of us. The grass in front of us was dark from something. "There's blood," you shouted. "There's blood everywhere." That was the smell. It was the smell of blood.

"Quiet," I whispered to you. "No matter what we see, we have to stay quiet." The trail of blood started at the street and led all the way to whatever it was that we had seen from the road. It was still moving. I took another step closer. I could see it better now. It was a man but he was in worse shape than anyone I'd ever seen before. I'd seen dead men in better shape. He was lying facedown in the grass. He was dressed entirely in black. He was wearing the uniform of an assassin— the same one that I had worn countless times. The movements his body was making were totally unnatural. His arms were moving in directions arms weren't supposed to move. It could have just been muscle spasms. I couldn't even be sure that he was still alive. We took another few steps toward him. Then I heard him moan.

We didn't have time for this. We were being chased. I was certain of that now. This man had something to do with it. How he'd ended up on the side of the road, I couldn't even imagine. "We have to leave him," I told you. I turned around and started walking toward the car.

"What?" you asked. "We can't just leave him here." You looked over at the body. "He'll die." That was the truth. What it had to do with us was beyond me.

"We're leaving."

"We can't just leave him!" you shouted. I held my hand up to my mouth again to motion to you to keep quiet. You lowered your voice. "You promised me there would be no more death!"

"I didn't cause this," I said, pointing at the squirming body with the muzzle of the gun. It was a lie. Somehow it was a lie. His groans became louder and more distinctive. He could hear us talking. He was trying to say something to us. The voice murmured through a mouthful of wet grass. I couldn't understand what he was saying. Then he managed to get out one word that I could understand. "Please." You looked at me. Even in the darkness I could see the pain in your eyes.

I walked back past you, back toward the body. When I got near you, you whispered, "Be careful." I stepped up toward the body. You stood only a few feet behind me. I kept the gun pointed at the squirming body. I told myself that there was no way this was a trap. There was too much blood for it to be a trap. I wasn't sure if I believed it, though. I didn't know what to expect. The groans had grown quiet, as if the body had used up all of its remaining energy trying to talk to us. *Please.* Now only soft, quiet moans came from the body as it quivered below my feet. I hooked my foot under one of his shoulders and lifted. He was deadweight. It took all my strength, but I was able to flip him over without getting my hands dirty. He was now lying on his back.

He was covered in blood. I'm pretty certain not all of it was his. His legs were twisted under him, corkscrewing, not flipping over properly with the rest of his body. He couldn't move them. His neck was broken. Once facing the sky, he opened its eyes. His face was cut up. Blood covered much of it but when his eyes opened they were a bright green. Even in the darkness I could see the color. "Help," he said now, more clearly. He wanted to say "Help me" but didn't have the strength to get out the second word. Punctured lungs. Broken ribs. I could diagnose a whole boatload of problems that I couldn't cure. You stepped around me and knelt down in the grass beside him. You brushed some of the dirt off his face.

I made eye contact with him. "You were in the car crash that we heard?" I asked. His head moved slightly, as much of a nod as we were going to get out of him. "This happened to you in that car crash?" Another nod. He was clearly the casualty of some chase. "And then they threw you out of the car? They left you here?" Again, his head moved; this time, I could see the sadness in his eyes. You grimaced, not being able to imagine how anyone could be so cold. I knew how. He was deadweight. He was slowing down a mission. Finding us was that mission. When you see death every day, one more death doesn't mean as much to you. They probably didn't even think twice before they tossed him out of the car.

"We have to do something, Joe," you turned to me and said as you held the dying man's head in your hands. The man looked up at you as you brushed his bloodstained hair off his forehead.

"There's nothing we can do, Maria." You knew I was right. Still, your eyes pleaded with me to try. I got down on my knees on the other side of him.

"Can you move your legs?" I asked. I could see the man's face strain. I looked down at his legs. There was no movement. "Your arms? Can you move your arms?" Again his face strained. This time one of his arms moved. The other lay still. It appeared to be broken. As he moved his arm, he let out another painful moan.

Suddenly, I heard another car coming down the road. There wasn't any time to find better cover. "Duck down," I said to you. We got as low to the ground as we could. The night sky flared up with light as the headlights moved past us. The sound of gravel churning grew loader and then quieter again. The car sped away from us. Soon, all that was left was the sound of our breathing and the body's wheezing.

"We have to go, Maria. It's not safe here." I could feel the panic rising in my chest. We were going to get caught because you were too kind.

"We can't just leave him, Joe," you answered, tears welling up in your eyes.

"Listen, Maria, you're going to have to make a decision here. Do you want to try to save this man or do you want to save our son? Because we're not going to be able to do both." You understood. I could see it in the expression on your face.

The dying man's head was still in your lap. You looked down at him. "I'm sorry," you said. You lifted his head up off your lap and stood up. You were trying to keep yourself from crying, which only led to sobbing. You turned away from the body and started walking back to our car. I looked down at the man, lying there. His eyes followed you as you walked toward the car.

I turned away from him too. I started following you back to the car. Then I heard another moan, this one louder. He didn't want to be left alone. He must have known that he was going to die but he didn't want to die alone. I turned back toward the body. "If I find a phone, I'll send help for you," I said to him. He slowly closed his eyes, knowing that help was never going to come.

When I got back into the car, you were already sitting inside. The tears had stopped. There was only determination in your face now. I turned the car back on and pulled back onto the highway. We started driving in the other direction.

"Where are we going?" you asked.

I had a plan now. Looking at that man dying on the ground had helped me formulate a plan. They knew where we were. That was for sure. They didn't sacrifice men like that for nothing. They knew they were close. I thought we could use that. We could use that to get some money before we left. We needed the money. We were down to our last few hundred dollars. It would take us a while to get settled in wherever we ended up next, and we were going to have to bring you to the doctor's if our son was going to survive. "We're going downtown," I answered.

"What? Why?" Downtown wasn't away. You just wanted to get away. In retrospect, maybe that would have been the right move.

"I still have my ATM card. We haven't used it because I was afraid it would give away where we are. Well, they already know where we are. This could be our last chance to get some money for a while. If we do it downtown, they won't have any idea what direction we go afterwards." I looked over at you. You looked skeptical. "We need to do this," I said. You knew I was right.

"Okay," you answered, sealing our fate. I stepped on the gas and we sped toward the city.

During our ride, everything remained calm, almost frighteningly so. Everything was quiet. We could see the city lights in the distance. It was still the middle of the night. The city would be asleep, but the lights were on. We crossed over the bridge leading into the city. My plan was to simply turn down a street with a bank, pull over, take out as much money as the bank would let me, get back in the car, and drive. I had to believe that my ATM card would still work. They would have wanted me to use it, knowing full well that it would give me away.

The city streets were almost empty. Every few blocks we would see someone walking down the street, heading home from a friend's house or from a night of drinking. We were in the rich end of town full of big houses and old money. There were highways leading away from the city in all directions. I hadn't even thought yet about which direction we were going to go in. One step at a time, I thought. You sat silently in the passenger seat of the car. I didn't know if you were thinking about the dying man we'd left by the side of the road or if you were simply trying not to think at all.

I glanced down a long street and saw a bank with an ATM machine. I stopped the car on the side of the road, pulling into a vacant spot near the front of the bank. I looked around us after putting the car in park. The street was empty. At least I thought it was. I unbuckled my seat belt and turned to you. "Wait here," I said. You nodded. "For real this time. Stay in the car." I opened the driver's side door and stepped out. I tried moving quickly, jogging to the door of the bank and swiping my ATM card so that the door would unlock. I took one last look back at you to make sure you were safe and then I stepped inside.

"Come on. Come on. Come on," I whispered to myself as I slid the ATM card into the slot and punched in the code. The screen came up and asked me how much money I wanted to withdraw. I punched in a thousand dollars but it wouldn't let me take out that much. Next I punched in five hundred. I waited. I heard the bills ruffling behind the machine. Then it spit out twenty-five twenty-dollar bills. It would buy us a little bit of time.

I turned to head back toward the car. I could still see you inside. You were okay. You looked safe. I was about the open the bank door and come back to you when I saw the phone across from the ATM machines. It wasn't just a bank help phone. It was a real pay phone. I decided to keep a promise I had made. I put the five hundred dollars in my wallet and put my wallet back in my pocket. Then I walked over to the pay phone, picked up the receiver, and dialed 911. I couldn't fight the feeling that I had somehow been through this before. My stomach knotted up. A dispatcher picked up the phone. "There's been a horrible accident," I said.

"Where?" the dispatcher asked.

"There's a man," I responded, "by the side of the road. He was hit by a car. He needs help now." I told the dispatcher the name of the road where we'd found the man.

"Can you stay on the line?" the woman asked.

"No," I replied. I was about to hang up the phone when the first gunshot echoed into the air. The first shot was crisp and loud. At first,

I didn't recognize the sound. It sounded too much like a firecracker. Then another shot rang out. The sound was less distinct this time, more muffled. It was coming from a different gun. All of a sudden I realized what was going on. I looked out at the car. You were still in the front seat, but you were hunkered down, trying to duck below the window. A bullet had already shattered the rear passenger-side window right behind you. I couldn't tell if you were okay. I started to run for the door. Just as I did, I heard another pop and the glass in the ATM booth shattered into a million tiny pieces. I kept running for the door, running toward you. I could feel my heart racing. In that moment, if I saw a bullet headed toward you, I would have jumped in front of it. But I wasn't even close enough to you to do that. There was another popping sound and a bullet ripped a hole in our right rear tire. I couldn't even figure out where they were shooting from. When I got outside the door, I realized that the bullets were coming from opposite directions. I could also hear you screaming. This wasn't good. The stress wasn't good. Unfortunately, the night had just started.

I ran toward the car. I could hear another bullet whiz by my head. I tried to figure out what direction the bullets were coming from. They seemed to be coming from everywhere. The reality was that probably only five or six shots had been fired but I felt like we were caught in the middle of a battle. I reached the driver's side door and swung it open. "Are you okay?" I shouted at you as I climbed inside.

"No!" you screamed back at me. I immediately ducked my head down below the window line. Then I turned on the car and stepped on the gas. I just wanted to get us away from the bullets. We'd have to leave the car behind now. We were short a rear tire. They had to have done that on purpose. We couldn't drive out of the city like that. We could, however, drive it out of the line of fire. Then we would have to go on foot. There was no way around it.

I stepped on the gas, lifting my head up just enough to see over the dashboard. I couldn't afford to hit anything. I couldn't afford another accident. As soon as the car started to move, I could feel the rear tire rattling along the street. People started turning lights on in the houses surrounding the street. I tried to ignore them. We just had to get away.

We veered back and forth along the street as we lunged forward. I tried to control the steering but the lost tire made it difficult. After four or five blocks, I couldn't hear any gunfire anymore. I pulled the car off to the side. "We have to get out," I said to you. You looked at me like I was crazy. "We're sitting ducks in here, Maria. We have to get out."

You reached down and unbuckled your seat belt. Then you crawled over the middle console so that you could climb out of the same door as me. I opened the driver's side door and stepped onto the pavement. I waited for a split second, expecting to hear another gunshot, expecting to hear another bullet whiz by my ear, but I didn't hear anything. I grabbed your wrist and pulled you to your feet on the sidewalk and then we ran down the next street. We ran for two blocks before I spotted an opening next to one of the houses. We ducked quickly inside one the few gardens without a locked gate. I lifted my finger to my lips to signal to you to be quiet. I had heard something. Someone was running down the street. I could hear footsteps pounding on the asphalt. We were lucky to have found shelter in the shadows when we did. A man suddenly ran past us. I looked down at his hands as he ran. He was holding a gun.

"What do we do, Joe?" you whispered to me when we couldn't see the man anymore.

"I don't know."

"How do we get out of here now?"

"I don't know." I tried to think. We didn't have many options. "How far is the bus station from here?" I asked you. You knew the city better than I did.

"About six miles," you answered. It was far. The night was dark and full of dangers. Still, it was our only option.

"We've got to get to the bus station," I said to you. Then I heard something else. I reached out and placed my hand over your mouth to make sure you didn't speak. Someone else was near us. They weren't running. They were walking. They were whistling as they walked. We hunched down together as low to the ground as we could. We tried to stay as obscured as possible. He was walking in the same direction the man with the gun had run. He didn't have a gun. Instead, he had a large knife in his hand. He was whistling the Louis Armstrong song "What a Wonderful World." We held our breath again as he walked passed us. It took another ten minutes before we felt safe that he was gone.

You picked up our conversation right where we had left it off. "I can't run, Joe," you said, placing both hands over your stomach.

"I know," I answered. God only knew what damage we'd already done to our child. We didn't talk about it. "What time is it?" I asked you. You looked at your watch.

"It's four in the morning," you said.

"Listen." I swallowed hard, barely believing I was about to suggest what I was about to suggest. "The first bus probably doesn't leave until around seven. Do you think you can walk six miles in three hours?"

"Do I have a choice?" you asked.

"No."

"I can do it," you said, nodding your head.

"That's my girl." I tried to smile at you. I don't know how it came across. I wasn't in the mood to smile. I took the gun out of my belt again. "Take this," I said, handing you our only means of protection.

"I can't take this," you said, holding the gun loosely between two fingers. "I don't know how to use it."

"Just take the fucking gun, Maria," I responded, exasperated.

"Please, take the gun. It's easy to use. I disabled the safety. All you have to do is point it at anything scary and pull the trigger." You looked at the gun in your hand. It didn't look right. Your hands looked too small for it.

"Why do I need this?" you asked. "Why don't you just carry it?"

I shook my head. "We'll never make it the six miles together. We need something else."

"So what are you going to do?" you asked, sensing that whatever my plan was, you weren't going to like it.

"I'm going to distract them," I said. I could see everything you wanted to say to me in the look on your face. You wanted to tell me that my idea was ridiculous. You wanted to curse me for even thinking about it. You wanted to tell me that we could make it together. You hesitated because you knew none of it was true. "Please, Maria," I said. "I don't know what else to do. This is the only way."

"Okay," you finally conceded. You knew that it was the only chance we had to save our son. You were gripping the gun with two hands now. Now it was your protector.

"Do you know where you're going?" I asked, stalling before the moment when I left you.

"Yes," you answered. Then I remembered the money. I pulled my wallet out of my pocket.

"Take this too," I said, handing you almost a thousand dollars in cash. Now I had nothing.

"We're going to meet at the bus station, right?"

"Of course," I answered, knowing that the odds of both of us making it there were slim. "But if I'm not there, get on a bus. Get on a bus going far away." I turned and looked down the surrounding streets. They were empty again. I never even heard a police car. Everyone must have thought that the gunshots were kids lighting off firecrackers. It looked clear to go. I turned back to you. "Give me a five-minute head start," I said. "Stay in the shadows and move quietly. Don't let anyone see you." You nodded. "I'm going to try to get them to chase me." Even as I said it, the idea sounded ridiculous. How long would it take them to hunt me down? For how long could I outrun a bullet? I wasn't trying to survive. I had to be realistic. I was only trying to survive long enough. I took a deep breath and readied myself to jump out of the shadows and into the light on the street. Before I did, you grabbed my face in your hands and pulled me toward you. You had the gun in your right hand and I could feel its metal on my cheek. You kissed me gently on the lips, then harder. Then I had to go.

"I'll see you at seven," I said. Then I ran. I stepped into the street and I ran like there was no tomorrow because, for me, there probably wasn't.

I didn't look back. I just ran. I ran south, away from the bus station. I needed to give you room. If I got away, I'd have plenty of time to get to the bus station. Only seconds after I stepped out of the shadows, I heard the first set of footsteps chasing me. Each step banged loudly on the street. There was barely any time in between footsteps. Whoever was behind me was moving fast. I didn't dare look back now. They had guns. All I had on my side was fear.

I knew I had to stay ahead of the person chasing me but I couldn't afford to lose him either. I needed him to chase me. I needed all of them to chase me. The only thing that I was more afraid of than getting caught was having you get caught. Then I heard the second set of footsteps, farther back but distinct. It now was like listening to the beat of two out-of-rhythm drums. I wondered how many there were. Were these the only two? Had there been only three of them before they dumped their partner by the side of the road, or were there more? If there were more, were you safe? There was no way for me to know. I had never heard of anyone working in groups greater than four. Even if there were five originally, they had already lost one in their accident. That would mean that there were the two following me and two others, lurking somewhere.

I expected to hear gunshots coming from behind me, but there was nothing. They must not have wanted to press their luck with the police. They must have thought that I wasn't going to be that difficult to catch. I had made it about six blocks before I realized that I was about to run into the southern tip of Charleston. When the city ended to the south, there was only water. I had already played that game, hiding in the black water at night. The only reason I'd survived it was because Michael saved me. I wasn't going to make that mistake again. I turned down the next street I could and kept running in a different direction.

I started running out of energy. My legs, arms, and lungs were tiring quickly. I needed to find a place to hide so that I could rest, even if it was only for a few minutes. The streets were still empty, lit up only by the old-fashioned streetlamps lining the sidewalks. On each side of the street was a line of old houses. The houses butted up right against the sidewalk. Most houses had a locked door leading into their private gardens. The only breaks between the houses were old churches and crowded cemeteries. I hadn't heard either set of footsteps turn the corner behind me yet. I saw a fence up ahead. It was a tall wrought-iron fence with spikes on the top. It must have been about nine feet high. I took two steps toward it and jumped. As I jumped I reached up and grabbed one of the spikes. I planted my right foot in between the two bars and pushed myself over the top. The left cuff of my jeans got caught on the spike for a moment, sending me spiraling down to the ground. I landed hard on my back. For a second, I couldn't breathe. The wind had been completely knocked out of me. Then my chest opened up and I inhaled, letting the cool night air fill my lungs. I had to remind myself that they were still behind me.

I quickly rolled over onto my stomach so that I could look through the metal bars in the fence and listen. I couldn't hear any footsteps. It was quiet. For a second, I was worried that they'd gone back to look for you. Then I spotted one of them. He was walking down the street, visually searching the alleyways. He wasn't holding a gun. Instead, he had a knife with a serrated three-inch blade in his hand. It was some sort of hunting knife. I looked around me to see if I could find a better hiding place.

That's when I realized that I was in a tiny cemetery. I had leapt the fence they'd erected to keep out tourists and ghost tours. There was a grave only a few feet from me with a large headstone facing the street. It would make for perfect cover. I looked at the man with the knife. I waited for him to look away from me and then crawled quickly behind the headstone. I got as close to the headstone as I could and ducked down. I could feel the cold granite on my skin. I looked down at the carving on the headstone. It was too dark to read. I could have been sitting on anyone's grave. Then I peeked over the headstone again toward the street. The man with the knife was still there, still looking for me. It looked like he was going to give up. He turned around. I thought he was going to go back toward you. I wondered for a second how you were doing, how much progress you had made, how our son was doing. Even more than you or me, I knew that it was going to take a miracle for our son to survive the night. Maybe if you moved slowly and stayed calm, he would be okay. Maybe if I could keep them at bay for a few hours, everything that we'd put ourselves through wouldn't be wasted. I was just hoping for a miracle.

Then I heard footsteps again coming down the street toward the man with the knife. I looked at him. He heard the footsteps too. He looked up toward them. His face changed. His eyes widened. He was suddenly afraid. He turned and ran. He ran fast, even faster than he'd been running when he was chasing me. If he'd run that fast when he was chasing me, he would have caught me. Only a moment later, I saw another man run by. He had a gun in his hand. It looked like he was chasing the first man, but that didn't make any sense. Nothing made sense. I watched the second man run by and tried to understand what was going on. My thoughts were interrupted by another sound, a new sound. It was the sound of shaking metal and it was coming from behind me. I looked back across the cemetery, past the hundred-year-old headstones. Someone was climbing the fence on the other side of the cemetery. The headstone that gave me such great coverage in one direction left me completely visible in the other. I hadn't even bothered to check behind me. They'd seen me. They were climbing the fence, coming for me.

I looked at the fence, shaking as one man pulled himself up toward the spikes. Another man was trying to help him up, pushing his feet up toward the top of the fence. I could see a gun in the hand of the one nearing the top of the fence. I couldn't tell if the other one was armed. I was sure that he was, though he didn't have his weapon handy. I could try to climb the fence on this side of the cemetery again, but without the running start, it would be a strenuous and clumsy climb. I didn't have time for it. The man with the gun would be able to pick me off the fence with one shot, as easily as if he were shooting a tin can off a fence post. I needed a running start. So I ran. I ran straight toward the fence the two men were climbing over. I saw the man on the bottom look up at me. The expression on his face was utter shock. That's what I was counting on, shock and chaos. I ran right over the graves in the cemetery, dodging a headstone or two. The cemetery was only one block long, so in seconds I was only a few feet from the fence the men were climbing. The man with the gun had reached the top of the fence before he even noticed that I was headed for him. He was standing on the top of the fence, about to jump down to the ground. I leapt, planting a foot between two bars, just as I had done getting over the fence last time. This time I didn't grab one of the spikes. Instead, I grabbed the man with the gun. I reached up and grabbed his knee, pulling myself up into the air. As I pulled myself up, I pulled the man with the gun down. He fell quickly. His leg kicked out as I pulled it and his body tumbled down. The back of his thigh hit the top of one the spikes. I heard the sound of the spike puncturing his skin and the cracking of bone. Then I was over the fence. I landed on my feet this time. I didn't look at the man I'd just impaled on the fence. I didn't look at his companion either. I just turned to my right and ran again as fast as I could.

Now I knew that there had been at least five of them. I had seen five. Two of those five were out of commission now. The man by the side of the road was as good as dead and the man on the fence, even if he survived, wasn't going to be chasing anyone else tonight. I was trying, Maria. I wanted to call out to you. I wanted to tell you to just keep moving. But I hoped that you couldn't hear me, that you were too far away.

I tried to figure out how much time had passed. Twenty minutes? A half an hour? Longer? I didn't know how long I'd lain there in the cemetery. I looked up at the sky. It was still pitch-black. I turned another corner to see if I could catch my breath. I found a shadowy indentation in between two of the houses and stepped into it. It didn't give me complete cover, but it would have to do for now. I tried to slow my breathing down. Then I saw another one. He was walking down the other end of the street. He had on a black pair of jeans and a black sweatshirt with the hood pulled up over his head. He had a gun in his hand. I tried to remember if he was one of the men I'd seen before, but I didn't think he was. That meant there had been at least six of them and there were at least four left. Six. Why would they send six people after me? It didn't make sense.

I stayed quiet and watched the man as he walked by, hoping he wouldn't notice me. As long as he didn't turn down the street toward me, I thought I'd be okay. He walked by and disappeared around the corner. I had seen six people. I told myself that there couldn't be any more than that. If I was right, then all the able-bodied ones were down here with me. If I was right, then maybe you were safe.

I listened. The night was quiet again. I stepped out of the shadows and began to walk slowly down the street. I tried to walk quietly, hoping that I would hear anyone before they saw me. I didn't know what to do anymore. I couldn't keep running all night. I didn't have the stamina for that. I began to wonder if I should go out looking for them, if I should start hunting them. I didn't have to wonder for very long. It wasn't that easy to simply become the hunter when you were the hunted.

I was lucky that I saw this one seconds before he saw me. He turned down the street I was standing on and started walking toward me. I had just enough time to duck back into the shadows of a doorway before he looked in my direction. He started walking closer to me. If he got too close, I was a dead man. There was no place to hide on the street. I thought about running but if I did, I'd run directly toward the others. I was trapped.

I reached behind me in the doorway I was standing in and grabbed the doorknob. I began to twist it. Mercifully, the door was unlocked. I opened it a crack and slipped inside the house. It was dark and calm inside. Even through the darkness, I could see the kitchen and the living room from where I was standing. Toys were strewn about the living room floor. I stepped forward, walking deeper into the house. I was still looking for a place to hide. There was a coat closet in the living room. I opened the closet door and stepped inside. Instead of closing the door behind me, I left it open a crack so I could see out. My heart was pounding in my chest. Waiting was almost more strenuous than the running. I could see the front door through the crack I'd left in the closet door. Slowly, it began to open. The darkness outside the door matched the darkness of the house. The man who was chasing me stepped quietly inside. He held the gun in his right hand up near his ear so that he could aim it quickly if he needed to. He did a quick visual scan of the rooms. I looked around to see if there was anything that I could use for a weapon, like a bat or a frying pan, anything. There was nothing. Then I noticed a light switch only a couple feet from the closet door. It was my only chance.

The man stepped farther into the house. He tried to walk without making any noise. He looked like he was going to walk right past me toward the kitchen. I didn't believe it, not for a second. He was only a few feet from me now. I could see his face. It looked pale in the darkness. I knew that he knew where I was. I knew that he was bluffing. I looked at him. I committed his position to memory, where he was standing, how he was standing. Then I reached outside the closet. I ran my hand along the wall until I reached the light switch. Then I flipped on the light. In a flash, the room was bright. I had counted on the brightness. The pale man tried to aim his gun at me but his eyes still hadn't adjusted to the light. He was virtually blind. I couldn't see anything but flashes of color, either, but I didn't need to. I stepped out of the closet, lifted up my right foot, and stomped down into where I remembered the side of the man's knee to be. I felt his knee buckle instantly and he fell to the ground. As he fell, he squeezed out one shot from his gun. I heard glass shatter as the bullet went through the kitchen window. Then, lights at the top of the stairs came on. I heard screaming. My eyes finally began to adjust to the light. I looked up toward the screaming. A woman was standing there in a nightgown. She was holding on to the railing at the top of the stairs and screaming at the top of her lungs.

I ran again. I began to feel like nothing more than a walking disaster, running from place to place, wreaking havoc everywhere I went. I began to feel like this night was a metaphor for my entire life. I ran out the front door. I ran from the woman screaming at the top of the stairs. I ran from the now crippled man with the gun. There was too much commotion this time. The others would hear it. All of them sneaking around in the darkness would be drawn to this one spot. I had to get away. I made it out to the street and started to run south again. The sky was beginning to change color. It was a dark purple when I stepped out of the house. Dawn was coming. I made it two blocks before one of them was chasing me again. He was running toward the house as I was running away from it, but when he saw me, he changed direction and started coming for me. I recognized this one. It was the second man at the cemetery fence. I wondered if he'd left his colleague behind like they'd left the man behind on the side of the road. My legs were heavy now. I'd been running for a long time. I couldn't run for much longer.

It didn't matter. There wasn't much more room to run. There's a park at the southeast corner of Charleston with oak trees and a small gazebo. Closer to the water there are old cannons and a large Civil War commemorative statue. After that, there's the water. By the time I got to the water, by the time I had run out of anywhere to run, I was exhausted.

The man chasing me had closed the gap between us until he was no more than ten yards behind me. When I got near the edge of the water, I turned to face him. I didn't recognize him. He didn't look like anyone I remembered. He didn't look like anyone I'd killed. I could have asked why he was chasing me. I could have asked him why he was willing to risk so much to kill me. I had asked that kid in Ohio. Now I was too tired to care.

The sky around me was turning from a dark purple to deep red. Soon the sun would come up behind me. The man lifted his gun and aimed it at me. I wondered if I'd bought you enough time. I wondered if our son was hanging on. I imagined you getting on a bus alone and riding west. I imagined you getting off the bus with no one chasing you. It made me happy to think about you getting away, but it made me sad to think that you'd be alone. It made me sad to think that, if our son survived, I was never going to get to meet him. What I would have given at that moment for even one day with our son. I looked up and stared into the barrel of my killer's gun. I remembered the last time I'd been this close to death, floating in the water off Long Beach Island. I remembered the pure instinctive drive to live that I had felt then, even though I couldn't think of one reason why I wanted to live so badly. Now, not only did I know that I wanted to live, but I knew why. Our son made the prospect of dying so much worse.

I didn't say a word to my killer. What was there to say? He didn't say a word to me. I just heard the gun fire and I felt nothing. Then I heard it fire again. And then again. I still felt nothing but the breeze blowing by me from the water. I opened my eyes. The bullets weren't meant for me. The first two shots struck my killer in his chest. The third hit him in the head. I opened my eyes to see my killer still standing there, blood dripping from his fresh wounds. His gun slipped from his hand. We made eye contact for only a moment before he fell to the ground. He didn't look scared, just confused. He didn't know why this was happening any more than I did. I looked around me. I couldn't figure out where the shots had come from. I didn't see anyone. For some reason, I had been spared when so many people had already died around me. For some reason, knowing why didn't seem to matter much to me at that moment.

I started running again, refreshed, revived. For the last time that night, I ran. It was a good seven miles to the bus station now but I knew I'd make it. I had been given another chance.

You were at the bus station when I got there. You were hiding in the corner, trying not to be seen. Two buses had left already but you had refused to get on them, waiting for me, holding out whatever slim hope you had that I would make it. Somehow I did. I didn't tell you what had happened. How could I tell you when I didn't know myself?

The next bus was headed to Nashville. We got on it.

———

You slept almost the entire bus ride. I asked you how you were feeling. You told me that you hadn't had any cramping and only a little bleeding. Then you told me that during your walk to the bus station, you felt our son moving for the first time.

I couldn't have gotten more than two hours' worth of sleep during the bus ride. Every time the bus stopped, I found myself eyeing each person who got on. I was sure that one of them was going to turn on us. They never did.

We didn't stay in Nashville for any longer than we had to. As soon as we got there, we bought another car. I found us an old beat-up Chevy for three hundred dollars cash. The guy who sold it to us promised me that the engine was in good condition. We didn't have time to haggle. I figured we'd drive it as far as it would take us and settle down wherever it finally died.

This time we'd go west. I wasn't going to stop driving until I physically had to. You had already been through too much for someone in your condition. It was time for you to rest.

Seventeen

I drove fast through the darkness. The land was barren and flat. We'd been on the road for hours already. I didn't even know how long. Day slipped back into night. I pushed that little tin can of a car as hard as it would go. The moon hung low in the sky and there were more stars than I had ever seen before. As I sped down the highway, the landscape became a blur around me but the stars never moved.

I looked over at you, lying next to me. You seat was reclined as far back as it could go. You were lying on your side facing me, your hands between your knees for warmth. You had slept nearly nonstop since Charleston. As soon as we stopped moving, we'd get you in to see a doctor to make sure that our son was okay. I didn't want to take any more chances.

You woke up while we were still on the long, barren road cutting through the desert. You flipped the lever on the car seat to make it sit upright. You looked tired. You stared blankly at the open road. "How long was I out for?" you mumbled.

"A few hours." You'd been sleeping since we stopped for dinner. I looked over at you again. Your belly looked even bigger when you were sitting up.

"Are we making good time?" you asked.

"This little machine won't go any faster," I replied. Then I motioned out the window toward the sky. "Check out the stars."

You leaned forward so that you could stare up through the front windshield. "Holy shit," you said, your eyes lighting up as if you were seeing the night sky for the first time. "They don't make stars like that in Canada."

"They don't in New Jersey either," I replied.

You stared at the stars for a few minutes. Then you leaned back in your seat again. I looked over at your face and could see the tears welling up in your eyes. You had held everything in for so long. You had been strong for so long. "Tell me that everything is going to be all right," you blurted out to me. You didn't look at me. You just kept staring at the road ahead of us.

I thought about how I should answer. "I can't," I replied.

You looked over at me, fixing your eyes on mine. You hesitated, taking a long breath. "Then lie to me," you said. The tears fell freely down your face.

I thought about it for a moment. "Everything's going to be okay," I assured you.

"You promise?"

"I promise."

I don't know how much longer I drove. You eventually drifted back to sleep. I just kept pushing the car through the night. I wanted to create as much distance between my past and my future as I could. Eventually, I must have gotten too tired to keep driving. When I was barely able to keep my eyes open any longer, I pulled the car over to the side of the desert road and slept. While I was asleep, I dreamt.

In my dream, a car pulled up in front of us as the two of us slept in our car along the side of the road. The car skidded to a stop, kicking up red desert sand, blocking any chance we had to escape. A man and a woman stepped out of the car. Both of them had guns in their hands. I recognized the woman. She was a pretty Asian woman. I couldn't place her at first because her face had changed, like it had been reconstructed somehow and not everything could be put back like it had been before. The man was a stranger. Every time I looked at him his face changed. Nose, eyes, hair color, lips, everything changed. Every time I looked he was a different person. He was everyone, everyone I didn't know, everyone I saw on the street and wondered which side they were on.

It was still night when they stepped out of their car. They ordered us out of our car. Then they walked us out into the desert. The sky was littered with stars. The man and the woman kept their guns pointed at us. I told them that you were only seventeen. I told them that you were off limits, that you were an innocent. They didn't seem to care. The man just kept asking me questions about the people that I'd killed. He kept trying to make me relive moments from my life that I wanted to forget. He was relentless, asking me about people I hadn't thought about for years, people whose lives ended at my hands.

I looked over at the Asian woman. I thought about Long Beach Island. I thought about Jared and Michael. I remembered that first night when Catherine had flirted with me. In a simpler world, I would have taken her home and we would have fucked until morning and then we would have gone our separate ways. I studied her face, her reconstructed nose and cheekbones. Her eyes looked the same but the rest of her face was different. She looked up at me as we walked. I expected her to be angry. She wasn't. "You look good," I said to her, my voice loud enough for her and only her to hear. She started to respond but thought better of it. She smiled slightly, her lips curling up in the corners. Even in my dream, I wondered which of the two of them would pull the trigger when they shot me. I hoped it would be her.

We walked a long way into the desert. The cars disappeared over the horizon. Eventually, I turned to the man. "Did you follow us all the way from Charleston?" I took a deep breath. The air was cool and dry. It smelled of earth and stone. I looked over at Catherine again. She wasn't looking at me. She was gazing off into the distance, into the seemingly endless darkness.

"We followed you all the way from Montreal," the man said. I didn't want to think about the bodies that had been left behind in my wake. No more. I was done.

"How are we going to do this?" I asked, turning to face the man without a face. All I could see was his ever-changing visage and the whites of his knuckles on his gun. He lifted the gun, his finger now tensing around the trigger. I stared up at the sky, not wanting the bullet to be the last thing I saw. Some of the stars had begun to disappear. The sound of the gunshot ripped through the air. I felt nothing. It was like Charleston all over again. The sun had begun to rise.

The sun rose over the flat desert like a fireball being lifted into the sky. There were no mountains to slow down the light from the sun, nothing to create shadows. The day came with the immediacy of a tidal wave. I turned to look at you, standing there in the purple light of early dawn. I turned to see whose gun had fired, to make sure that you were okay. You were fine. Your belly created the largest shadow in the entire desert. Its shadow looked like the shadow of a mountain on its side. There was silence. Suddenly I felt a burning in my left hand. I looked down. There was blood dripping from my hand. The ground was so dry that the blood pooled up on top of it instead of seeping into the earth. I looked at my hand. My ring finger was gone. I looked over at the man with the gun. His face had changed yet again. There was smoke coming from the end of the gun. He'd shot off my finger. The pain came slowly.

"What now?" I asked the man holding the smoking gun. I wondered if he was simply planning on dismantling me one small piece at a time.

"That's all we want from you," he said. He slid his gun into the waistband of his pants. "Let's go," he said to Catherine. She glanced at me and then at you and then she turned and the two of them walked away. They disappeared over the horizon.

I looked at you, standing in the sunlight. "He's moving again, Joe," you said.

I flexed my left hand into a fist. The bleeding had already slowed down. "How does it feel?" you asked.

"It's okay," I responded. I concentrated on the pain for a moment. "It's odd. I can feel the pain in my finger, my whole finger, even though there's no finger there anymore."

"Phantom pain," you said. "I used to volunteer at a hospital. I worked with amputees. They used to tell me that they could still feel their toes even though their legs were gone."

"When did it go away?" I asked.

"Never," you replied, shaking your head. "It's not so easy to let something like that go." I looked down at my hand. The bleeding had stopped completely now. Now there was just an empty gap.

"Are we going to be all right, Maria?" I asked you. I couldn't ask you in real life. In real life, I had to pretend that I knew. It was only in a dream that I could ask you.

"Yeah, Joe. We're going to be all right," you said.

"Why does it sound like a lie when I say it but the truth when you say it?" I asked.

"Because you've never been all right before, so you don't know what it feels like."

I woke up as the sun began to rise behind us. I've never been one to read too much into dreams. I was just happy to have had a good dream for once. It had been a long time.

I started the car, put it in gear, and stepped on the gas again. I had filled up our gas tank about 150 miles ago. We still had half a tank of gas. I drove for miles before I saw another sign of civilization.

Eighteen

We've been in Aztec, New Mexico, for over three weeks. I keep waiting for the other shoe to drop, but so far, everything's been calm. It's serene here. It's hot during the day but you seem to be managing the heat well. It's nice and cool in the evenings. We probably should have gone farther. We probably should have kept driving. Maybe L.A., maybe farther. Maybe Mexico would have been safer. I don't know. But here we are, still in Aztec. I think you've decided that you want to stay here. I don't think we'll leave unless someone chases us away. That could happen at any minute. We're ready. I think we're more ready than last time. But for now, this place seems like home.

It was a lot easier to find work here than in Charleston. I knew a trade now. At least I knew enough to lie about how much I knew. Frank was a good teacher. I like the guys that I work with here. My boss is Mexican. His son works with us too. He was born in New Mexico. I'm the gringo. They like that. They like that the white guy is the low man on the totem pole.

We found a place to live. Jumping from place to place didn't help us any before, so we decided that staying in one place might be less conspicuous. We're renting a small house out in the desert. We pay weekly, up-front, in cash. There's no one else around us. When you look out the back windows, you can see for miles. Most importantly, we got you in to see a doctor. He wants to see you regularly from now through the birth. I told him that there was only so much we could afford. He didn't want to hear it. "Just come in every two weeks," he said. Maybe someday we can repay him somehow. Our son is doing well. We're not out of the woods yet, but he's still growing, still developing. There haven't been any complications since we've been here. Still, on the doctor's advice, you stay off your feet as much as possible, lying in bed, reading books I buy for you from the convenience store in town. Your stomach gets bigger every day, your body changing shape for our son.

We never planned on staying, not in Aztec. When we got here, you needed to eat. You'd slept for almost twelve hours straight and were starving. We pulled into a small place for breakfast and sat at the counter. You began talking to the woman behind the counter who was serving us. She'd lived in Aztec her whole life. You started asking questions. She told us where we could find a place to stay if we wanted one. When I told her I was a carpenter, she mentioned a couple places where I might be able to find work. She didn't ask us questions. She didn't ask where we'd come from. She didn't seem to care. People pass through Aztec. That's just the type of place it is. I wonder how many people who pass through here are running from something.

After breakfast, we decided to take a little walk before getting back into the car to stretch our legs. It was a bright and sunny day. A few other people were out on the street, just enough to drive out the silence but no more than that. The little street was lined with shops. We seemed to pass a church every few blocks. You looked into the windows of the stores as we passed. I just kept looking at the faces of the other people on the street, looking to see if I would recognize one from that night in Charleston. We were walking slowly, worn out, and in no rush to get back into the car, since we didn't have a destination anyway. We were tired, tired of running and just plain tired.

One of the shops we passed advertised itself as a UFO museum, though it was a bit of a stretch to call it a museum. As soon as you saw it, though, you asked me if we could go inside. I couldn't see why not. The place didn't seem any less safe than any other place. We stepped inside, walking down a long aisle full of movies and books about UFOs that were for sale. There wasn't really much to look at except some old photos. You seemed to find it all fascinating. You walked toward the back of the museum, running your fingers over the old VHS tapes. Each one claimed to show, beyond a shadow of a doubt, evidence of alien visitations. While I didn't have an opinion on the matter, I didn't doubt that something like that could be covered up. The old man behind the counter looked up from his book for only a second, eyeing you as you perused his collection of memorabilia. He smiled at you and then went on with his reading. You walked to the back wall to look at some pictures. They were pictures taken at festivals celebrating the UFOs. You placed your hands behind your back and leaned forward, peering at the faces of the people in the pictures. You walked past more books, more videotapes. I stood near the door, trying not to forget that we still had to be careful. You pulled one of the VHS tapes off the wall, looked at the cover, and smiled. It was good to see you smile.

You put the videotape back and walked over to the front counter. I just watched you. You walked over to a large fishbowl that was on the counter, full of tiny plastic aliens. You picked one up out of the bowl and held it in your hand. It was a little green man with large eyes and a silver space suit. There was a sign on the fishbowl that said, "Adopt an Alien." It claimed that for one dollar you could adopt an alien and all donations would go toward UFO research. You lifted the little green man to show it to me. "Look, Joe," you said. "They love him." Your faced beamed, you looked happier than I'd seen you since the first week we spent together.

I adopted you an alien. We haven't thought about leaving since.

It's been over three weeks since that day. I'm sitting in a foldout chair behind our home writing this to you while you nap inside. I've started running again. Every day your belly gets bigger and you seem happier. Your skin is darker now, tanned by southern sun. You look vibrant. I look forward every morning to watching you climb out of bed and get dressed. You get up at the first light of dawn so you can cook breakfast for me before I go to work. Every morning I watch you in the dim blue light as you climb out of bed, pull off the T-shirt you were sleeping in, and get dressed. I know that you can feel me watching you. You don't seem to mind.

Nineteen

We went to the doctor again today. He said that everything looks great. The pregnancy has lasted longer than we ever expected. The doctor told us today that you are basically full term. He expects the baby to come any day now. We've now been in Aztec for as long as we were in Charleston. My past recedes further away into my memory with each passing day. I'm happy to forget most things. Some things, I try to remember, just in case.

You never asked me about what happened the night we ran from Charleston. When I asked you, you told me that nothing happened. You just walked. At times, you thought you heard strange noises but nothing ever happened. I don't think you liked to talk about it. I think the fact that it had been so easy scared you. I don't know what I would have told you about how I survived that night even if you did ask me. You never did. I think you've finally decided that there are some things you just don't want to know.

I still try to figure it out sometimes, how I survived, why I survived. I've got some theories but none of them really makes sense. Maybe I should chalk it up to divine intervention. Something stepped in and saved me and our son. I should probably follow your lead. Maybe there are some things that I just don't want to know.

Twenty

Our son was born today. He's beautiful. He's more than perfect. Perfection wouldn't be this special. His name is Christopher. He has your eyes. The doctor said that often, when they get older, their eye color changes. I hope his doesn't. I hope he has your eyes forever.

The doctor delivered him in our home. Apparently, it's not that uncommon an occurrence here. So many people, like us, don't have any insurance. He said he was just happy to help, that it was his favorite part of his job. You were so strong. I've never seen such strength in my entire life. You were quiet and determined, as if pain were just a nuisance you didn't have time for. I hope Christopher knows how lucky he is to have you for a mother. I hope he knows that nothing in the world will ever compare to the love and sacrifices that you've made for him. The look on your face when the doctor handed him to you for the first time was one that I will never forget. That look made everything I've gone through in my entire life all worth it. I've finally given something meaningful to the world.

I was glad we were able to have him at home. I was afraid of going back to the hospital after the debacle in Charleston. Besides, now Christopher was born off the grid. Now there's no record that he even exists. There's no way for anyone to know where he came from.

Officially, he was born to ghosts. Hopefully, that will help to keep him safe.

I don't even have words to describe how I feel. Maybe I'm too tired. Maybe the words just don't exist. Our son was born today. I feel like I was reborn with him. Thank you, Maria. You've given me such a gift. You've given me more than I deserve.

Twenty-one

It's a little after three in the morning. You're asleep in the bedroom. Little Christopher really hasn't figured out the difference between day and night yet. I'm sure it will come. It's only been a week and a half. It's nice for now. We couldn't afford for me to stop working, so this way I get to see our little boy. He's so small. He wakes up crying at pretty much the same times every night. Most of the time he's crying because he's hungry and you have to get up with him. But around three o'clock every morning he wakes up just because he wants to be held. I can't blame him. It's scary to be alone.

When he wakes up at three, I try to let you sleep. His feeding schedule has kept you pretty exhausted. Besides, I like having the time alone with him, just the men. I like that I can stop his crying just by picking him up and holding him. Sometimes I imagine that he cries at night even when he's not hungry because he's knows that I'll come for him. He knows that it's daddy who will hold him. When I pick him up out of his bassinet and place him in my lap he often reaches out and grabs hold of one of my fingers. Our boy's got quite a grip. He holds on to my finger like he'd go tumbling through the universe if he let it go.

He's asleep in my lap now. I could put him back in his crib, but I don't want to. I want to hold him for a little bit longer.

The moon is bright outside, bright enough that I can write by moonlight. I don't know how much longer I'm going to keep this journal. I'm not sure I need it anymore. I'm not sure if there's anything else that I can tell you about me. Now all anybody needs to know about me is bundled up in my lap. That's the only thing that's important.

I still can hardly believe that any of this has happened. I can't believe that I'm a father. I can't believe that I've abandoned the War. In some ways, it makes sense to me. I have a few random memories of my father from before he was killed. They are all from a time before I knew that the War existed. They're all innocent memories.

He used to take me fishing every Sunday morning. It was like our version of church. My sister would come sometimes but she didn't really like to fish. I didn't really like to fish, either, but I went because I liked spending time with my father. We'd drive down to a lake near our house. There was a little pier that poked out into the water. It was old and the wood was beginning to rot. I had never seen a boat on it. It was like our own private spot. We'd walk to the end of the pier and sit down, bait our hooks with worms, and cast our lines into the water. My father used to bait my hook for me because I didn't have the heart to push the hook through the squiggling little worm. Then we'd wait and we'd talk. I think I did most of the talking. I don't remember what we talked about. I don't remember my father imparting to me any fatherly wisdom. I just remember being there and being happy, waiting for a fish to nibble at the end of my line, half hoping that it wouldn't. In some ways, I think it's better that my father passed away before I learned about the War. I'm glad I never had to talk to him about it. I'm glad my memories of him are more pure than that.

Someday, maybe I'll take Christopher fishing. When I do, I'll bait his hook for him. We can talk all day about nothing and everything will be okay.

PART II

Chris,

I hope with every fiber of my being that you never have to read this, that when all is said and done I'll be able to protect you. If you are reading this, then something went wrong with part of my plan and I failed you for the second time. If something did happen to you, if I failed you again, then I think it is important for you to know who you really are and who your father was. Your name—the name your father and I gave you—is Christopher Jude. Your last name isn't important. It's probably better if you don't know it. My name is Maria. I'm your mother. Your father's name was Joseph. We had you when we were very young, myself especially. I know how dangerous the world I brought you into is. Trust me, I've seen the danger up close. I need you to know that I'm doing everything I can to protect you. I might not always make the right decisions, but I'm trying. Your father tried too. We so wanted a normal life for you. For a little while, we had illusions that we could give it to you.

You were born in New Mexico. After running for almost nine months, your father and I had settled down in a small white house on the edge of the red sand deserts.

We thought we had finally found a safe place, an oasis. We tried to stay to ourselves. We tried not to bother anyone. I'm sure you don't remember but for a little while, we were like a normal, happy little family. I remember beautiful moments when I actually forgot that we were running. I think that even your father, at times, indulged himself and let himself believe that they'd forgotten us. We were so naive, lost in our own little dream world, believing that wanting something bad enough could make it happen, hoping that what we'd already sacrificed would be enough. We gave up everything—everything but each other and you. You were such a blessing, a gift that goes beyond metaphors. Then they came for you. We had four weeks, the four most wonderful weeks of my life. In those four weeks, you gave me more than I can ever repay you.

I wish that there was some way that I could show you how much you changed your father. I remember watching him hold you. He'd put his hands around you and hold you ever so gently. At times you'd cry and all he had to do was reach for you and the crying would stop. He used to put you on his chest as he lay on that ugly green sofa we had in our living room and you'd fall asleep like a tiny angel. Your body would rise and fall as your father breathed. We talked about ways we could make the little house nicer so that you could grow up there and be like a normal kid. We had an old gray knotted tree in the backyard, the last tree before miles of empty desert. Your father talked all the time about tying a tire to one of the branches to make a swing for when you got older. I wish he could have given that to you. I wish I had real memories of your father pushing you on the tire swing instead of just dreams of memories that never existed.

Sometimes I tried to pretend that we really were a normal family. We wouldn't talk about the War for days on end. No matter how much we pretended, no matter how much your father acted like everything was normal, he never forgot who we were or what we were doing alone, hiding on the edge of the world. He was always thinking about it. I know because he used to talk to himself in his sleep. He used to mutter and scream. But during the day, he acted normal for my sake and for yours. We wanted so badly to spend our lives with you, to forget and to be forgotten. We just wanted them to leave us alone. But it wasn't over. They didn't forget us, Chris. If you only remember one thing that I try to teach you, remember that they never forget.

They came for you on a Sunday afternoon. Sometimes I feel like I have no memories except for my memories of that day, like every other memory I ever had was washed clean by five men with guns. It seemed like a normal, peaceful Sunday until I heard a knock on the front door. In the months that we had lived in that tiny house, not a single person had knocked on our door until that day. Who would knock? We barely spoke to anyone other than the doctor who delivered you and the guys your father worked with. Your father demanded that we keep a low profile for your protection. It was all for naught. They knew where we were from the very beginning.

The memory of the knock on the door still scares me. It made such a hollow sound on the door. I heard a loud thump and then there was a long pause as if whoever was knocking was waiting for the echo to disappear. I was sitting in the kitchen with you on my lap. At first I didn't think anything of it. People knock on doors. They just weren't supposed to knock on ours.

By the second *thump* your father had gotten to his feet and was walking toward us. He had been in the living room, lying on the couch, reading the newspaper. I tried to let him rest on Sundays, knowing how hard he worked all week. I watched him come toward us. He didn't make a sound as he walked. He had learned to walk like that, swiftly but silently, long before I ever met him. When I saw him walking toward us like that, that's when I finally realized that I should be afraid. You should know that before you were born, your father was a very dangerous man. I had done everything that I could think to do to tame him but it wasn't until you were born that he really changed. You made him happy and content. I saw it in him every day. When he heard that knock on the door, though, he changed back to that dangerous man almost instantly. I could see the paranoia come back into him and, I'll be honest, I was glad.

It wasn't until your father was a step or two away from us that I finally looked toward the front door. The front door was made of a light brown wood and was framed by two thin stained glass windows that threw colors—reds, greens, blues, and yellows—onto the floor. When I looked at the door, I saw two figures standing on the other side of the stained glass. Because of the colors, I could only see the silhouettes of two large, hulking bodies. The third man behind the door, the one knocking, wasn't visible through the glass. Your father, without any hesitation, stepped between us and the door, using his body to block the visitors' view of me and you, should the men press their eyes against the stained glass windows. When your father reached us, he extended his hand and slipped his thumb in your mouth. You immediately began to suckle his thumb like a nipple. Right after he stuck his thumb in your mouth, we heard the third knock.

I held you close to me. "Be right there," your father shouted toward the front door. Then he turned toward us and spoke in a whisper. "Take Christopher. Go out the back door." He paused for a second, waiting for me to nod so that he knew that I understood. I nodded and he went on. "Don't go to the car. Just get away from here as fast as you can. Go straight. Make distance." I wanted to say something but your father placed his free hand over my mouth. He shook his head to tell me that I shouldn't speak, that I shouldn't make a single noise. I was glad that he did it because I had no idea what I was supposed to say. "Go now. Whenever you have a choice, go north." I knew I should have been asking questions but I couldn't think of the right questions to ask. Fear had taken up all the space in my mind. "I'll find you," your father said to me, answering the most important question without waiting for me to ask it. Then he took my hand, held it in front of his face, and kissed the tips of my fingers. After he kissed my hand, he slid his thumb out of your mouth and slid in my thumb in its place. I felt you grasp my thumb with your gums and a split second later your father turned toward the front door. He didn't look back to see if I was doing what he asked me to. He knew that I would. I loved your father. I didn't want to leave him. But I had to. Your father wasn't telling me to run for my safety. He was telling me to run for yours.

I've gone over that afternoon in my head again and again, trying to figure out if I could have done anything to stop what happened, if there was any moment where I could have done something to change our fates. The idea haunted me for weeks. It ate up every moment of every day. Then I realized that I couldn't linger on the past. Even if I could have done something different, the fact was that I hadn't. The past is the past, Christopher. It's irrelevant unless it's got something to teach you about the future.

I turned back toward your father for a moment just as he was reaching his hand to the doorknob. The hulking shadows were still standing behind the stained glass. It was time for us to go. We had to get outside of the house before your father opened the front door and hope that no one saw us. We stepped out of the sliding glass door leading out of the kitchen. I was holding you in my arms, ready to run. I hadn't thought to take anything with me. We could worry about food and diapers later. Your father told me to run, so I planned on running. Straight lines. North whenever possible. Your father's instincts told him that the knock on the door meant danger and my instincts told me to believe him.

I stepped outside onto the hard red dirt, holding you against me. The sun was low in the sky but the day was still hot. I have vivid memories of how still the air was, like we were on a movie set. The desert opened up in front of us. It seemed endless. That memory has been burned into my brain. It tortures me. I had no idea if I would ever see your father again but I swear I didn't hesitate. I clutched you against my chest, my thumb still in your mouth, and didn't look back. I looked forward, past the tree with the ghost of the tire swing that had never been and would never be. Beyond that was just flat, sun-scorched land. I couldn't see a single other house or road. That's why your father had chosen that house. He thought the isolation would make us safer. I wanted to get you as far from the house as possible before you cried out. I had no idea what your father was planning on doing. Nothing would have surprised me. He had already volunteered to sacrifice his life for you once, before you were even born, when we were running from Charleston, but somehow he'd been saved. I didn't know what your father was going to do but I knew that my job was to run, so I ran. We made it about ten steps from the back door before I heard the horrible cracking sound. It was a sound that I recognized, a sound I was getting all too used to hearing. I stopped running, the noise lodged in my ear, caught somewhere between the sound of a whip cracking and the explosion of a cannon. The sound wasn't coming from inside the house like I half expected. It was coming from right behind me. I stopped short as if I'd run to the edge of a cliff. I held you even closer to me so that they wouldn't be able to shoot you without shooting through me first. I heard the cracking sound again—just one more time. This time, I saw dirt kick up five feet in front of me, like a tiny plume of red smoke rising from the ground. You started crying. Even with my thumb in your mouth, you began to cry louder than I had ever heard you cry before. I wanted to cry too. I wanted to cry with you. I knew that your father, if he was still alive, would hear your cry and he would know that I failed.

I turned and looked behind us. Two men were standing by the back door of our house, the one that we'd just run out of. One was holding a small pistol by his waist. The other had a rifle cocked up against his shoulder, aimed at the ground in front of us. "I'd suggest not running any farther," the man with the pistol said. His friendly tone didn't stop me from hating him. "Why don't you come inside with us?" he said. He was an ugly man, short and stocky with a bulbous nose. The other man kept the rifle up near his shoulder, pointing it in our direction and making it impossible for me to see his face. I walked back the ten paces toward the house. I didn't have a choice. Then I walked past the two men and into the house. I tightened my grip on you as we walked past them. I had no idea what they were planning on doing with us but I wasn't about to let you go, not without a fight. I pressed you into my chest, trying to make you feel like you had nothing to be afraid of. The two men followed us inside the house.

It was much cooler inside, out from under the desert sun. Once we got inside the house, I looked around. Everything seemed to be in order. There was no evidence of any fighting or struggle. The scene was eerily calm. Your father was sitting on the couch in the living room. From where I was standing, I could see another man sitting in a chair on the other side of the coffee table, facing your father. Two other men were standing by the front door. I recognized them as the men from behind the stained glass by their shape alone. They both had guns. The two men who followed you and me inside stopped just inside of the back door and stood there. Together, they had all the exits covered.

The man sitting across from your father looked up at me when we walked inside. I felt a chill run down my spine. Then he looked at you. Everything I needed to know, I saw it in that look. I saw hatred in that look. The man scared me. He turned back toward your father. "Come on, Joe," the man said, feigning disappointment, "you really thought that we wouldn't post anyone by the back door?"

"I didn't realize it was you, Jared," your father replied. "If I knew it was you, I'd have known that you would cover all your bases. Not everyone is as meticulous as you." Your father sounded despondent. I listened for any hope in his voice but heard none. I looked at the man sitting across the table from your father. I knew the name Jared. It was the name of your father's oldest friend. Your father had told me stories about how he and Jared grew up together. I wanted that to give me hope. It didn't. Not after the look that Jared gave you. Something was wrong. Something was very wrong.

"So there's the cause of all our problems," Jared said to your father, pointing at you like a witness identifying a murderer in a courtroom. He looked almost silly, pointing at a baby like that.

"His name's Christopher," your father said. "Christopher Jude." I could tell what your father was trying to do. He was trying to break through to his old friend.

"I really don't care what his name is, Joe. You shouldn't either." Jared's words were flat and emotionless. Jared reached into the waistband of his pants and pulled out a tarnished silver revolver. He placed it on the coffee table in front of him before looking up at your father again. When he looked at your father, all the hatred in his face was gone. It was replaced by something else, something more compassionate. "He's one of them, Joe." Jared spoke in almost a whisper, loud enough for me to hear him but quiet enough for your father to understand that the words were meant only for him. Jared was trying to break through to your father too.

"He's my son, Jared," your father said. Even in that moment, surrounded by strange men with guns, those words made me feel strong, but only for a moment. Jared nodded his head. I thought that maybe he was going to agree with your father.

"I always knew that one of you two was going to get into trouble," Jared said, shaking his head. "I just always figured it would be Michael." He laughed for a second and then stopped laughing as quickly as he'd started. "You still have time, Joe. I made sure of that. They haven't written you off completely. Give me the kid. Give me the kid and you can still come back into the fold."

"I can't do that, Jared." Now your father was whispering too.

Jared leaned further in toward your father, placing his elbows on his knees. "I really thought that once you had the kid—once you actually saw him—you'd come to your senses. I thought that once you realized what your kid was, you'd come back to us." Jared began to chew on his lower lip. "That's why we waited, Joe. That's why I've been protecting you all this time." My skin rose when I heard those words, before I even understood what they meant. "I just thought that if I gave you time, you'd come to your senses."

"So it was you that saved me in Charleston?" your father asked.

"You think you would have made it this far without me protecting you, Joe?" Jared responded. He almost looked like he was about to start laughing again, but he didn't. "Come on, Joe!" Jared raised his voice. He made a fist and slammed it on his knee. "Do you realize the risks I took to save you? We took three of their men out protecting you in Charleston. They accused me of using you as bait, of using you to draw them in. Do you realize what the penalty for that is, Joe? I risked everything for you." I couldn't tell who sounded more distraught, Jared or your father. "You're my best friend. I just kept saying, 'Give him some time. He'll come around.'" Slowly, it all started to come together in my mind. These people in our house, they were the reason why we made it out of Charleston together. They had been protecting us so that they could come back and take you from us.

"So was this all still part of your Fixer job?"

"Don't do that to me, Joe," Jared said. "You know that this goes way beyond that." Jared looked out the open window for a moment. "You know you're fucking killing your mother?" Jared said to your father.

Joe just nodded in response. I knew that he had already written your grandmother off. "What about Michael?" your father asked, wondering about his and Jared's other best friend, the third member of their trio.

"Michael doesn't get it, Joe," Jared replied. "He busted off when he heard you were on the run. You confused the hell out of that kid. He doesn't know what to do without you."

"So he's on the run too?" Some hope returned to your father's voice.

"No. Nobody's chasing Michael. He didn't do anything wrong. If I bring you back, he'll come back in a second. It'll be just like old times." Jared put his hand on the gun on the table. He pushed it to the midpoint of the table so that it was as close to your father as it was to him. I didn't understand if it was supposed to be a peace offering or a challenge. I still don't understand the rituals. I looked away from the gun. Everyone was too calm. I wanted to scream. You had fallen asleep in my arms. The sky outside was turning a dark pink as the sun went down. Long gray shadows began to emerge throughout the house.

"So what do you want from me, Jared?" your father asked.

"I just want you to do what's right," Jared answered. "It's just the kid, Joe. You can keep the girl." Jared motioned toward me with a nod of his head. I wanted to call him a bastard. I wanted to ask him who the hell he thought he was but I didn't dare make a sound. "This is for your own good, Joe. I've known you a long time. I love you. I'm trying to help you." Hearing the way Jared said those words, I almost believed them myself.

Your father rubbed his hands together. "I don't want my son involved in any of this, Jared. I don't want him to grow up to be a killer." Your father shook his head. His voice was full of a resolve that I had never heard before. "So if I hand Christopher over, what are you going to do with him?"

Jared leaned back in his chair. He knew the answer to this one. "I'm going to put him where he belongs. I'm going to hand him over to the other side. I'm going to follow the rules, Joe, just like you were supposed to."

"And when he turns eighteen?" your father asked, knowing the answer before he asked the question.

Jared shook his head. He knew that your father knew what he was going to say. "I'll kill the evil little fucker myself," Jared replied. I gasped when I heard those words. Jared heard me and looked toward us with nothing but contempt. That look told me what Jared thought of me. I had corrupted his best friend. I'd stolen his brother.

"No" was all your father responded, shaking his head from side to side as he did so.

"No, what?" Jared asked.

"No, you're not taking my son. No, my son's not going to be part of this War." Your father spoke the words like an incantation, like they could give him some control. But they were just words. No matter what your father hoped, there was no magic in them.

"It kills me to do this, Joe, but I've done everything I can for you. We're taking him. One day you'll thank me for this." Jared leaned forward and picked the gun back off the table. He stood up, tucking the gun into the back of his pants. "I gave you a chance to do this the right way. When you come to your senses, my door will be open. Hopefully, I will still be able to talk them into letting you back in." Jared walked toward us. "Take the kid," he ordered the others, pointing at you again. Two of the four gunmen stepped toward me. One of the others lifted his gun and pointed it at me. I suddenly realized what was happening. They were going to literally pry you from my arms.

"Wait," your father yelled before anyone reached me. Your father spoke with such authority that everyone in the room stopped for a moment. "Before you walk away, are you going to apologize to me, Jared?" Your father stared straight ahead at the wall. He didn't look at Jared when he spoke. He didn't look at us either. I thought he had given up.

"For what?" Jared asked, clearly believing that he had nothing to apologize for.

"For ripping my heart out," your father replied. They were the saddest words I've ever heard spoken.

"You first, friend," Jared replied with equal force. Then he gave a quick nod to his partners and they started to walk toward me again. The first man to reach me grabbed my arms with a grip like a vice. He stepped behind me and pulled my elbows together behind my back. As he pulled my arms apart, my grip on you loosened. I could feel you begin to slip from my fingers. Right before you fell from my grip, one of the other men grabbed you. He held you in front of him, not the way you hold a child, but the way you hold a wild animal.

"Don't let them do this, Joseph!" I cried out. I didn't know what else to do. "You're supposed to be his friend," I shrieked at Jared. I was crying now. I didn't know what I would do if I lost you.

"I am his friend," Jared whispered to me. He sounded angry now, like he wasn't used to not getting his way. Once they had you out of my arms, the first man let me go. My legs wouldn't hold me up any longer. My muscles didn't work. I fell in a heap on the floor. They were taking you and I didn't know how to stop them.

The sky had gotten dark outside. No one had turned on any of the lights in the house so it was becoming dark inside, too, making it difficult to see. I looked over toward the couch where your father had been sitting. I wanted to curse him for letting this happen. I wanted to scream at him for not stopping them from taking you, but I would have been screaming at an empty couch. Your father was gone. Jared and his henchmen were making their way toward the door. The man with the rifle was in front. The man holding you was right behind him. I looked over again at the empty couch and then I scanned the room to see if I could see where your father had gone. My eyes caught the deep purple of the sky and I noticed the open window. Your father was already outside. He was waiting for them. I wanted to do something. I wanted to help him somehow but I had no idea what your father was going to do.

The man with the rifle opened the front door. He stepped outside. The man holding you walked out after him. I could barely see the door through the backs of the other three men. I heard a sound, though, a deep, guttural sound of surprise. Then the front door swung closed. Jared and two of the men were still inside. Everyone just stood there for a second, confused. Then the sound of gunshots came from right outside the front door. I held my breath and listened, trying to figure out what the gunshots meant. I didn't dare breathe. I just listened and hoped. First there was silence. Then I heard you crying. I never thought I'd be so happy to hear you cry. Better still, your crying was getting quieter—not because it was stopping but because somehow you were getting farther away. It had to be your father. The henchmen would have come back into the house. Your father was abandoning me, leaving me in the house with these three horrible men and I never loved him more in my life. He was saving you.

I looked up at the three men who were left inside. The two henchmen still didn't seem to understand what was going on. They reached for their weapons before opening the door again. Only Jared remained calm. He reached for the front door and turned the knob. As he opened the door I could hear a car start out on the street. Your father was only seconds from escaping with you. I got to my feet. All I could think to do to help you escape was to make a mad rush at Jared. He stepped outside and, as he did, I ran toward the front door, past the two befuddled men standing inside. Jared had stepped onto the front porch. I could see that he was bending down to pick something up. I was outside now too. I knew that I had to try to tackle Jared, to hold him down, to keep him from doing whatever it was he was planning to do. But then I made my one mistake. Before I jumped at him, I looked up. I couldn't help it. I wanted to see you and your father. I wanted to know that the two of you were safe. I thought that it might be the last time I ever saw either of you. Your father was in the front seat of our car. I couldn't see you but I knew that you had to be lying on the seat next to him.

I looked over at Jared. He was leaning down to pick up the rifle. The two men who your father had ambushed on the porch were just lying on the ground, motionless. I could see blood. They were dead. Somehow, in seconds, your father had killed them both.

Jared picked the rifle out of the hands of one of the lifeless bodies. I ran toward him as he lifted it up to his shoulder. I tried to go faster but Jared saw me coming. In my moment's hesitation, in that moment when I looked up to see if you were okay, Jared saw me coming toward him. I lowered my head to try to bowl him over or at least hit him hard enough that your father would have time to drive away. I was about to hit him when Jared took his free hand and caught me near the base of my neck. He held me back with one hand before I had a chance to bury my shoulders into him. He dug his fingers into my collarbone while still holding the rifle in his other hand. He was so strong. I felt so weak. He lifted me up by my collarbone like I weighed nothing and flung me off the porch. I tumbled to the ground. When I stopped rolling, I turned to look toward the car. It was just beginning to move. Everything was happening too slowly. I looked back up at the porch and saw Jared lift the rifle up toward his shoulder. He aimed. He fired one shot. I turned and looked back at the car again. Jared had hit the right front tire. The car skidded to one side and fishtailed so that it was almost facing us. Through the darkness, I could see your father frantically trying to turn the steering wheel. Then, I looked back up at Jared again. He was aiming for a second shot. He took his sight and pulled the trigger again. I heard glass shatter before I even turned around. When I turned, the front windshield had already splintered, the crisscrossing lines of shattered glass creating a web centered on a hole directly in front of the driver's seat. Jared's aim had been perfect. I wanted to scream but I froze.

Jared walked back to the front door and yelled to the two surviving henchmen to come out. He ordered them to walk toward the car with him. "Grab the girl," he said to one of them as they walked by me. The man leaned toward me and grabbed a clump of my hair in his fist. He lifted me to my feet by my hair but didn't let go. Instead, he dragged me behind him. I stumbled, trying to keep up. It didn't hurt. I couldn't feel pain. I was numb. I prayed that the car would be empty when we got to it, that somehow your father had gotten out and run away with you. Jared looked over at me as we walked, his face full of hatred. "You killed my best friend," Jared said to me without the slightest hint of irony. My mouth was too dry to say anything back.

I could hear you crying as we neared the car and my heart sank. The sound was muffled but there was no mistaking it. You must have slipped down to the floor, beneath one of the seats, as the car spun. For a moment, all I was worried about was whether or not you had been hurt. Then I remembered all the other things that I had to worry about too. You were alive. I thanked God for that but that was all I had to be thankful for. "You can let her go but don't let her go anywhere," Jared barked at the man who was holding my hair. He tossed me aside. I fell to the ground again, my already bloody knees digging into the dry dirt. Even if I wanted to, I had no strength left to run. "You," Jared said, pointing to the other man, his orders now coming out with emotionless authority, "get the kid." I leaned forward so that I could see you as the man opened the passenger side door. He reached down to the floor of the car and grabbed you by one of your legs. He lifted you out of the car like that, holding one of your legs and dangling your body beneath his fist like you were a piece of meat. I hated him. I held my breath. You were covered in blood. I don't know if it was yours or your father's. I'm so sorry, Christopher. I'm so sorry I let them do that to you.

"You're hurting him," I shouted, but no one listened to me. Something inside me hurt physically, even though I knew that I wasn't injured.

Jared walked over to the driver's side door of the car.

He opened it and looked inside. I couldn't see what he was looking at. All I could see was the cracked windshield and blood. Jared took a long look inside the car. He didn't say a word. His face was impossible to read. His eyes were cold. Then he turned away again.

"Let's go," Jared said. He began walking toward the SUV he and his henchmen had parked up near the house. The two other men followed. They didn't bother with the bodies on the porch. You kept crying. Your face was turning dark purple as the man carried you upside down. I wanted to run to you, Chris. I wanted to comfort you. I was too weak. I couldn't fight. I could barely breathe. It felt like someone was standing on my chest. All the energy had been sucked out of my body. I didn't have the strength your father had. I didn't even have the strength to make one last, desperate try to save you. Death didn't scare me. Only the hopelessness did.

They walked past me, not three feet from me. For a moment, I thought they were going to pretend I wasn't even there. That was the worst part of it—their indifference to me. I would have rather had them shoot me than just let me lie there in my own uselessness. I wanted to be in pain. As they walked passed me, Jared turned to me one last time. I was praying he was going to lift his gun and put me out of my misery. Instead, he made eye contact with me and nodded toward the car. With a chilling indifference, he said, "He's still alive but he won't be for long. Don't bother trying to call for help because there's not enough time. Just go say your good-byes. Consider it my last favor that I'll ever get to do for my friend." Then Jared stopped walking for a split second and finished, "And then I suggest that you disappear."

I began to cry out loud again. I don't know how I had any tears left. I didn't have the strength to stand up. I knew that if I tried, I'd simply fall back to the ground. I just lay there in the dirt and watched as the three men got into the car with you. The man holding you in his fist climbed into the backseat. Once he was in the car, I couldn't see you anymore. He closed the door behind him and, when he pulled the door closed, the sound of your crying disappeared. The SUV's engine started and the men simply drove away, leaving me lying in the dirt. Just like that, you were gone.

I watched the SUV for as long as I could, knowing that you were in it. When I couldn't see the SUV anymore, I began to crawl through the dirt back toward your father. The car was only about twenty feet away, but I barely had the energy to crawl. I didn't know what I could possibly say to your father. I was ashamed. Your father was dying because he tried to save you and there I was, frozen, with scrapes on my knees.

As I neared the car, I realized that I couldn't hear any noise from inside. I thought that maybe I was too late. I tried to stand up, putting my hand on the car door, but my knees wobbled and I fell back to the ground. When I landed, I heard a small sound coming from inside the car. I looked up. The interior light of the car was on because the door was open. Your father was slouched in the driver's seat, a pool of blood on the front of his shirt. Jared had shot him in the middle of the chest. I could see more blood beginning to dry on the corners of your father's lips. He wheezed slightly as he breathed. I could see the pain in his face.

"I let him go," I confessed. I was already on my knees, in the perfect position to beg your father for forgiveness.

He shook his head. "You couldn't have done anything," he said to me, his voice growing quieter with each word. "You don't deserve any of this. You and Christopher, you don't deserve any of this." He looked down at the blood on his shirt.

"You don't deserve this, either, Joe. It's not your fault." I crawled closer to him and placed my hands on his lap.

He chuckled. It sounded painful. "No. You're wrong. This is exactly what I deserve. This was always how it was going to end for me." I didn't know what to say. In retrospect, I know what I should have said. I should have told your father how much I loved him. I should have told him that I was going to find you. I should have told him that I was going to rescue you and that you wouldn't have to grow up to be a killer. I should have told him that he was the bravest man that I ever met and that I didn't blame him for anything. Instead, I said nothing. He made one more request of me. "Kiss me," he said, his voice now barely more than a whisper. I hesitated, not sure if I heard him right. "I want the last thing that I feel to be your lips." The words were clear this time.

I gathered my strength and stood. I put one hand on the roof of the car to steady myself. I laid my other hand lightly on your father's chest. I could feel his blood through his shirt. I didn't care. I leaned in and kissed your father for the final time. I pressed my lips to his. The warmth was already receding from his lips but I could feel his heart beating weakly beneath my hand. As we kissed, I felt the beating stop.

You don't owe your father anything, Christopher. I would never put something like that on you. But you should know that he died trying to save you. Don't blame him for what you are. It's not his fault. He loved you. He gave everything just to try to give you a normal life.

It took me some time after your father's death to realize what I had to do. Now I know. I have to find you. I have to learn from your father's strength. I have to find out where they've taken you and I have to save you, for your sake and your father's. I hadn't been strong enough to stop them from taking you, but I can make myself strong enough to get you back. At least I can try. It took me a while to realize that I have nothing else to lose. I don't care how far I have to go or how long it will take. They followed us to a tiny, remote corner of the world. If they could do it, then so can I. They stole my child and killed the only man I ever loved. I've had enough running. Now it's their turn.

ACKNOWLEDGMENTS

I need to thank my wife, Carly, first and foremost. Dreamers can dream all they want, but without the pragmatist poking them and nudging them along, those dreams will never come to fruition.

Thanks to my agent, Alexandra Machinist, in part for helping me to navigate the funny industry we call publishing but mostly for believing in me and in my work and for standing with me when I was unwilling to compromise.

Thanks to my editor, Ben Sevier, and the rest of the team at Dutton. You've made me a better writer, and for that I am eternally grateful.

Finally, thanks to Drew Pitzer, Amanda Hulsey, Aron Gooblar, Jay Johnston, Noah Davis, David Menoni, Marty McLoughlin, Kevin Trageser, Stephen Szycher, and Michael Bedrick for reading and commenting on earlier drafts of this books. It would be a much different and far inferior book without your input. More important, thanks for giving me an audience to inspire me to keep writing, no matter how frustrated, frightened, or discouraged I became.

TREVOR SHANE lives in Brooklyn with his wife and son.

CONNECT ONLINE

---

www.childrenofparanoia.com

Read on for a preview of Trevor Shane's

Children of the Underground

Coming from NAL in April 2013

I remember the smell of blood. When there's enough of it, it's a pungent smell that you can never forget. When the scent hit me so many memories came flooding back.

I drove into Grand Case before noon. I brought a magazine with me, imagining that I could hide behind it as I searched strangers' faces for the man I saw on the pier. I was excited, not only at the prospect of finally finding him, but at the prospect of playing the game. For the first time in months, I felt like I had a chance to win.

Grand Case is small enough that I knew I would find Michael if he showed up. What I didn't know was how he'd react to meeting me. I knew there was a chance that he would blame me for your father's death. There was a chance that he wouldn't want anything to do with me. I didn't know how I was going to react to meeting him either. I'd spent nine months without the War, without violence or blood or terror. I'd need courage to go back. Sometimes life doesn't give you choices, Christopher. I made fun of your father for telling me that once, but he was right. Even if you have choices, sometimes you have only one worth making. I had to go back to the War. It's the only way I can save you from it.

When I got to Grand Case, I parked my car and walked toward the water. It was a quick walk from the street to the beach. The beach at Grand Case coils its way around the bay in an almost perfect semi-circle. From where I stepped onto the sand, I could see every bar, every restaurant, every sunbather, every ounce of sand as they all wrapped themselves around the blue water of the bay. I took off my shoes and began to walk, digging my toes into the soft, white sand. I walked the length of the beach twice, checking the inside of each restaurant and bar to see if Michael was already inside. When I didn't see him, I found a spot in the sand that afforded me a clear view of everything. I sat down and began scanning the faces of the people around me.

I sat in that spot for four hours before I saw Michael. When I did, it was as thrilling and as frightening as it had been the day before. I had so much riding on this man whom I'd never met. I spotted him coming out of the water. I recognized his face. I noticed the deep scar on his side from where someone had driven a knife into his abdomen while he was saving your father's life. It was shaped like a pair of eternally silent lips. I recognized the taut, muscular frame from the docks. Michael wasn't big but he looked strong and agile. Watching him gave me faith that he could help me. I thought for a moment that everything was going to work out. I didn't know that the next twenty-four hours were going to dissolve into a nightmare.

The beach was quiet and uncrowded. Michael was fifty yards from me but only a few people stood between us. I could hear the cries of the seagulls and the wind blowing through the flags on the boats anchored in the bay but I didn't hear any other sound. The water was calm. Michael stretched out in the sand and slept. Other than the rise and fall of his chest, his body didn't move. While he was sleeping, I took a cigarette out of my bag and lit it to calm my nerves. I was in the middle of my third cigarette when Michael sat up, put his shirt on and walked toward one of the restaurants overlooking the beach. I tossed my half-smoked cigarette in the sand, dusted myself off, and followed him. My plan was to let Michael get three drinks into him before I confronted him. I planned on telling him who I was and then telling him how often and how fondly your father spoke about him. I was ready to tell Michael that your father's last wish was that Michael get a chance to meet you. I was ready to lie. I was ready to do whatever it took.

By the time I walked up the steps leading from the beach into the shade of the restaurant, Michael was already sitting at the bar with a drink in front of him. I did my best to avoid staring at him. I sat down at a table overlooking the water. The waiter asked what I'd like to drink. I'd learned from your father's journal that you were never supposed to drink on a job. I remembered the stories where your father and his friends ordered club soda so that they could look like they were drinking. I needed a drink though. I ordered a margarita, thinking it would at least make me look like I was on vacation.

The restaurant was about half full when I walked in but it was quickly filling up. The day was slipping slowly into night. Men came in wearing loud Hawaiian-print shirts and the women came in wearing airy, spaghetti-strap dresses. Michael ordered a second beer. I ordered a salad so that the waiter wouldn't kick me off my table. I tried to eat some of the salad, realizing that I hadn't eaten anything since breakfast, but my throat closed up. I couldn't swallow. One drink down, two to go, I told myself. Then I saw one of the others for the first time.

He was sitting at a table in the corner of the restaurant. He appeared to be alone. He had a glass of wine on his table but it looked full, not even sipped. A plate of untouched seafood-strewn pasta sat in front of the man. He was doing what I was doing. He was watching Michael. At first I thought I was imagining things. I've had fits of paranoia before. When I was on the run with your father, they were frequent. I would suddenly feel every eye on me and think that everyone was out to get me. Maybe my brain could sense that I was near the War again. Your father taught me to trust my instincts, so I

kept one eye on Michael and one eye on the man in the corner. I
wasn't imagining things. He followed every move that Michael made
with measured ease, turning away only when Michael turned toward
him. Unlike me, he was no amateur. Michael didn't seem to notice
him.

My mind raced. I tried to think of what I should do. I felt like I
was trapped in one of your father's stories, only I was unprepared.
The man in the corner glanced at his watch. He reached out in front
of him and appeared to take a sip of wine. He was older than me but
younger than Michael. He had a thin face. His hair and eyes were
dark. He looked at his watch again as if he was waiting for someone.

I put my half-empty margarita back down on the table, vowing not
to drink another drop. I had thought that the only thing I had to fear
was Michael's reaction to meeting me. I'd been naive. I'd never
thought I had to be afraid that someone else would get to Michael
before I did. If anything happened to Michael, I was lost. He was all
I had.

That was when the second man walked through the door.

The second man and his partner were about the same age. I noticed the second man walk into the restaurant and glance at his partner in the corner. They made eye contact and the man in the corner
tapped on his watch and shook his head as if to admonish his partner
for being late. The second man was bigger than the first. He had
broad shoulders and deep-set eyes. He glanced at Michael and began
walking toward him. He was only a few steps away. I wanted to shout.
I wanted to warn Michael but I couldn't find the courage to speak.
The new guy reached Michael and kept walking. He eventually found
a place at the end of the bar. I began breathing again. The second
man ordered a beer though I would have bet my life that he wasn't
going to drink it. I looked at Michael again. He seemed oblivious to
it all. He drank his beer alone. The only person Michael spoke to was
the bartender. He wasn't nearly as alone as he thought he was. I felt

frozen, trapped watching everything that was happening as if it were a movie. Your father taught me how to run. He never taught me how to fight. I had to do something. I had to warn Michael. The restaurant was getting louder and the bar was getting more crowded. It was growing harder to keep an eye on Michael, let alone the others. I tried to think about what Michael would have done if our roles were reversed.

I stood up from my table and began walking toward the bar. At first my legs nearly gave out beneath me. I ignored the others as I walked. I pushed my way through the bodies of some revelers on the way to the bar. They smelled like a mix of red wine and coconut oil. At last I got past the final person and saw that the barstool next to Michael was still free. I hadn't had time to plan what I was going to say to him. *Run* or *They're after you* was all I could think of. Before I sat down on the stool next to Michael, I glanced at the thin-faced man in the corner. He was staring at me. He looked nervous. He wasn't expecting me. I turned away from him, trying to ignore the unease in my stomach.

I sat down on the barstool and turned to face Michael. As I did, the waiter who had served me my drink and my salad called out, "Miss," holding the check in his hand. "You forgot to pay." As he spoke the words, Michael turned and stared at me. Our faces were only inches apart. He was looking into me, through me. I wanted say something but I froze beneath his stare.

Without looking away from me, Michael yelled to the bartender, "Jerry, I gotta run. I'll get you next time, okay?" Then Michael stood up and began walking away.

The bartender laughed. "Sure thing, Michael. I'll put it on your tab." Michael walked toward the door leading to the street. I never opened my mouth. I never warned him. I never had a chance. I froze for a second and then looked over at the man in the corner. He had taken his wallet out and was dropping money on the table to cover his bill. I looked back toward the man at the end of the bar but he wasn't there. He was already gone. He must have gone out through the entrance to the beach as soon as he saw Michael leave. The man in the corner rushed toward the door to the street, leaving a wad of bills on the table. I sat there, frozen with panic.

"Miss, your bill?" my waiter called out to me again, waving the paper above his head. I didn't have time for him. I turned and ran toward the door. I wasn't going to lose Michael. I was too close. I didn't care that the thin-faced man stood between me and Michael or that the man with the sunken eyes was lurking somewhere in the darkness.

I made it out of the front door just in time to see the thin-faced man disappear into a crowd to my right. I followed him, moving as quickly as I could through the throngs of bodies now littering the street. I could hear the dissonant mix of reggae and jazz music echoing out of the restaurants as I passed them. I weaved through the crowd. I heard tourists laughing and bellowing out to one another. It was safe amidst the people. All Michael had to do was stay in the crowd and he'd be safe. He didn't have to run. I couldn't see the thin-faced man anymore. I kept moving, searching the faces of the people as I passed them. I came to a vacant little street that led away from the water. Dark, quiet buildings lined the street. The gaps between the buildings were empty except for shadows. I looked down the street. The only thing I saw was the silhouette of a man walking slowly away from the crowds. He was alone. It was Michael. I could tell by the way that he moved. He was walking away from safety and into the darkness. I didn't know where the others were. I'd lost them. All I knew was that they were out there. Michael was walking right into danger and he didn't even know it. I watched him until he turned down a smaller, darker alleyway branching off the side street. I broke into a run. I ran toward Michael. My feet stamped hard on the ground as I tried to follow the direction that his shadow had moved. I followed him into the darkness. I turned down the second, darker alley. Then I froze. Everything around me became quiet. The alley was empty, lit only by the half-moon reflecting off the broken windows around me.

I remembered to be afraid. I ducked into the shadow of one of the buildings. I didn't dare move. I listened. I heard the murmuring sound of people whispering to each other over the faint sound of music from the restaurants only a few blocks away. Then I heard footsteps, light footsteps, running away from the whispers. I couldn't figure out what was happening. I needed to save Michael. Without him, I had no way to find you. I moved. I jumped from one shadow to the next, from one gap between buildings to another. Each time I stopped, I listened. I heard nothing but silence.

I breathed slowly, deliberately, trying to control my anxiety, trying to remain hidden. Sheltered in the deep darkness between two build-ings, I leaned forward and peered around the corner. All I saw was moonlight shining down on the street. Then I heard a noise. It took me a moment to realize where the noise was coming from, one hor-rible, frozen moment. Something was behind me, hidden in the shad-ows. I didn't hear any footsteps, only a whooshing sound, like the wind. I saw a quick flash of light in front of me: the moonlight re-flected off a metal object as it moved by my face. Before I had a chance to react, I felt the hot blade of a knife pressing deep into my neck. I inhaled, trying not to breathe, knowing that any movement and the knife might break my skin. Then I felt an arm move across my body, clenching my arms at my sides in one strong, viselike grip. The arm pulled me backward until I was pressed up against a body. I couldn't move. I closed my eyes, trying to remember you one more time, thinking that it would all be over soon.

I couldn't see anything in the darkness. "You've got ten seconds to tell me why I shouldn't kill you," a voice whispered into my ear. I recognized the voice. I would have fallen if Michael hadn't literally been holding me up with the arm he had wrapped around my torso.

"People are following you," I whispered back to him.

"I know," he replied. "You're one of them."

I became confused. In my rush to warn Michael, I'd forgotten that he didn't know who I was. "No," I stammered, "I'm not one of *Them*." I said the word *Them* like your father used to say it, like it was the world's greatest insult.

"Then who are you?" Michael asked. I could feel the pressure on my neck from blade of the knife ease up slightly. My eyes were getting used to the darkness. I could almost see the knife blade now.

"I'm Joe's girlfriend," I answered.

Michael took the knife from my throat and spun me around until I was facing him. He kept a powerful grip on both my arms. For a moment, he just looked at me, staring at me through the darkness. We were close enough that I could see the expression on his face. He looked confused, surprised, and angry all at once. Your father had never been easy to read, but he wore only one emotion at a time. In one look, Michael wore hundreds.

"Stay here," Michael whispered to me. "Don't move. No matter what happens, don't move. If you move for any reason, I'll know that I can't trust you." I didn't know how to respond so I simply nodded my head. I felt his hands release my arms. Then he disappeared into the shadows. I stood there for a moment, relieved to no longer have a knife blade jutting into my skin but afraid because I was alone again. He had known that people were following him. I didn't know how it was possible, but he had known.

I stood alone in the darkness and listened to the night. I stayed as still as I could, trying not to move a muscle, hoping that my stillness would hide me.

Everything was quiet. I don't know how long the quiet lasted. It was impossible to measure the passage of time. Then I heard something moving toward me—the sound of barely audible footsteps.

Whoever was coming was placing each footfall carefully on the gravel, trying to move silently. I heard the footsteps only because my senses were heightened by the darkness. Then I saw a shadow move through the street in front of me. I held my breath. It was the man with the deep-set eyes. He was holding a gun out in front of him. His hands were trembling. All he had to do was look in my direction and I would have been at his mercy. I had never felt so vulnerable before. I stood there in the shadows, not daring to move. Losing Michael's trust now would be worse than death. Then, without warning, the man standing in front of me broke into a run, his feet pounding on the gravel. The footsteps sounded as loud to me as a drum. *BOOM, BOOM, BOOM, BOOM,* they went, and then, only seconds later, they stopped as abruptly as they had started. I stayed as quiet as possible, trying to hear what was happening. The sounds drifted toward me through the night air. I heard commotion that sounded far too short to be a fight. I heard the sound of feet sliding across gravel followed by a deep, guttural grunt. Then, even though I'd never heard it before, I heard the unmistakable sound of a knife piercing someone's skin. I heard a quick sound, almost like a popping noise, as the knife punctured the skin, and then I heard the knife slide deeper into flesh. I stood there, frozen. Then I heard a huffing sound followed by the piercing sound of the knife a second time. Everything was quiet for a moment. Finally I heard the last breath, gasping and horrid. Nothing else in the world sounds like the last breath of a dying man. I had almost forgotten what it sounded like. I wish I had. As someone else's breathing stopped, I breathed again. Someone was dead. I had stood there in the darkness and listened to them die. I only prayed that it wasn't Michael.

Then everything was silent again. I still didn't move, standing as Michael had ordered me to, hidden from the world only by the shadows, and waited for Michael's return. Michael didn't get to me first though. The man with the dark eyes found me first. I saw him before he saw me. He was moving down the street, trying to jump from shadow to shadow. The fact that he was still out there searching for something meant either that Michael was still alive or that they were done with him and were looking for me. I watched the man. His movements were clumsy. He looked younger than he had at the restaurant. For some reason, as he tried to make his way through the darkness, he didn't look much older than a boy, a scared and frightened boy. Like his partner, he held a gun. Without even realizing it at first, he turned toward me. He stared directly into the alleyway. He stopped moving, trying to let his eyes focus. Every single piece of my body told me to run but I didn't. If Michael was going to test me, I was going to pass. The man took another step toward me, still unsure of what he was seeing. He lifted his gun and pointed it at me. I thought he might pull the trigger, fire blindly into the alleyway just to be safe, but he didn't. He simply walked toward me, no longer bothering to hide himself in the shadows. "Don't move," he shouted as he walked closer, though I could still hear confusion in his voice. He made it across the street and stopped just shy of the entrance to the alley where I was standing.

He could see me now. He aimed the gun at my chest. We were standing less than five feet apart. "It's you," he said, his voice full of shock and anger, "the bitch from the restaurant." He lifted the gun so that it was pointed at my head. "Where's your friend?" he asked. I didn't answer. I didn't move. I stared into the barrel of the gun and was not afraid. No one could hurt me more than I'd already been hurt. "Okay, I'm giving you until three to answer me, and then I pull the trigger.

"One," he counted. I stared at him. I felt stronger than I'd ever felt before. "Two."

Michael moved so fast that I didn't see him. He must have made a sound, but I didn't hear him either. All I knew was that, the instant before the dark-eyed man said "Three," the gun wasn't pointing at me anymore. Instead, it was pointing toward the sky. The dark-eyed man's whole body was turned so that I could see his silhouette framed by the light from the street. Michael appeared, standing in front of the dark-eyed man. A knife blade was protruding from the fingers of Michael's right hand. Michael's left hand was clamped onto the dark-eyed man's wrist, pulling the gun toward the sky. Michael took his knife blade and jammed it into the dark-eyed man's throat. That's when I smelled the blood. That's when I remembered what it smelled like. It smelled like a mixture of life and death. Then Michael twisted the knife like a corkscrew and the dark-eyed man fell to his knees. I could see the blood now too, dripping from the man's neck onto the ground. In the moonlight, it looked dark and inhuman. Michael pulled the knife out of the man's throat. He wiped the blood from the knife onto the dead man's shirt. Michael let go and the dead man fell to the ground with a thud.

Michael turned to me. "What the fuck are you doing?" he shouted. "Are you fucking nuts?"

"You told me not to move," I answered.

"I meant not to move from here," Michael said, pointing around the dark alley I'd been standing in. "I didn't mean not to move at all. Jesus Christ." I didn't know what to say. I'd done what he told me to do.

"I wanted you to trust me," I said.

Michael stared at me like I was crazy. He shook his head. "Help me get rid of these bodies," he ordered me. "The other one is in a garbage can at the end of the street." He bent down and threw the dark-eyed man's body over his shoulder without another word. "Don't worry," he said, "I've done this before." His assurance didn't make me feel any better.

It took longer to get rid of the bodies than it had taken Michael to kill them. We dumped the bodies in the trough of water surrounding the landing strip of the Grand Case airport. I tried looking down into the water as we dropped the bodies in, wondering how many more bodies were down there, but all I could see was my own reflection on top of the shiny black water. By the time we were finished it was the darkest part of the night. It wouldn't be long before morning.

We barely spoke to each other as we worked. When we were done, Michael asked where I was staying. I told him. "Good," he said. "I'm staying with you."